The Lonebird

The Lovebird

NATALIE BROWN

DOUBLEDAY

NEW YORK LONDON TORONTO

SYDNEY AUCKLAND

This book is a work of fiction. Names, characters, businesses, organizations, places, events, and incidents either are the product of the author's imagination or are used fictitiously. Any resemblance to actual persons, living or dead, events, or locales is entirely coincidental.

Book design by Pei Loi Koay
Art by Malin Rosenqvist
Jacket design by Emily Mahon

LIBRARY OF CONGRESS CATALOGING-IN-PUBLICATION DATA
Brown, Natalie, 1978–
The lovebird / Natalie Brown.—1st ed.
p. cm.
1. Animal rights activists—Fiction. 2. Indian reservations—Fiction. 3. Identity (Philosophical concept)—Fiction. I. Title.
PS3602.R722375L68 2013
813'.6—dc23
2012032396

ISBN 978-0-385-53675-2

MANUFACTURED IN THE UNITED STATES OF AMERICA

1 3 5 7 9 10 8 6 4 2

First Edition

For Cheryl Lynne

No, the human heart
is unknowable.
But in my birthplace
the flowers still smell
the same as always.

— T S U R A Y U K I

Book One

Fuit puella maxima virtute et atque
*simillima matri.**

---
* She was a girl of the greatest courage and in fact very like her mother.

I SUPPOSE IT ALL STARTED WITH SIMON MELLINKOFF, though I hardly could have anticipated the consequences of our connection during that fateful hour I spent strewn on the sofa in his office. I was a college freshman with the flu—feverish, foggy, and fond. But even if, at eighteen, I'd had the foresight to see every curve of the course on which he would set me, and to know how long it would be before I would return to earth, I do not think I would have risen off that sofa, blown my nose, shouldered my backpack, and stepped outside onto a straighter, safer path. I think that, even with powers of prediction, I would have done exactly what I did, which was stay, and sigh, and squeeze pillows, and wait for him to come back.

Simon Mellinkoff was a freshly widowed professor of Latin. Our university in San Diego was as crowded as it was sprawling, but I was one of only twelve students who enrolled in his Intro to Latin course. On the first day of class, he appeared ten minutes late in opaque black sunglasses that contrasted with his fair, silvery hair. He left the glasses on for the entirety of his introductory speech, as if he could not yet bear to make eye contact with any of us. He had a lit cigarette in his mouth, which he stubbed out and replaced between his lips, where it gave his speech a clipped, crippled quality. Also, he was shaking, but I didn't think anyone noticed besides me. Perhaps this was because I had inexplicably taken a front-row seat while everyone else had opted for distant desks where they could idly doodle in their notebooks. I wondered what was the matter with Simon, and my left ovary, that radar for all things hurt and helpless, twinged.

Still, despite his initial distance, Simon managed to inspire a rather unorthodox sense of classroom intimacy, and counting him, we became a cozy baker's dozen. He exuded a curious kind of dark warmth, and soon it enveloped us all—even the back-of-the-room doodlers. He insisted we call him Simon. He cringed and puckered if we called him "Professor," as if our uttering it soured his mouth. He had little patience for the traditions and trials of academia, and was decidedly averse to consorting with his fellow professors or following any of their unwritten rules for ascending the nauseating spiral staircase to the top of the ivory tower. The only work he had ever published was an exposition on the love-hate relationship between Catullus and Lesbia—" 'May I Perish If I Do Not Love Her': Antagonism and Passion in the Love Poems of Catullus"—while he was still in grad school, long before his hair turned gray and his wife made her unfortunate exit, complete with its indelible effects.

Once, during the second week of class, while explaining the positive comparative superlative comparison of adjectives to us uncomprehending novices, Simon Mellinkoff called his colleague, the only other Latin professor at our university, a smirky Englishman with a supercilious affect, a "summus maximus bore." I don't know if he ever told the Englishman he was a summus maximus bore to his face. Well, I'm sure he didn't because, outside of his classroom, Simon was the sort who rarely had the time of day for anyone. That's why it was so surprising that he opened his office, his home, and, ultimately, an entire new life to me, Margie

Fitzgerald, a shy, skinny girl from suburban Orange County, an only child, a hunter for relics, a lifelong loner.

A week later, while seeking to illuminate the positive comparative superlative comparison of adjectives once more, Simon Mellinkoff stood at his lectern and said, "Rosy, rosier, *rosiest*," with ample pauses between each phrase. "*Beautiful, more* beautiful, *most* beautiful," he said. He said these things while looking right at me.

He was alone, with a little seven-year-old daughter to raise all by himself—too young of a daughter, perhaps, for a fifty-year-old dad. Theirs was an almost-family with a piece missing. I felt his loneliness from afar. Once, two months into the semester, I saw him sitting without a smile on a stone bench in the middle of a bustling quad on campus. (Subsequently, I examined this bench and found that it was engraved with a Latin sentence, which might have been why Simon was drawn to it: OFFICIA MAGISTRI SUNT MULTA ET MAGNA.*)

Students swirled all around him on their way to and from classes, but Simon was very still. I saw him sitting there on his bench and he saw me as I pushed my yellow bicycle across the quad. Our Latin class began in ten minutes, and I mentally recited that day's vocab terms and their definitions: *magister,* teacher; *bonus,* good, kind; *periculum,* danger, risk . . .

After spying Simon, I kept my head down, as was my habit back then. Today, it may seem hard to believe because of some *San Diego Sun* articles portraying me as a domestic terrorist, or because of a certain party I once threw in Little Italy during which I danced naked with only a bright green snake wrapped around my neck, but I have always been bashful. New to college, and living two long hours away from home, I led a solitary existence, sequestered in the moldy apartment I shared with a pair of

---

* The duties of a teacher are many and great.

fellow students, or hiding out at the university Crafts Complex, where I spent much of my free time. Already I had taken several weeklong crafting courses, including Intro to Stained Glass, Ceramics, Metal Fabrication, and Wonders of Weaving—Always Alone.

A nervous rose unfurled on my cheek when I passed Simon on his bench. I feigned fascination with the fallen eucalyptus leaves (our campus was groaning with groves and fragrant with their medicinal smell) that I crushed under my bicycle tires. I was a terrible Latin student and I knew it. I'd started out very strong. In fact, I'd aced the first quiz and finished it so fast that I'd had time to sketch an assortment of plump parakeets on the back. "Very complacent," Simon had written beside my drawings in the same red pen with which he had scrawled a decisive A on the front. But that was before I'd become baffled by declensions and conjugations.

I felt Simon watching me as I crossed the quad. Peeking at him sideways, I saw his silver hair glimmering in the sunshine. His hands rested on his kneecaps. Birds convened at his feet, as if he had scattered an abundance of seeds, but he appeared oblivious to them. Maybe he had watched me before that. Maybe, I mused, he had watched me wheeling my bike and walking to class every day since the semester had started, while I stared at my shoes or at the sky.

In class, just a few minutes later, in the middle of a lecture about genitives and subjunctives, he suddenly stopped speaking and stared at me with his gray-browed frown. He placed his unlit cigarette between his lips and pulled it back out again. Simon's stare, I sensed, saw right through my sundressed shell into the convoluted clockwork of my head, the hot little happenings of my heart. I stayed perfectly still in my seat. I wondered if its worn woodgrains were turning pink with my pervasive flush. Suddenly, it seemed as though only the two of us were in the room, he with his stick of chalk erect in his hand, I straightbacked with my knees pressed together in an attentive pose. The other eleven students telegraphed faint annoyance at their swift exclusion from Simon's universe, which was momentarily occupied solely by me. I had the feeling I used to get as a girl when I fell asleep with a dish of orange blossoms beside my bed and their neroli essence seeped into my dreams—a feeling of limitless longing.

He addressed me in a gentle tone, the kind he might have taken with a stray animal too scared to come into his arms. His question surprised me, for it had nothing at all to do with his lecture, and his asking it, I noted, perfectly illustrated a Latin term he had recently explained to us: *non sequitur*. "Do you—are you—" He paused. "Do you have any friends?"

I did not. But I didn't say so for fear of offending Jane, who I knew counted herself as my friend. She had sidled up to me after our very first Latin class and said, "You remind me of Audrey Hepburn. But with curly hair. So delicate!" and had complimented me several times on my home-sewn sundresses. No, I didn't answer Simon that day. Weeks later, when I sprawled for that hour on his office sofa, my temperature rising with the passing minutes, I tried to recall whether that had been the moment when he had charmed me, or whether it had been something else, such as:

his "rosy, rosier, rosiest" comment;

his smell, which was the clean smell of beach sand mixed with the essence of filterless cigarettes and, when he was close, of blue hyacinths—spring flowers that unfurl out of subterranean bulbs and are redolent of water, and especially of tears;

his wry, bone-dry delivery of jokes;

his Back East accent, which hinted at what would surely be beautiful bedroom whispers;

his tragic clothes, which he selected without the guiding hand of a wife;

his mystified, half-smiling, half-sad reactions to the strange drawings his golden-haired girl, Annette, made when she spent occasional afternoons tucked into a corner of our classroom, wearing the exact same canvas slip-on shoes that Simon always did, but in miniature;

his penchant for sitting on the top of his desk with one leg bent up and one forearm (he always rolled up his shirtsleeves) resting on his knee as he masterfully escorted us through a declension;

his mentioning that his mouthful of a last name had originally been Melnikov, a Russian moniker deriving from *melnik*, which means, he explained, one who mills grain, but that his father had changed it to Mellinkoff sometime in the early sixties when he decided the original sounded too unfriendly;

his confession that he had received seventy-nine parking tickets from the campus police for leaving his rattling, tomato red BMW 2002 in undesignated spots, and his insistence that he would never pay a single one of them;

his spontaneous proverbs and matter-of-fact tips for life ("Feet are important," he once declared apropos of what, I don't know, but our Latin readings mentioned all manner of body parts, and he gazed approvingly at my soft, sandaled, and cherry-tipped toes when he said it);

his habit of addressing his daughter by the diminutive form of her name, Nettie, and how easy it was to imagine him saying my own name with the same familiarity and intimacy because, being another two-syllabled term ending in "ie," it was not unlike the one he called the little lass he stirred from bed each morning and folded back in each night;

his unforgettable declaration that "marriage is like Chinese water torture," which burned itself into my brain, partly because of the shock of hearing it uttered by a widower (for weren't widowers supposed to glorify marriage, miss it, and mourn the loss of it?);

or maybe it was his perpetual aura of both vague happiness and vague unhappiness, and the quiet strength, the sense of moderation and temperance, he employed to ensure that he ventured too far into neither.

Oh, I still don't know just when or why it happened, but suddenly I was absolutely enamored with Simon Mellinkoff. It was probably the "rosy, rosier, rosiest" comment.

I WASN'T THE ONLY ONE WHO NOTICED Simon's humble but haunting charms. Jane—who reminded me of Marilyn because she had Marilyn's cloudy hair and cushiony proportions—noticed, too. Once, we commiserated over our shared fascination with him. "What a daddy!" she exclaimed breathily during our first study session in her bright apartment on Mission Bay. We drilled each other on vocab and drank PG Tips because Jane, a sophomore, had spent the previous summer in a study-abroad program in England. I regretted telling her about my own crush almost as soon as I uttered the words. Some of the juice, the succulence, was lost when I blurted it out of the private realm (a hidden hothouse, hand on hibiscus) in which it had flourished.

I didn't speak of my feelings about Simon to Jane again until much later, but they were still thriving when, at the end of our last Latin class before winter break, she and I lingered in the classroom to melodiously wish him a Merry Christmas. She hoisted her book bag over her shapely shoulder, and I stuffed my latest quiz into the pages of my textbook, somewhere between *cubiculum** and *cupiditas*.†

"Thanks," he said, "but I don't do religious holidays. I'm not a believer."

---

* bedroom
† desire

I resisted the urge to raise a hand to my chest and cover the Mary medal that always dangled there. "Oh," we fluttered and blushed, batted lashes and exited.

And my crush was still there after winter break was over and I dutifully attended Latin while in the throes of a severe illness, some physiological manifestation of mental malaise and holiday hopes unfulfilled—a consequence of home horrors, for home was where I'd discovered that Dad, dependent as ever on Dorals and glasses of Maker's Mark with a splash of water, had childishly stashed an entire month's worth of dirty dishes in the oven, and also where Old Peep, my pet parakeet, had disappeared under mysterious circumstances.

Jane waited for me as I packed up my *Wheelock's Latin* at the end of class. I paused to rest my heavy head on the desk, which was permanently perfumed with the sweet-and-sour smell of other people's palms. "I just feel so awful," I said huskily. The room was empty but for the three of us: me, her, and Simon. He paused on his way out the door to hover above me where I languished. Jane tittered and looked at him with deep blue bovine eyes.

"You're welcome to use my office for a nap," he told me, "if you want. If it would help." I swallowed, and strove not to show my shock. "I have to go teach another class," he continued, "so you'll have some peace and quiet. I can let you in right now." I collected myself and followed Simon outside, looking over my shoulder at Jane, who offered a few feeble, false sneezes.

Simon's office was in the Literature building at the very end of a musty, seemingly interminable corridor. All the other professors had decorated their office doors with postcards, cartoons, pictures of dead writers, and other nerdy ephemera—but not Simon. "You don't have any doodads stuck on your door," I slurred, pleasantly impaired by a potent concoction of cold medicine, PG Tips, and what I could only call love.

Inside, it was dim, brown, mannish. He pointed to the long, soft sofa. Sunlight snuck dustily through slits in the shut blinds, and slivers of the outside air—heavy and oceanic, full of seahorses and slippery kelp and phosphorescent diatoms—came in with it. There were a few Magic Marker mysteries scrawled by his pigtailed progeny and taped to his filing cabinet, and a picture of him as a much younger man, engaged in some improbable-were-it-not-for-photographic-proof athletic feat, hung up on the wall behind his desk. (In the photo, Simon's hair was black, showing that at one time he had more closely approximated the amorous dark-haired stranger who always populated my orange-blossom-infused dreams and held me in a front-of-him-against-the-back-of-me embrace.) "Doodads," he echoed, and I swear he was smiling when he shut the door on his way out, though the term had no Latin origin (*Doodad*: noun. Origin: rosebud mouths of cute coeds, friendless bicycle pushers, soft-soled sick girls, complacent Margies).

No, I never thought about leaving during that hour I lay in Simon's office, and I definitely didn't nap. I only waited for him to return. I reclined on the sofa in a state of fluish arousal, cuddly and clammy and coughing carefully into pillows lest any other professors hear me behind his closed door. I imagined him dismissing his class early and rushing back to me, lean legs striding inside his funny black-and-white-checkered trousers, wondering, hoping I would still be there, assuring himself that I must be eighteen because everyone in college is at least that, unless they're a genius or academically advanced, which, as my Latin scores of late evinced, I most likely was not, and then telling himself that whether I was eighteen wasn't any concern of his anyway, as what sort of guidance could an eighteen-year-old offer a motherless seven-year-old daughter? I lay, and I waited, dreaming of all these things, and of the things he had said and might say, and I shut my eyes tight, curled in my toes, and clung to pillows, swoony from the memory of having been declared rosy and beautiful, of having been seen, and wakeful with the possibility of being seen again.

When I finally heard his key turn in the lock, I shut my eyes and arranged my features in a tableau of dreamy unconsciousness, lips parted, forehead dewy. "Oh my," I heard him whisper. I was unaccustomed to attention from men, or even boys, and unsure of how to act. When he settled himself quietly into the chair behind his desk, I stirred and stretched and looked around as if uncertain of my surroundings. I gave him a slow glance. He stared at me with his hands resting palms down on his desk. "How was your nap?"

I stood, and he appraised me. My sundress was one of the many I had made after a course in Strategies for Simplified Sewing at the Crafts Complex. The fabric was printed all over with windblown stalks of wheat. The straps were slim and tied at my shoulders, and the bows they formed hung limply, skimming the bones of my back. I wondered if he was an Audrey man or a Marilyn man. I perused the books on his shelves while he watched me, statue-like, from his chair, palms still pressed into the desk. That was when I learned that Simon Mellinkoff had interests beyond Latin and the love poems of Catullus. His library included such titles as:

Animals Nobody Loves
Mammals and Morality
Tortoises, Today and Tomorrow
A Sand County Almanac
The Cookbook for People Who Love Animals
Elephants, Entertainment, and Exploitation: A History
Rattling the Cage: Toward Legal Rights for Animals
Research, Rabbits and Reform: An Animal Rights Reader
Our Ancestor the Ape

Animal Rights in the New Millennium
Dominion: The Power of Man, The Suffering of Animals, and
the Call to Mercy
Hymn of the Dolphin, Ballad of the Whale: Saving the Sea's
Cleverest Creatures
Cruel Science, Burdened Beasts

And these were just some of the books he kept in his office at school, a small portion of the vast collection, I would soon learn, that filled his study at home.

"You like animals?" I said, sniffing.

" 'The greatness of a nation and its moral progress can be judged by the way its animals are treated. I hold that, the more helpless a creature, the more entitled it is to protection by man from the cruelty of man,' " he said, not taking his hands off the desk or his eyes off my shoulders, my neck, my face, my hair so electrified by that long, soft sofa. "Mahatma Gandhi."

I knelt down to examine the books on the lower shelves. There, I found a misfit, a lone work of fiction. I read the spine aloud in a scruffy voice hemmed in by mucus and nerves. "*An Armful of Warm Girl,*" I murmured. I lifted my eyes to see Simon, finally, pull his hands off his desk. "That's a nice name for a book," I said. And then came the moment that led me to where I am today. The title of the book came true right in that room, and he had the armful, and I was the girl.

HOW—WHEN—DID I BECOME A DEVOTED DEFENDER of animal rights, a "domestic terrorist," as the *San Diego Sun* so dramatically put it? It happened sometime between the moment I first became a warm armful in Simon Mellinkoff's office and the afternoon he told me one daughter was more than enough, and I left his house with all of my belongings in the Strawberry Shortcake suitcase I borrowed from little Annette.

Before any of that, there had been only one man in my life: Dad, with whom I spent the winter break of that first semester at college, during which I became susceptible, I suppose, to Simon.

I had only been away from home for three months, but our stucco house in the Tierra de Flores tract seemed to have grown more grizzled in my absence. When I returned, I saw the peeling brown paint, the shutters missing slats, the jiggly doorknobs, and the torn window screens as if introduced to them for the first time, with eyes sharpened during the last semester by all of my Intros: Intro to Latin, Intro to Japanese Poetry, Intro to the Russian Novel, Intro to Romanticism. *Intro to your home, Margie. Grade: F.*

What did Dad think, I wondered, after showing and selling all those painstakingly cleaned, repainted, and remodeled houses every day, when he came home to ours? Was he blind to the Havisham-esque decay? Or did he find the evidence of time's passage comforting, a reminder that there would be an end to the sadness he endured just as there would be an end to the house, to all the sad things people lived in and lived through?

He seemed embarrassed by my efforts to tidy up. I vacuumed pebbly crumbs out of the serene blue carpet that Rasha, my mother, had selected nineteen years earlier. I pulled the teetering stacks of dirty dishes out of the oven and loaded them like dominos into the dishwasher. I emptied ashtrays overflowing with the stubby remnants of greedily sucked smokes. I threw away Old Peep's empty birdcage. Dad told me, eyes averted, that he had let our parakeet "go wild," but I suspected he was afraid to confess that the bird had died from neglect. I noticed there was no seed in Peep's dish or anywhere in the house.

"Don't do all that stuff, honey," Dad said, Doral dangling, pulling his hands pleadingly out of his pockets and then putting them back in, shuffling—with his head down and his cheeks flushing—out of whatever room I cleaned. He drove to the Christmas tree farm and returned with a Douglas fir fastened to the top of his Skylark, but I didn't dare decorate it due to my fear that Dad would leave it up indefinitely. I hated the thought of a trimmed and tinseled tree rotting in the family room in April.

I WAS TWELVE WHEN I FIRST FELT the twinge in my left ovary. It was growing up with Dad, I guess, that had made it so sensitive. When he came home from work, I noticed that his hands shook. After his five fifteen p.m. Maker's Mark with a splash of water and the usual string of Dorals, they stopped. He stayed up sipping and smoking at least until I went to bed at midnight, possibly after. Still, Dad made it to work at Sunshine Realty every morning.

And he added his florid autograph to all of my progress reports and school field trip permission slips, and paid for my annual physicals and my trips to the dentist, and brought home groceries (even making special trips to the pet supply store for parakeet treats and, once, a tiny mirror so Old Peep could admire his own pointy yellow visage), and dropped me off for CCD at Holy Rosary Catholic Church on Saturday afternoons, and remembered to take me out to dinner on my September birthday, and marveled over the handmade cards I presented to him on his March one, and gave me cash so I could go to the mall with Violet Holmquist, a girl from school, and Violet's mom to pick out my first bra, and subscribed me to magazines for teen girls, wherein I might discover the information about womanhood that he was too shy to explain. And he daydreamed, and never asked me any questions, and looked at me sometimes with a surprised expression, as if seeing me for the first time or trying to place me because I reminded him imprecisely of someone he had met before.

On weekends, when he was done mowing the lawn (his forehead burned by the relentless Orange County sunshine) and finished fiddling ineffectually with the increasingly plentiful broken things around our house, Dad disappeared upstairs into his den, where he kept the stash of old leather-bound photo albums featuring Rasha. She posed in front of ancient California missions, their adobe walls flaming with pink and orange bougainvillea. At the beach, she stood half submerged in the foamy waves, her long Beirut-brown hair black at the tips where it caressed the water like gorgeous Galilean seaweed. She shouldered a backpack beneath the Half Dome in Yosemite, her dusky cheeks dented with dimples and shining with excitement. She reclined on the grass in our front yard, eyes at half mast, smiling sleepily and sweetly at the man behind the camera, who held it so very close to her face, and, in doing so, made it a forever face.

I socialized with Violet Holmquist at her house, never mine. Her mother fed us floppy slices of processed cheese that came wrapped in plastic slips and miniature chocolate bars left over from Halloween and Easter. Violet and I studied our still-forming faces side by side in the mirror of her princess-themed bedroom (canopy bed, faux-crystal chandelier) and trolled the sidewalks scanning the look-alike lawns for other kids from school. They all knew Dad was a realtor, and their mothers commented to me with darkening eyes (as if the mere mention of Dad made their pupils dilate with desire for a handsome man so obviously in need of a hand) whenever they spotted his name on a "For Sale" sign in town.

He was nervous the night he escorted me to the eighth-grade Father-Daughter Dance. I wore a dress I had sewn especially for the occasion on Rasha's old Singer. (I had been a self-taught girl-seamstress of sorts until my more formal studies at the Crafts Complex.) It was fashioned from satin of a faded pink hue that the clerk at the fabric store had referred to as "antique rose." I trimmed the dress with several rows of flapper-inspired fringe because the dance had a Roaring Twenties theme. Dad, dapper in his dove gray suit, was careful not to shut the fringe in the Skylark's heavy door. On the way to school, though, he began to look panicked. I stared straight ahead and prayed that he would be okay, pressing my Mary medal into my chest. But his agitation worsened, and streams of sweat snaked down his high forehead toward his hooded Irish eyes. My left ovary throbbed, and I finally whispered a worried little "What?"

"It's . . . just . . . that I'm so . . ." I saw a look of self-hatred flicker across Dad's face that frightened me—eyes mournful, mouth drawn down, teeth clenched. "I . . . forgot!" he said.

Dad veered into the parking lot of a flower shop just as its

purple neon "Yes, We're Open" sign clicked off. He hurried
out of the car. I watched him gesture to an annoyed adolescent
employee on the other side of the locked shop's window. She
pointed to her wristwatch and shook her head. Dad persisted. He
said something to her through the glass, and from inside the car
I thought I could make out the word "daughter," but it sounded
as if it had been spoken underwater. She let him inside.

I turned on the radio, and since it was a song I liked, I sang
along. *Chances ar-r-re, 'cause I wear a silly grin, the moment you
co-ome into view* . . . Singing helped me to breathe. *Chances are you
think that I'm in love with you* . . . I fingered the silky fringe on my
dress and thought about whether I might make Dad laugh if I did
the Charleston at the dance.

Soon he emerged from the shop using both hands to carry
a clear plastic box out in front of him, like a birthday cake. I
switched the radio off. He slammed the car door shut and turned
to me with a smile that split his face into two faces: the top half,
where his eyes were, belonged to a despondent man; the bottom
half, where his mouth was, belonged to an overjoyed one.

"Margie," he said. "This is for you, Sweet." He proffered
a big pin-on corsage of roses, embellished with ribbon that
exactly matched my frock, freckled with an explosion of baby's
breath, and shimmering with sprays of tiny plastic pearls and
rhinestones.

Now, sometimes, in quiet moments, I think about Dad talking
his way into that locked flower shop and pleading for a corsage.
He looks at all the flowers, unsure of their names and their
mysterious meanings—the spidery chrysanthemums, the obscene
orchids, the sunny gerbera daisies, the voracious stargazer lilies.
He feels frightened and rushed, but then sees the roses and grows
calm, and chooses them, because they are what he knows, they are
the smell of the Virgin Mary, they are the totem of Saint Thérèse,
and they tell him all will be well, at least for a while.

I think of him watching that fledgling florist create the corsage, watching in that close way of his, with his long mouth compressed into a horizontal line. She scowls and wants to rush, but because Dad is hovering she has to do a good job and stick all the pieces together tightly with stem-green floral tape, and make a corsage that won't fall apart, not that night at the dance, and not after, not even after it is all dried up and laid in a shoebox where, fifteen years later, it will slumber alongside a few seashells, a red resin bracelet, a buffalo-shaped belt buckle of brass, a penny minted the year I was born, a recipe for invisible beauty, and four beaded amulets shaped like turtles, not ever.

I think of him watching her reach for a black or a white goes-with-everything ribbon, and I hear him say, "No, wait," and see him run his finger across the rack of ribbons, landing on the one that echoes my dress, because Dad has a talent for remembering the exact nuances and moods of colors, even after seeing them only briefly. "Use this one," he says. The girl asks in an impatient tone, eyes rolling, hot glue gun aimed skyward, "Rhinestones or pearls?" And he, unable to choose between the two, tells her, "Both."

I think of him paying, and tipping the girl an exorbitant amount for her trouble. He turns and sees me waiting for him, with my mouth moving to the words of a song he cannot hear, and he feels a little better, a little glad. This is what I think about, sometimes, when I think about Dad—these few minutes out of our lives.

In the car, I offered a sprawling smile to keep his uplifted mood afloat. He pinned the flowers to me, frowning at his shivery hands. "I don't want to make a hole in your dress," he said.

"It's okay."

A ladybug emerged from the dense ruffled petals of a rose. She crawled out, paused, and appeared to survey her unfamiliar surroundings.

"Well, look at that!" Dad exclaimed in amazement, as if the bug had nudged him out of the constant fog in which he lived, lifted the veil that hung between him and the rest of the world. "There's a lady with us," he said.

"Yeah." I bent my neck to study her.

"Should I take her off, put her out the window?"

"No, no," I told him. "She can stay." She crawled back into her bed of petals. Dad hummed as he drove.

The signature song of the dance was "Yes Sir, That's My Baby," a hit from 1925, and the school gym was decorated speak-easy style. We had our picture taken in front of a big paper mural featuring an assortment of jazzy horns surrounded by music notes. The photographer arranged us, coming so close I could hear the faint whistle of his nose when he breathed. He steered Dad into a glossy, high-backed leather chair and then stood me beside him with my hands resting elegantly, one atop the other, on his shoulder. I wondered if we had ever ended up similarly configured at home. "I blinked," Dad said when the camera flashed.

We danced a lot, and he even dipped and twirled me, which inspired the other dads to do the same with their daughters. When my arms got tired from reaching up, and his back got sore from bending down, we sat on the bleachers. We drank punch that stained our lips an unnatural red and ate cloying cookies that made me sleepy but had a revivifying effect on Dad.

He was abstracted under the swirling hues of the rented light machine. His magnetism, which was the pull of something beautiful but broken and in need of fixing, changed the air around us the same way it changed the pupils in the eyes of the neighborhood wives. His hair was coal black, and it contrasted with his light green eyes, the lids of which swooped down dreamily over the outside corners. His skin was translucent, the blood easily visible beneath his fine cheeks. His body was long, and his head was aristocratic, like one of the nineteenth-century sculptures our class had seen on a trip to the art museum. Some of the female faculty, who had initially dreaded their duties as dance chaperones, held themselves in strange, self-conscious ways whenever Dad and I danced past them. They abandoned the crusty cardiganed slouch of teachers' lounge lunches and Citizen of the Week certificate ceremonies, arched their backs to emphasize their matronly breasts, and sucked in their cheeks to resemble feminine fish.

Dad was oblivious to the women. He was as focused on me as he could ever be, joking, solicitous, smiling, until the last hour of the dance. Then he lost his equilibrium, not on the dance floor, but on the inside.

Maybe the music made him maudlin. The DJ had been punctuating poppy contemporary hits with occasional 1920s tunes, and one of those old-timey songs came on while we danced. I widened my eyes at him because it was called "Margie."

My little Maaarrgie, I'm always thinking of you, Maaarrgie, I'll tell the world I love you . . .

Or maybe it was the Beirut-brown color that my hair appeared to be under the golden glow of the slowly turning mirror ball.

A few other people might have noticed the tears before I did because I had my face tucked into Dad's chest. A movement there jostled my cheek, and that's when I looked up. He wasn't making any sounds, but his mouth was twisted down and his wet face looked like one face again, not two.

We left. By the time we reached the car, he had composed himself. He asked me if I'd had fun. He couldn't bear to mention what had happened. I said I had. At home, I went upstairs, took off my dress, put my corsage in the porcelain figurine shaped like a woman's palm that had always been on my nightstand, the same one that held my rose-scented rosary made of real rose petals, and tried to sleep.

Life got lonelier after that. Even if only a few people had actually seen Dad crying at the dance, it was, after all, a junior high dance, and messages among thirteen-year-olds spread faster than fire on a parched prairie. Soon, the whole school knew. Violet Holmquist retreated to a safe and snooty distance. She joined the girls who stood in gossipy gaggles and whispered "weirdo," "dad," and "drunk" sharply in each other's ears if I chanced to pass them. I did my best to feign contented absorption in a magical, private world of my own, wishing that someone would talk to me while also praying fervently to Saint Jude, patron saint of lost causes and desperate cases, that no one would. Meanwhile, my cheeks flamed in the manner of Dad's, and my feet felt far too big for my body. I buried my head in books.

WHEN I CAME HOME FOR WINTER BREAK after my first semester at college, I tried to be strong in the face of Dad's floundering. On Christmas Eve we watched *It's a Wonderful Life* and exchanged a few presents. I asked him if he wanted to go to midnight Mass, but he said no. We did pray together that night, though. I held his hand while we said the Our Father, and it didn't feel anymore like my little hand in his, but like his little hand in mine. When I went back to school for the second semester, I was very sick.

3   GERBIL   *(Meriones unguiculatus)*

AFTER I RECOVERED FROM THE MALADY that had inspired
Simon to offer me his office sofa, he invited me to dinner. He
wanted to take me to a restaurant he loved near the beach.
I agonized over what to wear. I had never imagined, when
I dreamed of dates on which I never went with college boys who
never talked to me, that anyone would take me to an actual sit-
down restaurant. The dark-haired dates of my daydreams unfail-
ingly escorted me to one of San Diego's numerous two-dollar taco
stands, where my homespun sundresses were always appropriate.

But, of course, Simon Mellinkoff was not a boy. And he, the
descendant of millers, had milled me in his office. And then, a
few days later, he had written, in his standard red ink, a message
at the bottom of my latest Latin quiz: "Will you have dinner with
me?" (It had been a daring move on his part, I thought, considering that, had I been capricious or conniving, or simply regretful
about what had happened between us, I could have handed that
quiz cum invitation straight to the dean. *Pretty complacent*, I
thought.) So I had to find something nice to wear, a task so chal-
lenging I actually solicited the opinions of my roommates.

"Um, who is the guy?" asked Amy, a pasty chemistry major

who subsisted on sugary fruit tarts and never cleaned their gelatinous drippings out of the toaster oven.

"Oh, just somebody I met at school." I cleared my throat. "In Latin."

I held up my only two *dressy* dresses: a floral-printed polyester frock with a lace collar and sleeves that verged dangerously toward puffy, which I'd worn to my confirmation at Holy Rosary at age fourteen (I hadn't grown much since then), and a vintage white sheath accompanied by a slender brass belt with a buffalo-shaped buckle that I had spontaneously and sneakily taken from Rasha's closet over winter break.

"If he takes Latin he'd probly prefer the white," opined Amy. "It's sort of toga-like."

Winnie was an exchange student from Taiwan who kept a pet gerbil in her bedroom. During one of our few social interactions, she had introduced me to the Double Happiness #1 Chinese Goods Emporium in downtown San Diego, where I'd bought a pair of intricately embroidered red cloth shoes that I believed by their brightness alone would bring me good luck. Winnie recommended the floral. "It will show him that you are a modest girl," she said.

In the end, I wore neither of those dresses but instead made a harried trip to the mall, where I procured a black jersey va-va-voom with no sleeves at all, the most grown-up dress I'd ever had, and a pair of high-heeled peep toes. I little suspected when I bought the peep toes, for which I took the time to put a fresh coat of red paint on my biggest and second-biggest toes (remembering Simon's feelings about feet), that I would wear them only once. But that was what happened because, after dinner, as he walked me to my station wagon with his arm wrapped around my waist, before whispering in my ear that I should follow him home, Simon looked toward the ground with a frown and asked, "Are those genuine leather?"

SIMON HAD CHOSEN A TINY MEXICAN PLACE for our rendez-
vous, but it was different from any restaurant I had ever visited
because, as I discovered upon reading the menu, every dish was
prepared without meat or dairy products.

"Wow, this looks delicious," I offered, genuinely intrigued
by the prospect of potato-filled taquitos smothered in soy cheese.
Simon nodded. He appeared as nervous as me and was charm-
ingly tongue-tied. After all, we had only been alone together once
before.

"Your dress," he said, and then drifted off. We looked at
the walls. They were adorned with Frida Kahlo prints and lots
of old black-and-white photographs of soldierly sorts wearing
big-brimmed hats and mustaches, all of them toting guns and
bedecked in bandoliers.

Simon saw me studying them. "Zapatistas," he said. Before I
could respond, our waitress came. Simon ordered for himself and,
just before I was able to tell her what I wanted, he ordered for
me, too.

"How did you know I wanted the potato taquitos?" I asked.
Warmth suffused my limbs, and my feet throbbed in their snug
shoes. Simon shrugged, grinned, fiddled with the pack of cigarettes in his shirt pocket. "Our waitress is so beautiful," I said.

"She's probably a vegan. It's amazing how a woman can
glow when she decides to stop consuming the products of
cruelty."

"Hmm." I nodded. Again, my gaze drifted toward the wall
decor, and Simon, growing more relaxed, went on.

"The Zapatistas. These were members of a guerrilla movement that formed during the Mexican Revolution almost a
century ago. They fought for the rights of the Indians who had
lost so much of their land. Brave people." My eyes landed on an
electrifying portrait of a young woman soldier dressed in men's

clothing. She stood with one hand resting sassily on her hip. In her other hand, she held an enormous rifle. "There were female Zapatistas, too," Simon said. "One of them was even a commander in the movement," he added. "A true warrioress."

The tortilla chips in a basket between us were warm and fragrant, and their bready scent—so wholesome, safe, right, and good—hovered over our table, creating a kind of enchantment. "It's one thing to have beliefs," Simon continued. He crunched a chip between his teeth, swallowed, and lifted a napkin to his lips. "It's another to actually act on them, fearlessly and passionately."

I HAD BEEN TOO EXCITED TO EAT much during our date. But from that night on, Simon sought to nourish me, in his way. "I feel like you're starved," he said one night as we lay beneath his cool bedsheet. "Not so much foodwise," he said, "but starved"—he rested his hand on my chest, where my heartbeat sped up slightly—"here"—then grazed the crooks of each of my elbows, which had so infrequently touched another body in an embrace—"and here"—then laid a palm on my womb, where my left ovary hummed—"and here."

All the characteristics over which I had swooned as a shy smitten student—the dry jokes, the secret Russian surname, the parking tickets, the accent with its promise of mischievous midnight murmurs—came together in one multifaceted and radiant whole, and now that I was close enough, I could actually see them all, shining sharply like cut gemstones, when I stared into Simon's eyes.

He hardly had to coax me to leave Amy, Winnie, and the gerbil to join him and Annette in their labyrinthine house in La Jolla. La Jolla was a quiet seaside town where none of the houses looked anything like the two-story rancher—which, in its pre-decay days, might have had an aesthetic best described as pseudo-Southwestern—that Dad and I had shared in the Tierra de Flores tract. They were sleek and shone like brand-new coins, and even the slightly shabby abodes among them looked as though their shabbiness was cultivated and carefully maintained, not a consequence of sadness. On the sidewalks, wealthy ladies walked little lapdogs with rhinestone-encrusted leashes. There were art galleries specializing in dewy oil renderings of dolphins, and breakfast cafés with offerings like brie-and-wild-blueberry-stuffed pancakes. In spite of my delight at being taken in by Simon, I felt alien as a desert flower in that moist and misty enclave.

Simon's shadowy dwelling was tucked away behind two doors: a heavy, dark outer door, which faced the sidewalk and opened to a courtyard, and an inner door, which opened to the house. Everything about the place was, as he termed it, "green." There were energy-efficient bulbs in each lamp, and the heating and cooling systems were powered by the sun. The various trash cans were all individually designated for different kinds of waste: aluminum, glass, paper, compost. The linens were organic cotton and laundered with earth-friendly detergent. I scanned the gleaming nooks and corners for traces of Simon and Annette—a stray sock or a slip-on shoe, a fallen flaxen hair, an old newspaper—but there were none. All the incidental signs of their lives were swept into oblivion by a maid who appeared thrice weekly. "I think you'll be comfortable here," Simon said.

He bought me bolts of fabric so I could sew as many sundresses with straps that came easily untied as I wished. He paid for my yellow bicycle to have a tune-up. He stared at me with interest even when I was engaged in the most prosaic of activities, such as cleaning the crannies of my ears with a cotton swab or tugging a comb through my uncooperative curls. He listened when I recited the poems I loved best from my Intro to Japanese

Poetry class. And he talked to me. He asked me all the questions he had wanted to ask when I had been nothing but a strange schoolgirl, when he had watched me just before class every day (yes, it had been every day) as I walked my bike across the quad while he sat on his stone bench surrounded by birds.

"Do you have any friends?"

This time I answered him. "No."

"Do you have a family?"

"Not really."

"Do you have a boyfriend?"

"Only you."

"Do you know how absolutely lovely, winsome, and precious you are?" he said, bundling me in his arms, the way a person holds a baby, after my shower.

And it was only then that Simon set about enriching my education. He was impressed with my overall intelligence, and did not care to drill me further in Latin (despite the fact that my grasp of it faltered further with each successive chapter in *Wheelock's*). Instead, Simon educated me about animals and their plight. He picked up where he had left off with the Gandhi quote he had recited in his office, handing me, one after another, all of the books whose titles I had read that day, followed by dozens more with a similar slant.

To feel seen was such a pleasure, and I supposed that if I let Simon make me into what pleased him most he would never stop looking. So I was Simon's girl for the shaping, and I read the books he recommended. But even Simon, incisive though he may have been, couldn't have predicted the depth of my response to all he showed me.

Dad had sometimes told me if I looked closely enough I could see that there was always a bit of heaven on earth. I knew he was right: I saw it easily in the orange blossoms, and in the sweet moments that sometimes flashed between us. But I had never considered that there was a bit of hell on earth, too, until I read about factory farms.

Those places, which produced most of the pork, beef, and poultry that I had long regarded as everyday sustenance, were home to practices so brutally inhumane I could hardly believe they existed in the twenty-first century. Personable pigs, gentle cows, and sensitive, sharp-witted birds who later became mere pieces of meat led, with far too few exceptions, completely confined lives full of emotional misery and physical torture.

I could no longer bear to eat the flesh of creatures who had known so much fear and anguish, who weren't free to feel the sunshine, flap their wings, or even so much as take a step, whose bodies were cut up in countless ways—their beaks, ears, teeth, tails, and more all sliced off while they were still alive, without painkillers—who screamed and cried out to no avail, who were separated from their young or else forced to nurse without ceasing, and made to dwell in the dirtiest of environments, sometimes among the dead bodies of their fellows.

"The meat available at the market today is not anything like it was one hundred years ago before the advent of factory farms. These animals have a completely different quality of life—they have *no* quality of life," Simon said. "Not that an animal's good or happy life is any justification for eating it," he added. "It isn't. Ever. They aren't ours to eat. The only solution is veganism." After all that I had read, it was easy to agree.

Medical, psychological, and cosmetic testing on animals were, I discovered, equally problematic, and much of what went on in labs shocked and saddened me. The animals used in circuses, rodeos, horse and dog racing, and wildlife parks were exploited, and often mistreated. Oh, how my ovary ached. There were too many living beings who were treated as unfeeling objects—and all so people could have the luxury of eating favorite foods, using particular products, wearing certain clothes, or being entertained.

I deposited my genuine leather peep toe shoes, along with all my other animal-derived adornments (an angora cardigan, a wool coat, glossy oxfords, the fur-lined mittens with which Dad had gifted me one Christmas that I'd never had occasion to wear), at the Goodwill. I stopped, as Simon had put it, "consuming the products of cruelty." My cheeks became silky, my hair shiny, my eyes bright.

Simon and I talked about animals every evening. "You're so beautiful. Your heart is so wide open," he said, looking amorous and awed after I summarized (with tears spilling from my eyes) the travesties about which I had most recently learned, or read aloud from an animal rights–angled essay I had written for one of my classes ("An Unnatural Life: The Practice of Beekeeping in Tolstoy's *Anna Karenina*").

Annette observed us quizzically from her perch in front of the extravagant three-story dollhouse her maternal grandparents had presented to her after her mother's passing. Sometimes she interrupted us with questions ("What is a 'bucking strap'?"), and sometimes she crawled onto my lap to comfort me, patting my forehead and cheeks and singsonging, "Don't worry, Margie. Everything dies at some time."

About six weeks after I moved in, Simon decided I had graduated from my survey of Crimes Against Animals and introduced me to what, were it to be included in a course catalog, could only be described as Collaborative Fieldwork.

"I can see you have a feeling about all of this, a genuine feeling, as I do," he said one night while I cleared the table of our dinner plates, which still held mostly untouched portions of a tempeh-and-fennel casserole that resembled shredded paper. (I had agreed to prepare our nightly meals but was new to the art of vegan cooking. "Dad, I'm still hungry," piped Annette, chewing on a fork tine.) "I lead an activist organization called Operation H.E.A.R.T.," Simon continued. "That stands for

Humans Enforcing Animal Rights Today. It has a small student membership. Would you like to take part?"

A FEW DAYS LATER, I PUT ON my lucky red Chinese shoes and Simon took me to Gelato Amore, a two-story café I had never before visited in San Diego's Little Italy neighborhood. Bluesy tunes came through the sound system. Upstairs, a narrow-faced fellow wearing a tweed newsboy cap sat alone, chewed his bottom lip, and studied a big book entitled *America's National Parks*. A smiling young man in a torn T-shirt came up the stairs with a tub full of dirty dishes and disappeared into a hidden kitchen, leaving an inexplicable smell of gardenias in his wake. A group of five college students sat around a table in an obscure corner. They heralded our arrival with a few waves. Simon introduced me. "We have a new crew member," he said with one hand resting impersonally on my shoulder, betraying no hint of his familiarity with the rest of me. "This is Margie Fitzgerald."

The members of Operation H.E.A.R.T. had all renamed themselves after creatures. There was a pretty blonde with a flower in her hair named Bear, a bespectacled gentleman in a wheelchair who called himself Ptarmigan, a girl with a blue-black bob who strummed a guitar and said her name was Raven, and a sturdy tomboyish type who tipped her hat and introduced herself as Orca. "And I'm Bumble B.," said a red-haired boy with baby dreadlocks just starting to appear in his hair. He set aside the digital compass with which he'd been tinkering. "That's 'B' with a period, not 'B-E-E.'" He shook my hand.

AS SIMON HAD EXPLAINED TO ME EARLIER, Operation H.E.A.R.T. had recently scored some significant coups against both local and large-scale animal exploiters. The slatternly owner of a puppy mill in Poway—into which the Operation crew had snuck one balmy night—appeared on the local news after she awoke to find her front door emblazoned with the purple-painted phrase "Kanine Killer!" ("The intentional spelling error made it more memorable," Simon noted). After neighbors told curious cops that the sounds and smells coming from the mill seemed "off," it was investigated and, because of its pitiful preponderance of malnourished pups, shut down. Then the Operation created a pamphlet entitled *The Circus: Hell for Animals,* and distributed thousands of copies of it citywide to coincide with the arrival of Barnum & Bailey. The size of the crowd inside the colorful tent, the *San Diego Sun* reported, was noticeably modest compared to previous years.

My first mission with the Operation concerned a Pacific Beach pet store that the crew had staked out for two months: Azar's Pet Palace. During that period, spies (Ptarmigan and Bumble) posing as shoppers had observed that numerous birds, including canaries, finches, and parakeets, had died from dehydration and unsanitary living conditions. The owner of the pet store, though generous with seed, was less conscientious when it came to refilling water cups and cleaning out cages.

"What we need," Simon said, "is to get someone in there who can get those birds *out.*" I couldn't help but think of Old Peep, who, under Dad's delinquent care, may have suffered before he died. And I was still so wounded by all I had learned during my recent reading spree that no effort to help seemed too small. I agreed with Simon: the birds must be saved.

When a "Now Hiring, Apply Within" sign appeared in the Pet Palace's window, the crew decided I was the girl for the job. "Look at her, she's, like, the dream employee," said Bear, adjusting the daisy behind her ear.

"Yeah, perfectly groomed, sweet, soft-spoken. With her rosy cheeks, who wouldn't hire her?" said Ptarmigan, lifting his animated hands, which compensated for his lifeless legs, into the air.

"Plus, she's cute as hell," added Orca, lowering her fedora smoothly.

"What's your work experience?" asked Simon. When he found out my résumé began and ended with the Shake Shack, where I had whirred blenders through all four years of high school, he manufactured me a new employment history. It listed an array of pet stores—all of them in faraway Kalamazoo, Michigan, where I was supposed to be from.

"Now go in there and get the job," Simon said with a slight squeeze of my arm that heightened my usual eagerness to please. The crew quivered with excitement, and then, as was our ritual, we gathered in a close circle, piled our hands one on top of another, and recited in unison—"Humans Enforcing Animal Rights Today!"

Azar was friendly. He scanned my application with unconcerned eyes and hired me immediately. "You seem like a very nice girl, Dolores," he said, calling me by the alias Simon had created. "I have trouble, such trouble, keeping the good people in here."

The crew had been right about Azar's inadequacies as a purveyor of pets. ("This is ninth American business I have run," he told me one afternoon, staring with solemnity into the bearded dragon's terrarium. "First pet store.") During my brief tenure at the Palace, I did my best to compensate for his failings and bring the assorted creatures, along with their varied habitats, into optimal condition. After two weeks of hard work, during which I impressed Azar with my skill in handling the animals, who all scurried in terror from his hirsute hands (and during which my left ovary never got a rest, surrounded as I was by so many doe-eyed dependents), it was finally time for the Operation to execute its plan.

Bumble came into the store, posing as a customer. He had

been in several times before, "browsing for a bunny," he had always said with a saccharine grin.

"Ah! My redheaded friend!" Azar rubbed his palms together. "So good to see you! I have many nice rabbits—er, bunnies?—in now, just came in. Many nice."

"Wonderful," Bumble said. "I think I am *finally ready to buy*." And that was our code, my cue to begin.

Swiftly, I darted toward the wide double doors at the front of the store. "It's stuffy in here, Azar," I said. "I'm going to open these for a while." The day was dazzlingly sunny. The wild birds outside sang siren songs. The sky was beckoning, the branches of the trees welcoming.

Azar ignored me, as I'd thought he would, so busy was he speaking to Bumble in the sultry tones of a seasoned if unsuccessful salesman. "But this one," he purred, "ahhh, this one, look at these markings, bea*uuu*tiful." He lifted a rabbit into the air by the scruff of its neck. Its little legs moved helplessly. I tore my eyes away and lurched in a half-walk, half-run toward the birdcages, where dozens of captive chirpers cheered me on. My heart pounded so fast that I, too, felt like a bird—like something nervous and fragile, with fine white bones, and like something expansive and surprising, something that stretched itself open to reveal a sudden and startling beauty.

One by one, I opened the cages. The birds, ten, twenty, thirty of them, emerged in a flurry of orange and cobalt, red and brown. Their wings made a thrilling sound.

Azar let out an uncomprehending cry. He dropped the rabbit into a mound of sawdust.

I was surprised at how readily they shot straight for the opened doors and fluttered up into the blue. They looked so bright, so foreign—like paint strokes of gold and violet and chartreuse—as they flew above the parking lot and into the trees where the common birds waited. I stood by the doors for a moment, mesmerized by their colors in the sun.

Only a few stragglers remained in the store, confusedly hovering and squawking in wonderment. Before Azar had time to open his mouth, Bumble, who I had learned possessed a fondness for high-tech gear, garments, and gadgetry, removed a specially made net with a retractable pole from his backpack. He expertly used the net to catch the lingering birds and release them outside. (He had practiced this technique for weeks with Raven, who had tossed small cat toys into the air for Bumble while she read her favorite magazine, *Billiards USA*.) All the while Bumble shouted at Azar, "You are an abuser and exploiter of animals and a killer of birds! We are friends of animals who watch when no one thinks we are watching, and act when no one expects we will act!"

I was silent, absorbed in trying to coerce a frightened lovebird out from between two bags of dog kibble. He was part of a family of two, a bonded pair, and I had often noticed how they perched side by side and slept huddled together, their breasts pulsing with synchronized beats. The lovebird's companion had already flown away.

"What is this?" Azar cried.

"We are Operation H.E.A.R.T.!" said Bumble.

"What operation?" Azar didn't understand. "I am calling the police!" He was purple in the face. I felt sorry for him, and for the lovebird.

Bumble was impressively adept with his net. "Margie!" he called. "They're all out! Let's go!"

"Who is Margie?" Azar yelled.

The lovebird could not be persuaded. "Come on, come on," I pleaded softly. I was dripping with sweat and could feel my throat thickening with tears. "Your friend is already outside," I said. "Come on!"

"Margie!" Bumble called.

"Please don't stay here. Don't be scared. It's better out there," I cooed. The lovebird blinked at me. He wouldn't move. Bumble's slick hand clasped mine. He dragged me out of the store. "Run!" he said. I ran, but I left a shard of myself with that lone lovebird who would not leave, and who reminded me of someone.

Bumble and I dove into our waiting getaway car, Simon's 2002, and Orca gunned the engine. Azar screamed at me from the sidewalk, "You little idiot!" As we drove away, I saw him staring at the sky, slowly turning in circles.

AFTER THAT, I DIDN'T GO HOME for visits with Dad. I just sent notes, or an essay I'd penned for one of my classes ("Radical and Revolutionary: What the Animal Rights Movement Can Learn From Fyodor Dostoevsky's *The Devils*"). I spent all my free time with Simon, Annette, and the crew, plotting the next campaign.

I THOUGHT A LOT ABOUT SIMON'S STATEMENT that marriage was like Chinese water torture. He had repeated it several times since the first. Of course, he was so characteristically bone dry when he said it that I could hardly tell if he was serious. The very ridiculousness of the idea of Chinese water torture, a made-up kind of torture said to induce insanity but not really used by anybody, led me to think that maybe he was kidding. (But it was always so hard to tell with Simon. Even when he looked straight into my face and shared the tenderest of sentiments—"When I watched you push your bicycle across that crowded campus quad, I saw beauty all around you"—his eyes had a dark, gemlike impenetrability. While I could see all the things I loved about him in their facets, I could not so easily see his feelings in them.) Still, it stung me a little to have something about which I'd dreamed for so long—union with another human being—spoken of in such a cavalier way. How could the snuggly, side-by-side peace and matching heartbeats of the lovebirds in Azar's be akin to the annoyance of having drops of water drizzled on your forehead, against your will, one at a time, forever? I remembered the one and only time Dad had spoken to me at length about his marriage to Rasha. Had there been anything torturous about their time together? It was only their being apart, I had always assumed, that tortured Dad.

ONE SMOGGY SUMMER DAY WHEN I WAS SIXTEEN, I wandered barefoot through our house, steeped in the torpor that occasionally overtakes teenagers, the feeling that something is about to happen but it is impossible to articulate just what—the feeling of waiting for life to begin.

Through the open windows I heard the distant buzz of sprinklers, and the closer one of flies, hot and iridescent and hungry. Dad was enclosed in his den, Doral dangling, long fingers wound around his glass of Maker's Mark with a splash of water. Predictably, I padded into the master bedroom to embark on my ritualistic hunt for relics, which is what I always ended up doing on such slow-motion afternoons.

I didn't hunt for the type of relics the nuns had always told us about in CCD, not the old alabaster bones of martyrs, or a russet lock of Mary Magdalene's hair, or a strap from Saint Francis of Assisi's sandal, or a stolen fiber from the Shroud of Turin. And I didn't hunt for almost-relics, like the one I had tucked in my top dresser drawer, a single rose petal glued to a paper card printed with the words "This petal touched to a relic of the Little Flower, Saint Thérèse," with which I had been presented after my first communion. I hunted for Rasha relics.

I turned into the master bathroom and pulled out a shoebox stashed under the sink. It was full of her old beauty supplies. There were several lipsticks. Their waxy surfaces, I had noted during countless previous inspections, were still lined with the prints of her lips. Had she bought them on impulse, I wondered, during a typical toilet-paper-and-toothpaste run to the drugstore? Had she tossed them boldly into her basket in hopes that maybe

Champagne Charm or Frosted Fuchsia would supply a spark
that may have been missing from what would ultimately be
her short sojourn in the suburbs? Had she tried them on alone
behind the locked door of the pink-tiled bathroom she shared
with Dad, taking slow, private breaths as she judged the effects of
their poisonous pigments on her eyes, skin, mood? And had she
filled the wastebasket with tissue after tissue streaked with smears
of dissatisfaction? Or had she liked the mouth that shone back
at her from the mirror? I pulled the cap off one, Peach Fizz, and
twisted it so that the shiny stick emerged from its cartridge like a
beacon. I waited a few moments, then twisted it back down and
replaced the cap. I had often thought about trying on one of the
lipsticks, but didn't want to erase the marks left by her lips with
my own.

In addition to the lipsticks, there was a pair of stray hot rollers
on which approximately six Beirut-brown strands had snagged
and stayed. There were tiny glass bottles of mysterious oils, their
Arabic labels faded and frayed at the corners, a three-pack of
velvety pink powder puffs with one puff missing, and a sterling
silver compact engraved with the words SHE WALKS IN BEAUTY
LIKE THE NIGHT. There was a half-used container of Pond's cold
cream that, when opened, revealed the impressions of two fingertips, an unopened box of Pears soap featuring a Gibson girl's old-
fashioned face, and an emery board with the ground keratin of
Rasha's nails still embedded between its minuscule grains. There
were a few bobby pins strewn on the bottom of the box. Because
they carried no traces of her, I had no rules against using them. I
inserted them into my hair to fashion a temporary updo.

Thus adorned, I sat on the closed toilet seat and waited for a
feeling of nearness, of completion, to visit me. The only feeling
I had was one of limitless longing. It hung over me stubbornly,
like the stifling summer air. I took the pins out and let my hair
fall onto my sticky neck.

Then I moved back into the master bedroom and opened the drawer of the nightstand on the side of the bed where Dad never slept. I pulled out a picture postcard. The photo had been taken from the sky and featured a cluster of white buildings beside a turquoise sea. "Beirut City" was printed on the image in a decidedly dated font (the letters appeared to have been dashed on with a thick paintbrush in early-eighties-style haste). The message side of the postcard was blank. Instead of putting the postcard back, I slid the drawer shut and carried it away.

Later, Dad saw me using "Beirut City" as a bookmark. He walked down the stairs while I walked up, my eyes flitting over the contents of an opened hardback: *Celluloid Sirens: Great Beauties of the Silver Screen.*

"Where'd you get that?" he asked with a startled expression. He slowly pulled a smoke from between his lips.

"The library."

"No, *that.*"

"Oh. The nightstand by your bed."

Dad wasn't bothered by my snooping or my snatching. He only leaned on the stair railing, stared down at the first-floor foyer where several of our shoes lay scattered, and said, "She sometimes missed Lebanon, I think."

This fascinated me. I almost could not believe that the woman in the photo albums who belonged so entirely to Dad, who gave her dimpled cheeks to the eye of his camera for immortalization, who still lived in half of his divided face (which half I couldn't be sure), whose hair still clung to curlers beneath the bathroom sink, had ever belonged to another place, and longed for it. "How old was she when she came here?" I asked.

"Oh, twenty-four. Almost twenty-five."

Had she bought the white dress with the buffalo-shaped belt buckle when she arrived? Was the buffalo the most American thing she could find, a symbol of her new home? Dad was still, but I sensed the possibility for conversation. He kept his Doral out of his mouth, suspended. And he had never, never told me enough about Rasha. I hurried out another question. "Why did she come?"

Like most immigrants, Dad said, she had hoped to find better opportunities. "She'd studied the art of perfumery back home in Beirut. She'd been apprenticed to a master there, an old man who made scents the ancient way, using only natural materials. Your mother was ambitious, and an artist. She always told me, 'A good perfume is an invisible kind of beauty.'" Dad smiled. "When the old perfumer died, your mother made the move to America. She had a cousin here. She brought her kit with her—a beat-up black suitcase filled with a hundred tiny bottles of attars and absolutes."

I imagined Rasha's kit, countless corked vials filled with extracts of every plant, bloom, bark, resin, and root in existence. Maybe she had sniffed and caught the essence of everything the earth had ever grown and could combine those spoils in infinite ways to create entirely new types of loveliness. Then I pictured her landing at John Wayne Airport, black suitcase in hand. "How did you meet her?"

She was working, Dad explained, at her cousin's dry-cleaning business in Anaheim. Dad stubbed his cigarette out on the oak stair railing, leaving a sooty black burn. He did this without realizing. "The day before I was supposed to show my first house, I went to that dry cleaners to drop off a suit. I rang a bell. Your mother came out of a great, crowded collection of clothes on mechanical racks—coats, skirts, blouses and sweaters, all this fabric, silk, corduroy, linen, velvet. And still, she was the softest thing in the whole place. So pretty. Have I ever told you what her name means?"

I nodded, and a gazelle ran from one end of my mind to another. Dad went on. "I don't know what I said when I handed her my suit, but she laughed. She had tiny sparkles of sweat on her forehead. She was a so golden. She had the sun in her—there were yellow flecks of it in her brown eyes."

Dad's facility with fanciful descriptions had served him well at Sunshine Realty, where he could make even the homeliest of hovels sound like a heartwarming hideaway. I wondered if he had first developed this talent while searching for ways to describe the comeliness of Rasha, if he had lain awake nights, lovestruck, composing secret songs about the girl at the dry cleaners. "She was wearing all white that first day I saw her," he continued, "and every time I came in, which was often. Everything I had in my closet, even blue jeans, went in and out of that place three times before I finally asked her to have dinner with me.

"On our date, she wore a white dress with a brass buffalo belt. She said it was hot in the dry cleaners and wearing all white made her feel cooler. She said most of the buildings by the sea where she came from were white, but from what she could see the buildings around here were painted all kinds of colors. She said it was a bit quixotic, but I knew she meant chaotic.

"After dinner, we took a walk around this neighborhood"—he extended an arm down toward our front door, on the other side of which sprawled the orderly rows of houses, the lawns (all of them but ours) fertilized to near-fluorescence—"the Tierra de Flores tract, brand new then, where I was selling my first properties. She wanted to see where I worked. We strolled through the half-built houses. They were like skeletons. Some had birds nesting in their beams. Our footsteps echoed on the fresh cement foundations. She took off her shoes and showed me how she danced."

She was living with her cousin who ran the dry cleaners, Dad said, and sleeping on a couch—though she didn't sleep much. "She told me she sat at the kitchen table every night experimenting with perfume formulas—or recipes, as she called them. She worked from the time the nightly fireworks show at Disneyland began—she watched it religiously through the kitchen window— until the early morning hours, just before that first slice of light sneaks into the sky. And when she fell asleep she always dreamed of where she wanted to live, in an apartment by the sea, with a white cat for company. 'There is a Ferris wheel at Newport Beach,' she told me. So she was saving up for her own place there, and was going to open a little perfumery.

"But one night she told me she loved my eyes." At this recollection, Dad looked right into *my* eyes, something he did so rarely it made me shy. "She said, 'I would love to have a child with you because he would have your eyes, with that green color, and the way the lids swoop down over them'—and she touched my eyelids, Margie!" Dad's cheeks flushed and his voice shook. "This woman who knew the names of all flowers, who could tell whether wine tasted of strawberries or soil, this woman who danced in her bare feet, she had told me about her child with my eyes."

"Then what happened?" I prompted gently. I couldn't help myself. I was greedy for more images of her, pictures with more dimension than the album-bound snapshots. I already knew how the story of our family ended. It was the story of how our family began that I wanted to possess.

"She was my bride," Dad said. "We were joined forever. Her cousin ordered us a fancy wedding cake and closed the dry cleaners for an hour to come over to City Hall and be our witness.

"I had been promised a great deal on a house here. We chose the lot we wanted. It had that big old magnolia on it." Dad nodded toward the front yard where our tree stood, the only one of its kind in the neighborhood. It was our home's sweet-smelling sentinel, a favorite perching place of birds, and with the passing years its beauty had increased in tandem with our house's growing decrepitude. "The builders were planning to rip it out, but

Rasha asked them to leave it. So instead of the sea, she got magnolias. But," Dad said with a faint frown forming between his eyes, "I thought she was happy.

"We didn't have any furniture at first, until my grandmother died and we inherited everything she'd had, including that painting of an Indian maiden in a canoe—it had hung in her bedroom for sixty years. The first thing Rasha did with the painting was smell it. She pressed her nose right up to it and guessed instantly the perfume that Grandmother Fiona, whom she had never met, had always worn. 'Mitsouko,' she said.

"She worked on her perfume recipes every night at the kitchen table. She finished her favorite one just before you were born, Margie." Dad closed his eyes. "Those were good months. We felt like two kids who had the run of a big castle. We always *chased* each other up these stairs."

I looked at the way the carpet at the center of each stair was worn. When I stared at it long enough, I could hear the thumping sounds of their feet rushing up.

THE SUMMER DAD TOLD ME ABOUT CHASING Rasha up the stairs was the same summer I started driving, and lots of late nights I took Dad's Skylark for solitary excursions. I loved the moon-coolness of the nighttime, and the nocturnes of the nightbirds, and the fine gloss of dew that slightly darkened the streets. The Skylark always smelled like Dad (a synthesis of Ivory soap and cigarettes), and of the leather of the bench seat (which had eight little tears mended with eight silver squares of duct tape), and of the coffee that he spilled when he drove from one newly listed home to another.

My night drives, like my lazy afternoons, all started out as meandering, but they invariably led to the same place. I tried to tell myself I was only going out for fresh air and a change of scenery, but really I was after a sensation that hit me hard, a heart-drug that made me both dreamy and desirous. I always got this feeling by driving out of our neighborhood to the houses in the hills.

The houses in the hills were relics of a different sort, left over from the time when there had been vast orange groves covering the flat land below, not endless tracts of homogenous homes like ours. The hill houses stood on streets lined with old-fashioned lamps that cast a mellow amber glow. They were covered in ivy, blanketed in bougainvillea, clutched by climbing roses, guarded by trellises. There were always lights shining out of their stained glass. And in the cool shadows of their low-hanging eaves and the fairy-tale tangles of their honeysuckle, where crickets bedded down to sing, the hill houses contained an almost unbearable romance.

When I parked the Skylark to sit and be near them for a while, I thought about the people who lived inside, the husbands, wives, mothers, fathers, babies, brothers, sisters. I would sit with my arm dangling out the open window and my head tipped back against the seat, watching, listening, and longing. I would glance over to the empty passenger seat, past the cellophane cigarette box wrappers and Sunshine Realty notepads bearing Dad's name and photo, past the pieces of newspaper folded into unfathomable origami airplanes that went nowhere, and I would almost see Rasha sitting there in a white dress with the backs of her legs sticking slightly to the seat. I would almost see her there, and then instead of me behind the wheel it would be Dad. I would be in the backseat, but I would be able to tell he was smiling by the curve in his right cheek, and "Chances Are" would be playing on the radio, and we'd be on our way home to our own house high in the hills because we were one of those families that the streetlamps shone above.

Once, in the middle of such a reverie, I caught a flash of my face in the side-view mirror. When I saw my ravenous expression, I felt embarrassed, even though no one was around but the cricket choir. I drove out of the hills toward home, hoping for one of the rare occasions when Dad had fallen asleep in his recliner and I could gingerly pull his reading glasses from his bowed, stubbled face, cover him with a blanket, and hear the soft purr of his snore, but when I arrived he had already gone up to bed, and his chair was empty.

I TRIED TO TELL SIMON about my night drives to the hill houses. "They gave me a feeling," I said. We lay in his bed face-to-face with our knees pressed together. Already we had talked, touched, and turned away from each other to finally fall into sated sleep. But, as was our habit, one of us had turned back around to face the other, and the other, sensing a stirring, had done the same at almost the exact same moment, so that, forgoing sleep a little longer, we could touch and talk again. He bathed my face in his hyacinths.

"What was it?" he asked. "The feeling?"

"I can't explain," I said.

"Try." The moonlight slipped into the windows through the trees that enclosed Simon's house. Annette was tucked in her room down the hall, a babyish stream of saliva slowly dampening her pillow. A nightbird crooned.

"It was," I whispered, "almost like this."

AFTER I HELPED TO FREE THE BIRDS from Azar's Pet Palace,
Simon drew me even closer and enveloped me even deeper in his
dark warmth. We whispered away many nights in his bed while
I stared at the sharp, shadowed planes of his strong Russian face
(it was easy to imagine him as young Melnikov, the dashing,
doomed soldier who was never mentioned in *War and Peace*),
and traced my fingertips over the broad high cheekbones that
rose up into his sad eyes, and petted his lush eyebrows and
eyelashes. I loved to pinch the plumpness of his earlobes, which
echoed the plumpness of the place where his thumb joined his
palm and betrayed the vague vulnerability I'd sensed the first
time I saw him.

Simon liked to keep the house completely closed up, but when
I saw the eager jasmine vines shooting up from his wife's garden,
which had been left to grow wild and weedy in her absence, I
begged him to open the bedroom window. He relented, and we
breathed the flowers all night.

With our noses touching, he told me about all the dreams
he had for the future of Operation H.E.A.R.T., about
the projects he envisioned, and about the offshoots of the

Operation he hoped to establish across the nation and, eventually, the world.

"The problems in this country are only a drop in the veritable ocean of animal suffering and injustice that drenches the globe. Look at Africa," he mused. "Just think of what we could do about the poachers there."

He asked me my opinion on many matters, for now that I had been in the field, albeit in what had only been categorized as a "low- to medium-risk situation," but in the field nonetheless, he trusted me to assess the feasibility of the other campaigns we had tentatively planned.

"After we are in Doctor Sorensen's office," Simon whispered, referring to the Del Mar veterinarian who catered to the moneyed crowd and made his own fortune declawing Persians and docking the tails of Dobermans, cruel and unnecessary practices, "do you think we will have enough time to pour purple paint all over his surgical instruments before the security company responds to the alarm system?" Purple was the Operation's signature color.

"Yes, but it depends on how many of us go in . . ."

"I want to take the crew to Tijuana so we can see how bad those bullfights really are. Who do you think I can count on," he asked me, "to stay serious and not just disappear for a beer somewhere on Avenida Revolución?"

"Ptarmigan, for sure," I replied. "Bear, maybe . . ."

And, on many nights, once he had finished soliciting my take on this idea or that, he asked me, with his hyacinth breath in my ear, "How long will you let me do this for?" and stirred in secret and familiar ways under the sheets, which were subtly scented with the sweat our skins seeped in our sleep, and with the narcotic smell of the jasmine that thrived despite neglect and clung with tenacious tendrils to the window screen.

"As long as you want," I always answered. And I felt a pleasant kind of cloak falling over my consciousness, softening my awareness of time, blurring the space between us, and stilling, for a few precious moments, the ladybug that so often wandered behind my eyes. I smelled jasmine and heard Simon's voice saying, again and again, "My girl, my dear girl."

SOMETIMES, ALMOST AGAINST MY OWN WILL, I gave quick consideration to how paltry—silly, even—Operation H.E.A.R.T.'s actions were, especially in contrast to Simon's ambitions. We:

smashed the windows of Superior Skins, a fur coat and fine leather goods shop in the Gaslamp Quarter, and destroyed its inventory with seven cans of purple paint;

staged a peaceful protest near the pony ride at the annual Lakeside Fair. ("These poor, put-upon ponies," Ptarmigan yelled into the camera, "deserve better!");

removed dozens of live lobsters more than once from the confines of an enormous saltwater tank in a chi-chi seafood restaurant called Laminaria, where Bear-with-a-flower-in-her-hair worked as a hostess, and transported them in the back of my station wagon to the shores of Ocean Beach, Pacific Beach, and Mission Beach during high tides;

infiltrated the cognitive research laboratory of our university with the help of a brilliant, wheelchair-bound exchange student from Prague, one Damek Kafka, a.k.a. our very own Ptarmigan in disguise, who surreptitiously slipped lab mice into secret compartments I had sewn into his voluminous sleeves and then released them into the eucalyptus groves;

and left harassing notes taped to the vehicles of employees at a cosmetics testing lab in Escondido, where, I imagined, there were dozens of bunnies smeared in Champagne Charm, Frosted Fuchsia, and Peach Fizz.

Still, despite their relative inconsequentiality, I was thrilled with these small successes, as were Bear, Ptarmigan, Raven, Orca, Bumble, and Simon. After all, we were each of us just looking for a way to make a difference.

Bear was an Iowa girl with yellow corn silk in her hair and auburn freckles sprinkled across her nose and cheeks. She was the oldest of eight children raised by a conservative preacher and his obedient wife who, when it came to looking after their offspring, were always, Bear said, "otherwise occupied." Consequently, Bear had been a mother of sorts to her brood of siblings. She was mild and milky, patient and soft-spoken, with a slightly distracted air, as if she had early on begun retreating into her own world (with a placid crescent-moon smile on her face) as a way to cope with so many children constantly clinging to her floor-skimming skirts. Bear's father had lately disowned her. Though she was a perfectly respectable nursing student, she also enjoyed reading philosophy and pursuing interests that were, he said, "ungodly" (astrological charts, chakras, dowsing rods, crystals, Kundalini yoga, etc.). Her mother echoed his disapproval, but she still sometimes sent Bear boxes of sugar cookies on the sly.

Raven had been orphaned at ten after her preppy parents, college sweethearts, died together in a paragliding accident off the rocky coast of Maine, her home state. She was shipped to California to live with her grandparents in Santee, a sleepy suburb east of San Diego where there was, she always said, "nothing happening of note." She found her father's old guitar in a closet and taught herself to play. Starting at the age of eleven, Raven made a habit of hitchhiking—instrument in hand—into the city so she could busk in front of a place called the Cue Club, where she spent all her earnings beating men three times her age at billiards. The "Santee Shark," as they called her, deposited her pool winnings into a college fund she established for herself and was now paying her way through school. As a math major specializing in geome-

try, Raven knew the exact shape of the invisible triangle a billiard
ball would trace atop a pool table when struck in a certain way,
and the precise trajectory at which her parents had fallen from
the sky.

Bumble was the son of a half–Crow Indian mother who had
caught the admiring eye of his father, an uptight army officer,
after she'd participated in the American Indian Movement
standoff at Wounded Knee in 1973 and her picture appeared in
the paper. Bumble was a self-described military brat who had
seen most of the world before his father was finally stationed at
Camp Pendleton. Having spent so much time immersed in army
culture, he loathed conformity, uniforms, and short haircuts but
had developed an obsession with all types of gadgets and gear.
Friendships had been impossible due to the frequency with which
he had been forced to move, but the greenish, glow-in-the-dark
radiance of a GPS device picked from one of his dad's pockets
was always a comfort to Bumble (who had also been, he had once
told me in confidence, "very fat"). He had hopes of becoming
an engineer, but was floundering in college because it was, he
believed, just another oppressive institution with too many rules
and regulations.

Orca was always unafraid to speak her mind and had once
boldly spoken her heart to her fourth-grade classmates when,
during Show and Share, she had held up a framed photo of Susie,
her towheaded second cousin from Georgia, and said, "This is the
love of my life. I get crushes on girls." After that, she felt she had
nothing to hide. She dressed exclusively in slacks, vests, and bow
ties, and often asserted that she was "handsomer than most guys."
With her curling black hair and arch smile, she was. After legally
emancipating herself from her parents, who shared none of Orca's
sense of peace with her identity, she began supporting herself as
a floral designer. (It was she who supplied Bear with the flowers
she always wore in her hair.) When she wasn't in her art classes at

the university, she worked at a popular flower stand in Leucadia, a bitsy beach town up the coast. Because she made the best floral arrangements in the county, customers didn't raise eyebrows when they noticed she had used a pen to draw a mustache on her upper lip—an occasional addition to her grooming routine in which she delighted.

Among the crew there was none sweeter or gentler than Ptarmigan. At seven, suffering extreme nearsightedness and in desperate need of spectacles (a fact to which his mother, who had refused to name a father when she'd borne Ptarmigan at the age of fifteen, was oblivious), he sped on a borrowed skateboard down a steep hill in starry Los Angeles and smashed right into a jacaranda tree, which he hadn't seen until it was too late. When the paramedics lifted him onto a stretcher, he was covered in hundreds of blossoms. They were, he said, "like little purple trumpets. I still like those flowers. They remind me of angels' trumpets, and I was born in the City of Angels, and I think angels must have been with me that day, because I only lost the use of my legs and not my life." Ptarmigan shared an apartment with his mom in the Kensington borough of San Diego. He stayed up late most nights writing plays because, he said, the defining moment of his life had not been the accident, but the first time he saw *The Glass Menagerie* performed by the theatre department at the university, which he promptly joined.

Despite the diversity of our backgrounds, we all had something in common. And it seemed as if the longtime loneliness we had each known would lessen the more we worked together toward our shared, if small, goals.

Still, sometimes I felt like the only one in the crew who had genuine and enduring empathy for the creatures we sought to help—a real piercing pain over their often pathetic circumstances. Even Simon, despite his passion for the cause, was oddly indifferent to animals as individuals, which confused me. There were many nights I could not fall asleep, so fixated was I on the left-behind lovebird at Azar's. Simon didn't understand. "You're sentimentalizing," he said. And though Annette found the companionship of her plethora of plush whales and bears insufficiently stimulating and routinely asked for a "pet cat, bird, dog, fish, or turtle," Simon refused. Pet ownership, he said, was yet another assault on the rights of animals. "The very idea of a 'pet,'" he declared, "is totally offensive, comparable to keeping a human enslaved."

"What about a hermit crab?" she suggested, sucking the bottom of her blond braid, hoping a crustacean might make the cut.

"No, Nettie."

"Didn't you ever have a pet when you were small?" I asked Simon one night after he had tucked Annette into bed with a stuffed chimpanzee clutched against her boyish breast.

"Yes," Simon answered. "Rupert. Our beagle. He went with my father." Then Simon told me that his dad had hastily packed his clothes, books, bowling trophies, shaving kit, and Rupert into his car and driven away from home for good one evening while Simon, his mom, and his big sister sat unawares through the usual Friday night services at Congregation Beth Elohim. They had all four of them licked sweet pancake syrup from their fingers as a family at eight that morning, and by eight that night they were a family no more.

That was the most Simon ever told me about his youth. He never spoke about the past, or about himself. The crew liked to speculate about Simon's background and pose possible reasons for the gemlike quality of his character—as hard and impenetrable as it was radiant and alluring. And they had known for months that Simon and I were amorously involved, so we all gave up pretending otherwise.

"You're good for Simon," Bear said as we all exited the

Sea Breeze Cinemas, where I'd dragged the gang for a special screening of *The Misfits*—ostensibly to examine the problem of wrangling wild horses for deposit to the dog food factory, but actually, at least for me, to steep in Marilyn's sad sweetness for a while. "Especially if it's true," Bear added.

"If what's true? That we're together? But it is."

"No." The others looked at each other. Ptarmigan nervously rolled his wheelchair backward and forward. "Just—" Bear began.

"—what some people say," said Raven.

"About what?"

"The truth about Simon's wife." Ptarmigan took a deep breath and stared into my face through his round little wire rims. "We've heard some rumors around campus—one of my professors in the theatre department teaches in the literature department, too. Some say that she didn't really die—she just left."

"Left?"

"Yeah, well, that's what some people whisper—" said Orca.

"But that's impossible," I said. "What about Annette? Her mother wouldn't just *leave* her." I felt a twisting in my stomach.

"Why not?" asked Raven. "People do all sorts of things. And Simon might have found it easier to tell his kid and everyone else that the wife just got sick and died."

Possibly I'd learned a secret about Simon, I thought, fingering the sharp edges of the *Misfits* ticket in my pocket. Possibly I'd learned *the* secret about Simon, shaky Simon who shaded his eyes and lived in a shadowy house, but I would not, I decided, say anything about it.

Simon had, with his tear-tinged hyacinth sighs, breathed life into me. I could feel his affection all around me. It was a vapor that enclosed me. And I lived in a state of elation because of it, and also a state of fear that he might one day pull his attention back into himself, tuck it behind his dark eyes, and I would wither without it. I tiptoed through my own happiness, hoping never to do anything to push him away. Maybe that was what Simon had meant by marriage being Chinese water torture—maybe by Chinese water torture he meant to describe the latent terror of losing what we most desire to keep.

"But, guys, you don't really know what happened," I said, "so what's the point of speculating?" The crew was silent. "Anyway," I continued, "what about the movie? What did you think?" And then there was no talk of Simon's maybe-wayward wife, or even of wild horses, only of Marilyn. "She's so tender," said Bear, "you just hate to think of anything bad ever happening to her."

I DIDN'T ADOPT AN ANIMAL-INSPIRED NAME like the others. The truth was—though I never said so—I couldn't bear to replace "Margie," not because I was proud or particularly fond of my hopelessly clunky moniker, but because it was something Rasha had given me. The crew didn't mind too much.

"I must say, though," Bumble said, "if you *were* to take a new name, it would have to be 'She-Bird.' "

"Indeed," seconded Ptarmigan.

"Not only," continued Bumble, "because of your affinity with avian creatures, which was so evident that day in Azar's"—he didn't know about the lone lovebird over whom I tossed and turned—"but because of your own seemingly inherent birdishness." He took a drag from one of the marijuana cigarettes he kept stashed in the futuristic fanny pack—it was called, he said, a marsupium, and it was, he added, waterproof—that encircled his waist.

"Yeah, and because you are delicate—" added Orca.

"I'm not delicate."

"—yes, delicate, and always looking around curiously at everything."

"She-Bird!" Bear hugged me.

ON MY BIRTHDAY, JUST BEFORE I BEGAN my second year of college, Simon, Annette, and the crew took me to the same vegan Mexican place where Simon and I had gone on our date. "Why does she get to have a monkey?" Annette asked repeatedly, pointing to a Frida Kahlo self-portrait on the wall. I stared once more at the photo of the female Zapatista, the warrioress. Between bites of potato taquitos, Bumble pulled a tiny box from his marsupium and slid it across the table to me.

"From all of us," he said.

I looked at Simon. He looked back in the familiar way that said he could see straight through my flushed face and messy hair into the nesty coils of my mind, and this was what he saw, I knew, shooting synaptic sparks: I had friends. *Yes,* I thought in answer to his question of so many months earlier, *I do have friends.*

Inside the box was a silver charm bracelet decorated with its first charm—a bird in flight, naturally. When I put it on, with Bear's help, the crew cheered, and Annette offered an exuberant "Woooo!"

Later that night, when we were snug in his bedroom, Simon gave me his present—a second charm for my bracelet. He dropped it into my hot palm and I savored its metalline chill for a moment. Then I remembered a fragment from the conversation I'd had with Dad a couple of years before, that day on the stairs when he'd told me about meeting and marrying Rasha. "Love," he had said, "is laying your head down on the tracks while knowing full well that the train is coming, and enjoying the coolness of the metal against your neck." I held the charm up to the lamplight. It was half of a broken heart. One side of the heart was curvaceous and smooth, while the other was jagged, like a serrated knife. "I have the other half," Simon said. I curled my arms around his neck, and just when I was about to utter the word "Where?" Simon put a finger over my lips and pointed once to his own bare chest.

THERE WERE MANY SATURDAYS WHEN, as I walked through the
cool corridors of Simon's silent house, where the air was always
sea-heavy and damp, I spotted Annette alone in her room, sitting
still as a sphinx, limp hands folded in her lap, staring into her
cavernous dollhouse with its miniature mother, father, son, and
daughter, its pixie furnishings, its dainty dishes, and I knew
we had more in common than a home. In such moments, I
recognized the perpetually waiting posture and hungry look of a
motherless girl.

Whether she really had died or just departed for greener
grass, Annette's mother was gone, and so was mine. Dad always
said Rasha had disappeared in a blur of red poppies.

Naturally, I wished I had a mother to talk to about Simon's
diamond eyes and broken edges, and about the irresistible pull
of hurt, helpless things. And I wished I had a mother to talk to
about the limitless longing I so often felt, a nameless longing I'd
first known as a youngster when the orange blossoms entered my
mind's own mythology.

In the old days, the blossoms had been abundant in our
neighborhood. But long before I was born, the orange groves had

been razed to make way for the maze of tract housing developments. The tracts were assigned romantic Spanish names that struck their inhabitants as enticingly exotic—Vista Verde, Via de Oro, El Sol Rojo, and of course our own, Tierra de Flores.

Still, there were a few lonely orange trees left standing here and there in our town, relics from the region's rural past. One afternoon when I was thirteen, suddenly curious to discover just how their blossoms smelled, I hunted the trees from atop my bicycle. When I found one, I stood on tiptoe, straddling my bike's seat, and broke off clusters of dust-filmed leaves where the five-pointed blossoms bloomed. I pressed my face into the waxy white stars and felt a tingling vibration, like a cello string plucked just once, in my womb. I realized the scent was one I had, in fact, smelled my whole life, that it had been there, in the air, all along.

I wondered how something could smell like love and like home at the same time. I made a habit of keeping the blossoms on my nightstand, floating in a chipped ashtray Dad had discarded. My dreams were of dark-haired strangers who pulled the back of me against the front of them in spooning embraces.

During the days that followed such dreams, I had that limitless feeling of longing, a nameless longing, so that the smallest sight, such as grass blades barely moving in the breeze, or a lone moth on a dusty porch light, made me sick with longing, longing to swallow the whole of life in one gulp, or to be kissed with deep, secretive kisses, to be loved by someone who could see me, the dark stranger of my dream life, someone who had known me forever in the dream world, who could speak my language, whose tongue would find my tongue. I had a searching feeling, and I was alarmed, so many years later, to find that I still had it, and I wondered why my time with Simon had not extinguished it, why it lingered. I wished I had a mother to talk to about it.

I knew something was missing. I looked and sniffed and felt around for it. And lying in bed beside mysterious Simon, listening to the rise and fall of his snores, or setting birds and lobsters free, or staging protests in front of ice cream parlors, or stealing into labs to liberate rabbits and rats, I whispered it—*something is still missing*—but I couldn't hear Rasha, couldn't hear her telling me just what it was.

I FIRST NOTICED JACK DOLCE just before one of our Operation H.E.A.R.T. meetings upstairs at Gelato Amore. I was standing in line downstairs, waiting to order a drink, running my fingertip across the jagged edge of my half-of-a-heart charm, when I saw him as if for the first time, though surely I had seen him many times before. It was as if I'd pushed partially through a bubble in which I'd been enclosed for the better part of a year, and there he was, with a secret beauty that suddenly revealed itself. He was like a red resin bracelet of Rasha's that I had once seen but not seen, and he radiated a romantic red amore essence that harmonized perfectly with his environs. I saw how the girls in line before me all had eyes gone glassy at the sight of his rich red mouth and his cocoa-colored doggy eyes, for he was a real Italian-American boy in Little Italy. In his warm rosiness and sensuousness   which was painted all over his face, audible in his voice, traceable in his movements—there were implicit promises of nuzzling animal love. Only the narrow-faced fellow in the newsboy cap, evidently a Gelato Amore fixture and the sole male in line, seemed immune to Jack Dolce's charms.

When it was my turn to order, I did so while looking not at him but at the menu, in which I feigned intense absorption. "Ginger ale, please," I said, squinting. I thought I saw him smile out of the corner of my eye.

"No gelato for you?" he asked, tapping on the cooler. It emitted a faint, constant hum I'd never noticed before, but now I could hear it even over the plaintive song (*In the evening, in the*

evening, darling, it's so hard to tell who's going to love you the best)
that played over the sound system. It sounded almost exactly like
the hum of the old-timey streetlamps near the hill houses back
home.

"No, thank you," I said. "I don't eat dairy."

"What?" Jack Dolce shouted, and it was impossible to tell
whether he truly had not heard me or was just incredulous.

He handed me my drink. Then he reached into the cooler
and, before I could protest, slid a pastel pink plastic cup my
way. It was spilling over with lush cream all dotted with fleshy
cherries, spring green pistachios, and chunks of chocolate that
matched his eyes. "Here you go, darling," he said. "Spumoni."
He winked. "That one's on me."

"He's not one of us," Bumble said, nodding vehemently, when
five minutes later, upstairs at our usual meeting table, I proposed
recruiting Jack Dolce as an Operation H.E.A.R.T. crew member.
Simon had not yet arrived. The untouched cup of gelato melted
into a pool before me.

"He's a rogue," Bear mumbled, pulling the petals from
the flower in her hair with what struck me as unaccountable
bitterness.

"He's so . . . coarse," said Ptarmigan, with lips pinched and
eyes squinched behind his glasses.

"We're talking about the kind of guy who lives to 'eat, drink
and be merry,'" added Orca. "Doesn't he even have that tattooed
on his arm?"

"He has no ambition." Raven wrinkled her nose. "He doesn't
care about anything. All he does with himself is work at this
place."

Simon slid into a chair beside me and we all fell silent.
The subject of the coarse rogue coiled into the ether with the
smoke of our captain's Camel. "What is that?" he asked, eyeing
the ice cream. But later that night, after our meeting was done

and we disbanded downstairs, I saw Jack Dolce—finished with his shift—don a holey sweater, mount a rusty red bicycle, and pedal into the moonlight. He was alone, and he was singing to himself in a surprisingly pliant and pretty voice. I sensed that underneath all of his seductive mannerisms, but not too deeply buried, there was an absolutely singular personality, a subterranean richness and complexity of character. Yes, there was something about him I vaguely feared and almost recognized, but couldn't define.

In an effort to solve the bothersome mystery of who or what he was, I dismissed the crew's views and began a sort of surreptitious study of Jack Dolce. I visited Gelato Amore for nearly an hour every afternoon. Always Alone. Pretending to pen that week's batch of Operation H.E.A.R.T. propaganda, I occupied a downstairs table where I had a good view of him. I learned a lot by eavesdropping on the conversations he had with customers over the music he played at a loud volume (almost always warbly songs by someone I had never heard of, a Cherokee folk singer he professed to worship named Karen Dalton). I discovered:

he had, in childhood, been an altar boy and attended Our Lady of the Sea Catholic High School, but, judging by the tattoo of a faceless Virgin Mary on his left forearm, he was even more of a lapsed Catholic than I, who had not attended Mass for well over a year;

he had, as the crew had so judgmentally noted, no career or worldly ambitions to speak of, and planned to continue working at Gelato Amore, he said, for as long as his boss and coworkers would tolerate his clumsiness (he sometimes slid the gelato cooler doors open with too much bangy zest and repeatedly knocked over a large canister crammed with hundreds of teensy tasting spoons, scattering them all over the sticky floor and rendering them instantly useless), his laziness (he often arrived to work late, with sleep still crackling in the corners of his eyes and the red

kiss-prints of one or more admirers on his neck), and his taste in
music;

he refused to drive a car because he thought it was unnatural
and, he said, practically a guarantee of premature death, and got
every place he needed to go on his crimson cruiser (paradoxically,
without a helmet);

he was, as his last name more than hinted, Italian, and though
his family had lived in San Diego for two generations, he was
descended from a long line of Tuscan dairy farmers;

he had many girlfriends, or, as he called them, "ladyfriends,"
all of them cutely tattooed about the ankles and shoulder blades
and succulently shaped;

he regularly gave the entire contents of his overflowing tip jar
to a homeless man named Baby Joe who often came into the café
slurring, "Hey, Dolce, loan me some change?";

he was absolutely free of guile, still had a little boy's smile, was
always kind to ice-cream-craving children, and only wanted to
gulp from what he termed "the good cup of life" for as long as he
could;

he embodied the earthy essence of those ancestral Tuscan dairy-
men who spent all day walking in fields among long-lashed milk
cows and all night rolling with pretty peasant girls in the grass;

and (this last characteristic I noted with delighted downcast
eyes), he liked me.

"Look at Margie Fitzgerald sitting over there, pretending not
to hear me," he would say to one of the regulars. "Isn't she something? The cutest, the kindest. Hey, Curly, look up! Let me see
those eyes." But I would only sort through my stack of Operation
H.E.A.R.T. flyers ("A Dirty Business: The Tragic Truth About
Greyhound Racing") and try to appear occupied.

After a couple weeks of this, I asked Jack Dolce in a very serious tone, frowning my smile into submission, if he would ever
consider joining Operation H.E.A.R.T.—*if*, I added, we were to

make him a formal offer. I pushed the disapproving faces of the
crew out of my mind. Jack Dolce gave me his guileless smile. "No
way!" he said, and then added, as if attempting to be more polite,
"I'm way too out of shape for that sort of thing." He patted his
very slightly protuberant belly. I reminded him that one of our
most effective members was in a wheelchair, but he didn't seem to
hear. "I've got a question for *you*," he said. "What's the story with
your boyfriend?"

I swallowed. "Excuse me?"

"The old guy with the beat-up Beemer and dark glasses."

I was disconcerted to hear Simon referred to as "the old guy."
Tongue-tied, I blinked.

"When I go upstairs to clean tables and you're having your
meetings, he's always looking around at everyone to make sure
they aren't looking at you. And if it wasn't for the way he looks
at you, I'd've figured he was your dad." Jack Dolce cleared his
throat and wiped an imaginary crumb off the countertop. "Forgive me for saying so, but it's kind of strange," he said.

He was the first outsider to comment on Simon and me, and
I wanted to say, "It's neither strange *nor* any business of yours!"
But I couldn't get the words out. All the protective pity I felt for
Simon came flowering up.

Still silent, I stood and began to gather my things. Jack Dolce
coaxed a napkin from a snugly stuffed dispenser. "I didn't mean
any offense," he said in a gentle voice. He wrote something down.
"This is where I live." He handed the napkin to me. "When
you're ready, come find me."

I rolled my eyes. I crumpled the napkin into a ball and shoved
it into my pocket. But I checked it with my fingertips for the
remainder of the day, finding it a soft sort of charm, one with no
sharp edges.

· · ·

I STOPPED VISITING GELATO AMORE ALONE and tried to cease
contemplating the curious creature that was Jack Dolce. The
Operation was more active than ever. Each week, we celebrated
another victory against animal exploiters, and we began making
headlines among the modest-but-still-worth-mentioning news
tucked within the middle pages of the *San Diego Sun*. In just one
month, we:

effectively canceled a rodeo in Ramona by stealing each and
every bucking strap on the premises (BUCKING STRAP BURGLARY,
RODEO RUINED, OPERATION H.E.A.R.T. SUSPECTED);

decreased attendance at the Del Mar Racetrack by approximately 15 percent when we intercepted visitors between the
parking lot and the entry turnstiles and horrified them with flyers
featuring disturbing behind-the-scenes photographs we had taken
on the sly (SECRET WORLD OF HORSE RACING "HORRIFIC," SAY FOR-
MER FANS. OPERATION H.E.A.R.T.'S INFLUENCE?);

snuck into a foul-smelling fur farm full of chinchillas, all
of whom we captured and left on the front stoop of the local
Humane Society under cover of night (RODENT OVERLOAD:
HUMANE SOCIETY GLUTTED WITH MYSTERIOUSLY ABANDONED
CHINCHILLAS, OPERATION H.E.A.R.T. AT WORK?);

and, at a particularly offensive booth at a craft fair in Vista, we
smashed fifty glass shadow boxes featuring captured rare butter-
flies pinned into permanent submission, which were for sale at a
hundred dollars each ("BRATS WITH BASEBALL BATS," VENDOR SAYS,
DESTROY BUTTERFLY ART AT COUNTY FAIR, OPERATION H.E.A.R.T.
AGAIN?).

The *Sun* had fallen in love with us, it seemed. Still, while
the headlines always held back from declaring us unequivocally
responsible for the acts of derring-do that brought, as Ptarmigan
put, so much "pizzazz" to the paper, they did bring us a certain
degree of notoriety. This, coupled with the fact that the police
evidently had more pressing concerns (understandable in a

crime-ridden county of three million people) than the shenanigans of a small group of college kids obsessed with animal rights, enveloped the crew in a kind of heady haze—one in which it seemed the only consequences of our actions were the flickering beginnings of fame and, of course, happier animals. "Good work, crew. We are *on track,*" Simon said.

The others were gratified by the glory of being mentioned in the paper. Bear even created an elaborate scrapbook comprised of all our clippings. Bumble, shaking his head at what he called Bear's "archaic habits," scanned the clippings into his computer. But I appeared, much to their perplexity, insufficiently excited. "Can you believe this?" Raven said, shaking another edition of the *Sun* in front of my face. I offered a slight sort of smile.

The truth was, a new desire had welled up in me, one that I couldn't bring myself to articulate to the crew, or even to Simon. It had happened gradually over the last several months, and now, I feared, it set me apart. Maybe, I worried, I had spent too much of my free time reading animal books—not just nonfiction treatises like the ones Simon had given me, but novels, and even children's books I'd purloined from Annette's room (*Misty of Chincoteague, Where the Red Fern Grows, Penguins!, Pat the Bunny*). Maybe my left ovary had twinged far too many times during our campaigns, leaving me in a permanent state of oversensitivity. Or maybe I had, a couple of years earlier, taken too many drives up to the hill houses to capture an ever-elusive feeling of closeness that I constantly craved. Whatever the cause, animals, the idea of animals, the feeling of animals—not just the physical fact of their existence or their suffering—had sunk straight into my soul.

I wanted to hold them all in my hands, to know their little touches, to press my fingers into the fleshy cushions of their paws, to hear the clacking hardness of their hooves. I wanted to grow goosebumps from the ribbons of air they exhaled against my cheek and into my ear, and to be softly sniffed by them, and tickled by wiry, weird whiskers. I wanted to be bitten, scratched, to have my blood drawn one droplet at a time by fangs and claws, and I wanted to sleep among them in a sighing, smelly pile. I wanted to tuck my beak into my feathered chest and fall asleep to my own breast's rising and falling, to warm myself, to make sad shrill songs in the night, to be a soloist. I wanted to smell every feeling before it was felt, to run, to dig, to dive, to breathe underwater, to open and close my silken gills without trying. I wanted to frighten, to surprise, to wiggle my antennae, to let my hair grow matted, to exude strange perfumes, to buck, bellow, bugle, and bray, to low, to preen, to stot, to trot. I wanted to bear young and lick them clean, to usher them forward on their wobbly legs, to nose the ground in search of the finest-tasting grasses and flowers, to live and move according to the seasons. I wanted to love because my body and biology willed it, to love without any threat or presentiment of loss, without any ladybug wandering behind my eyes. It was no longer enough to just help them. I wanted to be among them.

Among them, I knew, loneliness was an impossibility. I could feel that all of them, every species, even those carnivorous ones who hunted and ate others, were part of a community from which I and every person I knew were excluded. But I didn't know why we were excluded, always outsiders, and always manipulating a realm of which we were not even a part—*their* realm.

I wondered why there was a separation, and how people had ended up in a position that was so harmful to animals, and then in a position to try to undo the harm. The situation seemed artificial, somehow—that we must be "us" and they must be "them." I was troubled, a little, and so was my sleep.

One night, several weeks after he'd written his address on the napkin, I had a dream about Jack Dolce. In the dream, he stood beside the cooler at Gelato Amore. I approached him and said, "One small spumoni, please." He dropped his ice cream scooper and lifted up his T-shirt, and I saw that he had the proud, bulging, red-feathered breast of a bird. When he reached toward me, I saw that the back of his hand was covered in a thick, furry pelt, while his palm was soft, pink, and puffy. He was careful with his claws when he clasped my fingers. As he bowed his head and pressed his lips to my knuckles I saw, tucked beneath the dark waves of his mussed hair, two curved horns, like those of a goat. And when he slipped off his shoes, I noticed that his feet were webbed. Something in the way he smiled, lifting his long tiger's whiskers skyward when he did, told me that he was the happiest man I had ever seen. I awoke from the dream slick from the top of my head to the tips of my toes. My sweat-soaked nightgown formed a fine film on my skin, and, thus cocooned, I remembered that once, only once, I had looked up when I felt Jack Dolce looking at me, and allowed him to peer into my eyes. I rolled over and clung to Simon in fear, Simon, my Simon, my miller, Simon Melnikov of the silver hair and the nineteenth-century Russian army.

"A dream," I mumbled into his neck, searching for a hint of hyacinths. "Oh, a dream." I tugged at the plump lobe of his ear.

Simon stirred irritably and with a sudden sniff. Half asleep, he slurred, "Are you still worrying about that lovebird?" and then immediately started to snore, and I was left with nothing to do but press myself as close as I could against his hard back.

AFTER MY DOLCE DREAM I KNEW I was changing, but I soon discovered that Simon was, too. His change seemed to have happened suddenly. Later I realized it had probably been happening for a while and had gone unnoticed, the way orange blossoms can be smelled but not smelled, or a red resin bracelet can be seen but not seen.

I also discovered that, even though I might have been changing myself, Simon's shift cut my heart to such a degree that I would have, for my part, never begun to change at all and would have made sure Simon did the same, so we could have stayed near to each other always, with our noses pressed in the nights, with my thumb pushed into the cushions of his palm. I would have ignored utterly and forever any sense of something missing and remained an earnest explorer of his impenetrable eyes, a steady She-Bird. That was how I felt when Simon transformed, that I would reverse it, if only I could.

One Saturday morning in January I rose just before noon, my usual weekend wake-up time. During an unsuccessful search for Simon in the chilly chambers of the white-walled house, I found only Annette, still in her fleece footie pajamas. Simon had cut off the white vinyl tips of the footies to make room for her rapidly growing feet. Her bitsy toes hung out and now, encased as she was in the soft lavender fleece, she struck a slightly simian figure. She was in her bedroom, speaking intensely to one of her stuffed animals, an opossum: "I *told* you, Mrs. Gerkin, the *only* food that lasts forever is honey."

I stepped into the backyard wearing a pair of Simon's boxer shorts and one of his undershirts, crunching a spoonful of cereal in my mouth. Simon was in his wife's garden, stripped to his underwear, pushing a shovel into the dirt and squinting against the sweat that stung his eyes. His black-and-white-checkered trousers and button-down were in a pile next to a patch of pansies.

I saw that he had done much pruning, snipping, shaping, and weeding. The garden looked nearly groomed. And he had picked dozens of flowers. They snoozed beside him in a bucket.

"Wow," I said in a voice garbled by cereal and sleep.

"You're up bright and early as usual," he said. I smiled, but he did not. "And I see you've helped yourself to my clothes—"

"We look the same." I giggled.

"—and to some breakfast." He snapped the end off each word as he uttered it.

I didn't know what to say. He had asked me what my favorite type of cereal was as soon as I had moved in and had been faithfully bringing it home from the supermarket ever since.

"The garden looks amazing."

A full minute of silence passed. I tried not to chew too loudly. Then he said, "This is close to how she kept it."

He didn't say anything else, just stood back and studied a lavender bush from which he had removed a handful of dead flowers. He was without sunglasses, and his eyes were full of the pain I had, until that moment, always sensed but never seen.

He squeezed the dried lavender blooms hard in his hand and then uncurled his fingers to let them fall to the ground. Their smell, old and herbaceous and so very different from our rich and moony jasmine, wafted up to me. I went inside.

I TRIED TO BECOME AS UNOBTRUSIVE as possible. I knew Simon waged a perpetual and private battle against moodiness. And it had been his talent for temperance, for avoiding extremes of happiness or unhappiness, that had charmed me when I had been nothing but his admiring student—the way he walked a tightrope between the two extremes, so his smiles were always dry and wry, his laments always tinged with amusement.

I waited, outwardly patient and uncomplaining, for Simon to regain his equilibrium. I occupied myself with a Jane Goodall book. I didn't ask any questions when he stopped joining Annette and me for dinner. I switched on my book light to continue my reading when, after finishing his increasingly vigorous nighttime ablutions, he turned off the lamp, fell into bed, rolled over, and pretended to sleep.

I thought about all the nights we had lain, after talking and touching, with our backs turned to each other, and how a feeling—a mutual, tender uncertainty, the uncertainty of lovers—would paralyze us. I would lie wondering, *Does he still want me?* And he would lie wondering, I suspected, the same. And then one of us—it was always impossible to tell which one—would slightly shift and begin to turn, and the other would, at almost the same moment, also turn, and in a second we'd be facing each other again, our hands searching for each other and damply clutching, our arms encircling shoulders and waists, saying without speaking, *Yes, I do still want you, yes.* How many times had it happened? Four? Six? Sixteen? We had met. We had met in that sliver of a place, a sweet place.

And now there were only aching nights when Simon, after brushing his teeth and sliding under the sheets, lay with his back to me and I lay with my back to him, and then I began the turn and he did not follow it. He stayed still, and when I turned all the way around he still did not move, and even when I rested my fingertips against the back of his neck where his straight hair stopped and the skin was soft as a boy's, he remained where he was, and the hours passed, and we did not meet.

A couple of weeks after Simon first groomed the garden and brought it to a condition of such order and formality it rivaled the famous Roman Gardens of Lucullus mentioned in *Wheelock's*, I made my way down the hallway toward his study with a tray bearing dinner. I wore an apron I'd sewn with some of the fabric he had bought for me. It was printed all over with seashells. I hoped he might notice it. But instead of stepping right in to say, "Here you go, handsome," and smilingly setting down his plate, I stopped at the threshold.

Simon had his elbows on his desk. His eyes and forehead were crushed into the palms of his hands. He was encased in a box hammered together by his own thoughts. His back muscles twitched tensely beneath the fabric of his shirt, and he exhaled a deep, long sigh.

Watching him, I had the disturbing sense of almost-knowing, the feeling that comes when a not-quite-remembered word is on the tip of the tongue, or when a fast flash of a forgotten dream flickers into the mind and then flees, or when the secret truth of someone's heart sits like a snake pausing in tall grass just long enough to show the pattern of its skin and then slips swiftly away so the design is forever irretrievable.

Looking at Simon, I almost knew. I almost knew something about love, about marriage, about torture, but then he suddenly turned around in his chair, and what I almost knew flew like so many uncaged birds out of the room.

"Margie," he said. There was a period audible at the end of my name.

"Here's dinner," I said in a strained chirp. "It's that recipe I found, for wild-rice-and-tofu-stuffed bell peppers . . ."

"Okay," he said. I set the tray down. He looked at me with his soft gray eyes—the gray of the mourning doves that lived on the ledges beneath the eaves of his house. They were Annette's favorite animals. "I like their calls," she always said. When he looked at me and I looked at him, I got the usual warm stirring in my belly. *He's back*, I thought, and waited for him to call me to his lap. But instead he just repeated my name, and turned his face away, and told me that one daughter was more than enough, and that I needed to leave. "I'm tired," he said.

WHAT PERPLEXES ME IN RETROSPECT is that I didn't feel awful right away. If my heart were a peach it stayed unbruised and intact for several hours after Simon's declaration, which I'd heard clearly but, perhaps out of self-preservation, did not understand all at once. It was only partway through the next morning that the break happened—slowly at first, as if a pair of thumbs were carefully, even tenderly, splitting my peach apart right up the length of the cleft, causing the juice to seep out and make a sticky mess of my insides. And then, all of a sudden, it was halved. It made a sound like tearing flesh, and the pit fell out without any prying and rolled somewhere unseen where I was sure I'd never find it again, and I huddled behind the locked bathroom door, crying into my hands. I never wanted Simon to see me cry or to hear any of the questions that clustered in my clogged throat, and I left before he had the chance.

. . .

ON MY NIGHT DRIVES TO THE HILL HOUSES, I had always
loved to imagine the rooms where the children slept, warm and
dreaming with eyelids gently rippling, and especially the master
bedrooms—the bride and groom rooms, the mommy and daddy
rooms—where all the life-giving saps that flowed through the
houses originated. Those rooms, I knew, were kept safe in the
embrace of the climbing ivy, honeysuckle, and roses that covered
their exteriors, and set slightly aglow by the proud lamps that
lined their streets.

But after Simon told me to go, it seemed as if I had dreamed
the hill houses, that perhaps they had been nothing but images
beneath my own rippling lids as I'd slept in my girlhood bedroom beside the ashtray of floating orange blossoms. Perhaps
the houses and the feeling of closeness they represented were an
invention, and what was real was only this: People were separate
from one another, always, and could not really connect, could not
merge at all, and not only that, the ivy and honeysuckle and roses
cared little for us because people were divorced from the earth,
too, and from all of its creatures, who could not understand our
language any better than we could theirs, and it was just as the
nuns in CCD had always said, we had been cast out of Eden, we
were set apart from the earth and everything on it, estranged.
The old union that we had once known, ages and ages before,
had been severed forever, and there was no reclaiming it. Everyone was alone.

I MOVED INTO A STUFFY STUDIO APARTMENT and, for companionship, adopted Charlotte, one of the rabbits we had rescued
from an addiction research lab who had since been living at the
Humane Society. Simon had been adamant that I remain active
in the Operation, and when he e-mailed me an impersonal
notification about a crew meeting at Gelato Amore one week

after I settled into my new place, I dried my tears and quelled my constant nausea long enough to attend. I had not yet told the crew about my move or what had happened in case Simon changed his mind and we could go back, back, back. I hoped he wouldn't notice how much weight I'd lost. Our time together had confirmed that he was, after all, an Audrey man, but compared to me, emaciated by the loss of love, Audrey was positively zaftig.

Jack Dolce was gone that night. I shuffled up the stairs, walked past the man in the newsboy cap, who was scribbling intently in a journal, and collapsed into a chair at our usual table. "What's the matter?" Ptarmigan observed me with a furrowed brow.

"Are you sick?" Bear asked, stroking my hair.

Simon had his sunglasses on. I melted with sympathy for him the same way I had the first time I'd seen him. I felt sadder for him than I did for myself. He cleared his throat. "If I may have your attention, please," he said. "This meeting is very important. I want you all to listen carefully, and as you listen, remember the following: Change is part of life. It is inevitable, constant, necessary. Just as we, Operation H.E.A.R.T., seek to promote change, to be, as Gandhi said, 'the change we wish to see in the world,' so, too, must we undergo change."

Everyone stared at Simon. Bumble tugged on his shortest dreadlock. Raven played a few dissonant chords on her guitar. Ptarmigan nervously rolled his wheelchair backward and forward, over and over, until he ran atop Orca's toe.

"Watch it!" she shrieked.

Simon continued. His cigarette was unlit and nestled between his fingers. His upper lip trembled. "I'm officially resigning as the leader of Operation H.E.A.R.T."

The group sucked in a collective gasp. Raven swore.

"After much deliberation," he said, "I have decided that for the Operation to remain strong—to thrive, to flourish, to grow—

it requires leadership with more vitality than I—for reasons I
won't delve into—can presently offer."

"Who?"

"But—"

"What are you talking about?"

"Shh," Simon said. "I have one request that I ask—no,
demand—that you fulfill if Operation H.E.A.R.T. is to continue
on without me." Once more, I recalled the way Simon had spoken
about the female Zapatista commander when we'd shyly examined the wall decor during our one and only date. "A true
warrioress," he had called her.

"I request that Margie Fitzgerald," Simon continued, "succeed
me as Operation H.E.A.R.T.'s leader."

I swallowed and looked at Simon with big eyes. "I don't
want," he turned his face toward mine, "any questions or protests.
I've thought about this carefully."

I DIDN'T UNDERSTAND WHY SIMON BEQUEATHED the Operation
to me. Maybe, during those times when he had held me in his
arms after my shower and told me I was lovely, winsome, and
precious, he had perceived the depth and persistence of my longing, my limitless longing, and known that if he removed himself
from my life I would need something to do, to put my heart
into, and would only benefit from the added responsibility. So he
handed me a cause that would command my attention, occupy
my thoughts, and provide a channel for my emotions, which were
unwieldy as an unchecked garden.

Or maybe Simon felt, when all was said and done, that he
had taken something from me, and the least he could do, being
a decent man, was give me something in exchange.

THE STUDIO WHERE I LIVED with Charlotte was one of several
just like it in a huge Victorian house. I had to walk down a dark
hallway to use the steamy communal bathroom. There were
tall, spiney cactuses growing beneath a clothesline in the backyard. The rent was only three hundred dollars a month, and
the landlady, while showing me the studio, had used the word
character—which excuses all architectural and other oddities,
including slanted floors, unclosable cabinets, and century-old
smells—a dozen times. My new neighborhood was called
Middletown because it was halfway between the up- and down-
towns of San Diego, close to the airport and the interstate. It was
a burg that felt between worlds, full of ephemeral embellishments
and forgotten people. In Middletown, all the paint was peeling, but most of it was masked by the knotted masses of purple
morning glories that grew everywhere of their own accord. The
women wore pink foam hair curlers out of doors, the men stood
on the sidewalks every day feeding pigeons, and there was always
the rusty sound of a faraway accordion intermittently drowned
out by the roar of rooftop-skimming airplanes headed for the tarmac. Charlotte grew accustomed to the growl of engines overhead

and stopped hiding under the bed (for she was, and knew herself to be, prey to large, airborne things) after a few weeks.

Most nights I could not sleep (and not because of the planes, whose engines quieted after ten), so I slipped on jeans and my lucky red Chinese shoes under a white nightgown and walked like a ghost to the nearby Middletown Community Garden. It was a patchworked assemblage of wildly verdant plots that some neighborhood folk had established on a vacant lot. I climbed over the locked chain-link fence, careful not to tear my gown, and wandered among the moonlit blooms and grasses and leaves, whose secret saps flowed, I thought, most magically through their veins in the darkness and silence of night. I always sat for an hour or two on the same mound of moss-covered dirt, beside a patch of gourds, and rested my tearstained face in my hands. The vines of the gourds had fine coiling tendrils that seemed to stretch closer toward me the longer I sat. I imagined that if I rested there until dawn they would coil around me the way they did nearby sticks and stems, cling to my mussed curls and eyelashes, encircle my fingers and toes. Being in the garden helped to soothe the constant ache that originated in my chest and oozed into my limbs. And the spirited scent of the white, night-blooming moonflowers transmitted some vibration of gratitude for being alive, which had a heartening effect.

I wrote a letter to Dad to tell him about my change of address. Not knowing how to explain I had moved in with my Latin professor, I had never told him I'd left the mildewy apartment I'd once shared with Winnie and Amy. But now I was hankering for contact and, particularly, for comfort, paltry though it might have been, considering Dad's ignorance of my situation.

And since it was comfort I sought, calling would not do. Dad had never been a good phone talker. Our calls inevitably collapsed into awkward weather commentary before they'd even had a chance to really begin. Writing, however, could sometimes open

Dad up, as I'd learned during childhood stays at summer camps
in the Southern California pines. This was because upon receiving a letter he had time to compose his thoughts and string them
together in an engaging way. What sometimes arrived from Dad
via the USPS in response to a missive I'd mailed was more like
a pearl necklace than a plain letter—something to be treasured
forever, precious and Piscean, an enchanting expression of his
dreamy oceanic depths.

Then again, he was also capable of sending a five-word note
scratched in haste on one of his Sunshine Realty notepads. I
decided to gamble.

Dear Dad, I wrote, *It's been so long since we've talked. How are*
you? I miss you.

I moved. I wanted to have my own place so I might better concen-
trate on my studies. It's a gorgeous, historic apartment constructed
during the turn of the century, and overflowing with character
(I thought Dad might appreciate some realtor-like rhetoric).

I have a view of the ocean (that wasn't strictly factual, but "ocean"
sounded so much better than "airport"), *and an adorable pet rabbit*
named Charlotte. School is fine, and San Diego is as paradisiacal as ever.
I've spent time on the beach (I didn't mention that my time on the
beach consisted of releasing live lobsters kidnapped from a fancy
restaurant), *and in the country* (I decided to leave out any refer-
ences to fur farms, rodeos, puppy mills, and the like), *and seen*
some dazzling, exotic birds in a multitude of hues (I thought it best
not to note that I'd witnessed those birds flying out of Azar's Pet
Palace).

What's new, Dad? How's work and how's home?

I stopped writing and tried to think of what else to ask him,
but nothing came to mind, and I grew more and more melan-
choly with the waiting. That was all Dad had. Work and home.
He didn't even have me. I was away. And I had not visited for
over a year.

Well, Daddy, I just wanted to say hello. I hope you are well. I don't need anything.

XOXO,

Margie

The cap of my previously pristine pen was completely chewed up. I wanted to add a P.S. I never wrote a letter without doing so. A P.S. could be the very best part of a letter. Once, I'd had a pen pal in Tokyo with whom I'd connected through a free pen pal matchmaking service that advertised in the back of a magazine. As our correspondence progressed, I developed a habit of writing my pen pal very brief letters of only a few lines, followed by postscripts five times as long. She eventually wrote me saying she wished for a pen pal who wrote in a more traditional American style and did not want to correspond further, at which point I determined to try and shorten my postscripts, but vowed never to eliminate them.

I couldn't think of the perfect P.S. for Dad, though numerous possibilities came to mind: *P.S. Is this what heartbreak feels like? P.S. Am I going to end up like you? P.S. What makes a man want a girl and then not? P.S. Did you ever not want Rasha? P.S. What's wrong with me?* Exhausted, I put the unfinished epistle under my pillow and slept on it, fitfully.

Every morning I rose early and, smoking cigarettes I'd stolen from Simon before my move, drove puffy-eyed and perfunctorily groomed to campus for my classes. I transferred out of Simon's Intermediate Latin class, in which I had been earning an A (for effort, though not for ability), into the only other comparable course offered—one taught by the English fellow whom Simon had so dismissively dubbed a "summus maximus bore." Simon approved the transfer and so did Summus Maximus, who, when I entered his classroom for the first time, said with a smirk, "Yes, you're not the only person I've met who has experienced difficulties with Mr. Mellinkoff's teaching style," and my eyes welled as I remembered Simon the way I always would: seated on his desk in his black-and-white-checkered trousers and canvas slip-ons, with his shirtsleeves rolled up, telling us with his sweetly stilted semi-smile about Lesbia insulting a tormented and lovelorn Catullus in front of her husband.

But then I saw a familiar face in the back row—Jane, my old classmate and study partner, with whom I had once commiserated about Simon's crush-inspiring characteristics over cups of PG Tips. We'd lost touch after I'd grown involved with Simon and the Operation. "What are you doing here, Margie?" she whispered as I slid, sighing, into the desk beside her. Her smile dimmed when she studied me closely. "You've gotten so thin," she said, soft-eyed as ever.

"What are *you* doing here?" I whispered back.

"After Mellinkoff gave me such a bad grade last semester, I decided to try Professor Weatherbury. He's a lot easier— though not nearly as easy on the eyes." Weatherbury cleared his throat at us.

After class we made plans for a study session at my studio. Jane wrote down the address in bubbly cursive and tried to temper her excitement at the prospect of finding out all that had happened since I'd disappeared with Simon and left her faking a series of sneezes in his classroom so long before.

In her distraction, Jane transposed the last two numbers of my address, which was why one night, fifteen minutes after our study session was to begin, I peered through my limp lace curtains and saw an hourglass figure peeping tentatively into the windows of a cottage a hundred yards down the block on the other side of the street. I trotted down the saggy steps of the old Victorian and emerged onto the sidewalk.

"Jane!" I called. She tilted her head when she saw me.

"Margie?"

"What are you doing?" I asked.

"Looking," she said. "I thought you lived here."

"I live here." I gestured toward the crumbling edifice behind me.

"There?" Jane asked. Even from so far away, I could see her pert nose crinkle.

"Yes!"

"Shut the hell up out there, goddammit!" screamed a voice from a distant window.

Jane sashayed across the street. Inside, I poured two tall cups of red wine ("I brought us some tea," she said, setting down her thermos, "but I see you're drinking something else . . .") and lit a cigarette while she roved her eyes to take in my meager furnishings: an antique iron daybed that came with the studio, the desk Dad had bought me before I went away to college, and a nightstand. The nightstand bore a turtle-shaped lamp with a shell that glowed green, which I'd picked up at a yard sale down the street, several animal rights books from the downtown public library, a crumpled-up napkin, and the old white porcelain palm holding the rose-scented rosary made of real rose petals that I'd had for as long as I could remember.

"You smoke now?" Jane said. I exhaled through my nostrils, suppressed the urge to cough, and said nothing.

"How long have you lived here?"

"Since about three weeks ago." She wanted to know why I had left my old apartment. After several swallows from my cup, I told her the story she was dying to hear, the story of Simon Mellinkoff, beginning with that "nap" in his office and ending, despite my efforts to stifle them, with a stormy deluge of tears that made my cigarette too soggy to smoke.

"That predator!" Jane sat beside me on the bed and curled a marble-white arm around my shoulder. "I always knew he was a cad! So self-satisfied, always sitting on that bench in the quad, staring at everyone—"

"But you liked him, too! Remember?" Jane shook her head, disavowing the crush that had once prompted her to deem Simon a "daddy."

"And he wasn't . . . bad," I continued, "or . . . a cad . . ." I sobbed. "Really, it wasn't like that." I sucked in staccato breaths. "He was sad."

"Don't cry," she said, patting my shoulder. I wished I were in the Community Garden with the gourds. "You have to forget him. Just forget him."

I dried my face and, after we managed to enact some short-lived semblance of studying, Jane went home. When she was gone, I visualized her carefully and saw what I might have been had I not gone into Simon's office that decisive day, had I been the one who stayed behind. I saw a normal college girl, plump and smiling, humming pop songs under her breath, doodling hearts in the margins of her textbook, a girl with dancing feet in fashionable flats, a girl whose left ovary wasn't so relentlessly receptive. I felt so separate. How could I ever really confide in Jane—or anybody—about the ladybug behind my eyes, or orange blossoms tugging at a cello string in my belly, or the hill houses, or the under-the-bathroom-sink strands of Rasha's hair, or the way Simon shook, or the tears that hid behind the hyacinths of his breath when he murmured "my girl, my dear girl," or the Operation, or the pull and the mystery of animals, or little Annette, who had loved to comb my hair and then sit in my lap and let me comb hers. She had lent me her Strawberry Shortcake suitcase just before I'd departed Simon's house, where the window in the bedroom was tightly closed again, the way he liked it.

"OH, YES, PLEASE USE IT," she said in her shrill, babyish voice, clicking the suitcase open and waving a solicitous hand over its satin-lined interior. "I used to take it to my grandparents' house fairly often, but I don't go there anymore." She studied me with her bottomless blues. "Where are you off to?"

"I have to go away for a while," I said, gulping.

"Okay," she replied. "But please come back. We have so much fun." I realized I had been much more of a peer to Annette than a mother figure. She and I had both been Simon's girls—but she would be his for many years to come. I wondered what sort of life the strange sylph would have. "Fare thee well, Marjorie," she said after I'd packed the suitcase and clicked it shut.

Later, I unpacked the suitcase and discovered an exquisite drawing of a butterfly that Annette had snuck in. I taped the butterfly above the daybed and it hung there like an impossibility with its furred face, its jewel colors, its stained-glass wings outstretched—like something ahead of me but hard to believe.

UPSTAIRS AT GELATO AMORE, the faces that looked into mine were kind and open. Raven played me a new melody on her guitar. Orca wore her favorite bowler hat tipped at a saucy angle. Ptarmigan did not fiddle at all with the wheels of his chair, but clasped his hands elegantly in his lap. Bear pulled the daisy from behind her ear and passed it to me across the table. Bumble folded closed his laptop and leaned back, ready to listen. I had a feeling they had conferred amongst themselves and decided to accept me as their leader, or at least to give me a chance.

"I have some ideas," I said.

MY IDEAS FOR OPERATION H.E.A.R.T. WERE MANY, and my feelings for Simon fueled them all. He was always in my head, buried beneath everything I thought and did and dreamed of doing. His remembered voice, and the words I imagined it speaking, had a kind of mastery over my mind. His own mysterious mind, and the thoughts I imagined it thinking, gave shape to the smallest aspects of my days.

I remembered that first intoxicating sensation of being seen, the sensation only he had given me. The loss of that sensation was too painful to allow. And so, in my daydreams, he still saw me. If, in the morning, I put on my stalks-of-wheat sundress, I fancied that he might see me on campus later that day. "There she goes," he would think to himself, "that winsome girl I love so much. Wasn't that the dress she was wearing the first time I touched her? It wounds me to see it. I was a fool to let her go . . ."

Of course, never was this kind of dreaming more vivid than when I envisioned the future of the Operation he had entrusted to me. Every campaign I considered—establishing an official San Diego Spay & Neuter Day, encouraging local high school students to walk out of their frog dissection labs en masse via cleverly distributed flyers, exposing the truth about the dolphins at Ocean World who were literally driven insane by their confinement in the petting tank—was immediately followed by Simon's reactions as I foresaw them. Some of these reactions, of course, were better than others, but none would be as wonderful as the synthesis of deep, desirous love and profound pride that I most wanted to arouse in him.

Whatever we did under my leadership would have to be great. I wanted Simon to see a headline about us in the *Sun*. I wanted him to hold his breath in anticipation until he reached the end of the first paragraph, which would reveal our stunning exploit. And I wanted his mouth to fall open, to rustle the paper with an awed sigh. I wanted his gray eyes to widen, their lids to fall and rise with disbelief, and then to close with final pleasure as he tipped his head back in a capitulation to ultimate fulfillment. I wanted him to say my name, to murmur "Margie" as if into my neck, to utter it to himself in a tone of sated amazement.

These were the gestures I could no longer inspire Simon to make in person, in the jasmine-scented nights. Now I could only hope to make him do them from afar. And my love for the animals, enormous as it was, was rendered doubly powerful by my loss of Simon, who had taught me and tossed me away. Yes, whatever we did would have to be great. And so, for a long time, despite my abundance of ideas and the eagerness of the crew, we didn't do anything at all.

THEN, A NEW RESTAURANT OPENED IN TOWN. "'Untamed'— isn't that ridiculous?" said Raven, holding up a full-page newspaper ad. We were gathered around our usual table at Gelato Amore.

"Makes me want to throw up," said Orca, raising a hand to her inky mustache.

"It is truly offensive," added Ptarmigan, shaking his head.

Raven read the ad. "In the mood for something wild? Untamed, San Diego's most daring dining establishment, celebrates its grand opening in University Heights. Specializing in wild game meats from around the globe! This week we offer deer, buffalo, grouse, antelope, elk, snake, crocodile, kangaroo, camel, llama, emu, peacock, and, Friday night only, African lion meat. Sharpen your fangs, San Diego, and taste the difference. Meat the way it was meant: Untamed."

I snatched the paper from Raven's hand to read the ad myself. "Meat!" I exclaimed. "It isn't just *meat*. These are living creatures they're talking about!"

"*Were* living creatures," noted Orca.

"It's all so callous," said Bear.

"Yeah, and people are eating it up. Literally," said Raven. "They've only been open for a week and there's already a three-week wait for a table. I called yesterday. Every night, they are filled to maximum capacity."

"That's a lot of dead animals."

"As if it isn't bad enough," I said, "that millions of animals are already born and raised to be slaughtered and eaten, suffering the tortures of factory farms this very moment, now *other* animals, the ones ostensibly lucky enough to be wild, are being killed so that adventuresome diners with disposable incomes, no longer satisfied with run-of-the-mill flesh, can satisfy their spoiled palates." I took a breath. Out of the corner of my eye I saw the ever-present man in the newsboy cap lower his book and raise an eyebrow.

"Yes. *Exactly*," said Bumble.

"Hunting is always wrong," declared Orca.

"I don't know about that," said Ptarmigan. "I can see some impoverished family living in, oh, I don't know, rural Appalachia, surviving off the meat of one felled deer for a winter."

"But to hunt and kill *these* animals," I said, "peacock, kanga-roo, *African lion?*—this is just about people wanting to dine on something exotic and tell their friends."

"The hostess I spoke to when I called told me the meat tastes so much better," said Raven, "because the animals haven't been penned up—they've been using their muscles, they've had good exercise—"

"Yeah, dodging bullets!" cried Orca.

"Let's keep this in mind," I said. "Gather as much information about Untamed as you can. We'll meet again in three days."

"Three days?" asked Bear. "So soon, Margie?"

"Yes," I replied in an all-business tone. "We need to meet more frequently now. It's been a month since Simon resigned," I added, "and it's time to make some decisions."

"Have you heard from him?" she asked. Her face went soft and sorry when she saw the look on mine. "I mean . . . have you . . ." She bit her lip.

"It's okay, Bear," I told her, but my eyes stung. I put my hand on top of hers. Raven, Orca, Ptarmigan, and Bumble added theirs, and we recited our motto and disbanded.

"I LIKE THE DIRECTION WE'RE GOING," Bumble said. "It feels more . . . serious."

We lay on the steeply slanted roof of the old Victorian and watched the airplanes sail past. I'd brought up a blanket and a bottle of wine (I always kept one on hand now, and the mumbling man at the Middletown liquor store never asked about my age). Bumble had his digital camera aimed skyward. He'd been wanting to lie on my roof and take photographs of the planes ever since I'd told the crew about my new studio.

"It *is* more serious," I said. "I *want* it to be."

"I have to be honest." Bumble snapped some shots of the belly of a Boeing as it whooshed over us. "At first, I wasn't sure if you could handle it. Taking over, I mean. You seemed so fragile— well, more fragile—after the whole thing with Simon ended." I took a big draught from my glass. Bumble looked at me a bit bashfully. "I want you to know, I'm not going to ask what happened and I promise I never will." I noted wryly that I didn't really know what had happened myself. "Simon's a complicated guy," Bumble said, "and—anyway, it's none of my business. But I wasn't sure at first. About you. Now I am."

Another plane rushed overhead and, gratified, I lay back down on the blanket, letting the stirred-up air lift the locks of my hair. A few birds sent end-of-day trills out from hidden boughs. "Do you think any of those birds are the ones we let out of Azar's?" I asked. The wine was making me fanciful. Bumble laughed and said yes. I noticed he had decorated his red dread-locks, which had grown long and woolly, with a single plastic barrette of the sort Annette wore. It was shaped like a poodle. "I'm almost perfectly content at this moment," I said, and I was. The wine moistened and cooled my still-smoldering heart, the twilight delighted my senses, the planes seen from our perch electrified me, and Bumble was a bolstering companion. "You've grown so fiery on us, Margie," he said.

It was true: I had become more fiery, and not only because I wanted Simon to notice me and to be proud of the things I would accomplish as the leader of the Operation, but:

because I wanted there to be a reason I was born, so Rasha didn't disappear in a blur of red poppies and Dad didn't consume an ocean's worth of Maker's Mark with a splash of water for no purpose at all;

because I was alone, Always Alone, and wanted to be among, to be a part, to be a piece of a whole, to be a portion of all that was alive, linked to the tendrils and the peacocks and all the people of the world;

and because of the way Charlotte always sat on my chest and licked my face with her narrow pink tongue when I lay on my daybed staring at the ceiling, and I knew her mind was a finely wired web of perceptivity and sensitivity that my own could appreciate but would possibly never fathom, and I wanted to honor her and her kind.

And, since I was feeling so fiery, it was fire that captured my attention. I was interested in things that sparked and flamed, that contained and exuded heat, that built to a frenzy and then released their tension, that spent themselves.

I took to buying red taper candles and burning one beside my bed each night. I thought the warm, flickering light might help me to sleep, but I was always still awake long after my candle had disappeared.

I WENT TO GELATO AMORE FOR our next Operation H.E.A.R.T. meeting. While ascending to the second story, I met Jack Dolce coming down with a tub full of freshly cleaned and clattering dishes. They gleamed like his grin, and a few iridescent soap bubbles slid joyfully atop their surfaces. "Curly," he said. "Long time no see." He stopped and leaned against the stair railing. I stopped too.

"Hello," I whispered. I didn't mean to whisper, but he inspired such a feeling of shyness. With one glance I could see the brightness of his spirit.

"I've been missing a lot of work lately. You probably noticed."

It was true. He had not been at Gelato Amore for weeks, and I'd assumed (with a little pang of regret) that he'd finally been fired for clumsiness. Even now, a ceramic mug teetered dangerously out of the dish tub and threatened to bounce into bits down the concrete stairs. I flared my eyes at it, and Jack Dolce steadied it with his chin.

"Yeah," he continued, "I had mono. You know"—he winked—
"the kissing disease." I rolled my eyes. "Just kidding," he said.
"I really was sick though. With mononucleosis." He looked down
and leaned more deeply, with real weariness, into the railing of
the stairway.

I stole a good look at his fair face. There were bluish half-
moons beneath his eyes, and the vivid Tuscan ruddiness was
absent from his cheeks. Also, I couldn't help but notice that some
of his dark eyelashes were damply clumped together from the
steam of dish-doing. My left ovary flamed at the sight of frailty
in the fancy-free rogue. His singularly sweet quality was more
evident than ever, and I had an almost overwhelming impulse to
tell him all the sadness of my heart, as if he were my best friend in
the world. The gentleness of his brown eyes when he fixed them
on me made my own tingle with imminent tears, and I had to
look away. "I'm glad you're feeling better," I said, and resumed
making my way up the stairs.

"None of your pals are here yet," Jack said. "Neither is your
old man." I tripped slightly on a step. "Shall I bring you up a cup
of spumoni?"

"No dairy, thank you," I said over my shoulder, thinking of
how his favorite offering—ice cream—perfectly epitomized what
I was certain was his fundamental innocence.

Our table was empty, and the only person around was the
man in the newsboy cap, who was reading *Famous Rose Gardens
of North America*. We exchanged nods, and I sat down to wait. It
was early spring, almost Easter, and the air had a spun-sugar softness. I rested my face in my hands and stared out the window at
the traffic on the street below, at the green-gray ocean in the distance, and, hovering above it all, the dusk, the dusk shimmering
with specks of pollen spread by bees during the day, shimmering
with fibers of feathers shed from flapped bird wings, and shimmering with seadrops sprayed by whales, the dusk where the

secrets of all hearts hung suspended for a few delicious minutes before they were enfolded into the night and dissolved, before they closed like pink undersea anemones, only to be unpacked and hung out like almost-stars again at dusktime tomorrow. The moonflowers in the Middletown Community Garden would be unfurling soon. Jack Dolce came upstairs and pulled me out of my chair for an embrace. His T-shirt was damp from the sea air, from washing dishes, and from his own self. I felt his wet eyelashes against my cheek as he squeezed me close. A small seed sprouted in the center of my chest and flooded me with comfort. He lifted me up so my feet dangled with delightful helplessness five inches above the ground. His chin nuzzled my neck. He sent soothing rumblings into my ear, low and warm, and I recalled how, before I'd opened their cage, the lovebirds in Azar's had spent so much of their time side by side on their perch, so pressed, so pleasantly pressed, and I knew that *this* was the feeling of *that,* safe and animal and soft. I sighed. The man in the newsboy cap laid down his book with a thump, and I saw that I was in my chair with my face in my hands. One star had come out. Jack Dolce was still downstairs, and I was still alone.

"Lovely night," said the newsboy.

"Yes," I said. "What time is it?" I asked, and then, "What day is it?"

The discovery that I had not, in fact, known the day of the week was a disheartening one. Nobody from the crew had come because there was no meeting. The meeting was still one night away. I had been so much in my own world that I had lost track. I spent my days at school, my evenings staring at the ceiling, and my nights wandering wine-drunk through the Community Garden after my red bedside candle burned out. This routine never changed, and time had become indistinct. It wasn't passing so much as compressing into a lump of lonesomeness.

"Oh." I stumbled toward the stairs. "Goodnight." The man already had his face back in his book.

IN SPITE OF ITS ALREADY OBVIOUS POPULARITY, Untamed was aggressively marketing its offerings with more print ads and even a TV commercial. We all watched the commercial together on Bumble's laptop during our next meeting. Its star was Untamed's owner and head chef. Young and pink-faced, he wore a spotless white jacket and stood in the center of his crowded dining room. "I'm Zac, executive chef here at Untamed," he said to a spot slightly left of the camera's eye. He had a bleached-white smile and spiky hair.

"He looks so pure," breathed Bear.

"He has blood on his hands," Orca said.

Zac talked too fast. "This is meat the way the first humans enjoyed it: wild, flavorful, and free-range . . ." With his eager gestures and darting eyes, he was reminiscent of a rodent in a way I found unsettling.

"He reminds me of a squirrel," I said.

"I know," Bear agreed, "it's kind of cute."

"They serve that, too," noted Raven, tapping the menu she had obtained.

"Come," Zac said, "indulge your most primitive desires, and let your taste buds be . . ." Here he paused, counting three beats with a few unconscious bobbing movements of his head. ". . . Untamed."

The crew groaned (except for Bear, who giggled). "What if a bunch of emus came and hunted him down?" wondered Bumble boyishly.

"That will never happen," I said. "It's up to us."

AT HOME, I SAT IN THE DARK with a glass of wine and Charlotte on my lap. I knew Dad was doing the same thing, only instead of a rabbit he had an album of photographs opened across his legs and was drinking whiskey rather than wine. I could not stand the smell of whiskey, but Dad had said Rasha knew all about wines. I inhaled from my glass to see what I might know. There were hyacinths, predominantly, and the slightly metallic tang of an empty birdcage, orange blossoms of course, the sharp chlorophyll of just-cut suburban lawns, the powderish odor of old lipsticks, the sultriness of jasmine, the uncompromising finality of lavender, and the scent of my own breath, which was the smell of the wet dog that had sniffed and circled and curled around my heart again. He was a stray, and he had an awful keen, and jutting ribs.

I flipped on my turtle lamp. Charlotte twitched at the light and propelled herself off me by the impressive force of her hind legs. I lay back on my bed. A tear ran into my ear, always an unpleasant sensation. I heard the unfinished letter to Dad crinkling beneath my pillow, but still couldn't think of a satisfactory P.S.

I could always call the crew for company but didn't know what I'd say once I had them near. I was perturbed to feel such a yearning and to feel like a corked bottle, too, because none of them, not a one of them, would do. I recalled the frequency with which Annette had spoken to her stuffed toys—not always, I knew, because she was childish but rather, I suspected, because she was precociously aware of the occasional impossibility of uncorking oneself for any of the actual people in one's life. It was the longing, of course, the old feeling of limitless longing.

I reached over to the nightstand and picked up the crumpled-up napkin that had rested there, untouched, since the day I'd moved in. I uncrumpled it and read what was written over its soft folds. Then, for the first time in months, I fell into a deep sleep.

THE NEXT DAY, JACK DOLCE DIDN'T ASK any questions when I showed up at his Little Italy flat wearing my lucky red Chinese shoes. He was drinking orange juice from a jelly jar and playing a scratchy record on the patio. The cord from the record player snaked into the house through the open screen door, along with an army of ants and at least two lizards (one of whom I later found snoozing in my left lucky red Chinese shoe). When he saw me coming up the splintery steps, he rose.

"You finally came," he said. And then, for the very first time outside of dusk-dreams, we hugged. His warm neck left a salt residue on my lips. He smelled of gardenias, luscious tropical flowers with a thick, desirous scent.

He rode his red bicycle to the waterfront. When he returned, the front basket was filled with oysters. "Let's steam these!" he cried. I supposed, staring at the rough ruffles of their shells, that while I certainly would not eat any oysters, I couldn't force the unabashed bon vivant, who really was tattooed with the words "eat, drink, and be merry," to abstain. With some effort, I suppressed any thoughts of the sad sensations the beautiful bivalves might have felt upon being snatched from the watery rocks to which they had clung. For once, my own survival was my foremost concern. I was on the run from loneliness. And the extravagance of the oysters somehow reflected my own impulse to finally come and see about Jack Dolce.

His flat was cozy. There was a claw-footed bathtub in the kitchen and a surprising abundance of pampered potted plants. Jack Dolce kept everything spotless, and in the late afternoon it was so pleasant to see the white walls drenched in lemon light, as if there were no barriers at all between indoors and out.

A poster of an Indian chief hung above his bed. "That's Sitting Bull," Jack Dolce explained. "Probably my number one hero. He was a holy man of the Hunkpapa Sioux. All he wanted was to be true to himself and his people, and he died trying." I nodded my head in silence, wishing the crew, who had been so dismissive of Jack and derisive of his seeming carelessness, were there to hear him. "I respect American Indians," he said.

"Did you know Bumble is partly Indian?" I asked.

"The guy with the red hair? Really?" Jack Dolce's face turned dubious.

"Yes. His mom is half Crow."

"Crow, you say? Like Pretty Shield!" Now his face glowed. "She's one of my favorites. She was a medicine woman of the Crow tribe. The Navajo culture is wonderful, too—come here." He clasped my hand and pulled me toward his dresser. "I want to show you something." He kept my hand in his left one while using his right to rummage through the top drawer. My cheeks grew hot, though I wasn't sure if it was the hand-holding or the sight of Jack Dolce's underwear.

"I took a bus tour through New Mexico last summer and

bought this from a Navajo silversmith. Isn't it pretty?" He
showed me his trinket, a hammered silver hair comb inlaid with
real turquoise hearts. "I thought I'd send it to my mom, but . . ."
He bowed his head as if stifling some momentary sadness. His
hand grew slippery in mine, and he let me go.

"It is pretty, Jack," I said.

"It is, isn't it?" He panted on the comb a few times to make it
steamy, then polished it on his T-shirt. "Want to just hang out for
a while?" he asked. "Before we eat the oysters?"

"Yeah."

We lay side by side on his bedroom floor. Turning my head,
I saw a slim little bright green snake spiraled contentedly under
the bed. The snake lifted his neck to look at me and tested the
air with his tongue. "He's been here for a while," Jack said. Then,
with the snake listening in, I told Jack Dolce my story. When
I told him about Simon, I didn't cry like I had with Jane.

"You should quit that animal rights club," Jack said. He
tipped his head onto my shoulder for emphasis. "I don't think it's
going to bring you anything but heartache and trouble."

I told him about Dad. "He's a dreamer, and he drinks." And
I told him about Rasha. "She was from Beirut, and she was a
perfumer. She died while she was having me."

And so Jack Dolce became my good friend. I visited his flat
many evenings. Light from the setting sun moved through the
rooms and graced my face with warmth. I felt the worn wooden
planks of the floor as the trees they used to be, bending and creak-
ing in the wind and humming with persistent life through the
soles of my bare feet.

We drank wine, and Jack Dolce always ate oysters. Soon,
there were shells scattered all over the flat, their gorgeous glossy
interiors facing up to catch the light.

I often considered the oyster shells. Their two halves were
joined by a supple hinge. There was something about that

hinge that reminded me of Jack Dolce himself, as if he were
the link between one part of my life and another. I knew what
one of those parts was: the life I had lived and was still living.
But I didn't know what the other part would be, only that Jack
Dolce seemed to personify the promise that there would, in
fact, be something else. Maybe, I thought, there would even be a
pearl. This was partly why I drew so close to him. He was my
brother, my confessor, and just enough like me that in studying him I thought I might find some clue as to what, or who, or
where I—now without Simon, now in charge of the Operation—
would be.

I wanted the shells to be useful, so the creatures who had once
called them home would not have died in vain. I turned them
into receptacles for miscellaneous trinkets (a velvety leaf, a green
pebble, the tiny, tarnished key to a bike lock). This, I thought,
seemed in keeping with Jack Dolce's style of existence, which
was a tribute to simplicity.

As his penchant for bicycles over cars indicated, he had no
desire for convenient and contemporary forms of technology.
His only phone was a heavy black rotary model that predated
his birth, and instead of a computer he had a typewriter, a 1930s
Underwood portable. "This is the same model Kerouac used,"
he told me, pressing the space bar over and over with a childish
smile.

"Do you think I'm strange?" he asked me once after I peeked
into his middle and bottom dresser drawers and found just three
threadbare T-shirts and an equal paucity of pants. "I mean, for
the way I live?"

"No," I answered in earnest. "I think you are rare and beautiful, and like an endangered species."

"I know people look down on me—some of them—and think
I'm some sort of loser, because I'm not plugged in, or ambitious,
or what have you." He shrugged. "I can't say I care." He held

up a record, Karen Dalton's *In My Own Time*. "Have you heard
this? Sweet Jesus, what a voice!" He had many records. After
rent was paid, he spent what remained of his modest earnings on
music, food, and drink. And he was fond of giving me little gifts,
including:

an old brass bell blotched with a glorious green patina;

a stuffed kitten with whiskers of fine wire;

a box of colored chalk so we could graffiti the flat's front
porch;

a set of jacks so we could play outside at sunset while admiring our front porch artwork;

a turtle (who lived at the flat and befriended the green
snake);

a beat-up old paperback titled *Teenage Temptress,* with a
pressed flower tucked into every other page;

and a baby blue plastic rosary he bought from a Mexican boy
who wandered the streets with rainbows of rosaries dangling
from his skinny arms chirping "One dollar!"

Jack Dolce bought me the rosary in spite of the fact that he
was not, he asserted, a believer, certainly not in *her,* the one to
whom the rosary was meant to be prayed, and once, when I
suggested that he give a face to his faceless Virgin Mary tattoo,
he challenged me. "Prove to me that she's real!" he said with
a sudden and surprising ache in his voice, revealing that underneath all the seductive smiles he directed at his would-be
ladyfriends he was just a heartbroken boy who would never
get enough womanly love, for his own mother, he eventually
confided to me, had abandoned him when he was just fourteen
years old for a new life with a travel trailer salesman from
Tucson. That was why so many girls were mad for Jack Dolce.
They perceived his want of mother love. He inspired ancient
feelings of tenderness and motherliness. Of course, I was far too
fixated on Simon to regard Jack Dolce in the same smitten way

the other girls did. For me, it was different. We were like the two children on the Six of Cups card in the tarot deck Bear always toted in her purse, two motherless children meeting in a garden.

"You're kind of an endangered species yourself, you know?" Jack told me.

"What?"

"You know, like a dying breed."

"Hardly."

"Yes. You go around sniffing everything. You probably got that from your mom. And you truly love animals. You're connected to the earth, sun, moon, and stars. So few people are earthy anymore. I mean, in a real way. They care way more about *stuff*." I considered Bumble and his assortment of gear, which had lately grown to include a sleek new jacket fashioned with unpronounceable synthetic fabric, and a twenty-four-pocket backpack that expanded like a concertina. He was passionate enough about the Operation, but those acquisitions were what really made his heart pound.

Jack Dolce was as special as I'd suspected, and I wanted Bumble and the others to see it, so Jack and I threw a party at the flat. In addition to the crew, there were people from Gelato Amore, including the man in the newsboy cap and homeless Baby Joe, and people whom Jack's little-seen roommate, a grizzled, divorced fortysomething who had a rabbit's-foot keychain and drove a bicycle taxi in the Gaslamp Quarter, brought home on his rickshaw. Even a few old Italian grannies, who had lived in Little Italy since it had been nothing but a stinky fishing village, were charmed into joining us after scuffling to the front door in their slippers and black housedresses to tell us to quiet down. They huddled around the record player and enjoyed cigarettes with the same sneaky relish they had felt as young girls forbidden by their husbands to smoke. It must have been the oyster shells that enchanted them. They echoed the nacreous glow of their prim pearl earrings.

The rest of us danced, and talked loudly about inconsequential things. For the first time in a month, I forgot about Simon for a full five minutes. I even ran outside and jumped into the shallow neighborhood fountain, and watched the full moon shatter like a plate on the water's rippling surface. I returned to the flat smiling, with my clothes thoroughly soaked. I took them off with abandon, draped the green snake around my neck, and offered shouts of encouragement while we set about discovering that Jack Dolce could yank a tablecloth out from under a dozen oyster-laden dishes without disturbing any.

But my plan to promote some sort of camaraderie between Jack Dolce and the crew went unrealized. They, perhaps jealous of my new friendship and scandalized by its effect on me, ignored him, and he, wounded by their indifference, did the same. This saddened me. In some ways, he would have fit right in as a crew member. But he wasn't supportive of Operation H.E.A.R.T. More than once he had termed it "an ineffectual exercise in folly." When Jack dashed out into the moonlight to tear a handful of rosemary from the neighbor's porch, the crew crowded around me for an impromptu meeting.

"I'm exhausted," Bear said. In accordance with my instructions, she had parlayed her experience hostessing at Laminaria into a new job as a waitress at Untamed, where she was our spy. She had just finished a shift that night. "I smell of death," she continued. "The customers are brats."

"And what about Chef Zac?" I asked.

"Hmm? Zac? Oh . . . Zac is . . ." Bear's weary eyes brightened. "He . . . he's a double Scorpio," she breathed, "with a forked love line. And he is so good about letting me wear my hair daisy, even though it's not part of the official Untamed uniform—"

"Bear—" I began, incredulous at her crush.

"But . . . well . . ." She hesitated. "He's a killer. Obviously. We throw away two hundred pounds of bones a night, at least." Ptarmigan clucked in wonderment.

We discussed a few other matters. Life was growing increasingly miserable for the dolphins in the petting tank at Ocean World, Ptarmigan said. They had lately been demonstrating signs of real psychological distress—deliberately banging their heads against the cement walls of their tank and refusing to come up for air—as a result of being confined to a space that was, he explained, a mere one ten-thousandth of 1 percent of the size of their natural habitat. Moreover, he added, there was so much chlorine in their water that they couldn't open their eyes, and their skin was peeling away. A flashy pet store in Hillcrest was illegally selling abductees from foreign jungles—spider monkeys, yellow-shouldered Amazon parrots—out its back door, Bumble told me. And Moi Moi the baby panda, Raven reported, was still looking pretty depressed at the zoo. "What's our next campaign? You said you were ready to make some decisions, remember?" Bumble prodded. They were antsy. And I was overcome by that familiar ovarian flare.

Jack Dolce returned with a few rosemary strands, appetizingly aromatic and speckled with tiny blue flowers. He curled them into a ring and rested it atop my head. Then he led me to the sofa, where he told me to stretch out. The crew stepped back to watch, shaking their heads. I was still naked, except for the green snake. Jack rummaged in his top drawer for the silver Navajo hair comb and pushed it into the curls above my ear. "Now," he said, cupping my face in his warm palms, "turn your head just a little . . . good."

He found his camera—the same one he'd had since boyhood. "My portrait? My portrait!" I cried. "Rosemary for remembrance. Now I'll never forget this moment," I added.

There were exactly three shots left in the camera. In the first photo, I was tentative. In the second, a smile bloomed over my face like a red and white flower. In the third, I looked accidentally away from the lens and off to the side, as if gazing at a future I could not quite see.

A FEW DAYS AFTER THE PARTY, the crew and I convened at Gelato Amore. They were relieved that I came, for they feared my new friend would lure me away from them and the animals. "Good to see you with your clothes back on," said Orca, who had just won a regional floral design competition and proudly wore the first-place ribbon pinned to her vest. "Well," she grinned, "not really, but . . ." Bumble hugged me so tight I bumped into his marsupium. When Ptarmigan maneuvered toward me to peck my cheek, his wheelchair was completely silent. He had upgraded to a glossy black Rolls-Royce model because his well-to-do British aunt had died in a polo accident and left him an inheritance. From a distance, the man in the newsboy cap eyed the chair with the sort of admiration usually reserved for cars and motorcycles.

Bear gave us another Untamed update. Chef Zac had recently shot her an unabashedly hungry look that, she confessed, made her "knees turn to mashed potatoes." He'd told her she had the "elegance of an egret" as she waited on tables, daisy in place, radiating her milky magnetism. Their relationship had progressed and this slightly complicated, though did not compromise, her position as an infiltrator.

"An egret?" scoffed Raven.

Blushing, Bear shared her latest findings. "Zac got an A from the county food facility inspection people. No customers have reported any food poisoning, or even so much as sent a plate back to the kitchen. The crew from *Rise and Shine, San Diego* came last night to film Zac giving a cooking demonstration, which aired this morning." She paused, as if considering, then dutifully reported, "He made smoked swan omelets."

"Heavens!" exclaimed Ptarmigan.

"All the meat—er, I mean, slaughtered animals—comes from one wholesaler, who obtains it from various sources around the globe," Bear continued, reading aloud from a diary she kept beside her bed and scribbled in by flashlight every night after the lusty chef fell asleep. "Everything is inspected by the USDA or the state before it is served. Oh"—with a guilty expression, eyes shining, she interrupted herself—"and Zac is *so* happy that I'm *so* interested in the restaurant and ask *so* many questions about what he does."

"Don't worry about it, Bear," Raven said. "I don't really see how we can do anything, anyway. The guy isn't breaking any laws. The place is untouchable. Maybe we should shift our focus to Ocean World and those dolphins—"

"I don't agree," I said. "I'm very disturbed about the dolphins, but we can't just allow this to go on. It's so brazen, so deliberate, so *celebratory* . . ."

"I'm with Margie," said Bumble. "We could distribute some damning flyers—"

"Or stage a protest in front of the restaurant," said Ptarmigan.

"Maybe mildly harass some customers and employees," added Orca.

"No," I said. "Those are the sorts of things we have always done." Simon would see, I thought. He would see the story about us, would release a satisfied sigh, would smile. "I want to take this to another level."

"What do you mean?"

"I have something in mind," I whispered, thinking of my series of bedside candles and the flickering of their flames. The candles melted down to red puddles that reminded me of the red poppies Dad had seen blooming on the white sheets of Rasha's hospital bed the day she died. I'd come early, and because I was a "small and well-positioned baby," the hospital report said, it was a "precipitous labor"—meaning I'd come too fast. "Next time, we'll meet in my studio," I told the crew. "This is too sensitive to discuss here."

THE FOLLOWING AFTERNOON, JACK DOLCE AND I played jacks on his porch. "I think I'm going to take down that awful restaurant," I told him. The turtle stood amiably beside us. "It is a blight on this city."

Jack Dolce scooped three jacks into his palm and grinned. "I win," he said.

"I think Operation H.E.A.R.T. should tame Untamed."

"I don't want to know anything about it," Jack said. "It's crazy, Margie. Please stop all that stuff. Quit the Operation." And then he added (rather inexplicably, I thought), "Give up your apartment and come stay with me forever. I'll ask Hank to go. Maybe he can sublet your place."

"No," I murmured. "That won't work." I fed the turtle a leaf of lettuce. "A fire . . ."

"You're going about this all wrong," he said. "Violence and destruction are not the way. Please, Margie. I know I'm right."

"What about all those Indian warriors you like so much?" I asked, thinking of the female Zapatista Simon had praised, the warrioress.

Jack Dolce laid down the jacks and sighed. He released the two red rubber balls and watched them roll down the steps. "When you first came to visit me here, you told me you were tired

of tears running into your ears at night. I haven't seen a single
tear since you've been hanging out with me." He tried to catch my
gaze, but I could only stare at the turtle until it grew hazy. It was
true. I had completely stopped crying, until that moment. And
the ladybug had come back. She was crawling around behind
my eyes again. "What reason is there to go to such extremes? For
some silly animal rights group?"

"It's not silly—"

"You're too much under the influence of that Simon, that's all.
I wish it wasn't so."

"You're just jealous," I said.

"You're right. I am. Not of the Operation, but of Simon, yes.
I'd make you mine if I thought I could take your mind off him
for more than a minute or two."

I looked at Jack Dolce. I looked at his clear open eyes, his
guileless grin, which even in the middle of our argument he proffered as a plea for peace. I looked at his uncombed hair, the red
blood beneath his cheeks. He was a warmhearted creature.

But there was a rigidity in me. I had studied Jack Dolce to
see a vision of my future, and he was showing me one, but now I
would not bend to it.

"I just . . . can't . . ." I said. "I have to make a difference. There
is so much work to be done. Those swans . . ."

"Those swans?" Jack Dolce hid his face in his hands. He
stayed like that for a few moments. Then he looked my way
again, and I couldn't believe the rosy-mouthed rogue for whom
hundreds of glamorous, gaga girls had stood in line now had wet
eyes for skinny me. "Margie," he said. "You are connected to the
earth, sun, moon, and stars. Just like I've told you. You already
are. Don't you see? You don't have to be so desperate to 'make a
difference,' like you're always saying."

Some part of me thought he might be telling the truth. Still, I
felt a stiffness in both of my shoulder blades, as if I had sprouted

invisible wings in want of exercise and was helpless not to flap them.

"Just live your life," he said. "It's not your fault your mom didn't make it."

"This *is* my life." My voice shook. Who had ever dared to say such a thing? "You don't understand."

"I think I understand more than you think I do."

And there, on the porch, Jack Dolce and I turned away from each other. All at once, our sweet siblinghood was gone. Crushed, I walked inside the flat and looked under the bed for the green snake. He was gone, too.

I heard the scrape and squeak of Jack Dolce pushing back the kickstand of his bicycle and pedaling away.

Crying noisily now, I took the baby blue plastic rosary, which I had been wearing as a necklace, and laid it on Jack Dolce's pillow. Then I left the flat, and as I walked the new stiffness in my shoulder blades subsided slightly. I traversed the sun-striped sidewalks of Little Italy, past the red-and-white-checkered tablecloths of outdoor cafés, past the shop windows festooned with garlands of chili peppers and garlic, past the Virgin Mary statue where I'd left many offerings of oyster shells, and saw a wedding party come foaming out the door of a spaghetti restaurant. The bride was adorned in endless snowy layers of tulle, and a gust of wind came along and carried her veil into the sky.

BACK HOME IN MIDDLETOWN, I ran into my landlady, who was patching a hole in the hallway. Her oxygen tank was stationed beside her. "Sweetie," she said in her scratchy voice, "your phone's been ringing like mad for the last hour." She stepped toward me, towing her tank behind, and peered into my face. "What's the matter? You've got boy trouble? Forget it, girly. My only husband was a miserable bastard. It took me forty years to get up the courage to leave. By that time, I was sixty-five, and it was too late for me." She cleared her throat with a guttural growl. "You're young. You've got your whole life yet."

I wondered what little conciliatory gift Jack Dolce had waiting for me in his bicycle basket when he'd returned to the flat and found I had gone. I was sure he had brought one. He called me on his old rotary telephone that night and for many nights thereafter, letting the rings number into the sixties, the seventies. He typed me letters on the Underwood and sealed them shut with a drop of green wax embossed with an *M*. But I stayed away. I knew that if I tarried with Jack Dolce, I would never save anything again.

I ORDERED STRANGE MANUALS AND HANDBOOKS off a few obscure websites and learned there were many ways to start a fire. (My guides were cheaply xeroxed, haphazardly stapled, full of spelling errors and typos, and, in one instance, personally inscribed by the author: "Good Luck!" he had written above a winking smiley face.) It was hard to decide on just one method, but I did. I prepared a presentation consisting of a series of illustrated poster boards that summarized my findings about all things fiery. My final three posters explained how to construct what some of my slightly more academic resources had termed an "incendiary device." During our next Operation H.E.A.R.T. meeting, the crew crowded into my studio to watch the presentation.

I used a telescopic pointer I'd swiped from Professor Weatherbury to gesture toward my pictures. My charm bracelet clinked softly with my every point, so that while I told the crew about fires and clever ways to start them, the two charms told the story of one brokenhearted bird.

"But Margie . . ." Ptarmigan searched for the right words

when I was through. "A firebomb? It all seems . . . a bit . . .
excessive."

"I expected that reaction," I said, swilling from my wineglass.
"However, the point is not to hurt anyone. And we won't. The
point is to make a statement."

"Which is?" said Orca, one eyebrow raised.

"Which is," I said, "what it has always been, and what all of us
gathered here tonight"—I swept my arm theatrically across the
studio, where my five companions sat smooshed together on
the floor and Charlotte chewed rapturously on the wooden leg
of my desk chair—"know to be true: that animals are sentient
beings; that they are worthy of our protection; that their rights
must be respected; and that those who dare to disregard the rights
of animals must receive a message—"

"A message," Bear interjected. "But that could be, like, a
letter, or—"

"A letter doesn't do anything!" I snapped. "People need to be
shocked into paying attention." I took another swallow from my
glass.

"It's okay, Margie," Bear said soothingly. "I was just thinking
out loud is all." Bear spoke to me in the same mild tone she must
have used with her bevy of baby brothers and sisters, and I was
instantly contrite for being sharp.

Still, I was glad when Raven said, "Margie's right. People do
need to be shocked into paying attention. That's why I started
dyeing my bangs green in junior high."

"Listen," I continued, "we can keep repeating ourselves. Or
we can evolve. We, as Operation H.E.A.R.T., can embark on a
novel journey in a new direction." I paused and made eye contact
with each crew member, one at a time, before adding, "Say you'll
make the journey with me?"

Bumble nodded. "It's time," he said. "We've made good
progress in the past. We've got some momentum going. Let's
keep moving forward."

"I'm with Bumble," Orca said. "I think Margie has made some good points tonight. Even if she is kind of drunk."

"Friends," Ptarmigan said, "I am in agreement about momentum and moving forward. But I am only on board if no one gets injured."

"I'm sure nobody will be around if we go late enough," conceded Bear. "The whole staff always goes out for drinks together after closing. Except for Zac." Her face clouded. "He likes to come home with me. But it's time for me to let him go, anyway." She shook her head. "Outside of loving, we have very little in common."

Bear spent one last night with the chef. And while Zac snored in the way only a man with a belly full of meat can, she stole his restaurant key.

THERE WAS SOMETHING UNREAL about the burning. It had the feeling of a fairy tale, a story Rasha, had she lived, might have read to me one night in my girlhood room, in bed, beside the porcelain palm holding the rose-scented rosary. Yes, when it was over, it had the quality of something I had read, but had not done. The heroine and her friends conjured flames as if by magic. They moved in the earliest morning hours, when all was dark and the air was full of the scent of shy night-blooming flowers that would soon close themselves again, all at once like a choir going silent, in defense against the smoke. Long-tressed Bear unlocked the door using the stolen key she had strung on a silk ribbon around her neck. It glinted under the light of the moon. She disengaged the alarm system, pushing a secret code. She took one last look around her lover's palace and went weeping to wait in the getaway van with Ptarmigan, who perched like a sovereign in his ebony chair, and Orca, who waited behind the wheel, her fedora pulled down low, her mustachioed mouth stoic and still, as if manning a charmed chariot. Across the street, Raven painted a purple message on the sidewalk in her best calligraphy. The heroine and Bumble B. stepped into the darkness of the kitchen, where a hundred bodies—once feathered, once furred—lay stacked in the freezer. The two whispered things to one another, things neither of them would remember, words that would become ash. They touched hands, laid down their strange instrument. It would make a music of hisses and crackles after an initial percussive pop. And only the heroine, who was under the spell of a prince, a miller of wheat, could coerce it into singing. She had a stick in her pocket that came all the way from a star. She scratched that stick, and it sparked into five points like the white blossom of an orange. Then she ran with her friend. She ran. We ran.

ZAC WAS ON THE NEWS LATER THAT MORNING, tripping sleepily through the smoldering remains of Untamed. "We will rebuild," he said, coughing. The camera panned over the words Raven had painted in her careful cursive on the sidewalk across the street, where we knew the fire would not erase them.

"Zac, do you have any idea what—or who—could have caused this?" a reporter asked him.

"No, I really don't," he said.

"It's true, he really doesn't," Bear sniffled, snuggling her head into Orca's shoulder. "He's not very smart." We were all squished on the couch in Ptarmigan's apartment, where we had gone after leaving the restaurant. His mom hadn't noticed we'd borrowed her van, and she looked surprised to see us when she departed for work at seven, widening her heavily mascaraed eyes in our direction before kissing Ptarmigan goodbye. "Love you, William," she said. He straightened his glasses sheepishly.

The fire had been featured on three morning news programs. And, had we not known otherwise, we might have thought Ptarmigan's TV was an old black-and-white model, because as we flipped from one channel to another all we saw was the dark, charred skeleton of the restaurant against the white sky—completely overcast with clouds—of a San Diego morning.

I thought of Simon in his black-and-white-checkered trousers and wondered if he was watching.

The *Sun* printed an article the following day. For the first time, Operation H.E.A.R.T. had made it to the front page: LAW ENFORCEMENT FINDS RESTAURANT FIRE SUSPICIOUS, OPERATION H.E.A.R.T. AT WORK? "A popular local restaurant called Untamed," the article read,

was destroyed in a fire early yesterday morning. No one was hurt in the blaze. The damage to the building was thorough, according to Untamed's owner and head chef, Zac Valentine. "We will have to start over from scratch," said Valentine. "Fortunately, our insurance will allow us to do so."

Pending further investigation, the cause of the fire is undetermined, but local law enforcement has one reason to suspect arson. On a sidewalk close to the restaurant, police found a message written in purple paint: "Animals: Friends, Not Food!"

The appearance of the graffiti coincided with the fire and has led police to suspect animal rights activists might have played a role. "This restaurant specializes in meat—wild game, specifically," said Detective Adam Wood of the San Diego Police Department, "which might have made it a target of activists or, as we and the FBI would call them in this case, considering the damage they have done and the threat to human safety they pose, domestic terrorists."

Operation H.E.A.R.T., a San Diego–based animal rights activist group, has been associated with purple paint in recent years.

This publicity excited the crew, but I thrilled at the thought of just one person seeing the article. We had done something big, and we had done it completely. I slept soundly. I had a dream in which I wandered through an unfamiliar house, opening doors and discovering one room after another, each of them different from the others (one had orange-tree wallpaper, one had jasmine vine drapes, one had a carpet of red poppies standing strong and straight), and they all filled me with a sense of possibility, of delight.

"WE'RE ON A ROLL NOW," I said during a merry meeting on the roof of the old Victorian. "Let's keep growing. Maybe it's time we brought in some new people, so we can accomplish even more . . ." A plane droned overhead and zoomed toward the tarmac, taking the rest of my sentence with it. No one seemed to mind.

"We *don't* want Jack Dolce on the crew," said Orca. The others echoed her.

"That isn't who I mean," I said, and my elation dimmed when I thought of him, the tenderhearted Tuscan, learning of my exploit. I shook my head as if doing so could dislodge the image of his disappointed face. "But consider who else might be out there, and the contributions they might be able to make."

"But it's always just been *us*," Bumble said.

"My point exactly," I countered. "And Simon said change is necessary, remember? And he had big dreams for the Operation. He told me about them." Did he remember telling me, I wondered, remember touching me? "We just took a big step, and we succeeded. If we continue to allow ourselves to change, the animals will benefit. They *need* us." Before the sun sank, I convinced the crew of the correctness of my view and was secretly surprised at the ease with which, once again, they followed my lead.

Bumble designed a flyer that we distributed throughout the city. It featured a drawing of Charlotte, who we decided would

henceforth be our mascot. "Are you a friend to animals?" read the
thought bubble that floated above Charlotte's head.

> *Do you want to make a difference fighting for their rights?*
> *Operation H.E.A.R.T., a local animal rights activist organization,*
>   *is recruiting new members!*
> *Come to a free information session upstairs at Gelato Amore*
>   *Café in Little Italy.*
> *Bring your questions, your ideas, and your heart.*

On the night of the information session, the entire upstairs
of Gelato Amore was packed with prospective crew members,
most of them college students. Some smoked slouchily with suspicious faces while others prepared to take notes. They crowded
around the usual café regulars, including the man in the newsboy
cap, who hid his head in a book with his trademark timidity and
appeared undisturbed by the invasion.

The crew and I faced the crowd from a makeshift stage of
sorts. We sat in front of a rolling chalkboard purloined from an
empty classroom at the university. Much to my own surprise,
I was not nervous. I, who had been forever shy, who had been
Always Alone, was actually excited by the prospect of talking
to a room full of unfamiliar faces. I was making a difference, I
thought.

I wrote on the chalkboard with professorial zest: "Operation
H.E.A.R.T.—Inaugural Information Session—Welcome!—Your
Host, Margie." I smoothed the front of my strawberry-printed
sundress and peeked at my lucky red Chinese shoes.

I cleared my throat and addressed my audience. "Hello
and thank you for coming." The crowd applauded. Behind me,
the crew applauded, too. "Operation H.E.A.R.T. is a small
group of passionate activists who love animals. We were
established by a local intellectual who has since retired from
the organization.

"As you know, we hope to welcome some new members into our existing crew, which includes myself and the five individuals you see seated behind me: Raven" (she strummed a single chord on her guitar), "Bumble" (he saluted, military style, and then looked embarrassed), "Bear" (she flashed a peace sign), "Orca" (she tipped her Little Tramp derby hat), "and Ptarmigan" (he smiled wide, as if for a photograph).

"After a few more comments from me," I continued, "I will take your questions. I will do my best to answer them, but please know I cannot reveal any information that would compromise the success of our future campaigns."

A pair of chocolate eyes melted into me. In the very back of the room, leaning against the wall, stood Jack Dolce, arms folded across his chest, dishrag dangling. I had not seen him in weeks. I had avoided Gelato Amore since our fight and, tonight, had forgone a ginger ale and marched purposefully upstairs without checking to see if he was working. There he stood, missing his usual red-mouthed radiance. Unlike every other face in the room, his looked so sad, so sorry. A bit of the spark seeped out of me, and, disconcerted, I went on.

"We will make our decisions regarding new membership democratically and base them on the merits of the applicants, specifically assessing their commitment to animal rights, adherence to a vegan lifestyle"—many in the audience nodded receptively—"unique skills, valuable connections to and/or knowledge of perpetrators of animal exploitation, and"— I paused, noting once more the slightly blurred beauty of Jack Dolce's faraway face. It wasn't that he looked sorry *about* me, or about the two of us and our failed friendship; he looked sorry *for* me, I was sure of it. Forgetting what I'd meant to say, I awkwardly added, "and, of course, we will consider every applicant's level of physical fitness."

A husky boy sighed and snuck out. My own composure was equally fleeting, thanks to Jack Dolce's eyes, but I forced a smile.

What was it he had meant, I wondered, about earth, sun, moon, and stars? *"If,"* I continued, "after this info session, you remain interested in joining us, we ask that you turn in an application form tonight and, within the next week, submit a one-page essay via e-mail explaining what you can offer Operation H.E.A.R.T. Any questions?"

Suppose he had been right, Jack Dolce? And it all really was an "ineffectual exercise in folly"? What if Simon neither remembered me nor cared about any of this? What if nothing would ever make sense? And we would always be separate from the animals, divided into an "us" and a "them"? Now I *was* nervous. The strawberries of my sundress deepened in color as I grew damp.

Bumble had given me several gentle warnings before the meeting began. ("Be careful what you say. Mention no specific campaigns. Take responsibility for nothing. We don't want to get in any trouble, after all.") But his admonitions had been unnecessary, at least at first. The questions were all easy to answer, even in my shaky state.

"How many hours per week do you expect crew members to devote?"

"How much travel is required?"

"How much hands-on experience with animals would one need before becoming involved?"

There was one question I knew I shouldn't answer, and didn't: "Were you really the group that burned down Untamed a few weeks ago?"

"Next question, please."

There was a question I probably should have avoided answering—"Do you make use of incendiary devices in any of your campaigns?"—but answered anyway, with what I'd hoped was delicacy and grace. "There is a possibility we may use such tools in the future. However, we would never put the lives of any humans or animals at risk."

And there was yet another question I most certainly should not have answered, but did.

I answered because I was distracted by questions of my own: What was the point of earth, sun, moon, and stars? What was the *point* of such things when there were so many who needed saving? And then, as if he'd heard me pose those questions aloud and was aggrieved that I should have to ask them at all, Jack Dolce slowly made his way through the crowd toward the stairs. I saw him shaking his head as he descended.

I also answered the question I shouldn't have because I was surprised. The person who asked it was not one of the kids in the crowd, but the man in the newsboy cap. I never suspected he had any interest in the Operation, though he had been in the vicinity of many of our meetings and had even come to the party at Jack Dolce's flat (he had been a wallflower that night, speaking to no one, recoiling from the green snake wound around my neck, and declining a glass of wine with a quick shake of his head). He laid down his tome on U.S. presidents and raised his hand.

"I don't mean to keep the conversation focused on, er, fire," he said in a nervous, high-pitched voice. He fiddled with a cell phone on the table before him. I both noticed and did not notice it. "But, I'm curious about incendiary devices. If we were to use them, how would we make them?"

I had never noticed his eyes before. They were a hard, icy blue, and they contrasted with what was in all other aspects a seemingly benign and bland face. Thinking of those eyes, and of a ring of rosemary speckled with blue flowers, a blue plastic rosary bought from a little Mexican boy, and the blue hearts in a Navajo silver hair comb, I answered his question. I answered almost automatically, for it was a subject I had lately studied, always with Charlotte asleep on my back as I perused my handbooks. Every passage I had highlighted, every illustration I had circled came back with ease. The man in the newsboy cap awkwardly repositioned his cell phone. I both saw and did not see it. He nodded, and wore a flattering expression of fascination while I spoke.

I spoke of gasoline. I spoke of plastic milk jugs. I spoke of batteries, timers, igniters, the power of one match. I spoke of fire. I even picked up a stick of chalk and started a sketch on the chalkboard before Bumble, who had been staring my way with the incredulous eyes of a lemur, stood and shushed me.

"*Thank you,* Margie," he said, shooting a smile at our onlookers, all of whom had raised eyebrows and open, rapt mouths. "I think that about wraps things up. And thank you all for your questions, everyone. We'll now begin taking your application forms." He feigned a few friendly pats on my shoulder in an effort to push me down into a chair.

And then, just as I took my seat, I noticed it again: the cell phone. I saw the cell phone of the man in the newsboy cap clearly now, as if for the first time, positioned upright on the table in front of him, and it gave me a sudden sick feeling.

Yes, even though I had no notion of what was about to happen, I had a sick feeling, sick and scared, a sensation no warrioress would feel, worse than the feeling of watching Jack Dolce descend the stairs in disapproval, worse than the feeling of dozens of Dorals dangling from a downcast dad's mouth, worse than Rasha's red poppies—it was a feeling of doom that clung to me like the strawberries of my sweat-soaked dress, so dark now that they looked overripe, unappetizing, rotten.

BUMBLE CAUGHT UP TO ME AS I SPEEDWALKED to my car. Jack Dolce had given me a wistful wave when I'd passed the downstairs window of Gelato Amore, and I could feel something salty brewing behind my eyelashes. "I think that went well,"

Bumble said. "You did start running off at the mouth there toward the end—what was that all about?—but all in all, it was good. Some promising people in the crowd. Let's go have a beer at the Ould Sod." The Ould Sod was a bar in Kensington that had an actual chunk of Irish earth mounted on one of its walls. Bumble liked to tell me the color of the oft-touched soil matched my hair. "Celtic chocolate," he called it, not knowing how much more I loved Beirut brown. He lightly socked my shoulder. "I'll buy."

"I can't," I said. "I don't feel right. I think I'm coming down with something." I ducked into my station wagon and slammed the door after me. Bumble frowned, squinted into my eyes. "I'll see you soon," I said through the glass and steered myself home.

THE NEXT MORNING SOMEONE KNOCKED on the door of my studio. I was sluggish from the bottle of red wine I'd imbibed the night before in an unsuccessful effort to drown my feeling of dread.

I let the knocking persist for several minutes. I tried to convince myself that Bumble or one of the others had come to discuss the applications we'd collected (none of which I had so much as given a glance) or to tell me the latest news about a chicken ranch in Escondido with a modus operandi abundant in the usual atrocities (birds driven mad by their living conditions, by the heartless hacking off of their highly sensitive beaks) or an underground sushi restaurant in the Gaslamp Quarter (hidden door, big bouncer) that was secretly selling endangered sea turtle to select patrons. But in my belly, I knew.

I rolled over with a little groan. Charlotte sat beside my head, watchful. "Oh," I whispered to her, "oh . . ."

Then I heard a voice, nasal and newly familiar, on the other side of the door. "Margie Fitzgerald," it said. There was no question mark after "Fitzgerald."

For five minutes, I listened in vain for the sound of retreating footsteps. Then I heard my name once more.

I stumbled to the door and opened it, wild haired.

I saw two men in suits. "Good morning," I said.

One of the men used to be the man in the newsboy cap. "Ms. Fitzgerald," he said. His cap was gone. "I'm Agent Fox and this is Agent Jones. We're with the Federal Bureau of Investigation."

At that moment, I had a memory. It wasn't a remnant of a dream snaking its way through my brain, never to be seen again. It was a memory of something true. I remembered a red resin bracelet that had belonged to Rasha.

"May we come in?" Agent Fox said.

I was self-conscious about the condition of my apartment. A gang of fruit flies hovered over a pile of cherry pits in the overflowing trash can, and Charlotte had left a smattering of droppings beside the chair in which Agent Fox took a seat. He pretended not to notice, as I pretended not to be amazed that the man who had habitually sat upstairs at Gelato Amore staring into a book (by all appearances a meek man with neither a lover nor a job, a café loiterer, a gelato addict) was the very same proud personage who now, suited and badged, seemed to take up so much space in my shabby studio.

Then Agent Fox told me in polite, almost tender tones that "the Federal Bureau of Investigation" was in possession of "recent video" of me "teaching the making or use of an explosive," which was, he added pointedly, a federal crime. I looked at Agent Fox, the very one who had baited me to "teach the making or use of an explosive" with his question, who had obtained the "recent video" with his cell phone, and he looked back at me and did not blink or shift his gaze. My cheeks grew hot with humiliation. He said

I had demonstrated that I could be a serious threat to my country as a possible domestic terrorist, one who endeavored to spur others to commit violent acts. And, finally, he said what was at once inevitable and unimaginable, what I prayed to Saint Jude, patron of the lost and desperate, would not be true: I was under arrest.

AFTER ALLOWING ME A FEW MINUTES to dress and set out some
rabbit food, the agents drove me to the county jail, where they
took my photograph (a joyless image with no rosemary crown, no
green snake necklace) and my fingerprints (unfathomable hiero-
glyphs with all the secrets of my destiny in their swirls). I waited
there while the crew arranged for my bail (I had placed my sole
allotted phone call to Bumble, for I could not conceive of calling
Dad). During my confinement, which I spent alone in a locked
cell with a disinfectant smell that stung the insides of my nostrils,
I had time to think. It was only then that I realized why I had
suddenly remembered Rasha's red resin bracelet upon opening
my door to the agents: the cell phone with which Agent Fox had
recorded me at Gelato Amore was not the first object I had both
seen and not seen.

It had happened with the bracelet, too. When I was younger,
fourteen or fifteen, I found it while poking through a drawer
of miscellany (tape measures, decade-old coupons, plastic forks,
pencils too short to write with but too cute to throw away) in
the kitchen. I put it on, wore it on a whim to Sunday Mass, and
then—it seemed—lost it. Later that afternoon, I noticed it wasn't

on my wrist anymore but could not recall just when or where I had taken it off. I hunted all over for it and finally resorted to chanting the special prayer for lost objects the nuns had taught us in CCD: "Saint Anthony, Saint Anthony, won't you take a look around? Something has been lost and must be found." But this was to no avail. I lay awake in my bed all night, listening to the broken song of a nightbird who stood in the magnolia tree, worrying, wondering where the bracelet had gone.

My search continued well into Monday. My bleary eyes and the dark circles beneath them convinced Dad that I was sick and should stay home from school. As he left to show a house in the Rio de Lágrimas tract, he suggested I make myself a hot toddy with his Maker's Mark, wrap myself mummy-style in a blanket, watch TV, and try to "sweat it out."

Once alone, I frantically turned over and looked under absolutely everything, even in cobwebby corners where I had not trod in years, until, breathless and despondent, I threw myself belly down onto my bed and sobbed.

I could not bear it, the feeling of having lost anything of hers.

Then I turned my face and saw the bracelet sitting on my nightstand next to the white porcelain palm that held the rose-scented rosary, exactly where I'd already glanced a thousand times, where it had been seen but not seen, and, reverent in my relief, I sniffed it. It was the most radiant of relics, a vermilion icon, a piece of picked fruit, still fragrant from Rasha's wrist—there, all along.

GENEROUS PTARMIGAN PAID TO HAVE ME SPRUNG from the slammer. He used all that remained of the funds bequeathed to him by his aunt who had expired in the polo mishap. "You're a bird, Margie," he told me. "I always think of you that way. And no man—no honorable one, anyway—can abide a bird's confinement in a cage any more than he can a chimp's, or a mouse's." Once free, I kissed him on both cheeks, and then pulled off his glasses to kiss his shut eyes, where I tasted salt, to my surprise.

I found an attorney in the phone book. His name was Ronald Clack, and the photo accompanying his ad depicted a cocksure young upstart with arms folded across his chest. He seemed to wink at me from the page. I was mildly comforted by the familiar tone he took with me when I called. "It could go either way, Marge," he said. "We could be talking months, we could be talking years. Or, best case, we could get you off. Everything has changed since the terrorist attacks of 2001. And forget the red scare of the 1950s—we're in the midst of what I like to call the 'green scare.'" He paused, as if waiting for the import of his words to sink in. "Enviros and activists like yourself are the targets now. I think what we're really dealing with here is a freedom of speech issue. Why don't you come over to my office and we'll hash this thing out."

During our meeting, Ronald Clack had gourmet takeout fare the likes of which I could not normally afford delivered right to his office door. "Dig in," he said, but I was too worried about my future to eat. My trial date, set for just three months away, loomed. My hands shook and I couldn't stop blinking. "Am I going to be locked up again?" I asked. Ronald Clack's desk was buried under layers of paper—notes he said he'd made while brainstorming ways to get me out of my mess. He seemed sincere in his desire to help, and because he had just begun practicing he was not quite as costly as most other lawyers. Still, even if I gave him the rest of my student loan money, it would not have been enough to cover a mere week's worth of his services.

BACK ON THE ROOF OF THE OLD VICTORIAN, I stared out at the lights lining the airport tarmac and wondered what Dad would do when he learned I was going to jail. The unfinished letter was still tucked beneath the pillow on my bed, and I fretted over the prospect of writing any sort of postscript now. *P.S. One more thing, Dad: it looks as though I'll be going away for a while.*

I heard steps behind me. "I knew you'd be up here," Bumble said. He sat down and curled an arm around my shoulders. "I always sensed there was something funny about that guy, Agent . . . what's his—"

"Fox."

"I just never imagined it was this. I'm still trying to get to the bottom of it. I even called Simon, but he never answers his phone."

"What difference does it make?" I said. Pride, along with persistent heart-pain, had prevented me from reaching out to Simon myself. And, on the rare occasions when I chanced to pass him on campus, he always looked at the ground, and had a hunched posture, as if weighted down by a bag of burdens he couldn't unpack, not even for me. "What's there to get to the bottom of?" I flopped back and searched for a star, but they were all hidden from me. "I'm doomed."

"I've been working on that, too," Bumble said. "And I don't think you're doomed. But you have to leave. A lawyer doesn't seem like a possibility. And a public defender will be of no use—I'm sure they're all in cahoots with the feds anyway. I talked to my mom. She's been making some calls. She has some relatives you can go stay with. Well, friends, really. Or, I'm not sure—it's different with Indians—everyone acts as if they're related."

"What are you talking about?"

"People like us, we're not just activists anymore, we're enemies of the state. *Domestic terrorist?*" Bumble shook his head. "This is a witch hunt, Margie. I'm sorry that you're the one they singled out. I'm sorry for everything. But it's best if you just get out of here before you're made an example of. Start over. We've had our thrill."

"But, what are you saying? Indians?" I thought of Jack Dolce with his poster of Sitting Bull.

"I found a hiding place for you," Bumble said, "in Montana. You can stay there until we come up with something else."

"Montana." It was a place to which I had never in my life devoted a single thought. "What's in Montana? Nothing's in Montana."

"Exactly. But there are seven Indian reservations there, which are basically, like, invisible places. And one of them is the Crow Reservation. That's where my mom's friend lives—"

"Bumble," I said. "Aren't Indian reservations supposed to be like third-world countries?" But he was too busy explaining to hear me.

"—a friend she met back in the seventies, when she was a lot cooler. Anyway, this friend of my mom's has a son, and this guy—"

"No guys." I covered my eyes, thinking of my fractured friendship with Jack Dolce, whom I had wanted for a forever brother, and of Simon, of course I thought of Simon, who had first milled me so long ago on the soft sofa of his school office. "Nothing personal, Bumble, but I'm weary of guys."

I watched a moth flap crazily past us in the gray evening, searching for the kind of warm bright lights that had not yet been lit. Bumble lifted his digital wristwatch, pressed a button. "There you go, friend," he said, and the moth alighted there, magnetized by its glow. He went on, undissuaded.

"It's not just a guy, Margie, it's a family. I'm trying to tell you."

"Do you know them?"

"Well, no. I've never been out there. Frankly, I'm embarrassed by how little I know about my mother's people."

I sighed, bit down on my quivering lip. Loneliness was all I felt—the loneliness of my future. I imagined the loneliness of living with strangers, which had to be worse than the loneliness of living alone or the loneliness of living with a despairing dad and a Beirut-brown ghost.

"No," I said. "I don't like this idea."

"Now listen, Margie," Bumble said. "Do you want to go to jail or do you want to go to Montana?"

I didn't say anything. It was a case of, as Simon had been fond of saying, *a fronte praecipitium a tergo lupi.**

"It sounds kind of nice, actually. They live way out in the middle of nowhere on the western side of the reservation, on a chunk of land that's been in their family for, like, over a hundred years. It's probably pretty peaceful. There's the guy, and he lives there with his mother—that's my mom's friend—and his daughter, a little girl who's got no mother—"

"Oh, come *on,*" I protested. "Are you *kidding* me?" Another motherless one, I thought. There were so many of us. "Is this a joke?"

"No, for real. Her mom's in jail. Her dad drives to Billings every day for his job at a printing press or someplace. And so the grandmother and the kid are left alone. Like, out on the prairie. The grandma insists that they stay out there. That parcel of land means something to her, I guess. Now, my mom told me that they would be willing to shelter you, to hide you, and they don't even *know* you." Bumble shook his head in amazement.

"It seems so clichéd," I said. "I'll be the lost white person who is saved by magical Native Americans."

"What's wrong with that?" Bumble replied. "What would be so bad about that? A little human kindness? People like to help each other, Margie. It makes them feel good. My mom said they would enjoy having a young woman around, someone who can

---

* A precipice in front, wolves behind

be a friend to the girl. They say they have no real fear of the feds. And apparently the grandmother is very intrigued by your story. So, if you need to disappear—and you do, Margie—there's no better place. It's very isolated where they are."

THE FOLLOWING AFTERNOON, the crew came to my studio and watched while I stuffed a handful of sundresses, the lucky red Chinese shoes, the porcelain palm, the rose-scented rosary, *Wheelock's Latin*, and the unfinished letter to Dad into Annette Mellinkoff's Strawberry Shortcake suitcase. Bear and Orca stood arm in arm with solemnity. Ptarmigan forlornly petted Charlotte, who snuggled in his lap and ground her teeth with pleasure. Raven lamented, "I don't know why it had to be you who got into all this trouble and not all of us."

"It's my own fault. I'm the one who got greedy and over-excited and wanted to hold that stupid info session." I stood facing them all with my hands dangling at my sides. "I'm going to miss you. You were my first real friends."

"I did a tarot spread for you," Bear said, wiping her wet, white face. "It looked—"

"Please don't tell me." I cut her off and clicked the suitcase closed. "I honestly don't want to know."

I stepped outside to check my mailbox and found a letter from Dad, forwarded from the apartment I'd once shared with Amy and Winnie. It surprised me, slipped among the usual abundance of junk mail. A few flaky Doral ashes, cancerous confetti, fell out when I tore open the envelope. The paper came from one of Dad's Sunshine Realty notepads, the ones he ordered in bulk and left on people's front porches as a form of advertising. A black-and-white portrait of him, looking buttoned down and dapper, was in the upper left corner, and his name was printed across the top ("Mark Fitzgerald: Finding Families Homes for 20 Years").

Other realtors had abandoned the now-nostalgic notepads and moved on to glossy refrigerator magnets embellished with full-color head shots that highlighted the dazzle of their sharky grins, or to ballpoint pens with their names printed on the side—useful items that people might actually hold on to. But Dad preferred paper, pieces of ephemeral paper on which strangers would scrawl their grocery lists, their Things to Do, and then discard, crinkling up his face and name.

This was not, I could see, going to be one of his rare and wonderfully long missives. The sheet of paper had been pulled from the pad in evident haste, for the top was carelessly torn. *Hi Honey,* Dad wrote, and then proceeded with a series of fragmentary sentences, all of them lacking the first-person pronoun ("I" in English or *ego*, as Simon had taught me, in Latin):

> *Hope this finds you happy and healthy.*
> *Cleaning out the attic.*
> *Been thinking about you.*
>
> *Miss you,*
> *Dad*

I stepped back inside and turned to Bumble, who was going to drive me to the Crows. "I just have one quick trip I need to make before we leave."

He shook his head. "We should get on the road."

"I won't take long," I assured him. I told the others, "You can all share my station wagon while I'm in Montana." Turning to Ptarmigan, I added, "I want Charlotte to stay with you now."

Then, as was our habit, we all drew close together in a circle, extended our hands, and stacked them. But this time, no one spoke, and there was no triumphant declaration of our

organization's name. We stood touching each other, and for a
moment we were all of a piece, in need of no one and nothing
else. Somewhere, a wing flapped, an antenna quivered, a hoof
turned up dust, a beak snapped shut, and our hearts with their
varied wounds were momentarily mended, and the world with its
menagerie of inhabitants was right again, and there was no such
thing as an "us" or a "them," only a giant "we," otherwise known
as a family, and we savored that sensation of wholeness until the
dream flickered away as suddenly as it had come, and Simon's
Operation was done.

I DROVE TO ORANGE COUNTY BY MYSELF. I hadn't been back
home in over a year. Our house was the same dun color, but
seemed several shades lighter. The magnolia tree was a bit
taller and bright with blooms. Dad, of course, wasn't expecting
me. Several minutes elapsed between my second, amplified
series of knocks and his arrival to the front door. He was clad
in a bathrobe and dress slacks. When he saw me standing on
the porch, hidden behind my big black sunglasses and shaking
from stress, he blinked and stepped back. "Margie?" Maybe he
didn't remember sending the note. In my arms, he was stiff with
surprise.

Inside, I quickly surmised that "cleaning out the attic" really
meant removing everything from that shadowed, spidery upper
realm and scattering it haphazardly around the first and second
floors. There was an antique Louis XV–style chair turned upside
down on top of the coffee table, leaving just enough room for Dad
to place his *TV Guide* and remote. A stickered steamer trunk,
reeking of mothballs, was stashed in the hallway, requiring me to
turn sideways on my way to the bathroom. Half of the sofa was
occupied by boxes of old *Life* magazines, along with a phono-
graph, dull with dust, inherited from one of the long-deceased

Fitzgeralds, as well as the curvy dress form Rasha had used to sew some of her clothes. The stairs leading to the second floor were lined on both sides with additional debris—a doll-sized stroller, a set of golf clubs, a remote-controlled toy car, three skis, an old black suitcase, and a ladies' fan fashioned from faded pink flamingo feathers—and I wondered if my bedroom was still habitable or if Dad had rendered it a repository for more of his attic discoveries.

I stood in the living room, unable to remove my sunglasses. I poked my finger through a hole in a Depression-era quilt assembled by Grandmother Fiona, she of the Mitsouko perfume. Then I let my eyes rest on a porcelain wedding cake topper. It featured a pair of blushing lovebirds snuggled side by side. A faintly glittering crust (fossilized frosting?) was clumped around its base.

"Are you thirsty, Sweet?" Dad asked. He patted the oversized pockets of his robe as if they might contain a small box of juice complete with its own bendy straw, or a sippy cup of milk.

"No, I'm good."

He smiled. "You look beautiful. I'm happy to see you. The place is a mess. I didn't know you were coming. How's San Diego? You have a lot of friends?"

Without going into too much detail, I told Dad that I had met with some trouble, withdrawn from school, and was going to move to Montana for a while. A frown furrowed the top half of his face, but the bottom half still smiled.

"Montana?" he said. His voice was soft with awe or confusion.

"I wanted to come and say goodbye," I said. "Goodbye for now," I added, swallowing. "Not forever. I promise I'll write."

There was a breadbox on top of the hi-fi in the foyer. On top of the breadbox sat a fat photo album. But it wasn't a snapshot shrine to Rasha. It was one I had never seen before, with a dark green vinyl cover on which Dad had markered his (or my) initials: *M.F.* I touched it in curiosity. "Oh," Dad said. "That didn't come out of the attic, honey. That's usually in my den, but I brought it down here. I look at it often."

WHEN BUMBLE DROVE ME AWAY toward my hiding place in Montana, and I had an embarrassing bout of tears lasting all the way from Salt Lake City to Pocatello, it was the green album that I was thinking about.

THE ALBUM'S SPINE WAS LOOSE, FLEXIBLE. It opened with the ease of oft-opened things. The first two pages contained thirteen photographs of me. They were wallet-sized pictures, one for each stage of school, from kindergarten to senior year. I hadn't known Dad had saved them, much less arranged them with such care (he had written my name and the date beneath each one in his baroque cursive). Glancing over them, I remembered a ritual I had hitherto forgotten: Dad had spent many a morning styling my hair, and the imperfect results of his earnest labors were evident in all of the earlier photos. There were uneven pigtails, weirdly woven braids, and bangs freshly snipped at accidental angles across my forehead. I thought of us standing together before the bathroom mirror, the everyday intimacy of it. I imagined us staring into a circle wiped clean of steam, he behind me with his hands in my hair, and I helpfully offering instructions in my chirping child's voice. What had we talked about, I wondered, when I was six and Dad had spritzed my curls into submission? What morningtime murmurs had we exchanged? Had we smiled at each other in the mirror and spoken of the dreams we'd had before waking?

The next pages in the album featured little relics of sorts—items with a bit of bulk that prevented the pages from lying flat with perfect smoothness. My face flushed as I flipped through them, for I was unaccustomed to the sensation of seeing myself memorialized. There were several baby teeth taped to one page. They resembled sunbleached pebbles and might have just as easily been scooped by Dad from the seashore as from beneath my pillow. There was a stray pink anklet, toddler-sized, with no companion. There was a thin gold baby ring with the following note written beside it: "Gift from Aunt Yalda, Sent from Beirut, Worn, Swallowed, and Spat Up On Easter Sunday, 1986." And there was a collage comprised of dried black beans depicting an elephant that I had created in kindergarten.

I turned more pages, passing over painstakingly printed book reports and moody sketches, and found the program from the "Yes Sir, That's My Baby" Father-Daughter Dance, followed by the photo we took that night—Dad in that regal leather chair with me standing beside him wearing my corsage of roses. His eyes were closed in an involuntary blink against the glaring flash, but he wore a wide smile.

Then I came upon a series of essays with consistently ungainly titles ("The Haunted Huntress: Why Hunting Foxes Hurts Natasha in *War and Peace*"). They were the papers I'd written during my second semester of college while in the first flush of my animal rights romance, the ones I had sent home to Dad after I'd stopped visiting him.

Upon receiving them, Dad must have gathered that I had grown deeply interested in animals, that the affection I'd once held for Old Peep, our absent parakeet, had morphed into an obsessive regard for "all things both great and small," to quote the Coleridge poem I had used as an epigraph for several of the essays. I wondered what he'd thought of it all. And I wondered if he intuited that the "trouble" I'd run into had something to do with the animals. He was silent as he watched me glance over the essays. I noticed he had drawn a star on "Needless Desperation: How a Dog Could Have Saved Werther from His Sorrows"— perhaps to indicate it was his favorite.

The last page contained a memento I couldn't place. It was

neither a photo nor an essay, neither a trinket nor a tooth, but a fine sheet of paper bearing a handwritten column of text, with numbers and measurements, too. It might have been a poem. "Twenty years," Dad said.

"Hmm?"

"Your mother's perfume formula, honey—or recipe, as she called it. It's almost twenty years old. It's the one she finished just before you were born, the one she called her favorite. I've been saving it for you. It's something of hers that you helped her create."

"What do you mean?" I asked. "I ruined her whole dream . . . and yours, too." It was the first time I had ever said such a thing, and as soon as I said it, I felt it, hot, in my eyes.

"No, Margie. Please don't say that. She told me she was never as inspired as when she was carrying you. She could smell everything!"

I took off my sunglasses. The paper was goldening with age, and the penciled words were soft and silvery. Rasha's handwriting, which I'd had so few occasions to see, was sweetly slanted toward the right and featured lush, bulbous lower *g*'s and *y*'s, and tall, elegant *l*'s and *t*'s. It was lovely to look at, like a drawing, regardless of the words it spelled. But when I read some of the words—*magnolia, orange blossom, jasmine, lavender, grass, roots, cherries, tobacco, wild rose, peach*—I realized they *were* a poem, both poem and enchantment, recipe and prayer, a code for an invisible kind of beauty to be conjured with the things of the earth. "I've been waiting for the right time to give it to you," Dad said. "I suppose this is as good a time as any since you are going so far away." His voice faltered at the last two words. "Go ahead, honey. Take it out."

I did, and I couldn't help but smell it, as if the words and figures might exude the scent of the perfume they outlined. The sheet was transparent, like tracing paper. I held it up in front of me and looked through it, looked between the words, to see Dad standing, hands pocketed, watching me with expectant eyes.

Yes, I lifted the recipe to my face, and after a moment Dad blurred, and I could not see him at all through my tears. "Dad," I said. "I can't believe it." I didn't just mean the recipe. It was the very existence of the album that surprised me, the photos, the relics, the essays. I had lived, and grown, and Dad, in his way, had watched. He had kept track. And everything, all of it, was safe behind sheets of that clear plastic film that adheres so gently to whatever it contains—inconspicuous but always present, always pressing, always protecting—there, all along.

Book Two

Terra homines fructibus bonis alit.*

---

* The earth nourishes human beings with good fruits.

1 ❧ LION *(Panthera leo)*

ON THE DRIVE TO MONTANA I THOUGHT once more about the hour I'd spent in Simon's school office on that fluish day and retrospectively studied the seconds that had comprised it for portents—unnoticed at the time—of what had since come to pass. I recalled the books I had found crowding his shelves. And I pondered writing my own book, one that might someday be slid among them. Thematically, it would fit right in. I would call it, I thought, *Montana, My New Loneliness: The True Story of an Animal Rights Activist on the Lam*.

Montana really was a kind of loneliness, as if the feeling of loneliness had cloaked itself in earth, capped itself in sky, and become a place. How is it, I wondered, that of all possible locales I've ended up in the one that is the geographical embodiment of the very condition from which I have for so long been running?

But I knew Bumble had meant well when he suggested I escape to the Treasure State. And he had been extra cautious, using a fake ID to rent the tiny blue economy car that carried us all the way from the saline sweetness of San Diego to the prairie of eastern Montana, where the season was not summer or winter or spring, but unsettlingly in between.

Long before we reached our destination, homesickness began to hurt my stomach, then shape-shifted into an invisible elephant who stood upon my chest. There were no orange trees in Montana, and no occasional oceanic odors. And what about Dad? Robe-clad Dad with his Dorals dangling, Dad in our crumbling house with the furniture so crazily arranged, Dad with his photo albums, Dad with an old lovebird cake topper complete with ossified frosting? The ladybug began to stir behind my eyes, causing a tingle that I knew was preludial to tears, and I had already had a sloppy cry during which Bumble tried to comfort me with shoulder patting, hair smoothing, and, finally, with singing. His singing voice was showy and surprisingly high, but his spontaneous choice of "Oh My Darling, Clementine" proved to be ill considered, because when he melodiously declared "you are lost and gone forever" the elephant on my chest grew almost unbearably heavy.

I studied Bumble's profile. Not only had he found me a hiding place on the Crow Reservation, but he had insisted on staying behind the wheel for most of the twenty-two-hour trip. He said he wanted me to relax. He was exhausted but he tried not to show it. Still, he looked tired—tired and serious and boyish and more human, somehow, than he ever had. Maybe I'd been mistaken, I thought, for assuming that Bumble's love affair with gadgetry and gear betrayed a lack of inner warmth.

"Bumble," I said. "Thanks again for this, for driving, for singing, for everything."

"Of course, Margie. And please don't worry. Everything's going to work out." I remembered the night I'd met Bumble, when Simon brought me to my first Operation H.E.A.R.T. meeting upstairs at Gelato Amore. A year and a half had passed, but remembering it was like recalling an incident from childhood— a moment so long ago it seems, when viewed from what feels like a great distance through memory's misty eyeglass, imbued with sentiment. Bumble's red dreadlocks were just beginning then, and his face had still been cushioned with a pillowy layer of baby fat that, in the ensuing months, had melted away. "I'm Bumble B.," he'd said, shaking my hand. "That's 'B' with a period, not 'B-E-E.'"

What has happened, what has happened? went the secret refrain in my brain. *How can I ever go back to school? Or do anything at all? Wanted by the FBI? A fugitive?* I rested my head against the seat and stared out the open window. The prairie air blew against my face without tenderness. Black ravens, heavy with carrion, flapped lazily off the road just in time to dodge our wheels and observed us from fence posts, only worsening my sense of being watched.

After a few minutes, Bumble spoke again. "Remember, it's only temporary, Margie. And what comes after this is up to you." I stared, listlessly.

We entered the reservation and drove through a small town called Crow Agency, where countless fluffy white tufts—cottonwood seeds, Bumble said—drifted from the trees and floated through the air, looking delicate and celestial amid the weathered buildings and the cars, which were older, louder, more beat up, and more creatively patched together than any I had ever seen. One stretch of asphalt we traversed was blotched with gleaming shards of broken Beirut-brown bottles, and Bumble drove around the glass with care.

"Nobody will find you here," he continued. "Just hang out until things die down. It's not as though you hurt anyone, after all. I mean, what on earth?" he exclaimed. "I know we've talked about it a million times, but I seriously doubt the feds are going to stay worried about some freckle-faced college girl who wanted to help out a few animals."

"But you're the one who told me I should go away because of

what Ronald Clack called the 'green scare'—the witch hunt, you said. Remember?"

"Just wait it out. Wait a while."

"What's 'a while'?" I asked. "How long is 'a while'?"

Poor Bumble didn't know, so he pretended he hadn't heard me. Crow Agency was behind us in minutes, and we were once again surrounded exclusively by earth and sky. Driving north through Idaho, we had seen a few patches of persistent snow lingering in the shady places beneath roadside pines, though the first day of summer was just weeks away. Now the landscape was vacant and vast. There were too few trees to make shade for stubborn snow, and nothing new had grown in winter's wake. The land was neither white nor green—it was an uninspiring shade of khaki and it had the quality of something incomplete, something waiting.

"Look at this place," Bumble said. The prairie was so foreign, so full of secrets, and I had no key to unlock it. The softly sloping hillocks rolling away in every direction looked to me like a lot of lions sleeping. There were mountains in the distance that— with their absence of angles and their curvy shapes—seemed gentle, but I did not know their names. "No distractions," Bumble went on. "Perfect for getting your thoughts in order and starting fresh. It's so quiet. No more airplanes! And," he added, "if it gives you any comfort, you don't have to think of yourself as being in the U.S. or even in Montana anymore, but in Crow Country, because the way my mom explained it, the tribe is a sovereign nation all its own."

"Hmm." I watched the prairie pass in a blur of beige. The land was dotted here and there with abandoned cars and pieces of farm equipment dissolving into rusty crumbles. We passed through a town called St. Xavier where no one appeared to live. I saw a log cabin that had been converted into a church, a rusty trailer tipping precariously into a ditch and painted with

the words EAR CLINIC, and a place called Pretty Eagle Catholic
School. Pretty Eagle's exterior was embellished with a chipped
mural featuring an Indian boy and girl, their heads bowed in
prayer and a basketball hovering between them. It was early
afternoon and all the students were out of sight, hunched over
desks. St. Xavier was quiet, and as we left it I continued to search
in vain for signs of life, studying the hillocks to see if the slumbering lions might awaken.

After a while, I did see life. I spotted a bent figure fifty yards
from the road, carrying a short stick and making measured progress over a bluff. The person was long skirted, and the softness of
her shape was reminiscent of the distant mountains. She paused,
then crouched and pierced the ground and pulled something
from the soil. She deposited her unearthed treasure into a sack
slung over one shoulder. Wondering at what I had seen, I stared
at the woman as we passed, poking my head out the window to
watch her shrink to a speck behind us. She stared back, lifting
up a hand to shade her eyes.

Bumble checked the hand-drawn map he'd received from
his mother. "I think we're getting closer," he said, consulting the
digital compass he had strapped to his wrist. "Yep. This is it." He
turned onto an unmarked dirt road, which we followed until it
ended at a humble house that looked as much like a child's drawing as an actual abode—perfectly square and symmetrical, with
curtained windows, a peaked roof with a black stovepipe poking through, and a spotted dog lounging near its front door. The
dog lifted its head at our approaching car, then lowered it again,
unimpressed.

Bumble parked alongside an old tan-colored Cutlass with a
raised hood. Its engine parts were all on the grass but arranged
neatly into groups, categorized according to characteristics and
purposes unknown to me. I took a curious comfort in their
orderliness. There were also dozens of oily black tools, but these,

too, were tucked tidily away, stationed in a splintered shelf that appeared to be a fragment from an old row of elementary school cubbies. A forgotten name, "Ruteger," was carved in callow cursive inside one of the compartments.

"Well," Bumble said. He shut off the engine.

"Well."

"Guess we should go say hello."

But no one came to the door, though we knocked at a grandmother-friendly volume. And we could see through the parted gingham curtains that no one sat in the small kitchen, where bright blue dishcloths hung from nails in the wall above the sink, or in the living room, where white lacy ovals covered the armrests of a pair of faded recliners.

"Maybe they don't even live here anymore," I said, summoning a halfhearted hope. "Maybe they just moved away, and we'll have to go back home."

"I'm sure they still live here," Bumble finally said. "Look at this dog. She's not even hungry. We'll just wait."

I remembered the tiny flashing tongue of the green snake who had lived under Jack Dolce's bed in Little Italy—Little Italy of the lemon light and the luminous oyster shells. The snake had used his tongue to test the air. Now I tested the air. I perched on our car's hood, lay back against the windshield, closed my eyes, and breathed in. The prairie was sunwarmed, and it exuded a rich, lively smell, similar to the way skin becomes more fragrant when the hidden workings of the body heat it. There was a smell like baking bread in the blond grass, and also a dark, secretive smell like mushrooms, and, from further below, the fresh vegetal smell of the slick tangles of pale roots that formed subterranean nests. Throughout my life I had smelled the swoon-inducing saps of flowers and the salty tang of beaches, but never had I known such a strong smell of earth.

I sat up and opened my eyes to look around, wondering how

such a colorless place could say so much to my nose. The only trees nearby were three gnarled sentinels at the front of the house. No birds rested in their branches, but in the trees' rippling whispers there was a salve for scared hearts, a secret lullaby. I leaned back and closed my eyes again. And then I caught hold of something that had eluded me for weeks: sleep.

I DREAMT OF A BUTTERFLY, THE ONE drawn by Annette Mellinkoff that I had hung above my bed in Middletown. It fluttered away at the sound of a truck driving onto the grass beside me.

MY HEART POUNDED. I had forgotten where I was and, once I remembered, could not believe I had fallen asleep in that strange setting, and on the hood of the car, too. The truck was big and noisy. I slid onto my feet, shaking with shyness. Bumble appeared beside me and we faced the driver, a big boned, black-eyed lady with blunt bangs across her forehead and breasts that brushed up against her steering wheel. A young girl sat beside her. For what felt like five hundred years, they looked at us and we looked back. The truck rumbled and vibrated. Bumble smiled.

"You the animal rights kook?" the woman yelled. My cheeks flamed. I nodded affirmatively.

"Welcome!" she shouted. "Here's Cora!"

The girl emerged. The truck bore her with a creak and swing of its door, and her long narrow feet, encased in purple sandals, fell upon the grass. She regarded us through a pair of cat-eye spectacles. The thick lenses seemed hefty for such a slight child.

"Granma should be back soon," the woman told us, "and Jim's usually home by seven or so." The girl slammed the door of the truck shut with one spindly brown arm and stepped wordlessly into the house.

Like Bumble, I offered an awkward smile. "Okay, thanks!"
I said to the woman. My arm rose with the beginnings of a bashful wave, but the truck had already spun around and stirred up
a cloud of dust.

"Who was that?" I asked.

"I don't know. But the girl, Cora, she's the one I told you
about. She lives here."

Even with Cora in the house, Bumble and I weren't sure if
we should enter or continue to wait outside. We shuffled, biting
nails and clearing throats, until another person appeared in our
midst without a sound. She was scarcely taller than the girl but
considerably rounder and slightly stooped, with a sharp-ended
stick in one hand and a flour sack hanging over her shoulder. Her
silver hair was wound into a knot at the nape of her neck. Her skirt
was so long it tickled the ground, and she wore a man's western-
style shirt with pearlescent snaps. She, I realized, was the person I had seen digging on the prairie. She, I supposed, was the
grandmother.

"I'm Granma," she said. Her voice was low and womanly.
The dog rose and nipped at her skirt hem with adoring whimpers. "You must be our guest," she said to me. She gave Bumble
a slow nod, her eyes dancing over his unusual hairdo. "Welcome.
This is Belly, our dog. She's an old gal like me." She hoisted her
sack up higher on her shoulder and, as she made her way toward
the house, I saw why we hadn't heard her approach. Her gentle
steps were rendered nearly silent by the thick soles of the bulbous
orthopedic sneakers peeking out from under her skirt. They had
Velcro closures. She used her back to hold the screen door open
for us. "Please come in," she said.

"Would you mind if I turned on the television?" Granma
asked. "I have a show I try not to miss." She clicked the remote
until she arrived at what was unmistakably a soap opera. That
day's episode had already commenced, and a woman wearing

too much eye makeup insisted weepily, "But Slade, I swear, the child is yours!" Granma shook her head at the screen, whistling through her teeth in disbelief.

Bumble and I sat in the twin recliners. Granma stood and emptied the contents of her sack onto a glitter-flecked Formica table that wobbled on its metal legs. Dozens of roots rolled out of the bag, and a lush, loamy odor filled the room. She rolled the roots under her tanned hands, freeing them of the dirt that clung to their surfaces.

Bumble ventured a question. "What are those for?" Granma didn't reply. Her eyes were fixed on the TV. A white-coated doctor stepped into a hospital waiting room. "Charmaigne is alive!" he said.

"Is she deaf?" Bumble mouthed to me. I shrugged.

Granma began to peel the bark-like skins off the roots. When that was done, she deposited the roots into a collection of old coffee cans she pulled from the kitchen. After a long while she said, "Jim will be home any minute."

TWILIGHT DARKENED THE SKY TO PURPLE. Granma fed Belly, and Bumble and I ate the peanut butter and jelly sandwiches she prepared for us after we, the virtuous vegans, politely refused everything else she had offered. She disappeared down the hall with a plate of food for Cora, who had been hiding since our arrival. Finally a truck—smaller and kinder sounding than the growling monster of the afternoon—pulled up outside. A door closed, footfalls crunched the grass, Granma emerged from Cora's room, and the screen door opened.

I detected the fragrance of orange blossoms, a familiar solar sweetness, creamy, bright, and inexplicable on that unblooming prairie. I wondered if my homesickness was so severe as to cause an olfactory hallucination, a neroli memory.

Then I saw stained fingertips, stained hands, speckled and splattered all colors of the rainbow.

"Hello!" the painted man said, smiling. He looked toward me, then turned to Bumble. "You must be Bumble." He extended a hand. "I'm Jim." He seemed so quiet, but not because he spoke softly. In fact, his voice was rather sonorous. Still, he reminded me of a church with no one in it, the way Dad and I had found Holy Rosary on the rare occasions that we'd arrived early for Mass—glossy wood pews empty, votive candles glowing, streaks of sunlight through the stained-glass windows making visible the millions of motes that hung in the air—more complete and inviting than it ever was when bustling with activity. "And you must be Margie." He directed his gaze away from mine and toward my left shoulder. I noticed a deep furrow between his eyes. "Welcome. I hope you'll feel comfortable here and know you can stay for as long as you need."

"Oh, thank you."

My hand, for the quick second that he shook it, disappeared in his. "Sorry about the ink," he said. He dropped a kiss atop Granma's head. "Hi, Mom." He set down a lunch pail and thermos and washed his hands in the kitchen sink until only a few persistent flecks of violet and orange remained. I tried not to look too long at the vertical crease between his eyes. It lent a wounded quality to his friendly smile that made my left ovary flame.

We joined him at the table under the glow of the star-shaped lamp that dangled from the ceiling, and Jim and Bumble talked. I mostly listened to the conversation between the two men—or, more accurately, between the man and the boy, for even though Jim was, I learned, twenty-nine and only five years older than Bumble, beside him Bumble seemed increasingly puerile, fiddling fondly with his compass watch, gnawing on a dreadlock. "I wish I knew more about Crow culture," he said. "Is it true that you, like, worship the buffalo?"

I wondered what had happened in Jim's life to carve that little line of hurt between his eyes. Then I considered how juvenile and ridiculous I must have seemed, a girl in trouble with the law, an animal rights kook, and I sat in self-conscious silence with my chin in my hand. I was just as relieved as I was perturbed that Jim would not look at me on the occasions that he directed a question my way. His eyes, so heavily lashed as to appear half closed, always fell just right or left of my face, but never on it.

"It's been nice for our moms to reconnect," Jim told Bumble. "They were friends long ago." Granma nodded from her recliner. "And I think your mom's dad was actually married to one of my mom's cousins, though, you know, in Crow we don't even have a word for cousin.

"We're glad we could help out with all this," Jim continued. "What a mess, huh? The federal government." He shook his head. "We tribes have had our share of conflicts with it, too. Even though we're supposed to be a sovereign nation all our own, the feds still have jurisdiction here when it comes to cases like yours. But this is a decent hiding place. And you—" He turned his face once more in my direction. "You can stay with us as long as you need. I know I already said that, but we're glad to have you."

"Thank you," I said. "I know I already said that, too. But I am so grateful," I added, reddening, "for your help. I hope I can be as much of a help to you, and to Granma, and—"

Cora stepped out of the hallway. She wore a nightgown, and her loosened hair streaked down her back in a straight and shining waterfall. She crushed her small body up against Jim's big one. "Have you met my daughter yet?" he asked.

"Hi, Cora," I said. "I'm Margie." With some prodding, she faced me, and slid one of her hands into the other with the quickness of a mouse vanishing into a hole. Standing with her hands thus arranged, she looked both dignified and demure.

"I like your glasses," I said. She still had on the cat-eyes. They were tortoiseshell, with constellations of rhinestones on both sides. The points of the almond-shaped frames extended beyond the perimeter of Cora's pixie face, which she promptly turned away from me. The glasses were of the same sort that a certain set of San Diego twentysomethings had been wearing for the last several years. I'd seen them for sale at steep prices in twee vintage clothing shops that specialized in adornments from yesteryear, most of which were meant to be worn with a tongue in one's cheek. I had a feeling Cora wasn't wearing the glasses ironically, but I also did not have any idea what to say to her, so impenetrable did she seem, as locked away from me as the mysterious prairie. So I asked, "Are those prescription, or are you just wearing them because they're cute?"

"They're subscription," she mumbled after a long pause and a slight, encouraging jostle from her dad.

"They're beautiful on you."

"Thanks." She frowned and looked at her bare feet, which she curled kittenishly, as if she hoped to hide them.

I watched the way Jim ruffled his broad hand over the top of Cora's head, the absent, innocent enjoyment he took in the softness of her hair. "Did you eat?" he asked us, and Granma brought him a sandwich stacked with sliced meat of unidentifiable origin, and Cora disappeared back down the hall, and Jim and Bumble talked some more. And Bumble was familiar to me in his grunts and foibles, in his fundamental goodness, and I could sense the vestigial traces of home on him like I could on nothing else in the room: they were folded in his speech, floating in his breath, woven invisibly among the fibers of his high-tech clothes, and I wanted to bottle them up, to keep them under my pillow for all the nights I might spend in that square and snug house among strangers. When he stood up with a stretch and said it was time to go, I fought the urge to cling to him in a way that the unwritten rules of our platonic palship had always prohibited.

"You should just stay the night here," Jim told him. "It's awfully soon to get back on the road after the drive you've had."

"Oh, that's okay. I already made arrangements for a hotel room in Billings. The War Bonnet Inn." Bumble blushed after saying the name.

My throat swelled with stifled tears, and I half-whispered a little "no," which no one acknowledged having heard. The star-shaped lamp above the table flickered.

"Well, at least Billings isn't too far," Jim said, and he told Bumble how to get there using a shortcut, and to beware of the black cows who sometimes ambled onto the reservation roads and were invisible on dark nights when the moon was just a sliver, and Granma rose, her knitting clutched in her gnarled hands, to bid him farewell, while Cora snoozed or, more likely spied, in her hidden chamber. Outside, Bumble clutched my shoulders and leaned close to whisper in my ear things I was too scared to hear, and handed me the Strawberry Shortcake suitcase (but not the dozen bottles of red wine I had bought special for the trip, because Granma said I could not have alcohol in the house). As he drove down the dirt road that had led us to that place so many hours earlier, I watched his taillights wane and dissolve. I tipped my head back to see the stars, and they seemed to swell and contract, swell and contract with every beat of my heart. I stood that way for a long time, listening to a melodious bird send out its short song again and again into the night, and watching the stars throb in time to it. Then my own name came clear to me, and I realized the birdsong was Granma, calling me inside.

GRANMA SHOWED ME TO CORA'S ROOM. We crept in, careful not to disturb the girl who, I was surprised to see, slept on a bunk bed. "She's always had it," Granma whispered. "It will come in handy now." The top bunk was for me.

I lay there, just beneath a ceiling I could not see, for that night on the prairie was as black as Jim had said. I stayed awake for hours, listening to the occasional chirps of insects through the opened window, to the mellow rustlings of the grass, to Cora's sleep sounds, and to the squeak of a wheel in constant rotation— presumably the exercise device of a small pet rodent.

I missed Charlotte, who had habitually slept beside me, and I wondered about everything under the slumbering sun: about Agent Fox and all the books I had seen him pretending to read at Gelato Amore, about Bumble snoozing at the War Bonnet Inn, about the handwritten recipe at the bottom of my suitcase and the loveliness of its ingredients, about the houses in the hills and how far away from me they were now, about miscellaneous Latin words whose meanings I had already forgotten, and about the dark-haired stranger of whom I had so often dreamed, the one who held me in a front-of-him-against-the-back-of-me embrace.

My mind spun relentlessly, in tandem with the ceaseless circulations of Cora's caged creature, until, at what had to have been an hour before dawn, I heard the front door open.

Certain that Agents Fox and Jones had followed the trail of the bright blue car all the way to Montana and simply breezed into the house to retrieve me, I instantly began to sweat, and a cavern opened up in my chest. Then, through the window, I heard the sound of footsteps going out of the house rather than in. I surmised by their near-inaudible softness and by the slowness of their pace that they were Granma's. Possibly Granma sleep-walked in her orthopedic sneakers, I thought. My chest mended itself partially, and I lifted my head from my pillow—carefully, carefully, so as not to disturb Cora, who, on the bunk below me, seemed to answer my every minute movement (a wiggle of toe, a blink of eye) with an annoyed-sounding sigh—and pulled away the window's makeshift curtain, a pillowcase printed with daisies. I peered into the night. By the light of one star, I saw Granma walk away from the house and climb a distant hillock. She stood there, wrapped in a blanket, unmoving and silent, for a long time. I decided I would watch to see what she might do, and it was only then, while straining to see her against the charcoal sky now lit by a single streak of gold, that I fell asleep.

I WOKE UP IN THE MIDDLE OF A DREAM in which Bumble, wearing a war bonnet and biting into a doughnut, told me, just as he had when he had first spoken of the reservation, "It's very isolated where they are." The room was yellow with sunlight, and I squinted, unsure of where I was. Then I saw the daisy-printed pillowcase curtain, smelled the grassy prairie air, and remembered. And I thought about isolation. Was it merely a consequence of too much open space? Or did it also live in cluttered houses on suburban streets, and in the pages of photo albums

where sad eyes had too often looked? Was it the lifeless down on
my arms when there was no one beside me to stroke me awake?
Or the sound of a strange child breathing?

Soon I heard Cora rise and scrape her spectacles from
her dresser. "Daphne," she said in a scruffy voice. The nighttime wheel spinner, a cream-and-brown hamster, wiggled her
nose with exuberance before burrowing into a bed of cedar
chips. A small sign bearing Daphne's name in precise penman-
ship hung from the cage. Beside it stood a row of books arranged
in perfect alphabetical order (*Anne of Green Gables; Apsáalooke
Nation: A History of the Crow Tribe; Are You There God? It's
Me, Margaret*). Cora added a handful of pellets to Daphne's food
dish and said nothing to me at all. When she opened the
bedroom door and exited, the smell of something savory and
sizzling curlicued into my nose. It was forbidden, fleshy food,
I knew, but my stomach drummed with desire, and soon I
stepped shyly out of my top bunk and into the day, one ladder
rung at a time.

IN THE KITCHEN, JIM FILLED HIS THERMOS with coffee and his
lunch pail with assorted pickings from the refrigerator and cupboards: an apple, a hunk of cheese, several strips of some sort of
jerky, a few pieces of bread, and, from a tin canister painted with
ducks, a handful of sunflower seeds. Still, he avoided my eyes.
"How did you sleep, Margie?" he asked.

"Oh, fine," I said. Cora darted a dark glance my way, having
caught me in an untruth. I realized she had been as sensitive as
I'd suspected to my every move on the bunk above her. She took
a peach from Granma's extended hand and pushed it into her
mouth, holding it there while she tied her shoes, careless of the
juice slipping down her chin. Granma worked the tangles out
of Cora's long locks with her fingers before weaving them into a

single braid that snaked like a stroke of paint down the girl's narrow back.

"Ow! *Basahkáalee!*"* Cora yelped.

"All done," Granma replied, soft and husky.

I stood near the table and sipped from the cup of coffee Granma handed me. I was uneasy in my robe and felt suspended somehow, as if I were waiting for instructions. What do I do here, I wondered, in my new but temporary life?

Jim donned shoes and kissed his mother on the head—"Love you, Mom"—and spoke to me—"Margie, I hope you have a good day and find everything you need"—while Cora stuffed her backpack with a sack lunch and zipped it closed, and soon they left the house together, the screen door squeaking shut behind them, a pair of dancers who had completed a well-rehearsed and prosaic morningtime routine à deux. I watched Jim's yellow truck disappear down the dirt road, like a sun that chased the horizon instead of rising above it. It was only seven—the earliest I'd risen in years.

"Jim takes Cora to school?"

"Yes, he drops her off on his way to the press," Granma said as she tinkered in the kitchen. "And Josie, Jim's sister, picks her up."

"Oh, Josie's the lady with the big brown truck? She's your daughter?"

"She's my own sister's daughter. The way we understand things, she is Jim's sister. We have no cousins here." Granma said that as a member of her clan, the Whistling Waters, Josie was considered her daughter, Jim's sister, and one of Cora's mothers. "Have you ever seen what happens to a single piece of driftwood in a river?" she asked me. Confused, I nodded yes, even though I had not seen many rivers up close. "It gets tossed around in those currents, pushed into rocks, beat up. Have you ever seen a big

---

*   Grandmother!

cluster of many driftwood pieces gathered together against a bank in a river?" I nodded again, sheepishly sipping from my mug. "It's a strong bunch. Those pieces don't move. They're all woven together like a nest, and nothing bad happens to them. That's why we say *ashammaleaxia* when we talk about Crow families. It means 'driftwood lodges.'" I thought of Bumble, Raven, Orca, Ptarmigan, and Bear. Without the Operation to bind them now, would they float apart from each other in different directions like stray pieces of driftwood? And Dad and I, what kind of a lodge had we ever made? I frowned. "Sit down," Granma said.

I sat, and she put a plate in front of me. It was heaped with fried eggs, scraps of the same jerky Jim had taken in his lunch pail, toast, and a puddle of deep garnet jam speckled with tiny berries. I looked at it all, marveling at how good it smelled while wondering how to explain again to Granma about being a vegan. "Oh. Thank you, I—"

"Just eat what you're comfortable with," she said. "You won't hurt my feelings. The eggs are from our own chickens—they live in our backyard. We treat them well. The jerky is called pemmican—that's meat from a buffalo we got at last year's hunt, mixed with dried chokecherries. And there's toast and choke-cherry jam. I picked the chokecherries myself last summer. We're going out to dig roots today."

"You and Cora?"

"No, honey, me and you." She smiled, and I noticed she had a few teeth missing. Their absence lent her an endearingly youthful look—as if she were a girl who had lost some baby teeth—rather than an aged one.

I spread the jam over my toast and ate it all in a few bites, thoroughly seduced. The chokecherries wavered flirtatiously from sour to sweet and back again. Gratified, Granma got up and sang to herself while she washed dishes. Still, I sensed her atten-tion. I scrutinized the eggs and, anxious about being a rude guest,

reasoned that since they had come from happy, home-raised
chickens rather than poor birds crammed into cages with no
access to sunlight or fresh air, they were acceptable fare, and ate
half of them. I relished the yielding yolks, which were a deep
golden hue. They reminded me of Saturday mornings at home
with Dad, when I used to cut heart shapes out of slices of bread
and fry our eggs inside. I left the pemmican untouched. "Good,"
Granma said, snatching it from my plate. "I'll snack on this when
we go digging."

"Can I help you clean up?"

"It's done," she said. "Take your time getting dressed. I like
to knit in the mornings."

Back in Cora's room, I rummaged through the Strawberry
Shortcake suitcase for a sundress. No, I had not seen many rivers
up close, only the sea. I had seen the sea and set lobsters free,
and let phosphorescent waves wash over my bare running feet.
Then I sat on the floor, bent so far forward as to bury my face in
the suitcase, and cried, silently, so Granma would not hear. After
mere minutes alone, my thoughts went immediately back to the
dreamlike incomprehensibility of my situation. Bumble, I knew,
had already left Billings to get an early start and was headed out
of Montana without me. Dad was preparing for another day at
Sunshine Realty, sleepily shuffling his way through a house
chaotic (or, as Rasha might have said, quixotic) with attic artifacts.
I put my hand on my chest and expected to feel nothing but air,
like the vacancy left after a cannonball blasts through a brick
wall, but there was skin, warm to the touch inside my robe, and
beneath it, bone, and under it all, a beat that still came at regular
intervals. Then I heard a rustle and sat up. The suitcase's contents
were damp from my tears. The rustle sounded once more, and it
came from Cora's dresser. Daphne had emerged from her cedar
chips to curl her minikin fingers around the wires of her cage and
study me twitchily. "Hello," I said in a clogged and quavering

voice. I gathered my things and found my way to the bathroom. It was still steamy and soap-scented from Jim's shower.

I HAD NEVER KNOWN SUCH QUIET. All I could hear was the movement of grass, the calls of birds, and the occasional creaks of the house, as if it were a living thing that had grown up out of the prairie. Still, despite her silence, I knew Granma was there. In the short bits of time I had spent with her, I had memorized the feeling of her presence. She had a soothing effect on my left ovary. I had grown so accustomed to the sensation of its excitement, its pangs and flares, its melting aches. But Granma, I had noticed, softened it, made it uncoil and breathe a sort of sigh of relief, because there was nothing in her that inspired pity, no strain of sad helplessness, no heart-crushing vulnerability. She had a quality that seemed like it might mend those aspects in others. I didn't exactly understand it, but already I knew how I felt when I was near her. Showered and with my hair still dripping, I wandered in my lucky red Chinese shoes, seeking her out. I worried for a moment that I had already become the cliché I so feared, the wayward white girl romanticizing a wise old Native American. But, apart from a few cantankerous schoolteachers, I had not been around many older women in my life, and I knew it was Granma's pronounced femininity, not her ethnicity, that attracted me.

She was not in her room, the entirety of which I could see from the hallway—a bed draped in a quilt featuring a giant star made of scraps from old blue jeans, a nightstand covered with framed photographs of faces I could not quite make out. She wasn't in Jim's room, which was opposite hers. Giving it the briefest of looks, I saw a brown woolen blanket, a basketball, and a buffalo skull propped against the wall. And she wasn't in the kitchen or the living room.

She was outside on a makeshift porch of sorts, a square of packed dirt under a place where the metal roof extended out a few extra feet to make an awning. She sat in a chair, knitting. The dog lounged at her feet in a posture of profound satisfaction, her chin resting on a ball of yarn. "Beautiful Belly," I said, stroking her enormous, triangular ears.

"The chickens are around back," Granma said after a long time. She had folded the subtlest of suggestions into her voice.

There were eight hens, round and pale in shades of white, cream, and fawn, with bright red combs, and when I stood among them they made worried, watery warbles. They scratched at the ground and examined it with their beaks. I looked into their coop, a structure evidently fashioned in a spirit of improvisation with assorted scraps of wood in varying sizes and shapes, and spotted one lone egg. When I picked it up, it was still warm. I had never seen or touched a freshly laid egg before. I held it out to Granma.

"Good!" she said. "That can go in the fridge."

When I returned from the kitchen, Granma glanced at my lucky red Chinese shoes. "Those are beautiful," she said.

"They're good luck. Or at least that's what I tell myself."

"I know what you mean. It's so interesting, the way certain things we wear seem to help us along. But they won't be good for digging. We're going to walk a lot. What else do you have?"

"Some sandals. Well, rubber flip-flops. I don't wear leather."

Granma was silent again. She studied her knitting with great concentration. Then she said, "That's okay. I have some sneakers that will fit you."

I PULLED THE VELCRO STRAPS of the nylon orthopedic shoes—identical to the ones Granma wore—tightly over my feet. "It's good to have a spare pair," she noted. "Sort of like Cora's top bunk." They were more cushiony and comfortable than any other shoes I had worn. And, dissonant though they were with my standard sundress, I did not want to take them off. Granma put some snacks (pemmican for her, apples for me) and water in a backpack, which I carried. She took up the antique flour sack I'd seen slung over her shoulder the day before. SNOW WHITE DELICIOUS CAKE AND PASTRY FLOUR the sack read, and I could barely make out an old-timey image of Snow White herself wielding a rolling pin. The Disney princess was an incongruous image on the prairie, an emblem of my own home turf. (I wondered if Rasha, who had watched the Disneyland fireworks through the kitchen window every night during her first months in Orange County, had known much about Snow White—the motherless girl who dodged an unpleasant fate by escaping to a cottage in a hidden place, the girl who was cared for by strangers, the girl who communed with birds.) Outside, Granma found a slender spade for me, retrieved her stick from its resting place beside the front door, and we left.

We walked past the chickens and went on for miles. I saw lots of slinky prairie dogs who poked their heads out of holes in the ground and sometimes darted through the pale grass with expressions of great alarm. Granma was not a fast walker, and it was noon before we arrived at what she called our digging place—a rocky slope at the base of some low rolling foothills. "Let's eat a little," she said. She chewed her pemmican slowly, sitting in a small square of shade thrown out like a blanket by a lone tree.

Soon she rose and pointed to a plant. "This is what we're looking for," she said. "*Ehe*. That's wild turnip. Prairie turnip." Then she crouched down and used her stick to dig all around the plant. "My digging stick is made of chokecherry wood," she told me. "It was my grandmother's. She was a root digger." She pushed the stick deep into the earth, taking care not to pierce the plant's root. "It's the root that we need," she said. She coaxed the plant and its root out of the soil and whispered a word—"*A-ho*"—and pushed the displaced dirt back into the hole. Then she pulled the leaves off the root and tossed them onto the ground. "The seeds from the foliage will fall and make more turnips," she explained. Finally, she put the root into her sack. "That's what we do."

"What are you going to do with them?" I asked.

"Same thing my grandmother and great-grandmother and great-great-grandmother did," Granma said. "Use them to feed my family. These wild turnips are kind of like bread to the Crows. They're so nutritious, and they have their own distinct flavor. We eat regular, store-bought bread, too. You saw. But these are a special food for us, one that we've been eating for a long time. *Káalixaalia** gives us so many good things to eat. It's all here for us." Granma watched me for a few moments while I stood with my short spade, staring at the ground. "Go ahead," she said. "Now you try."

"So . . . just . . . dig?"

"Just dig."

I pushed my spade around the circumference of another of the plants. Its leaves resembled small hands with five fingers, and they greeted me with lazy little waves in the breeze. I thought about Simon digging in his wife's garden on the morning I'd found him there, with a bucket of flowers beside him. I wondered what it was he'd been looking for, and I knew it hadn't been the flowers. Soon, the image of Simon faded as I focused more on the pleasurable sensation of pushing a spade into the ground. I heard Granma say that phrase again—*A-ho*—softly while she dug.

When I accidentally snapped off one of the root's slender arms with my spade, I forgot my fledgling pleasure and felt a fast flood of panic. I cried, "Oh!" and remembered Agents Fox and

---

* Mother Earth

Jones and my own uprootedness. I had left so many fragments of myself back home, where the ground had drowned in cement, the dolphins had chlorine rashes, the people had smoked swan for breakfast, and the men had broken hearts.

"It's okay," Granma said. "Just keep going." I managed to lift the root out of the ground and, turning it around in my hands, saw that it was mostly intact. "Perfect," she said. "Now the top." I tore the leaves and purple flowers from the root and watched them bounce along the ground as the breeze ushered them away.

"Am I supposed to say that word you are saying?" I asked.

"I'm saying thank you," Granma said. "*A-ho*. Yes, you can say thank you, too." She smiled.

I held the turnip in my hand and told it, "Thank you," before tucking it into the backpack. When I moved on to another, I recalled the shy, almost secretive beauty of the plants in the Middletown Community Garden, how they had thrived beneath the roaring of airplanes in that realm of chain-link fences and cracked sidewalks, how they had soothed and stilled my heart and mind on many a restless night, how it had never occurred to me to thank them. I wondered if they had sensed how I needed them, how glad I had been to be beside them. Then I stopped thinking about those plants, and of the Community Garden, and of San Diego altogether, of Agents Fox and Jones, of Dad, of the Tierra de Flores tract, of the Operation, of Bumble driving farther and farther away from me, of Ronald Clack and my legal woes left dangling, of darling Jack Dolce and his bicycle basket gifts, of Rasha's bathroom cabinet relics and of the blood-red poppies that had bloomed out of her. I stopped thinking completely. I just dug, and it seemed all I had ever known were wild turnips on the prairie.

With every push of my spade, I felt myself falling. And the roots, the fragrance of the earth, the salty beads of sweat on my

forehead, the *A-ho*'s and thank-you's, the cracked skin of Granma's hands, the inquisitive peeps of the plain brown birds who
lined up alongside each other on one tree branch as if posing for a
photograph—all blurred together so that each became indistinct
from the others, as if part of a tapestry into which they had been
deliberately woven.

We dug for hours, until Granma said it was time to head back
and meet Cora coming home from school.

"And catch your soap," I said.

"That too." Before we left, she walked behind the tree, lifted
up her voluminous skirt, and crouched. "Don't look," she said,
giggling. I heard a stream of liquid hit the dirt. I followed her
example a moment later and thought I heard the birds above
titter.

When we were halfway home, we stopped to drink. "Do you
usually do this alone?" I asked Granma. "I saw you yesterday
when we drove past."

"Most of the time," she said, "unless I go with Cora when
she's not in school. She'll come with me a lot this summer. She
just turned eleven and she has to learn this. All of it." I wondered
what "all of it" was. "And I hope you'll come along, too," she
added.

"O-oh," I stuttered, "y-yes." I wanted to come along. I wanted
to feel that sense of forgetting and falling again, that delicious dissolving. "If I'm still here."

"Of course." Granma's face was flushed and slick, and I
thought I saw her hand shake when she screwed the lid back onto
her water jug.

"Do you want to sit for a while before we start again?" I asked.

"No no," she said. "We'll go," and the certainty with which
she set off made me feel foolish for thinking her fragile.

. . .

BACK AT THE HOUSE WE WERE GREETED first by the chickens, who encircled Granma with urgent clucks, then by Belly, who praised her with yips. I washed my hands in the bathroom sink and watched brown rivulets of dirt spiral down the drain. In the mirror, I noted without surprise that a day of sun had awakened all kinds of freckles on the tops of my cheeks and nose, but I was startled by my eyes. I didn't recognize them at first as my own. They had none of Dad's swoopy sadness, but were shining and appeared infused with something new, brimming with a substance other than tears. I stared at them and wondered what I had done that was so remarkable besides walk for a long time over the prairie with Granma and lose myself in digging.

We unpacked the roots and found we had dug dozens of them. Against the dramatic dialogue of her soap, Granma showed me how to peel away their rough outer skins. Soon, Josie's truck pulled up outside, and the roots shivered on the table. Cora stepped through the screen door. She made me nervous. I was sure she didn't like me, and I could feel the fragile joy of the afternoon stealing out of my eyes, retreating to the mysterious prairie that had bestowed it.

"Why doesn't Josie come in?" Granma asked.

Cora pulled a stone from her mouth. "She says she will tomorrow." The stone was rough but glistening with saliva. "She has to go home and get ready," Cora continued. She let her backpack fall to the floor, sucked in a big gulp of breath, and fluttered both of her hands with excitement, twin birds flapping at her sides. "She says she has a date with Pete Sings Plenty!" An explosive laugh escaped from Cora and she pushed the stone back into her mouth. Granma, too, stifled a snicker.

"Who's Pete Sings Plenty?" I asked.

Cora actually answered me, though only because the subject was irresistibly amusing to her. "A really skinny guy who works at the rez casino and spends all of his paycheck there, too!"

"Shh, shh, Grandchild. He has a good heart," Granma said. "What's that rock?" She cupped her hand beneath Cora's pointy chin.

"It's not a rock. It's the peach pit."

"Give."

"No, I want to keep it."

"Say hello to Margie."

"Hi," she piped. Her manner was different from the night before, more confident and careless. She looked at my hands, squinting through her glasses at the brown crescent moons under each of my fingernails.

"Margie went root digging with me today," Granma said. Cora was silent.

"It was so nice," I said.

Cora blinked, and her warm amber eyes went frosty. Slipping one hand into the other, she turned away from me. "Granma," she asked, "what's for dinner?"

A WEEK AFTER GRANMA TOOK ME ROOT DIGGING, Cora returned home from her last day of school and asked me a question. Apart from telling me about Pete Sings Plenty, it was the first time she had spoken to me directly without being prompted by a reassuring squeeze from her dad or a whispered Crow word from her grandmother.

"Why are you here?" she said. Granma was outside feeding the chickens.

I noticed, when she asked me, that her tongue was blue. I supposed this was due to a lollipop that a teacher—or (I imagined with a sudden shudder) a pedophiliac school janitor, lurking near the drinking fountain, dreaming of brown-skinned Lolitas— must have handed her as a parting gift. Her backpack, I could see, was much lighter because she had returned all of her textbooks but one—*The World of Math*. She unpacked that tome while awaiting my answer and slid it onto a splintery shelf alongside several framed photographs of her many relatives.

"Why do you still have that book?" I asked. My voice shook with uncertainty. I badly wanted to be accepted by the sharp-elbowed sprite, the long-tressed light sleeper, Cora of the bottom

bunk. Her bold question left me feeling as crushed as I had
been when Violet Holmquist and the other junior high girls had
deemed me unworthy of acknowledgment, much less friendship, after Dad's conspicuous crying jag at the "Yes Sir, That's
My Baby" Father-Daughter Dance. I swallowed. "I thought
students were supposed to hand in all their books on the last day
of school."

"I asked you something first," she retorted. She pulled her
peach pit out of the tiny side pocket of her backpack and squinted
with great consideration at its intricately grooved surface. Then
she proceeded to roll it back and forth on the tabletop with the
air of one who could wait all day to find out what she desired to
know. And I had thought the purpose of my fleeing to that lonely
landscape was to leave all threat of interrogation behind.

"Your tongue is so blue. Did you know Chow dogs have dark
tongues?" I asked.

"That's what I mean," she replied. Her eyes burned with
intimidating intelligence. "That's why you're here, isn't it?"

"What?"

"People say you're here because you like animals. Like, way
too much." One of Cora's eyebrows rose above the upper rim of
her sparkly frames.

"People who? What people? No one is really supposed to
know why I'm here."

"Well, just Josie, really. Only she knows. And us. Granma says
it's a secret. And Dad says if I tell anyone about why you're here,
I can't dance at Crow Fair this year. Josie says you are an animal
rights kook. She also says you are a hippo. And that all hippos try
to act like Indians." Cora paused and took in a big breath—her
habit, I noticed, when speaking of matters of importance to
her (the sum of a square, neatly braided hair, Crow Fair)—before
asking me questions two, three, and four: "Why are you so
skinny? Why are your cheeks so pink? Is that makeup?"

"I'm not a hippie," I replied, "assuming that's what Josie actually said. It's not makeup. I was just born this way. And I'm skinny because it's my body type, I guess, and because I haven't eaten any animal products—except for the last week I've spent here—for over a year."

"Why the heck would anyone do that?" Cora asked, mouth agape.

"As for being an animal rights kook, I'm not a kook, I don't think. I just did a lot of things to try to help animals. Some people decided some of the things I did were wrong. Against the law. They, federal agents, wanted—*want*—me to go to jail." Hearing this, Cora stilled the peach pit on the table and held it beneath her pinky finger. Her tiny fingernail was like the smallest of seashells. "So I have to hide," I said. "That's why I'm here."

"But why did you want to help animals? Animals can help themselves."

"In the place where I come from, a lot of the animals need help. It's not like here on the reservation. People breed them, and eat them, and use them—"

"People breed animals here, too. And eat them and use them."

"It's different . . ." I felt myself fumbling for all the reasons why, and wondered what Simon, articulate and erudite Simon, might say.

"You mean like the worms we dissected in biology?"

"What about the math book?"

"I just like it."

"Who gave you the lollipop?"

She scooped up the peach pit and cupped it protectively in her palm.

"How did you know about the lollipop?" she asked with a glower. "Are you some kind of spy?"

"Your blue tongue."

"Oh." Cora seemed relieved. "Just my teacher, Mrs. Pennyray. She gave them to us for the last day of school."

Then I was relieved. I couldn't bear the thought of anyone predatory, cruel, creepy, or otherwise unworthy of cat-eyed Cora, a mathematician in the making, hovering over her, handing her a lollipop, or so much as looking her way. I felt protective. Something about Cora had coerced a sleeping lioness out from under the prairie hills and placed it in my heart, where it paced watchfully in front of her. Maybe it was the vulnerability inherent in her knobby knees, or in the sweet sag of her nightgown when she stood, barefoot, freshly showered and soggy-haired, to kiss Granma goodnight before slipping into her bed where, I knew, she snuggled with a stuffed fawn.

Still, as her pointedly impolite question had made clear, Cora most definitely did not reciprocate my regard, not like the other girl I had known, Annette Mellinkoff. But then Annette had never inspired such a protective impulse in me, though I knew that with her flaxen hair and her father's mysterious, gemlike eyes she would someday suffocate under an avalanche of advances from leagues of libidinous boys whom Simon, I suspected, would be far too weary to repel. Little Annette used to climb (plaintively mewing) onto my lap while Simon and I discussed the different ways we might rescue cats from the research labs at the university.

Yes, in her sisterly sweetness Annette had loved to have me comb her fine, fair hair and to help me set the table each night for the weedy dinners I prepared. I didn't think Cora would ever deign to do such things with me. Though a petite, elfin eleven, she wouldn't fit quite so easily on my lap. But even if she could, her apparent distaste for me—and my accoutrements—would likely prevent her. Just a few days earlier, I'd seen her lift a discarded dress of mine from her bedroom floor with the absolute tips of her forefinger and thumb (lips pursed, eyes rolled heavenward) and hang it gingerly over one rung of the ladder leading up to my bunk. Since then, I'd been careful to keep all of my belongings tucked into the Strawberry Shortcake suitcase, out of her spiteful sight.

But why, I conceded, should Cora like me? Unlike Annette Mellinkoff's mother, Cora's mom had not died or disappeared. Her place in the world was known and, evidently, fixed. She was in prison. And that, I suspected, was why when I explained to Cora that I was hiding in her house to avoid landing in jail, her eyes suddenly outsparkled the rhinestones on her glasses. She appeared to ponder, with mathematical logic, how she might trade me in for her mother, how she could subtract her mom from the prison population and add me to it, in the same way Granma had paid money in exchange for her best beaded belt, which a sticky-fingered relative had sold to a Billings pawnshop.

I didn't know what Cora's mother was serving time for, but I did know she had been locked up for eight years, and no one spoke about her as if she would be coming home anytime soon. And when I had asked Granma, a few days after my arrival, why she had refused to let me bring in my case of red wine, she pointed without comment to a photograph of a woman with a face like Cora's, except the delicate pointed features had been hardened by misfortune. Granma had meant, I assumed, to warn me of the harm wrought by certain substances.

"Oh yeah," Cora murmured, more to herself than to me, reaching once again into her backpack. "I almost forgot. Josie went by the post office on our way back from school, and I got the mail. Granma!"

"I'm right here, Grandchild," Granma said. She stood just inside the screen door, rubbing the dust from chicken feed off her hands. I wondered how long she had been there.

"What's this?" Granma outstretched her arm in the direction of Cora's peach pit.

"The pit from the peach."

"Give it to me. The peach is done."

"No, I want to keep it." Cora dropped the pit into the pocket of her shorts while Granma shook her head. "Granma, me and Josie got the mail."

"Goody," Granma said with a gappy grin. "Cora, turn on the TV, will you?" Charmaigne, the true love of Slade, threw a crystal vase at Victoria. "Oh, my," Granma said. She sat down at the table and sorted through the stack of envelopes. She pushed some toward one end of the table, some toward the other. "These are Dad's," she told Cora, "and these are mine—"

"And I already know," Cora said, "that there's nothing for me. In a matter-of-fact voice with which no words could possibly be minced she added, "I checked. She didn't write."

Granma looked at Cora sideways, studied her slyly, and, satisfied by the child's sturdiness of manner, went on sorting the letters. "It's okay," she said in her purring way. Her hands floated with uncharacteristic indecision over an elaborately illustrated envelope. It featured a killer whale leaping triumphantly over a surfacing submarine—a symbolic and hopeful image of sea life somehow surviving the devastating effects of navy sonar. I knew immediately that Bumble was the artist, but I was too shy, too desirous, to say anything. My throat went dry, and my palms grew hot with yearning for the note, something from the world I had left behind.

"This isn't ours . . ." Granma examined the whale in fascination. "Wonderful!" she said. Then she flipped the envelope over.

"That one's for Margie," Cora told her. "No return address."

"It is," Granma said, smiling and sliding it across the table to me, "for Margie."

"Is that from your boyfriend?" Cora asked me.

"Shh, shh, Grandchild," Granma admonished Cora. Then she turned her own twinkling, curious eyes my way, awaiting my reply.

"N-no," I said. "I think this is from the friend who drove me here. Bumble."

"Do you have a boyfriend?" Cora asked.

"Bad girl!" Granma chided Cora before fixing me once more with an anticipatory look.

"No. No, I don't." Both girls (for Granma seemed to have straightened up out of her slight senior-citizen slouch and matched Cora's natural air of perky prepubescence) bowed their heads as if my answer to the question was of no consequence whatsoever, as if the question had not even been asked, while I was momentarily lost in a montage of memories of my first and only boyfriend, my miller, my Melnikov.

UP ON MY BUNK, I OPENED THE ENVELOPE, careful not to tear the whale.

> *She-Bird of the Crows,*
>
> *Hope this finds you happy, healthy, and not too homesick. It is I, your loyal servant, Bumble B., with information for your entertainment and elucidation. (I think it's safer to write than to call.)*
>
> *Agent Fox is still hanging around upstairs at Gelato Amore. Can you believe it? Always in that repulsive little hat of his. I think he suspects you split, Margie. He actually talked to me and Raven the other day. He said he "hadn't seen you around" for a while and that if "for some reason" you weren't able to "show up for your trial in September" they could always "make other arrangements." And he smiled. He is so pleased with himself. He asked us, "And how are the animals of San Diego County surviving without your friend's assistance?" Raven looked so mad I thought smoke might come out of her ears. She started playing a scary song on her guitar.*
>
> *I don't believe he knows your whereabouts. I am completely confident we weren't followed on our drive.*

Ptarmigan asks me to tell you that Charlotte is thriving, loves cantaloupe, and cannot possibly miss you as much as he does.

Bear says she is sending you rays of pink and gold light to keep your heart chakra open, and that there is much wisdom to be gained when dwelling among the Native Americans.

And Orca kissed this paper HERE [examining the spot, I could see a faint black smear left by Orca's markered mustache].

I suppose you should know Agent Fox isn't the only one who seems to have noticed your absence. Of course that deadbeat Dolce asks about you constantly and we tell him, naturally, nothing. But Simon saw me on campus just yesterday and asked where you've been. (I thought you left his Latin class a long time ago, but he must have been keeping an eye out for you anyway.) I said you were just home with a nasty flu. He didn't seem to believe me, and I couldn't tell if he had or hadn't seen the latest article in the Sun, *which I have enclosed.*

Much love and support from all of us,
Bumble B.

I found the newspaper clipping to which Bumble had referred. LOCAL ANIMAL RIGHTS ACTIVIST ARRESTED, the headline read, above the photograph of disheveled me taken on the morning I was booked.

Maggie Fitzgerald, a member of the San Diego–based animal rights activist group known as Operation H.E.A.R.T., was arrested by federal agents less than 24 hours after giving a speech about incendiary devices at Gelato Amore Café in Little Italy. Fitzgerald posted bail shortly after her arrest. Her trial is set for September.

Fitzgerald is accused of violating United States Code 18,842 (p)(2)(A), which specifies that it is unlawful for any person to teach the making or use of an explosive with the intent that the teaching or demonstration be used for, or in furtherance of, an activity that constitutes a federal crime of violence.

Local law enforcement has reason to believe Fitzgerald played a role in a series of acts of theft, vandalism, and harassment over the last several months. "She may end up facing additional charges," said Detective Adam Wood of the San Diego Police Department, "and other members of Operation H.E.A.R.T. may be charged as well. This is all pending investigation, of course, and that's no longer in our hands since the FBI has stepped in."

I wondered how the *Sun* could have possibly obtained the scoop on my arrest, considering that it had been made in the privacy of my own slovenly studio. But when I read the next paragraph, I realized who had told them my story.

Ronald Clack, a local attorney and self-described acquaintance of Fitzgerald, spoke to the *Sun* about the activist's arrest. "She's been dubbed a domestic terrorist by the feds," Clack said. "Her case is not as atypical as it may seem. In the last couple of years, I've seen more and more evidence of what I like to refer to as the 'Green Scare.' Contemporaneous with the trend toward greener, more holistic ways of living and more humane treatment of animals, there has been a kind of backlash, a real crackdown, if you will, by law enforcement on those like Ms. Fitzgerald who are perceived as taking their admirable commitment to a more earth- or animal-friendly lifestyle too far."

I was impressed with Ronald's rhetoric in spite of the fact that he had, I was sure, called the paper and told them about me just so he could secure a bit of free publicity for himself.

According to Clack, if Fitzgerald is found guilty, she could serve several years in a federal penitentiary. "It has happened to activists who were far less bold than she—allegedly—was," Clack said. Neither Fitzgerald nor any of her fellow Operation H.E.A.R.T. members could be reached for comment.

I crumpled the article into a tiny ball and crammed it under my pillow. I was confounded by my legal fix and terrified of being discovered in my hideout, full of affection for Jack Dolce, as well as for Bumble and the rest of the crew, hopelessly homesick, craving an interminable cuddle with Charlotte, embarrassed that I, my exploits, and my arrest had been the subject of a newspaper article, glad my first name had been misspelled, and, most of all, sentimental about Simon, who had asked about me.

He had not said so much as one word to me since he'd handed me the Operation, but he had thought of me and, I now knew, watched for me. He had watched for me, just as he had once watched from his bench on the busy campus quad before class, while I passed before him with my yellow bicycle and a litany of Latin vocab words running through my brain. I wanted to write to him, even if I wrote a letter that I would never mail. I wanted to tell him everything, how I was living with a family that was not my own on an Indian reservation in the middle of nowhere, could summarize the latest happenings on TV's most popular daytime soap, was digging roots out of the ground, had prairie earth tucked under each of my fingernails, and wore a pair of old-lady sneakers, all because I had once been his armful of warm girl.

I pulled a pencil and notepad from his other girl's suitcase, lay belly down on my bed, and wrote, with the soft tones of Cora and Granma's conversation humming in the background. "Don't bother her," I heard Granma say, "she needs time to herself." I wrote while the light turned dusky and dim, and I wrote through the grumblings in my stomach when I heard dishes clanging in the kitchen. *I am lonely,* I wrote. *I am living with the Crows. I am hiding. I will never understand you or what happened.* I wrote and wrote, and I only stopped for a few moments when I heard Jim come home.

I paused to consider how after just one week I had unwittingly memorized the hallmarks of Jim's presence. I recognized the sounds of his homecoming like a dog does those of his two-legged companion—the rhythm of his footfalls on the grass outside, the gentleness with which he opened and closed the screen door, the metallic scrape of his lunch pail when it met the tabletop. I heard him say my name with a question mark at the end. "She's resting," Granma answered. Even hidden away as I was in a distant room, I detected his rich dark odor of blue and black and purple inks, and the odor of his body's efforts at work. And I thought of all my yearning to be among the animals and a part of their world. Maybe, when we shared one shelter and grew familiar enough with each other, like the imagined families in the hill houses whose closeness I coveted, we were already much more like the animals than most of us ever realized.

But why had that animal familiarity never suffused my time in Simon's shadowy home? What had been missing from that place and from us, the people who had shared it? I wrote more, to try and find out. I wrote until long after dinner was done and Cora went to sleep below me and the house was silent, the prairie black. And there was something, I realized, about writing in the dark that mirrored my life as it felt to me then: I couldn't see the letters I was shaping, but I wanted to go on writing anyway.

THE NEXT MORNING, A SATURDAY, I woke to the sounds of Jim working on the old Cutlass, just as I had on the Saturday before. I heard him humming through the window beside my bunk.

I burrowed down into the bed and slid my hands under my pillow, where they found the crumpled-up newspaper article from Bumble, and the folded pages of my long letter to Simon. I struggled to reconcile them with the sound of Jim's wordless melody. I felt in between places and in between lives, the way sometimes it is possible to feel in between sleeping and waking, poised on a threshold. After a few minutes of lying with my eyes closed tight against the strong prairie light, listening to Jim's air (a mournful tune I remembered, though I didn't know from where), I climbed down the ladder.

From her bunk Cora regarded me with the blank, inscrutable gaze of a still-sleepy child. Daphne watched from behind the woven wires of her cage and I thought about feeding her but decided not to risk arousing Cora's annoyance. When I reached the bottom rung, Cora let her stuffed fawn roll away and sat up. She yawned hugely, and her bangs poked up at crazy angles.

"How was your sleep?" I asked.

"Mmmumph," she replied, reaching her arms toward the ceiling and shaking rather violently with the stretch.

Outside, I found Granma on the porch with her knitting. "Good morning, honey," she said.

"Good morning, Granma." I peered at the mass of yarn in her lap. "What are you working on today?"

"Oh, it's a little cap. For one of my young relatives over in Lodge Grass. He's not born yet, but he'll be here any day now." She held it up, and it resembled a fuzzy blue bell without a clapper.

"Have you always been a knitter?"

"Oh, not always. They made us learn knitting at the boarding school I was sent to as a girl." Her face darkened for a moment in a way I'd never seen, but she was quick to offer me a grin and add, "I made dozens of caps like these for Jim before *and* after he was born, more than he could ever wear. Can you believe his head was once this tiny?" She giggled.

I looked at Jim as he bent over the Cutlass. It was true that his head wasn't small, but then no part of him seemed to be. His face was broad and benevolent. His plum-colored lips were full. His smile was wide and generous when he bestowed it in his vague way. And I almost could not look at his hands. I had been studying them surreptitiously for days as they accomplished the most ordinary of acts—wrapping around a doorknob, pulling out a chair, turning on the faucet in the kitchen sink. They, too, were big, and beautifully formed, with expansive palms and long fingers. And they seemed even more attractive because they were always stained with ink, the same ink that, on paper, told thousands of true stories to readers of the newspapers and magazines that wound their way through the press every day. I thought it fitting that his job ensured his hands would be marked, always marked, and, that way, always set apart. Even while he tinkered with inanimate engine parts, they looked like such caring hands, as if they might make right whatever—or whomever—they touched.

Cora, I noticed, always had the pleased, eyes-at-half-mast look of a drowsy cat after he rumpled her hair. And Granma always fell asleep as soon as he began to rub the joints of her fingers after she'd spent a long time at her knitting. The chickens always went silent out of sheer contentment when he held them, which he did on occasion, and for no reason other than it seemed to give him satisfaction. And Belly, fittingly, always flopped down to display her stomach in absolute deference and delight when he scratched her ears. I could see Jim's heart in his hands, and, just once, I had caught myself wondering what it would be like if he ever put them on me.

That had been a daydream, I told myself, born of my abject homesickness and basic yearning for comfort. I was certain Jim did not have even the most fleeting thoughts of touching me. He didn't even look at me. He was the opposite of Simon, who had watched me so intently. When Jim spoke to me, his eyes were always drawn to the side, as if he were addressing some ethereal companion hovering a few feet in front of his left or right shoulder, an invisible angel.

Then, possibly because he felt me studying him, Jim looked up from the Cutlass and waved. "Morning, Margie," he called. "How's everything?" He frowned in the glare of the morning sun, and the line between his eyes was perfectly perpendicular to the horizontal line of his smile. I thought of Cora's *World of Math* and what little I recalled of geometry, and wondered about the intersection of those two lines—what was buried beneath the point where they met?

"Everything is great!" I replied, with far too much eager-to-please enthusiasm straining my voice. Why, I wondered, couldn't I sound soft and breathy like Marilyn, or sweet and vaguely continental like Audrey, or deep and thrilling like Granma? Why must I be so wispy, so nervous, so girlish? I remembered the night of the Little Italy party when I had sprawled, sans clothes, on Jack Dolce's couch to pose for his camera, my throat husky from shouting over the music, my eyes snoozy from wine, my neck adorned with the green snake, how relaxed I'd felt at that moment (the rosemary moment I swore I would never forget), like something juicy, something ripe for the picking. Jack Dolce had given me a green-snake glimpse of the red thread of joy that wove through me and all of life, that had even stitched us together as siblings for a spell. And just how right about everything had he been? I supposed he had been right about the foolhardiness of my fire fixation. All I knew for sure was that, looking at Jim, standing on a porch of packed dirt in my bathrobe, I felt about as far from that night as I ever could, too tightly wound with my tentative smile.

"Ready for another day of root digging?" Granma asked. We had gone twice more since the first time. "I want to make sure Cora joins me at least once this year before the wild turnips are out of season, so she is definitely going to come. But if you'd rather stay home today, I understand. Jim will be here, working on the Pronghorn. That's what he calls this car—after those antelope who can run so fast across the prairie."

I looked at him ministering to the Cutlass. His hands had disappeared into her hood, and his shirt was sticky from sweat. I had not yet been alone with Jim. Jim and his invisible angel.

"No," I said, "I'd like to come with you."

"Good girl." Granma reached out and squeezed my hand. "There's lots to learn if you stick with me. Though Jim could tell you plenty, too."

Cora pushed through the screen door and stood barefoot and bleary-eyed on the other side of Granma. She munched on an apple. "How were your dreams, Grandchild?" Granma asked.

"Good." Always verbose with her grandmother, Cora continued, "I had a lot of dreams about seahorses. Did you know seahorses are raised by their fathers?"

"I did know that," I said.

"It's true." Cora squinted straight ahead at her dad. She was not wearing her glasses, and she looked touchingly tiny and fragile without them, as if they served as some sort of sixties-style armor. "Seahorses. I had a lot of dreams about those. One of them was a baby. She flew out of the water. She had the sweetest breath." She paused to crunch into her apple and went on. "I finally found that shoe of mine that Belly ran away with last week"—Belly, hearing her name, cocked her head—"in Dad's room, under his bed. It is *utterly* destroyed. I've been thinking a lot about how I want my leggins to look at Crow Fair this year . . ."

Jim approached, wiping his hands. He ruffled Cora's bed-head. I watched his face while he listened to his girl describe her dream "leggins," and looked for a sign of distraction in his eyes, and listened for a false note to slip into one of his encouraging "mmm-hmms," and waited for a bit of boredom to sneak into the shape of his smile when he bobbed his head up and down, but all I sensed was interest—a degree of interest that would have made me suspicious, so strange would it have seemed had I ever perceived it in my own sad dad. Dad, as the green photo album had shown, could sometimes summon the strength to grasp at fragments of life as they passed and tuck them away for preservation, for resurrection in some distant future, but it wasn't as easy for him to engage with such moments as they were happening.

At the end of Cora's monologue, Jim asked her a couple of follow-up questions: "Did you give Belly your other shoe?" ("Not yet, but I may as well.") "How much will the supplies for your new leggins cost, about?" ("I don't know . . . not too much?") Then he turned to Granma, who answered his query about her plans for the day half in English, half in Crow, so the only parts I understood were my own name and Cora's, along with "walk" and "turnip." She also said "stars," and I wondered if she was telling him about some predawn celestial happening she had observed when she ventured outside before sunup, as was—I had come to understand—her habit.

Then it was my turn. Jim tilted his face toward me. "Do you like going out and digging roots, Margie?" His eyes fell somewhere to the right of my body, and I wondered why he had even asked me the question if he was already so disinterested in the prospect of an answer.

"Oh, yes, very much," I said. I absently drew an X in the dirt between us with my toe. "I feel like I can forget myself and my troubles when I'm doing it." He just nodded and was silent, and soon I went back inside.

WE WALKED TOWARD A NEW ROOT-DIGGING PLACE that Granma had in mind. "The world is greening up," she said. She was right. The prairie was no longer a bland expanse of beige. It was alive with emerald grasses and all kinds of plants I had never seen.

She pointed to the soft, rounded mountains I had first noticed when Bumble and I drove across the reservation. They had an unostentatious beauty, as if they knew they were pretty enough without having to show off a lot of sharp crags or cloud-piercing peaks. There was something comforting in their easy slopes. "Those," Granma said, "are our Bighorns. We Crows are so lucky to have those mountains here with us. Cora, why don't you tell Margie about the Bighorns?"

"Mrrrr." Cora gave a resistant little groan.

"Go on," Granma persisted. "I want to hear you tell about them." Granma seemed to be giving Cora a kind of test.

"*Basawaxaawúua*—" Cora began to speak in a ringing, authoritative voice that vibrated with her bouncy steps.

"In English, Grandchild," Granma said. "So Margie can understand."

Cora started again. "The Bighorn Mountains"—she paused to

suck in a great gulp of air—"are sacred to the Crows, who
are more accurately known as the *Apsáalooke*—that means
'children of the large-beaked bird.' Belly, c'mon!" Belly was
interested in gobbling one of the prairie dogs who periscoped
their heads out of innumerable holes in the ground, but she obedi-
ently trotted up behind Cora. "No Intestines," Cora continued,
"was the first leader of the Crows after we broke apart from our
old friends, the Hidatsa. That was a long time ago." Granma,
closing her eyes, smiled to herself. "No Intestines was just a teen-
ager then, but he knew we needed to find a new place to
live, and he led us on a long journey in search of it. He knew
when he saw tobacco seeds, that would be the sign that we had
come to the right place. Good girl, Belly." She reached down
to stroke the top of Belly's freckled head. "No Intestines was
117 years old by the time he found these Bighorn Mountains.
He climbed the highest one, Extended Peak. When he was up
there, he had a vision. He saw that the tobacco seeds he had been
searching for were lying right at the base of that peak. He saw
them shining like stars. He knew then that he had brought his
people to the place where they belonged. That's why the Crows
are here today, and that's why the Bighorn Mountains are the
heart of our world."

Granma looked as though she might explode with happiness.
Cora, too, was deeply pleased. "That's a fantastic story," I said.

"But it really happened," Cora said. She turned toward me
and her eyes had a dreamy look behind her spectacles. "The
tobacco seeds were shining like stars." I could tell that was her
favorite part. It reminded me of my orange blossoms, which had
also always shone like stars for me—white scented stars at the
heart of what had once been my world.

"And that's why," Granma said, "if you really want your
prayer to be heard, it helps to burn some tobacco and let the
smoke rise up to the stars. Tobacco and stars are very connected."

"I don't have any tobacco!" Cora said.

We came to a rocky spot similar to the one where Granma and I had dug. Cora had her own root-digging stick, which was much like Granma's. She set about digging straight away, and we followed her lead.

I thought about the man named No Intestines. I imagined him on the mountaintop when he had his vision. His expression must have been one of absolute enchantment, and of relief, because the long journey was finally over. Maybe he had even wept and smiled at the same time. I could see his face. He had a vertical line between his ecstatic eyes—the mark of all the hardships he and his people had endured before finding the Bighorns. Yes, he had a vertical line between his eyes, just like Jim. And I realized I was imagining him *as* Jim, with Jim's hands and Jim's sideways gaze. Then I accidentally snapped off the entire bottom half of a root with my spade. "Ohhh," I moaned.

"What is it, honey?" Granma plopped down on the dirt and rested with a freshly dug root in her lap. She stretched her legs out in front of her and winced. I heard her knees pop. Cora was digging in a distant patch, and I could barely hear her flutey voice trilling "*A-ho, a-ho.*" I sat close to Granma with the broken root in my hand.

"Granma."

"Yes, Margie, what's the matter? Getting tuckered out?"

"No, I'm fine. It's just, something's on my mind."

"Yes, I can see that, honey. Do you want to tell me about it?"

"I—it's hard for me to say—I don't know what to say, really. It's just—" Granma laid her digging stick on the dirt. She looked as if she had all day and night to listen to me ramble, and that made me feel guilty for being so hesitant. "It's just Jim," I blurted. "I worry. I worry that I'm an intruder here in your home and that—that he doesn't like me." I glanced at

Cora, who was, thankfully, immersed in her work. I would
have been embarrassed had she seen my tears.

Granma shook her head. "Margie! Honey, how could you say
that now? We are all enjoying you so much here. Of course Jim
likes you. It's possible that, at first, he may have thought having
you come here was another one of my funny ideas—it *was* my
idea, did you know? I'm the matriarch after all, and what I say
goes." She winked. "So, Jim was probably surprised—why would
we hide somebody in trouble with the law? But when I learned.
just *why* you were in trouble, I was intrigued. I wanted to meet
the person who had those kinds of feelings about animals, even if
her actions were a bit . . . unusual. It was the feelings behind the
actions that captured my interest. But," she patted my leg, "that's
all beside the point. I know Jim likes you. What's not to like?"

"But," I brushed my cheek with the back of my hand and
caught a salty drop, "he never looks at me."

"What do you mean, he never looks at you?" Granma's eyebrows raised.

"I mean, never, ever. When we talk, he always looks a little
away. Like he can't *stand* me, or—"

Granma's eyebrows returned to normal. She nodded and said,
very slowly, "Ahhhh," as if she comprehended everything already.
I felt slightly relieved. So she had noticed it, too, I thought.

"Honey," she said, "have you never been around any Indians
before?"

"Well, no. I mean, Bumble is, I guess, a quarter Crow, because
of his mother, but . . ." Again I thought of Jack Dolce, how the
long arms of his lush houseplants climbed and stretched all over
his sunlit flat, because if he had to bide in a wood and stucco
dwelling he would at least bring the feeling of the outdoors
inside, how little he cared for the things of the world, like clothes
and cars and computers, and cherished the simplicity of his
existence, how he adorned his wall with an image of Sitting Bull,

and how much he talked about the earth, sun, moon, and stars. Admittedly, I knew nothing at all about Indians apart from what I had seen in a few Hollywood movies that portrayed them as either feather-bedecked fiends or, conversely, mystical and gentle magicians who could turn the wind. But Jack Dolce seemed like the most Indian person I had ever known—before I'd come to Montana. I told Granma about him, leaving out the depressing detail of our friendship's demise. "He is an endangered species of a man," I said.

"Well, that guy sounds interesting, honey, but *we're* not an endangered species. We're now one of the fastest-growing minorities in the United States. And most Indians only live 'simply,' as you put it, because they're too poor to do otherwise. Now," she said, "here's what you need to understand." Granma took my hand. "Even though we live in the same country, there are lots of differences, cultural differences, between Indians and"—she paused again, as if hunting for the right word—"non-Indians. There are even lots of cultural differences from one tribe to another, but it's like this: generally speaking, white people are big on eye contact. Indian people aren't. You never heard that, did you, dear heart?" I shook my head. "Our grandparents felt it was rude, or invasive, or in some cases even aggressive, to look someone in the eye. So that's why it seems we aren't looking at you. And when I say *we,* I mean *we*—I'm sure Cora and I are no different from Jim. After all, I raised him, and he and I are raising her." Granma was thoughtful. She stroked one five-fingered leaf of the prairie turnip in her lap as if it were an infant's hand. "Why does it only bother you," she said, "that Jim looks away when he speaks to you, but not that she and I do?" Her eyes twinkled with some subterraneous mischief, as if just beneath their glossy surfaces there grew sly little roots that grasped absolutely everything.

"I—don't—didn't—"

"You didn't notice it in us? Only in him?" She looked as if she was trying hard not to smile. And then I had the urge to smile, too.

Cora approached with a fistful of the most slender, sleek young roots—the kind that Granma said tasted best. "What's so funny?" she asked.

"Good job, Grandchild. These are my favorites. And now I see a patch over there," she pointed to some faraway purple flowers, "waiting for you."

"Oh, I get it. I'm not wanted. Humph." Cora only pretended to be offended. She was playful, bright with the pleasure of root digging, and she sang to herself as she departed.

"Now," Granma said, laying a hand on my shoulder, "I'm not going to claim to know why this habit of ours bothered you so much in my son and not in Cora or me. But you shouldn't take it personally."

"But Granma, Cora doesn't like me either. I notice it differently with her. She—"

"Shh. Nonsense. Cora just has trouble trusting. Her mother let her down early on. Don't worry. Just be yourself. Cora will be your friend soon enough. And I think it's good for her to have you here, to have a young woman around. She'll always be a *káalisbaapite*, a grandmother's grandchild, but it's good for her to know a younger woman's ways."

"It's strange to hear you say that," I said.

"Why?"

"I don't think of myself as a woman."

"What do you think of yourself as? A She-Bird, like your friend Bumble called you?" Granma's smile was full now.

"I think of myself," I answered, "as a girl."

"You're a girl as long as you allow life to happen to you. You become a woman when you start living according to your own instincts, your own intelligence, and your own desires. You're a woman when you take hold of yourself." Granma scratched the dirt with her stick. "It won't be much longer."

THAT NIGHT BEFORE BED, Cora was especially spirited. Her eyes still had the glint of a day spent digging on the prairie—the same glow I had been so surprised to see in my own. And maybe it was because we had gathered roots together, or because she had told me the story of No Intestines and the Bighorns, or maybe Granma had pulled her aside for a private talk, but for the first time, she spoke to me with some friendliness, some familiarity. "Do you want to pet Daphne?" she asked, standing before me in her nightgown. Her hands, the twin birds, flapped at her sides. Of course I did. Cora opened the cage.

She cupped the hamster with exquisite care. Daphne curled one of her own fairy hands around Cora's finger. "One of my relatives got her at a pet store in Billings," Cora said. "Her name used to be Roxy. Then my relative moved away to Great Falls with a truck driver and said I could have her. I changed her name to Daphne. It's my favorite." Daphne hunkered down happily in Cora's hand, clearly enamored of her mistress. "I think she's happier here."

ONE END-OF-JUNE AFTERNOON, Granma and I stood together in the kitchen, surrounded by hundreds of wild turnips, the spoils from our digging excursions. Jim was at work, and Cora had accompanied Josie on a trip to Crow Agency to visit friends. Before Cora had left that morning, I'd passed my long letter to Simon into one of her fluttery hands, and she'd agreed with an officious nod of her head to mail it for me. "No problem," she'd said, studying Simon's mouthful of a moniker on the envelope with an inquisitive squint. "You can count on me." She was warmer with me now than she had been in weeks previous, but it was a warmth tinged with wariness, and her smile as she slipped out the screen door had been but a fleeting flicker.

The turnips lolled on the countertops and on the glittery Formica table. They appeared alive, like terrestrial starfish. Granma showed me how to weave the limblike offshoots of the roots together to make a braid. We would store the roots that way, braided together, and she would pull them off as she needed to make wild turnip flour for thickening stews and baking breads. "Cora does love to do this," she said, "so we'll make sure to save some for her to braid when she gets home."

"How did you learn about all these things?" I asked. "Digging roots and storing them and using them for food? And choke-cherry jam? And pemmican?"

"I was like Cora," Granma said, "a *káalisbaapite*, a grand-mother's grandchild. That means my grandmother raised me and showed me everything she knew. My own mother was gone. She was sick from drinking. She was lost to us." I thought of Dad and wondered if that was the best way to describe what he had always been: lost to me. Still, it was possible to miss someone who had never even been entirely there, and I longed to see the delicate drape of his eyelids over his Irish eyes, to pull his glasses gently from his sleeping face as I had so many times when I was younger.

"My grandmother knew all the secrets of the earth," Granma continued, "things my mother's generation had been told they were supposed to forget. I think my grandmother was very disappointed that she could not help my mother, so she turned all of her attention toward me. She took me—my big sister, Ruby, was raised by some other relatives. We lived right on this spot—it was a different house then, one that my grandparents had built—and we walked together all over this prairie. She managed to keep me here with her until I was Cora's age— that's when two men in suits came and took me away to a boarding school for Indian kids." Granma made a mistake in her braiding and unwove a few roots so that she could start again. "It took me many years to find my way back to my home," she said.

"You were really taken away?"

"Mmm," she nodded. "It happened that way sometimes. The law said we had to go. They had already come out here looking for me twice before, and my Granma told me to hide under her buffalo blanket, which I did." Her hands shook a little while she twisted the roots. "Eventually, though, they figured it out and found me, and I went. But I hollered and carried on the whole way."

"How long did you have to stay at the boarding school?"

"Seven years, honey. Until I graduated."

"Did you learn a lot?"

Granma was silent, and for several moments all I heard was the soft rustling of our work. "It was more like I unlearned a lot," she finally said. "You see, my grandmother was very traditional. Even though she lived after the turn of the century, and after the reservation had been established, she really clung to her old ways."

"Things like this?" I said, lifting the beginnings of my braid off the countertop. It smelled of clean earth, and I resisted the urge to press my face into it.

"Yes." Granma nodded. "And she was a healer. She understood all about plants, and she loved animals, too—the prairie dogs were her helpers. She began teaching me what she knew when I was a very small child. So I grew up in the Crow world that my grandmother had been taught to keep by her grandmother. And that *she* had been taught to keep by *her* grandmother. And so on, all the way back to No Intestines. Remember him?"

I nodded, thinking of Jim's vertical line and ink-stained hands.

"My grandmother taught me every day. I spoke the Crow language, ate traditional Crow food, prayed Crow prayers. I was a happy girl. I slept under a heavy buffalo blanket beside her every night. And every morning, at *iisakchihpashé*—that's dark face time, when the Creator comes closest to the earth—I felt her rise and go outside to pray."

With a sudden flutter in my belly—the kind that comes with unexpected discoveries (a shiny quarter on the ground or a lost red resin bracelet found)—I realized what Granma had been doing every morning before dawn when the screen door squeaked and I heard her step outside. She had been praying. I couldn't imagine forcing myself out of bed every morning at dark face time to pray. Even thinking of it filled my limbs with a lazy feeling. It would be easier to stay awake until dark face time, like Rasha had done when she'd worked on her perfume recipes while living at her cousin's place. Maybe that had been a sort of prayer, too—the effort to create an invisible kind of beauty.

"So that's what you do every morning? Pray like your grandmother did?"

"Yes, honey. But I haven't always done that. You see, when I was taken away to the boarding school, I was emptied of all those things my grandmother showed me and filled up with other things, new things. It was all part of assimilation—that was the word they used at the time, people like the two men in suits and the teachers at the school. They said Indians had to be reeducated in white ways and become functioning members of white society. It wasn't okay for us to do things our way anymore." Granma peeled a lingering strip of skin from one of the roots. "Did you like school, Margie?"

"No." I recalled shuffling self-consciously through high school with a stack of books, my only companions, perpetually pressed to my chest. "I was really lonely. I kept to myself, and my dad was . . ." Granma looked my way with interest, and suddenly I felt protective of Dad, too protective to talk about how once he had cried in front of everybody at the Father-Daughter Dance because he drank and was irredeemably sad. ". . . and . . . yes, I just hated it."

"I hated it too. At the school I went to, some kids actually died from sickness. I think they died from homesickness, home-sickness so strong it broke their hearts. Oh, I used to feel so sorry for the kids at the boarding school," Granma said. "That was why I hated it so much. I always felt so sorry for everyone. They lost their homes and families. They were made to forget their language and were punished if they tried to speak it. They were made to forget their prayers and religion, and given new prayers and a new religion. They really had lost their entire world. I used to feel so sorry for them, so sorry my chest just *hurt*. And then, sometimes, I realized I was no different from any of them. In fact, I *was* them. Of course, after a while, most of us got used to it. And after seven years, well, I was a very different girl coming out than I had been going in."

"After you graduated, did you go back home?"

"My grandmother had died while I was in school. I didn't feel like I had a home to go back to. If I went back to the Crows as I was, with my hair all curly from my permanent, speaking my slangy English, wearing my hat and gloves and a cross on a gold chain around my neck, knowing how to read, write, and type, it wouldn't make sense. I was no longer a part of the place I had belonged to as a girl. I would feel like . . ." Granma hesitated, hunting for a word. "An *akihkéetaahawassdaawe*—an astronaut. Someone who's been to a different planet.

"And also," she went on, "I was afraid that if I returned to the reservation, that would make me a failure. At the boarding school, they had taught us that the reservation was no kind of home, no kind of life. It was poor and behind the times, they said. They wanted us to be a part of the so-called civilized world. I didn't know if I believed that. Actually, I didn't know what I believed at all. But I got a job as a secretary in St. Paul, Minnesota."

I stared at the turnips to hide the surprise in my eyes. It was so hard to imagine Granma as I knew her—Granma with her floor-skimming skirts and button-down cowboy shirts, Granma with her Snow White flour sack and root-digging stick of choke-cherry wood, Granma with her grin full of gaps—as a big-city secretary, a professional girl in stockings and a silk blouse, wielding endless papers and pencils and pens instead of knitting needles.

"Really?" I said. "A secretary?"

"Mmmhmm. I did it for about twenty years, too. It wasn't always easy. My skin wasn't light enough. That always posed some difficulty. And I lost a few jobs because my bosses thought I was disrespectful for never making eye contact." She poked me playfully with her elbow. "I guess that's one habit the school never managed to extinguish. But for the most part, I did pretty well. I always had a nice apartment, all to myself. But," she paused, "that was just it: I was always alone."

I nodded. I knew what that was, to be Always Alone. I remembered what Simon had once stopped to ask me in the middle of Latin class on that long-ago day when he had turned his attention, his hyacinths and gemlike eyes, his unlit cigarette, entirely toward me, and I had warmed and blushed in my chair. I asked a similar question of Granma. "Did you have any friends?"

"No," she said. "Not really. Boyfriends came and went. But it was hard for me to make connections. I felt so different, inside, from everybody. I didn't know how to explain myself to myself, much less to anyone else. I didn't feel Crow. I wasn't white. I was just in between."

I pictured her as a girl the same age as me, working in a world she could not quite call her own, strolling the crowded city side-walks with a sideways gaze so as not to intrude upon another's space with her eyes. I could see her hands, smooth and agile, clasped tightly around the straps of her prim purse, with no bits of Montana earth lingering beneath her fingernails. And I saw her as a thirty-year-old woman, a lonely woman who ate dinner while standing over the stove, who missed the grandmother she remembered and wondered about the mother she didn't, whose face sometimes took on a secret startled look when an old Crow word, coughed up by some cranny in her brain, flew like a lost bird into her head and then back out again. And for the first time, I felt a mournful twinge in my left ovary for Granma—not for the way she was now, in the kitchen, silver haired and sure of herself, but for the way she had been then. "It makes me sad," I said.

"What does, honey?"

"Thinking of you like that. So alone. Like you said. In between."

"Well, I didn't stay that way forever, now, obviously, or I wouldn't be here with you today. I came out of my shell eventually," she said. "What happened was, I began to hear about something that was happening in Minneapolis. I kept reading about it in the newspaper. The American Indian Movement. They called it AIM. A group of Indian activists had come together because they were tired of police brutality in the city. And then it developed into something more. They began saying that Indians should be proud of who they were and reclaim the knowledge, the traditions, the identities they had lost. One night, after work, I drove over and sat in on one of their meetings. I looked around me, and it was as if all those kids I had felt so sorry for at the boarding school, they were all grown up, and they wanted it all back, everything that had been taken from them, from their parents, their grandparents, from all their ancestors."

"What were they talking about?" I asked. I thought of Bumble, Raven, Ptarmigan, Orca, and Bear, how they had looked the first time I'd seen them sitting around a table at Gelato Amore.

"They wanted to end the poverty of Indian people," Granma said, "get back the millions of acres of land that had been stolen from the tribes, and see all the broken treaties made right. For the first time since I was a little girl, I started to feel excited. This was something I could do, I thought, and then that empty, lonely feeling seemed like it would leave me."

I could hardly believe Granma's words. Our lives had been so different and yet so much of what she told me was achingly familiar.

"I had saved up so much money over the years, living as quietly and working as hard as I had, that I was able to quit my job and give all my energy to the movement. I wasn't a leader, but I was always there, on the sidelines. I was there when we seized the BIA headquarters in Washington, D.C. That was how I met Bumble's mother. I was so happy she was Crow like me. I was at all kinds of protests. I helped to burn down a building and two police cars. I was always writing pamphlets and flyers. It was my life. I put all my effort into it. I wanted to make a difference. Maybe you know that feeling?" Granma stopped braiding and studied her roots with intensity, waiting for my response.

"I do."

"I got involved with one guy in the movement," she continued, "then another. Sometimes it seemed like we were all working toward the same goal, but other times it seemed like we were all in our private worlds, all floating in different directions."

"Like driftwood?"

"Exactly. There was so much unhappiness. And too much anger. And, eventually, too much violence. In 1973, we had a standoff at Wounded Knee, over on the Pine Ridge reservation. Back in 1850, the U.S. Army had massacred 150 Indian people there, including women and children. We returned to that place to hold a protest. But then it turned into something else. And the FBI got involved. People started shooting, and one of the men I'd had a relationship with was killed." Granma shook her head, remembering. "I had touched his body, known him well, knew his laugh, cooked him food, even seen him cry. And then he was gone, and for what? I started to wonder if anything we had done had really made a difference at all."

She considered for a moment. "It's not that the movement was a waste. It wasn't. But . . . for me, well . . . The feelings I had wanted to escape from were still there. And the things that I had wanted to reclaim, the peace I was searching for, it still felt so far away from me."

Granma's braid of roots had grown so long she pushed one end of it into the sink to make room on the counter. My own was short. I was too absorbed in listening to her to get much done.

"And part of me," she continued, "was just so tired. After Wounded Knee, a lot of my friends were in trouble with the FBI and they had to go on trial. I pulled away from everyone and everything. I slept a lot. I was so tired, honey. You can't imagine. And I started to have a memory, all the time, just before I fell asleep, of quietness. I guess it was more like a memory-feeling, you know? And it wasn't just the complete absence of sound that I was remembering, that I had not known since I'd gone away to the boarding school, but a real deep quietness, in my body, in my mind. I think I was remembering my childhood, and lying beside my grandmother under her buffalo blanket. And that's when I decided I wanted to go home."

The afternoon was at its ripest moment, at the peak of richness just before it would begin its descent into evening. Granma looked through the window at the gold sky. Her eyes were dark, her mouth closed tight but still mobile, as if struggling to separate the words she wanted to speak from the tears that had collected around them. She was equal portions happy and sad, and in the space between the two there hung her beauty, a weathered and generous beauty born of strength.

"When I drove into Crow Agency," she finally said, "I was forty years old. I had not been on the reservation since I was eleven,

when the two men in suits took me away. I found my way back
out here, back to this piece of land. The house my grandparents
had built was still standing, though it was empty and all torn up
inside—plenty of animals had made themselves at home in it over
the years." This charmed her, and she laughed. "But it was mine.
So I lived. I got a job at a market in St. Xavier, and I worked
there in exchange for groceries.

"And sometimes, waking up in the morning, I felt it, that old
quietness, coming back into me, as if I had only been away for
a month, a week. I felt . . . home. I found that what I had been
looking for, what I had been missing, had been right there, all
along. She was here, right here, waiting for me. It was her, and
even though she's everywhere, I found her here."

I wasn't sure if Granma meant her grandmother, her mother,
or someone else. "Then after a while, I met Jim's father," she
said. "That's Ray." Her face bloomed open when she said his
name, and a russet gladness colored her cheeks. "He was a
good man, ten years older than me. We met at the Baptist
church over in Pryor. I used to go every Sunday. My friends
back in AIM would have questioned me for doing it. I don't
know why I went the first time. I guess I was ready to be among
people again, and the people there were nice. I kept going because
I was curious about Ray, and he kept going because he was curious about me. One Sunday, after the service, a bunch of us were
standing around outside in the sunshine. I went up to Ray. He
was standing all by himself. I asked him, in a low voice so nobody
would hear, 'Do you really believe any of this stuff they tell us
in church?' I don't even know what got into me, why I asked
him that."

"What did he say?"

"Ray didn't say anything at first. He really squinted in that
sun, I remember. I thought to myself, 'He's handsome.' Then he
stepped a bit closer to me. 'Actually, Evelyn,' he said, 'I do, in my

own way, but I still believe all the things my grandmother taught me, too.' Well, I rushed over to my car and drove away as fast as I could. And when I got back home, I climbed under the covers. I had a terrified feeling, but I also couldn't stop laughing. You see, honey, I just knew."

"Knew what?" I asked. But Granma didn't seem to hear me. She was living the story as she told it.

"Ray came out here to visit me. I knew he would. And I knew exactly *when* he would. I was waiting outside for him in a dress and sandals with a pot of coffee heating on the stove when he came. And after that, he and I were never apart. I had been just about freezing to death in the winter in my grandparents' old house, and so we tore that down and built this house together, and we lived out here as a pair. We told everyone we were married, and we were, in the Indian way. He was quiet, never had much to say, and after my years in the city and my time with those activists, I thought, 'I like this guy. He's so calm.' And he was kind to me. When he talked, he talked to me in Crow, and then," she sighed, as if with relief, "I began to remember. I remembered a lot of things. I went for a long walk every evening. When I saw certain plants, like these turnips, and touched them, and smelled them, I remembered what my grandmother had taught me. Smelling the prairie, seeing it, feeling it . . . it all came to me through my senses, and I remembered. It was like she was calling me back. Back to my home and back to myself."

Josie's truck came growling up the road. Belly ran alongside it as fast as she could, celebrating its approach with staccato barks.

"Ray and I didn't think we could have any children," Granma said. "Then Jim came along when I was forty-four. He surprised us, and we were so glad." I thought of Jim as a baby wearing an endless succession of hand-knitted blue hats, baby Jim the surprise with no line between his eyes. "Ray died twelve years ago. And now there's Cora."

Granma stopped braiding and pressed her hands close together. We could hear Cora's high, strident voice rising above the rumble of Josie's truck as it pulled up alongside the house. "... and wild roses in dark pink and light pink beads up the sides ..."

"It will be better for Cora," Granma said, almost to herself. And then she did something I hadn't anticipated. She took the dangling ends of her long braid and wove them into the dangling ends of my shorter one, so that our two braids became one very long garland. She did it so swiftly I hardly saw her hands move. "This makes sense, doesn't it?" She smiled up at me. "And I think everything is going to turn out for you, too, Margie."

Cora came through the screen door as if a gust had blown her in, and she tumbled breathlessly into the kitchen on her tripping feet. "I mailed your let—" she started to say before laying her blazing brown eyes on the garland. The rhinestones on her spectacles had a stellar quality—just like, I thought, the tobacco seeds of No Intestines's vision. And I realized at that moment that the glasses—wherever they had come from—had been destined for Cora. What had at first seemed incongruous and even burdensome on her babyish face actually made perfect sense. The glasses were shining like stars. "You braided?" she bellowed. "Without me?"

"No no, Grandchild. We saved you all of these roots to braid, and when you're done, we'll add them on." Cora examined the remaining roots and decided they were sufficiently plentiful.

Later, after Jim came home from the press, he stood in the kitchen, streaked in shades of indigo and slate and midnight blue that echoed the sky outside. He watched while Granma gave instructions and Cora and I stood on chairs and hung the long garland of braided roots on the wall, affixing it here and there to nails that had evidently been set in place for that purpose years earlier. "Here? And here? How's this?" Cora asked. The garland was so long we had to hammer in new nails to hold it up, and even drape some of it across the tops of the kitchen cupboards. "I think we have enough," Granma said, "to keep all of us full for a very long time."

JIM RETURNED FROM THE PRESS AN HOUR LATE one night, and he came bearing gifts.

Granma knitted in her recliner while Cora and Josie played a game of Go Fish under the glow of the star-shaped lamp. They were accompanied by another relative, Fern, age four, whom Josie was looking after for the night. Fern held her own cards but mostly watched, laughing impishly whenever Cora told Josie to go fish. Cora uttered the command with great solemnity, though I could see her twitchy efforts to stifle a smile every time. Josie, who since my arrival had begun to address me less as a curiosity and more as a misguided if well-intentioned soul, invited me to play.

"Join us, Margie," she said, peering into her fan of cards through the curtain of her long bangs. She looked stately sitting with her elbows on the table, her brown skin smooth, her teeth white, her bosom imposing, like a T-shirted queen of Crow Country, proud of her generous proportions.

"No thanks," I said. "I'll just read." I sat with my *Wheelock's Latin* opened on my legs, which were sticky with summer night warmth, but I could no more give it my attention than I could engage in even the most uncomplicated of card games because

I was nervous. Jim was coming home. I listened for his truck. I looked over and over again at the screen door. I thought about retreating to my bed and staying there, but I couldn't allow myself to cave in to such a cowardly impulse—I, who had set San Diego's most popular eatery ablaze!

This had been happening for weeks, the nervousness. I felt like one of Cora's fluttering hands. Although Granma had explained that Jim's avoidance of my eyes was not a sign of dislike, I was still uncomfortable in his presence. In fact, much to my own confusion, I was even more ill at ease than I had been before her reassurances. Still, I resisted the temptation to flee when I knew his homecoming was imminent. I forced myself to wait, to watch him come through the door, to notice what he might say or do. And, most confounding to me of all, there was something delicious, something almost unbearably rich, in all of it—the nervousness, the waiting, the watching. I looked down at my lucky red Chinese shoes. And now that he was an entire hour later than usual, I was damp, quivery, even a little nauseated, and my head ached.

Time slowed down when I finally heard the purr of his truck, so that it might have been another hour that elapsed between his parking and his appearance in the house. During that span of time I stared into the pages of *Wheelock's* (*victus,* food; *aeternus,* forever; *mell,* honey). He carried a giant plastic sack.

"I got paid today," he almost sang. "I stopped by Sammy's Secondhand and brought us back a few presents." He dropped his lunch pail and thermos on the floor and shook the bag enticingly, like some sort of ink-splattered, summertime Santa. As always, his exuberant smile ran in the direction opposite to the little line of hurt between his eyes.

Fern squealed with uncontained anticipation. Cora slapped her cards on the table and rushed to his side. "Whad' they have?" she piped. Granma and Josie both beamed at him with the kind of excitement they might have felt as girls when confronted with the prospect of any kind of treat. Watching them all, I knew: Jim was beloved by his women. I was overwhelmed by the idea that in his bag there was a gift for me, that somehow I would be enfolded into this familial love, and how could that be possible? I was Margie, a stranger from California, a criminal, a kook. I feared I might drown in the atmosphere of unspoken affection and, no longer able to resist the urge, I scooted out of my chair to make my weird, worried way down the hall to the safety of my bunk.

"Wait, Margie," Jim said. "Don't you want to see?"

"Oh, y-yes." I watched his hands disappear into the bag. First, he pulled out a shiny red teakettle.

"For you, Mom," he said.

"Oooh, honey, it's so pretty. Thank you."

"And this, too." He unveiled an old wooden pencil box with a sliding lid painted like an American flag. Granma pushed the lid back to discover a collection of metal knitting needles in pastel pink and purple and aqua. She gasped with delight.

"Hmmm . . ." Jim said. "And what's in here for Cora?" He squinted into the bag, dipped his head all the way inside of it, and sighed out a sleepy-sounding "Let's see . . ." until feisty Cora darted at him and tried to snatch the sack away.

"Dad!" she shrieked.

Jim emerged with a pair of headphones on his head and a portable stereo resting in his hand. "It plays CDs, too," he said. "Should work great—just needs batteries." Cora had some difficulty arranging the headphones just so over the frames of her glasses. Once she got them in place, she kept them on, listening to nothing but imagined music and the muffled sounds of our voices. She bobbed her head back and forth in a rhythmic, funky way.

"Sister," Jim said, and regal Josie sat up even straighter in expectation. "I'm glad you're here tonight because I found something for you, too."

Josie's gift was a carved bangle bracelet made of dark, grainy wood. It suited her splendidly. She slipped it onto her wrist, rested her head in her hand as if to model it, and batted her eyelashes. "Jim" was all she said.

"And for Fern, who is so sweet . . . I have . . ." Jim reached into the bag, and I wondered if he really did have something for Fern, because her presence was unexpected, but he came through. ". . . *this!*" He held up a stuffed koala, which Fern passionately embraced before pushing her chubby fingers into its pouch. There was a quarter inside.

"And, last but not least," Jim mumbled and fumbled for a cumbersome something at the very bottom of the bag. "For Margie."

I leaned with precarious composure against the wall. "You didn't have to get me anything—"

"I know." He let out an abrupt laugh. Granma, Josie, Cora, and Fern all stared at the bag in silence and waited with burning eyes, curious to see what Jim had selected for me, and when he lifted out a cookbook, each looked disappointed in her own way: Granma silently shook her head, Josie recoiled backward as if she smelled an offensive odor, Cora stopped shimmying for a moment and yawned, and Fern stage-whispered "Oh, no" into the ear of her koala.

Jim passed me the book. I noticed his hand shook slightly. *Three Hundred Thrifty Thirty-Minute Meals!* the cover shouted. I flashed back to my months in Simon Mellinkoff's kitchen, the many nights I'd spent fussing over meticulously prepared meat-free fare because Simon required the most ascetic concoctions. And now, was I supposed to cook for a household of unrepentant omnivores when I was still (with the exception of occasional fresh eggs) holding fast to my vegan diet? How long, I wondered once more, recalling what Bumble had said about the duration of my stay, was "a while"? I struggled to cork a sudden fantasy that Agents Fox and Jones would discover my whereabouts after all and liberate me from what might turn out to be several months of sweaty stove-based servitude.

But I could not hurt Jim's feelings. "Wow, this is wonderful." I flipped through the pages. "Thank you, Jim. Mmm, it all looks delicious. And," I rambled, "I have been thinking I should do more to earn my keep around here, so this is perfect. I'll start cooking—"

"Actually," he interrupted, "that's not exactly what I had in mind." He looked askance, as usual, and went on with the same shake in his voice that I'd seen in his hands. "I was thinking that maybe a couple of nights a week—well, on the weekends— you and I could whip something up together."

Evidently, he had, with that statement, redeemed himself in the eyes of our onlookers, because Granma uttered an enamored "Oh!" Josie shook her head back and forth slowly, as if she had just watched her favorite basketball player make an impossible shot, and Cora was impressed enough to let her mouth fall open. "Good idea, James," said the plainspoken Fern.

"I thought we could liven up the menu around here," he continued, "and also give Mom a break. So, maybe you could pick some good recipes and then tell me what ingredients we need on Friday mornings, and I'll swing by the supermarket in Billings on my way home from work. Of course, we can make a vegan version of everything. We can cook up some good meals, you and I, together. On Saturday and Sunday nights." He cleared his throat. "For everyone."

I looked into the kitchen. I considered the diminutive two-burner stove, the single sink, the stubby countertop. I pictured Jim and me stuffed in there, side by side, smilingly stirring spaghetti. Was there a teaspoon—a pinch, even—of genuine, not obligatory, friendliness simmering somewhere in his proposal? The long garland of braided roots undulating against the wall seemed to express a definite yes, but when I looked at the wet blue towels drooping from the rusty nails above the sink, I wasn't sure.

"Gosh." I smiled dumbly down at the book and saw that his hands had left some orange, yellow, and green fingerprints on the cover. I opened it randomly to Marinated Chicken Breast on a Bed of Aromatic Rice. "Thanks, Jim," I said. "That sounds like a good idea." But he had already turned away to ask Cora to take off her headphones.

"Cora. The moon's coming up and it's full," he said.

She stopped gyrating. "It is?"

"Yes. I watched it my whole drive home."

"You know what that means, Fern," Cora said. "It's a night for jumping."

Fern laid down her koala and hurried outside.

"What is she doing?" I asked.

"They don't do it in California?" said Josie with a teasing squint.

"Do what?"

"She's just jumping at the moon," Granma said.

"It's something we do, we Crows, when we are young," added Jim.

"Kids know they'll grow up good and strong if they jump when *bilítaachiia* is rising," Josie explained, no longer teasing but serious.

"Where do they jump?"

"You know. Just up. Should we let her see?" Josie asked.

"Of course," Jim said hastily. "Of course she can see. Come on."

Outside, the air was hot. A lone lark, seduced by the moon into nightsinging, sang a stop-and-go song. The moon was high, but not yet as high as it would be. It was still rising, as if hung

on a transparent cord and lifted heavenward by the stealthiest
of hands. Beneath the bird's aria we heard a recurring thud, the
sound of feet falling on dirt.

We saw them in the distance. Cora, too big for jumping,
stood still, her body slender and dark against the blue prairie.
She watched Fern leap again and again toward the white light.
When the child rose, the moonglow reflected off her outstretched
arms, her splayed little legs. When she landed, it shone off the
top of her head. She looked like a star, one that was bound to the
prairie and belonged there somehow, as if a star could flourish
anywhere at all.

THE NEXT MORNING, I WOKE BEFORE DAWN after a dream
I couldn't remember, but it was one that made me throb.
I worried I may have even made a sound—a moan or a
murmur—and disturbed Cora who slept so lightly, but her
breathing was peaceful and regular, punctuated by occasional
chirps from the previous night's lark, still singing outside. My
neck was stiff because, apparently, I'd been using my pillow as
something to cling to rather than lie upon, and my legs were
twined tightly around it. I was damp everywhere, from the
pads of my bare toes to the place where my forehead met my
hair. My throat was parched and my lips were chapped. I lay
still and concentrated, and tried to follow one fine thread of
the dream back to its spool of origin, but I couldn't. The
thread only shivered a few more times with some electric desire
and dissolved. The lark called and waited for an answer that
didn't come.

I had not pressed my damp skin against anybody else's for
so long—not since I had left Simon's house. Had the dream,
I wondered, been about Simon, who had milled me, who had
made me his own in a musty office where the light snuck in

through the slits in the shut blinds? Simon, who had plump earlobes and plump palms, whose dear girl I had been? It might have been about him, but there were no vestiges of jasmine in my nose, no hint of the hyacinths with which he had bathed my face on so many nights before he tended his wife's wild garden and told me he was tired. A lot had happened since then, all of which I had chronicled in my long letter to him, and I wondered if he had read it yet.

I heard the soft squeak of the screen door open and close. I rolled onto my belly carefully, soundlessly, and bent my head to spy out the window. I saw that the star quilt Granma kept on her bed was wrapped around her shoulders and her feet were bare, and I wondered if there was dampness on the grass the way there was on me. I watched her walk out to a low hillock where she stood, unmoving, to pray.

Sometimes her head was tipped upward, sometimes down. Sometimes she looked in one direction, sometimes another. She was too distant and the light was too dim for me to discern the words her mouth might have been shaping. Even so, my gaze felt like an invasion and I moved my face away from the window. I lay on my back and stared at the ceiling above me.

At Holy Rosary back home, the ceiling was an enormous concave circle, representative of the sky, painted the same shade of blue as Mary's cloak the way it was rendered in so many paintings of her—Virgin Mary blue, I always called it. I used to tilt my head back to look at it when Father Murphy prompted the parishioners to pray and everyone else bowed their heads. I used to look up at the ceiling and know that the actual sky, the one that arched over us all out of doors, was also the cloak of Mary. Yes, the sky was her cloak, the orange blossoms her crown of stars, the swaying forests her eyelashes, the Sierra Nevada mountain range her spine, the sand at the beach the skin on her elbows, the magnolia blossoms on the tree in our front yard the whites of her eyes, and the September Santa Ana winds her sighs. She wasn't just the mother of God, I thought—she was the mother of all creation.

Once in CCD a sister asked, "Where are your thoughts and your hearts during Mass, children? In what direction do they turn?"

I believed she meant the question to be rhetorical, but still I raised my hand and volunteered an answer, explaining the many earthly manifestations of Mary I pondered when I looked up at the skylike ceiling of the church.

"That sounds pagan, Marjorie," the sister said. "Stop thinking so much about nature and how things smell. The mother of our Lord is not *sand* at the *beach*." But my ideas, unorthodox though they might have been, remained in place. And even though I never attended Mass after I left home for college, I still had those Mary thoughts, and when I saw laboratory mice or undernourished birds or frightened chinchillas, I always (unbeknownst to Simon or the crew) said silent prayers to Mary, because I knew she must be the mother of all animals, and that was why I never stopped wearing the Mary medal Dad had given me to commemorate my first communion, and why even during my visits to Jack Dolce in Little Italy I often walked at sunset down the block to Saint Anthony's Church (where the same gray-haired matrons who had come to our party knelt in their black dresses) and paused at the Mary statue to leave a few oyster shells at her feet (for oysters, I thought, were the muscles of her heart, and she was the sea, too, because in Latin, I'd learned from Simon, the sea is *mare*). Jack Dolce always shook his head at me. "She's not real, Margie," he said. "She's an image. *Made up*."

I contemplated all of this at dark face time while Granma stood outside in prayer. Then, as I always did, I fell back asleep before she returned to the house.

CORA AND I SAT ACROSS FROM EACH OTHER at the table and
ate bowls of cereal in sleepy silence. Beside her, Cora had
placed her peach pit, which she had refused to relinquish to
Granma.

At night, Cora stored the peach pit in a jewelry box on her
dresser. Once opened, the box displayed a mechanical ballerina who pirouetted to a tinkling tune. Cora always spent a few
meditative minutes examining the pit before bed. When she was
through, she placed it in her jewelry box and lowered the lid with
secretive swiftness. I wondered if the ballerina kept on pirouet-
ting after the lid was closed, and if she and Daphne's exercise
wheel and my dreams and Cora's would spin together according
to some mysterious nocturnal choreography while all else in the
world was still.

Now, I noticed, the pit was slightly worn down on one side,
and after breakfast I discovered why. Cora stepped out onto the
porch and blinked in the bright morning sun. She removed her
spectacles and polished them with the hem of her nightgown.
Then she sat on the ground, picked up the brick that Granma
used to hold the screen door open when she craved a breeze,
placed it before her, and set about rubbing the pit against the
brick's rough surface.

"What are you doing with the peach pit?" I asked.

"Making a ring."

"A ring? To wear on your finger?" Cora nodded. "How?"

She sucked in a big breath, and I knew it was a subject of
significance to her. "You rub away one side and then the other
until you see the seed on the inside of the pit. Then you pull out
the little seed that's in there. Then you shape the inside, sort of,
and . . ." Cora's voice faltered. "I'm not sure yet what you do after
that, but I'll figure it out when I get there. My mom told me about
it a long time ago."

"Oh?" Cora had never spoken to me about her mother.

"She said *her* mom taught *her* how to do it. They came from Georgia, where the peaches grow."

"Really?"

Cora was silent. Had there been a jewelry box with a ballerina twirling inside of it right there on the porch, she—I was sure—would have tucked the topic of her mother inside it and closed the lid tight. I decided to change the subject.

"Did you hear me talking at all in my sleep last night?" I asked. "Or this morning?"

"No. Why? Were you dreaming a lot?"

"I don't know," I said, thinking of the dark-haired dream strangers who always held the back of me against the front of them in spooning embraces. "Yes, I guess I was."

Jim stepped outside smelling of the soap from his shower. He kissed the top of Cora's head. "I'm not even going to ask what that's about," he said, baffled by the peach pit.

"It's going to be cool. You'll see."

"Did you get a chance to look through that cookbook, Margie?" He sipped from his coffee mug and stared at the horizon.

"Oh, I—yes. I did." It was true. I had looked at the book just before falling asleep. But I could remember nothing from it, nothing at all, apart from some sort of raspberry tart drizzled in ribbons of red glaze, because when my eyes had scanned its pages my thoughts, as they so often were, had been in another place. "It's a nice book," I said. "Thank you again."

As if he hadn't heard me, Jim said, "Well, I'm off to work. Have a good day you two. And keep Granma out of trouble."

Cora and I watched Jim's truck depart until it became a tiny yellow prairie flower that finally blew away in the breeze.

"I dream a lot," she said. "Granma says it is because my mind is sorting through all the possibilities for my future." She scraped the peach pit against the brick several times in silence, then eyed me sideways through her cat-eyes. "What were you dreaming of?" she asked. "Or who?"

THE MOON WAS JUST A SHY CRESCENT on the night we all sat around the table and ate the stuffed bell peppers—some made with meat, some with rice—Jim and I had prepared together. They were our first attempt at collaborative, *Three Hundred Thrifty Thirty-Minute Meals!*—inspired cooking, and they were received by Granma, Cora, and Josie with great greed and enthusiasm.

During our time together in the kitchen, Jim had asked me about my charm bracelet after it jingled against a can of tomatoes. "Oh, it was a birthday gift," I said.

"I like the bird."

"Thanks." I lifted my wrist in front of the window and let the light from the sinking sun glint off the silver. "My friends used to call me She-Bird."

"She-Bird?"

"Yes. I think it sounds like an Indian name."

"Kinda does." My wrist remained raised for a few more moments as if suspended by a puppeteer, and we both looked at the other charm, the half of a heart with its jagged edge. I hadn't bothered to take it off, for it had always seemed an integral part of the bracelet. I didn't say anything about that charm and Jim didn't ask about it, but still the image of Simon pointing to his own bare chest, as he had on the night he gave it to me, flashed through my mind.

The preparation of the peppers took decidedly longer than half an hour (which led Cora to declare the cookbook's title "false advertising!") and was punctuated by several seemingly interminable silences, occasional nervous laughter, and three bodily collisions—inevitable in the cozy kitchen. But Jim wore his mother's rose-printed apron while we cooked—more for the purpose of putting us both at ease, I suspected, than to protect his unfancy clothes—and it was amusing to see him wrapped in flowers with a big bow tied at his back.

We lingered at the table after the food was gone. Josie burped. "Oh my," she said. "That was delicious. I actually liked the meatless ones just as much. Who knew?" Outside, Belly whimpered for scraps that didn't exist.

Just as I got up to gather the empty plates, Cora's eyes went wide. "Oh," she said. "I almost forgot!" She disappeared into her room and emerged with a big, golden manila envelope. "This was at the post office today. It's for you." She slid it across the table and Jim's eyes watched it closely, the way they never watched me. A drawing of Charlotte, unmistakable with her droopy ears and dark fur, decorated the envelope's front.

"Funny bunny," Josie noted.

"This looks like it's from Bumble," I said.

"Bumble-not-your-boyfriend," Cora singsonged. Jim blinked.

"Right." I blushed.

"If you write him back," Granma said in her soft way, "give my regards to his mother." I nodded. "And go enjoy your letter in peace, honey. We'll handle the dishes."

. . .

UP ON MY BUNK, I TORE OPEN the envelope only to find another
envelope inside. It was wrapped in a sheet of paper on which
Bumble had printed a note.

> *Bird, Simon asked me to give this to you. I admit I held onto it for*
> *a while. I didn't read it, I promise. I just wasn't sure if I should*
> *send it. I've been hoping your life is peaceful, and I don't want*
> *anything to upset you.*
>   *No news here. No run-ins with your nemesis, Agent Fox.*
> *No more newspaper articles, either. The gang says hello and Char-*
> *lotte, as I believe her portrait illustrates, is doing great! I think*
> *going away was a good decision. I think the whole thing is going*
> *to blow over. I'd say you can return to civilization in a couple*
> *of months, and start fresh in a new city, with a new name, so long*
> *as you promise to stay out of trouble forevermore, and give up*
> *driving to eliminate the possibility of being pulled over. NYC?*
> *Why not?*
>   *I'll keep in touch. In the meantime, here's this . . .*
> *(drumroll) . . .*

Simon's sharply slanted cursive spelled out my first name across
the envelope. The sight of it gave me a Ferris wheel feeling. The
envelope was fat with many folded-up pages, and I found that his
letter to me was almost as long as mine had been to him. Upon
reading the first sentence, however, I realized Simon had not
received my letter before he had written his and given it to Bumble.

> *Margie,*
>   *I read about the restaurant fire in the* Sun *and, in light of your*
> *conspicuous absence from school, have guessed that you've gone*
> *away somewhere. Bumble is unwaveringly loyal to you, and*
> *refuses to inform even me of your whereabouts, but I persuaded*
> *him to do me the favor of sending you this letter.*

Where to begin? At the beginning, I suppose, when you had the misfortune of meeting me.

You touched me very deeply with your aura of a sad little girl who is always trying to be brave. I will never forget the sight of you with your bicycle, the sight of you always alone. From the moment you first appeared in my classroom, it was all I could do not to stare at you unceasingly, not to have conversations only with you, not to forget my job altogether. I swore I would never allow myself to be alone with you, but I couldn't help it. When I led you to my office that day, I didn't know I was leading you to an eventual life on the run (assuming you are not just two hours north of me sitting in your shambles of a house with your tragically remiss father, which wouldn't be much better). If I had known, I never would have done it.

Don't misunderstand me: I loved the time we spent together. I loved having you in my home. I loved sharing the Operation with you. It was fear—no, pragmatism—that broke the spell—that and the specter of my wife, with whom I wage a constant battle, one that persists even now. But I'll get to that shortly. I sent you away in part because, I admit, I was not yet entirely over Anna. She haunted me and at times my anguish was unmanageable. But mostly I sent you away because, deep down, I knew there was no way you would stay. Being young, bright, and so beautiful, it was only a matter of time, I was certain, before you would come to feel you had no use for an unhappy, dried-up old man like me—a man with a rather distasteful history. I sensed your restlessness. One night at Gelato Amore I overheard you talking with the crew about that unkempt ice cream boy who worked downstairs, and there was such a dazzle in your voice. I knew how sedate and gray I must have seemed to you, or would seem to you soon enough. I saw the way strangers looked at us when we were together. What would happen when I was 70 and you were barely 40? It was too ridiculous to even consider. The feeling of waiting for you to tire of me, as you inevitably would, was one of unbearable suspense. I couldn't stand it.

Also, I saw Annette's sisterly attachment to you growing—how could it not? She sensed your inner beauty and your gentleness—and I couldn't stand to think of her being disappointed in the future. She has suffered enough loss already. True, I was entirely to blame for having created the situation in the first place, but I let romance and hope overpower reality and common sense. Can you blame me, Miss Red Shoes?

I couldn't explain myself to you this way then because of course you would have simply told me I was wrong, bitten my earlobe and insisted on staying. And by that point I would have been in no position to argue because, my dear, you were so seductive, though you did not know it, which was partly the reason why. So, I put it to you the way I did. I know it was cruel and swift, but it seemed to me to be the best way. Oh Margie, you must forgive me. Not only for hurting your heart, which I know I did, but for unwittingly helping to land you in this fix.

I gave the Operation to you because I was too tired and depressed to keep it up, and you so clearly needed a family and a cause to give your heart to. I should have known that you, with your passionate nature, would take it further than I had ever dared with that bold campaign—a fine finale, if I do say so—concerning Untamed. Still, your subsequent information session at Gelato Amore should not have resulted in this mess. And it wouldn't have, were it not for the fact that you were being watched by people who were just waiting for you to say the wrong thing. And I believe you—we—were being watched before I retired from the Operation. And that, I suspect, was the specter's doing.

Contrary to rumors you may have heard, my wife really is deceased. It is true that she left me. She died after. She did both— the leaving and the dying—in a state of bitter rage against me that, obviously, I will never be able to assuage.

She was the original animal lover. Anna was a brilliant scientist who had grown completely opposed to the use of animals in laboratory tests. It was she who converted me, much as I did you. Initially, I went along to please her, but in time my concern for animals—which led naturally to my commitment to a more earth-friendly way of living, as you observed during our cohabitation—became genuine. We established Operation H.E.A.R.T. together, recruited a few friends, and set about enacting small-scale campaigns much like the ones in which you participated shortly after you joined. Anna and I did have some fun. For all her cerebral precision of thought and manner, she was capable of great moments of total and ecstatic abandon, such as when we vandalized a fur coat boutique or staged a noisy protest at a petting zoo, but then I don't think she had been able to express herself much as a child. In any case, it was an exhilarating abandon of which she was, to my disappointment, absolutely incapable in any other circumstance.

In those days, the Operation had a completely different crew. Among them was a young woman, a colleague of my wife's, with whom I became inappropriately involved. I won't go into detail, except to say that it ended badly. When Anna discovered the affair, she left, and took Annette with her. She was too prideful and, in her way, too punishing to even demand stewardship of the home for which she had singlehandedly paid. I stayed, alone, waiting for her to come back.

The Operation limped along for a while, then dissolved. I could not persuade Anna to return.

A year later, she got sick. The cancer was merciless, and she went fast. Annette came back to live with me. Our devastation was mutual, if different in its origins and nuances.

After she died, I reestablished the Operation with entirely new membership. Why did I do it? Because I missed her? Because I wanted to honor her memory? Because I wanted to appease her? Because I wanted to resurrect something I had ruined? I did it for

all of these reasons, along with a handful of other, shadowed ones
of which I cannot pretend to be completely aware. This is all my
own tangled and overgrown mental mess, and it is my burden to
weed through it. It was nothing you could have ever understood or
remedied. Yet I'm afraid the punishment she hoped would fall on
me is now hovering unjustly over you.

You see, I believe that sometime between her leaving and
dying, Anna contacted law enforcement about my sometimes
criminal, albeit relatively harmless activities as an animal rights
activist. I didn't realize this until just recently, as I've been thinking of virtually nothing but how and why this has happened to
you. As I mentioned, she was a very smart woman. And I know her
well. That was exactly the sort of spiteful action she would take,
endeavoring to see me caught and punished for the very activities
she had inspired, and in which she herself had once gloried. She
knew all about the "green scare" your lawyer friend described in
that silly article. And she knew that someone like me would be a
potential target for those whose job it is to crack down on so-called
domestic terrorists. I am sure it was Anna who prompted the FBI
to turn its gaze on Operation H.E.A.R.T. Why else would they
have worried about a humble and, I am not too proud to admit in
hindsight, fairly ineffectual assemblage of six college students and a
middle-aged professor? And there the gaze remained, until you, my
misera avis* gave them cause to take action by committing an offense
they could spin as truly serious—much worse than mere vandalism,
breaking and entering, or the theft of some lobsters.

Margie, I'm sorry! Please forgive me. If I can help you, let me
help you. I'm not sure that running away and hiding was the best
course of action, as you are officially wanted by the FBI. I fear
you will only make matters worse for yourself in the long run.
I understand it was a case of a fronte praecipitium a tergo lupi,

---

* unfortunate bird

and that you lacked the funds to pay for a lawyer, though evidently you spoke to one. In truth, I don't have much money to offer, either. As you know, I am unlike Weatherbury, that summus maximus bore in the tweed blazer, not a tenured professor, and my salary is meager. But I can offer you support. You needn't go through all of this alone. Who are you with? Where?

Simon

Stunned, I lay on the bed in complete stillness for an hour. Simon had finally shown me what his gemlike eyes never had, the secret of his heart, the secret that had almost revealed itself and then slipped away from me on that final evening when I had walked down the hallway to deliver his dinner and found him sitting with his head in his hands. Simon, I now knew, shook for sadness. He shaded his eyes for shame. He was so lonely that he had compelled me to come close, and so afraid of being lonely in the future that he had pushed me away.

I felt myself returning back to him, and the quality of his presence was as vivid to me as if I had been beside him that very day. The hyacinths of his breath were all around, and the heat of his cushiony palms was on my waist. His voice with its many mysteries was in my ear. And all the life I had led after leaving his house blurred and paled like a fading old photograph. My time in the Middletown studio where the tears had run into my ears was the equivalent of a single moment. My maudlin meanderings in the Community Garden compressed tautly together into three economical images: white nightgown, chain-link fence, tendrils. Even my connection with Jack Dolce seemed diminished. And my month on the reservation took on the quality of a dream, one populated by turnip roots, knitted baby caps, a peach pit, printing press ink stains, tobacco seeds shining like stars, and a vertical line between two dark eyes. The big blooming roses of Jim's apron closed into tight buds and disappeared. With his letter, Simon had reasserted himself as the foremost figure in my mind. He was unparalleled in his power to overwhelm my consciousness.

Still, for all its length, I had a strange sense that there was something missing from Simon's message, but I couldn't tell just what. Something about it made me uneasy. And it wasn't his confessed infidelity to his wife or her rage. I had forgiven him and pitied her as soon as I had read of both. It was something else.

I rolled onto my side and watched Daphne board her wheel in preparation for her all-night run. Cora tiptoed down the hall-way, passing the door to her room slowly and glancing in with an expression of impatience. She looked as though she had passed that way, with that face, many times. "Oh, Cora," I called. "It's okay. You can come in."

"I wasn't sure. You looked so worried and, I don't know, I wondered if maybe you got some bad news."

"Oh, no. No, not bad. This is your room. I don't want you to feel like you can't come in anytime you want." Cora undressed. She sighed with contentment when she slipped her nightgown over her head. Though I could not see her, she exuded a complete and cozy comfort at simply being in her habitat, at being tucked away safely for the night in the only home she had ever known, and I thought of what Granma had told me about the peace and pervasive quietness she had felt as a girl sleeping beside her grandmother under a buffalo blanket.

Could he help me, I wondered? Simon said he wanted to help me, if only by making me less alone. How did he mean? Did he mean for me to go back to his shadowy house with its white walls? My heart pounded at the memory of it.

I was tired, though it wasn't very late. I heard Josie leave and my eyes fluttered shut and then opened again at the sound of Cora's voice. "Want to turn off the light?" she asked.

"Okay," I whispered.

She stood at the doorway again, slender and dark against the glow from the hallway, her long arms dangling, ready for the ceremony that took place every night. "I love you, Granma," she called.

"I love you," came the answer.

"I love you, Dad," she added.

"I love you," he replied. And, thus enveloped, she was asleep in minutes, and soon I was drawn into dreams of my own by her long and regular breaths.

I DID NOT WANT TO ACCOMPANY Granma, Cora, and Josie on a trip to Billings to buy supplies for Cora's new Crow Fair leggings, which were to be part of her traditional dancing regalia. "Crow Fair is coming up," Cora had informed all of us on numerous occasions. "I really need to make new leggins. My legs grew."

"Well, I guess we'd better get over to the craft supply store then," Josie had replied one day when she dropped off a pile of mail and a paper plate laden with a stack of her homemade fry bread.

Cora sucked in her breath. "When? When? When?" she wondered, executing a few steps of the Fancy Shawl Dance—her specialty—in the living room, and causing the pair of matching lamps stationed beside the recliners (bronze bucking broncos straddled by cowboys with yellowed shades for hats) to shake. Josie did not name a date.

One afternoon a few weeks later, however, Josie rolled up unexpectedly in her truck, left the engine running, and called to us through the driver's-side window. "You all ready to go get some beads and whatnot for Cora's Crow Fair clothes? Come on, let's do this!"

"Yaaaaoow!" Cora let out an elated yelp, scooped up her portable stereo, and dove out the door. Granma clicked off the TV just before Charmaigne was about to break the big news to Victoria that they were half sisters. She tucked a ball of yarn into her shirtsleeve for the road. I looked up from *Wheelock's*. I had been trying to translate a letter by Pliny the Younger about the "Delights of the Country." So far, I had written, "Picture to yourself an immense amphitheater, such as only nature could create."

"Well," Granma purred. "Get your shoes, honey."

"Oh, that's okay." I drummed my fingers on Pliny. "I'll hang out here. You three go on—"

"Why don't you want to come? This is important."

"I know, but I—I don't feel safe out there."

"What are you going to do with yourself, Margie? Stay hidden in this house forever?"

"No." I closed the book. I thought of Simon's letter, as I had for the entire week since its arrival. *If I can help you, let me help you.* "I'm not going to stay forever."

Granma raised one silver brow. "Where are you going to go?"

"Well, I . . . That's something I've been thinking about. I . . . I'm considering . . ." But what had he meant? And would the covey of mourning doves still be there, calling to each other from under the eaves, if I returned? "When the time is right . . ." I fumbled. Granma studied me in silence.

"You can't just stay cooped up in here all day," she said. "It isn't healthy." Her words sparked a reverie during which I imagined myself falling into a state of frail health within that tiny abode, and exhibiting the strangely flattering signs of tuberculosis—wet and shining eyes, slightly opened mouth, twin apples ripening on my otherwise chalky cheeks. I saw myself lounging insensibly on Granma's fully extended recliner, my damp curls spread extravagantly across a pillow. I saw Granma nursing me with mysterious tinctures made from roots and prairie plants. I saw Belly cooling my fever with lavish licks and nuzzling my face with consoling whimpers. And I saw Simon as a slouchy, cowboy-hatted silhouette in the doorway, with a rectangle of sunsetty orange behind him. "Oh my," he uttered under his breath, and then he stepped closer to lean over me, anoint my forehead with a kiss, and say, "I'm sorry I led you into this mess, Precious."

And just when I imagined him scooping me up and laying my languid body over his white horse (Annette waited beside it on a small strawberry roan of her own), Josie gave her horn an impatient honk. Cora cried out to us, but her thin little voice was swallowed by the engine's roar.

"Honey," Granma said, "today I think you should come to the city. It will be good for you. Now, come on. I want your company."

ON THE DRIVE TO BILLINGS, Cora crowned herself with her headphones and bobbed her head to the beat of whatever played through her portable stereo. She didn't seem bothered at all by the sonic competition coming from the truck radio, which Josie had turned up to top volume. Only when I studied the rhythm of her head's movement (back and forth, back and forth, in the manner of the nervous turkeys the Operation crew and I had stealthily liberated from their crowded cages at a filthy farm one late November night) did I realize she and Josie were tuned to the very same station.

We stopped for gas on the reservation. Josie stepped out to pump, but a rangy fortyish fellow who had pulled up just behind us hopped hurriedly out of his own rusty rig and beat her to it. He was, Cora told me in a laughing whisper, Pete Sings Plenty, who, she added, had been hankering after Josie's body for years. "Shh, shh, Grandchild," Granma said before turning her face away to hide her grin.

Pete Sings Plenty wore an exceedingly wispy mustache that blew weakly in the Bighorn breeze. He held the pump in Josie's tank and eyed her with longing while the gas gurgled in. When he waved goodbye to us as we drove away, Josie asked no one in particular, "What is the point of growing that mustache?" She watched him in the rearview mirror and slurped greedily from the giant slushie Pete had bought for her at the mini-mart. "Indians don't have the facial hair for that sort of thing. Doesn't he realize?"

I SPIED THREE COP CARS within five minutes of our arrival in Billings. Josie, I noticed, thought using her turn signal and stopping at bright red hexagonal signs were optional facets of the driving experience, their execution dependent on how cooperative she was feeling at any given moment, and when I politely asked her to please drive carefully to avoid being pulled over, she blinded me with a big smile, stained orange from her slushie, called "What?!" and turned the radio down one fraction of a notch. Granma knitted obliviously, and Cora knocked her sharp knees together over and over in bead-anticipation.

The city was a shock after the weeks I had spent immersed in what Pliny would have called the delights of the country. There were so many cars, buildings, fast-food restaurants, parking lots—all the same sort of sprawl that characterized my Orange County home. (There, Dad was driving his Skylark from one open house to another and waiting, I worried, for a letter I'd promised but still had yet to send.) But I knew none of the secret charms that lay beneath Billings's unbeautiful surface. The streets were noisy, and the sun's brightness seemed harsher and sharper-edged—glaring cruelly off the windows of the downtown buildings—than it did on the prairie. To my surprise, I missed the reservation, and not just because I was uneasy about being seen.

Even my first glimpse of new faces in over a month left me disappointed and vaguely sad. On one street, a jowly man in a business suit walked fast while he jabbered into a cell phone and devoured a hamburger before disappearing behind the behemoth doors of a bank. On another, a woman Granma's age pitifully pushed a shopping cart full of aluminum cans and grimaced against the cutting sunlight, as if smiling at some secret thought or person no one else could see. "It's so *crowded* here," Cora said.

We passed a shoe repair shop, a sporting goods store, a place called Whole Woman that sold plus-sized dresses, and an old movie theater that had been converted into a church of indeterminate denomination. The marquee that had once flashed the glamorous names of great silver-screen beauties now read: FEELING THE HEAT? THIS CHURCH IS PRAYER-CONDITIONED.

The sky was the same one that extended endlessly over the reservation, but it looked paler somehow, its cerulean more diffuse. Even the green leaves of the trees lining the sidewalks had a washed-out, overexposed quality. When I pulled down my sunglasses to see whether the bleached effect remained, another cop car pulled up alongside us at a red light. I slumped down, shielding the side of my face with my hand.

"You have that weird look again," Cora said.

"What look?"

"The one you had the first night you came to our house. The one you get whenever my dad talks to you. Like you don't know whether to smile, cry, or maybe run away. Why do you get so nervous, Margie? Geez."

"Cora," Granma said.

THE CRAFT SUPPLY STORE WAS in a new strip mall on a treeless avenue. Inside, I followed Josie, Cora, and Granma to an aisle lined with clear plastic canisters of seed beads in every imaginable hue—as if all the colors missing from the city had been captured and condensed into the tiniest of spheres.

Cora wanted wild roses to climb up both sides of her leggings, so we examined beads in various versions of pink. "I want them bright, but not neon." She frowned through her spectacles. "And also we need greens and maybe some browns for the stems and leaves and thorns."

We four stood close together, our heads bowed, considering—Cora the girl-child, me the almost-woman, Josie the Whole Woman, and Granma, the wise woman. And it was feminine work of the finest sort, I thought, to decide which colors would best bring the five-petaled prairie rose (a flower I had yet to see firsthand) to life on Cora's dancing legs. For a moment, I was blissfully forgetful of all but the task at hand, and the sound of our own wondering voices cast a kind of enchantment up and down that aisle of beads.

We selected dozens of different colors, but each of us had a favorite. Cora loved a pure fuchsia for the brightest of the petals, Granma a grasshopper green for the healthiest of the leaves, Josie a burnished brown for some nuanced portions of the foliage. I was most partial to a dusty antique rose—the very color of the dress I had sewn and worn to the eighth-grade "Yes Sir, That's My Baby" Father-Daughter Dance. At first, Cora eyed it dubiously. Then she conceded that it might work for some of the unopened buds.

While they moved elsewhere to examine threads and needles, I explored the store alone. I found all manner of merchandise, including frames, fake flowers, and feather boas. I came to an aisle stocked with plain baseball caps, T-shirts, tank tops, and aprons, each one awaiting embellishment. Simon's writing that I was "wanted by the FBI" had somehow made that fact even more true, as was the case with so much of what spilled out of the miller's mouth or pen, and I decided to look for a disguise that went a bit further than my Audrey sunglasses. I chose a cap in navy blue—a safe color, a patriotic shade, a conformist cast—and tried it on. I tucked my hair inside and pulled it down low, so the brim bumped the top of my glasses. I felt hidden, but when I passed the sewing section, Cora lifted her gaze from a tomato-shaped pincushion, pointed at me, and said, "There she is!

"What is that hat?" she asked. "And why are your sunglasses on? Does the light in here bother your eyes?"

At the checkout counter, I dipped into my small stash of cash to pay for the cap. "That's a lot plainer than the stuff you usually wear," Cora noted. To pay for Cora's supplies, Granma pulled a few bills out of an envelope she carried in her tote bag, which was embroidered with the flag of the Crow Nation. "Your dad has been setting this money aside especially for this," she explained to Cora, whose eyes closed with gratitude behind her glasses.

For fear of offending me, I knew, Josie and Cora walked far ahead of us back to the truck to discuss the deer that Josie had killed the previous year. They would use its skin to make the new leggings.

Granma held on to my arm as we strolled and talked about the money in the envelope. "It's true, we don't have much. Jim's wages are low, and most of them go into Cora's college fund. I want Cora to go to college so she can be a master of both worlds—the Crow world and the outside one. I want her to thrive in both," Granma said. "We live on the reservation by choice, because it's what is best for our family. Jim is a member of the Tobacco Society, like his father was. They're in charge of keeping the tobacco garden on the reservation, because that plant is sacred to us. Cora gets to learn the language and culture and history of her tribe, and to know her many relatives. And I get to be on the land that I love."

In the truck, Josie asked, "Should we stop by the press and say hello to Jim?" Granma said that it "would be nice," and Cora asserted that we should "bring him something," so we stopped at a convenience store. Josie, Granma, and I waited while Cora darted in, hands in flight, to buy a candy bar and a newfangled drink comprised of nothing found in nature, which fairly fluoresced from within its bottle. "I bet Dad's never had this one before," she said, exhaling one long excited breath. "He'll love it."

I supposed Cora was probably right. Observing Jim's eating habits had been a revelation of sorts for me, especially after Dad's diet of Dorals and Maker's Mark with a splash of water, and Simon's strict and skimpy vegan regimen, and Jack Dolce's decadent but streamlined steamed oyster habit. Jim's tastes were comprehensive. He accepted and consumed all. Nothing was off limits, and not all of it was nutritious. He ate everything, from store-bought cold cuts to homemade pemmican, from fiberless loaves of airy white bread to Granma's wholesome deer-and-prairie-turnip stew, from tepid TV dinners to the thirty-minute meals he and I prepared together, from sugary sodas to tea made with wild mint plucked from the prairie, from black coffee to buttermilk by the glassful, from sunflower seeds out of Josie's garden to potato chips shining with grease. And still he embodied absolute health from the ends of his short black hair to the tips of his toes. Though he wasn't plump, he seemed stuffed with vitality. He had a health radiance, I thought, as the buildings passing outside the truck windows ushered us closer to the press. Of course, I kept my observations of Jim, his vertical furrow, his hands, and his radiance all to myself. It was like what the nuns in CCD always told us about Mary, how she treasured things away in her heart, and pondered them. I pondered.

"WHOA, WHAT'S THIS?" JIM BOOMED, holding his beverage up for examination. Behind him, an enormous black printing press—so huge that it filled an entire warehouse—spat out pile after pile of colorful pages. I smelled metal, ink, sweat, and trees. Jim's coworker that day was an obvious neophyte who seemed barely out of high school, and who navigated the churning machinery of the press with the lost, gangling air of recently foaled livestock. He stared at us from a distance with the same sort of gaze I had seen on so many startled animals.

"Better put these in!" Jim said. He reached into a bucket for four small boxes of earplugs and handed one to each of us. When he gave me mine he added, "I like your hat." Granma had trouble manipulating the squishy plugs, so Josie inserted them for her. She cupped Granma's wrinkly chin delicately in her palm. Jim hugged Cora, and when she stepped away the resultant ink spots on her clothes exactly mirrored the ones on his. "Thanks for the drink!" he said. "I'm thirsty. This looks exotic."

I stood apart as I so often did, watching. And, because he was so much on my mind, I tried to imagine what Simon Mellinkoff might think of it all—and specifically what he might think of Jim. I pictured them standing side by side, Simon in his sunglasses, his canvas slip-ons and black-and-white-checkered trousers, his silver hair, his frame slim from his meager meatless meals, and Jim in his work clothes of heavy canvas, his richly shining if evasive eyes, his smile, which he flashed between swallows of his daughter's sweet gift. I wondered what Simon, who had no close male friends, would think about Jim, who had no college education, no cause, and no cares as far as I could see, apart from the trio of dark-eyed females who stood before him with plugs in their ears.

"So what brings all you ladies to Billings today?" he asked.

"We came to get the stuff for my leggins!"

"Great!"

"They're going to be so gorgeous, Dad."

I approached the press and picked up one of the freshly printed pages, warm and damp as a newborn. It was an advertisement, meant to be tucked into a newspaper. "Be careful," Jim said into my ear. His voice penetrated the plug. "Don't stand too close." He lifted the paper from my hand, let out a groan, and shouted to his partner, who slouched and nodded at the ceiling while dreamily picking at his cheek. "Larry!" Jim yelled. The boy turned lackadaisically at Jim's voice. "Is this supposed to be navy?"

"What?"

"Blue!"

"No! Red!" Larry, bewildered, shifted his weight from one lanky leg to the other.

Then Jim, moving more swiftly than I'd ever seen, climbed a ladder to a platform at the top of the press and adjusted an assortment of levers that controlled the distribution of ink. Each time he moved one, a different color seeped onto his hands. I saw that the press was a kind of giantess that bled all over him. And that, I realized, was how he got so stained every day. Every day he tried to manage her, not to dominate her, because he never could, but just to steer her, to draw her hues out with great sensitivity, to lift her levers, to coax her to release her gold, her magenta, her green. And he came home multicolored, with an inevitable spot lodged in the crease between his eyes. From down below, I watched the papers change slowly as the press spat them out. The SALE SALE SALE heading transformed from dark blue to indigo to purple. Then it began to blush.

"Margie!" Jim yelled to me. "How's it look?"

"What?"

"What color is it now?"

"Getting rosy."

He waited a few moments, tinkered with the levers. "Now?"

"It's getting rosier."

"Now?"

"Red . . . pretty red. It's red now! Beautiful!" I was stirred by what seemed like a symbolic transformation. There was something magic in it, and Jim had been the magician. And the roses of his mother's apron, which had shrunk into such tightly closed buds a week before, bloomed open again.

He descended the ladder. "It's a good thing you came over here, or I might not have caught that." He jerked a thumb toward his partner. "And that one sure wouldn't have." Larry was robotically throwing stacks of too-blue papers into a waste bin.

"What happened, Dad?" Cora asked. She took a bite out of the candy bar she had yet to present to him.

"Margie just helped me out."

Cora was silent for a moment, chewing. Then she said, "Yeah, she helped me out at the craft store, too. She picked out some good beads."

I bent my head in shyness, hoping my new hat would hide the thrill in my eyes.

DAYS LATER, GRANMA GUIDED CORA as she practiced decorating scraps of fabric with perfect pink petals of beads. Once she grew adept, they would work together to create the new leggings. "We want you to help," Granma told me.

"Me? What can I do? I don't know how to do this stuff."

"Well, how can that be, honey? We know you can sew."

"Yeah. We've seen all those crazy dresses you've made," said Cora.

"Have you beaded before?" Granma asked.

"Beaded? No . . ." I recalled my courses at the Crafts Complex, where it seemed I had done everything but bead.

"Cora, go get your amulet to show Margie."

Cora appeared with a turtle that fit in the palm of her hand, made with seed beads in deep oceanic shades of green and blue and brown. It was glossy, dappled, pebbly to the touch. "See, this is a good example of the kind of beading we do," Granma explained. "We sew the beads by hand right onto the material, to make a dense pattern." With considerable ceremony, Cora placed the turtle into my hand. It was light, yet there was a kind of buzzing energy to it, a mysterious substantiality.

"What's inside this?" I asked. "I mean, what gives it dimension? So that it's not just flat?"

"It's my umbilical cord amulet," Cora said. "My umbilical cord is in it." My stomach tumbled in surprised delight. "The cord that connected me to my mom when I was born. They saved it and they made it into this. Who made it, Granma?"

"Me and Josie."

"I wear it at certain times. Like when I dance."

I wondered about our cord—mine and Rasha's. What had become of it on that day when I—too small, too well positioned— swam out and she lost all her blood? There had been no magician there to adjust a lever, to slow her outpour. Now I could see more clearly the source of Cora's disconcerting confidence, which so intimidated me. She was tethered. She came from a place where the line that links a girl to her mother is preserved, and worn when she dances on the earth—a place where she always knows who she is and where she comes from, because they set the information aside for her, they sew it up safely after her birth.

BY MID-JULY THE HEAT ON THE PRAIRIE actually made a sound, a subtle hum, like the electric hum of the streetlamps that stood over the hill houses back home, like the hardworking hum of the ice-cream cooler at Gelato Amore into which Jack Dolce was surely reaching the faceless Virgin Mary of his left arm while I, a thousand miles north, sweltered. It was audible under Jim's musical hum when he tinkered with the Pronghorn. It was the sound of some invisible burning, some hot internal effort, and it was also the sound of myself, for I lived in an anxious state, always waiting, always wondering about when I might leave.

I was beginning to think I had hidden for a long enough "while," though exactly where I would go I did not know. Bumble's latest missive suggested that I "stand by." He'd written to say he was in conversation with a friend in New York who might be able to provide me with a part-time job at a bakery and a couch so I could find my footing and start, as Bumble had termed it, "from scratch." But I wasn't sure about the Big Apple. And I had yet to pen a letter in response to Simon's lengthy confession, over which I was still mulling. I sometimes murmured to myself in a confounded tone that drew an inquisitive gaze from Cora.

Jim's Pronghorn was slowly becoming complete. There were fewer and fewer parts scattered outside of her with every passing week. Now only ten or twelve pieces lay on the grass, waiting to be tucked into their right places, where they could whirr and purr and pass juices and propel her forward over the hot grass. All summer, Jim had worked on her steadily, most every weekend, humming to himself and marking his shirts with oil. He lay on his back and looked up into her underbelly, or stood and stared into her opened hood with an absorbed expression.

One steamy Saturday he took a break to visit with Cora and me on the porch where we wilted. My new navy baseball cap had gone mysteriously missing, and even under the metal awning there was no real respite from the sun's blaze. Granma was flushed and breathless and had decided to lie down after break-fast. "How are you two holding up over here?" Jim asked.

"Hot." Cora looked up from *The World of Math*, which she had opened on her lap. Her glasses were foggy and her face was pink.

"How's the Pronghorn?" I asked. Through my sunglasses, I watched him wipe his hands on his pants, on his strong straight legs. Even in the heat his signature health radiance was aglow. He had a persistent succulence. All the nutrients in the meal we had prepared together the night before—Confetti Salad of Pasta and Vegetables—deepened the plum color of his lips and shone out of his clear eyes. Sometimes, looking sneakily at Jim, I recalled the images of snug sleeping babies that had always been part of the fantasies I'd constructed around the hill houses. In truth, I had never felt any specific desire to make babies with anyone. But when I looked at Jim in all his unwavering wholesomeness, which was evident to lesser degrees in both Granma, his progeni-tor (with her girlishly round cheeks and rich voice), and Cora, his progeny (with her fluttering hands and explosive laugh), I under-stood the impulse to reproduce. Jim's body held a beauty in it, one that wanted to be made flesh again and again.

"Aw, she's making progress, but there's still work to be done."

"Where did you get this car?" I asked.

"She belonged to my dad, and he passed her on to me. I drove her for a long time until I got my truck. I decided at winter's end to rebuild her engine and fix her up. In a few years, I'll pass her on to Cora. What do you think about that, Cor?"

Cora could only offer a parched "Hmp."

Jim looked sympathetic. "What do you say," he said. "Should we go for a swim?"

Cora slammed shut her book and rose. "I don't have a bathing suit," I said. Jim averted his face completely.

"We'll find you something," Cora said. "Come on." She tugged at my hand. "It's the most fun."

WE WOKE GRANMA AND DROVE to a place on the Little Bighorn River. The hum was inaudible there. The only sounds were the hurried whispers of the water, the wind ruffling the leaves of the cottonwood trees that stood all along the bank, and the papery rustling of the cattails, whose slender stalks were capped in brown, furry cylinders that broke apart to release soft tufts into the air as if surrendering to the heat.

Cora immersed herself and moved through the water sleek and straight as a muskrat, with just her head poking up above its greenish surface. Her movements made only the faintest of ripples, and they radiated away from her in rhythmic rings.

Jim laughed when he entered the river. His splashy swimming reminded me of a cacophonous and tuneless band. Still, he managed to stay afloat. Then he dove down and disappeared. He was gone for so long I began to feel worried, and to stare unseeing into the opaque depths. When he finally surfaced, his eyes had a sleepy look, and his smile was enormous. "Brrrufff," he said, shaking his head like a delighted dog.

I slid in shyly, wearing one of Jim's black T-shirts. Once wet, it hung almost to my knees. The river had a fertile smell of mud, moss, fish, ducks, and the slick green plants on the banks. A rash of gooseflesh spread over my arms and, grimacing, I slowly sank down until the water reached my chin. I stood still for a few moments and savored the blood-stirring sensation of the chill. Soon I wasn't cold anymore and began an aimless half hop, half swim. When my feet no longer reached the bottom, I quickly moved back to a place where they did. Once, a blue dragonfly paused on my shoulder and sipped the droplets there. I tipped my head back and felt the water climb, slow and delicious, up the back of my scalp, soaking my hair, and I sucked in my breath at the sweetness of it.

Granma sat on the bank beneath a cottonwood. She pulled back the Velcro straps of her sneakers and slipped her feet out. Then she peeled off her socks and laid them side by side on the grass like a pair of freshly caught fish. From my place in the water, I saw that the soles of her feet were a pale brown color that darkened to deep rose at the balls and heels. Her left sole bore a small, leaf-shaped birthmark, and it seemed fitting for the part of her body that came in frequent contact with the earth to be thus embellished. She wiggled and spread out her toes girlishly before reaching for a ball of yarn ("Booties," she had told me in the truck, "for a friend's baby in Lodge Grass") and her needles. The needles (aquamarine metal ones from the American flag pencil box) glinted in the sun.

All was quiet for a long time. Then Jim snuck up alongside Cora, who was absorbed in swimming, and scooped her swiftly into his arms so she was cradled. "Dad!" She pretended to protest but her face was aglow. She curled her hands into tiny fists and hammered Jim all over his chest.

"Oh, you want to be free?" he asked.

"Yes!"

"Okay!" Jim tossed her high into the air above the water. She screeched with delight before landing with a splash. Then, thrilled, she swam immediately back to her father and piggy-backed him, encircling his throat with her arms.

"Dad!"

I turned my face away from their display. Something in it hurt me even as I smiled.

Cora shouted in the magisterial manner of a river queen, "Get her! Get her!"

"Oh no," I said, shrinking backward toward the bank. Jim approached with a devilish "Mwa-ha-ha-ha," and Cora, clinging to his back, cried, "Yes! Yes!" I made a quick dart to the left but was no match for Jim, who appeared so clumsy in the water yet moved with a secret kind of stealth. At the prospect of being touched by him I panicked and made a dash to the right, but in a moment he had both hands curled around my waist and I screamed. Cora cheered when he lifted me out of the river, and I felt prettier than I ever had under the rambunctious gazes of that daughter and dad in my long saggy shirt, my soaked hair and wet, shining face, and she cheered louder still when he dropped me back in. And so the afternoon passed.

We climbed out of the river and sat warming ourselves and grinning without obvious cause. Granma broke from her knitting to walk along the muddy bank and pull the shoots off the cattails. "These will make a good salad for us tonight," she said.

"What about the wild plums?" Cora called to her. "Are they ready?" Granma squeezed one purple globe hanging from a gnarled shrub. She said they were not.

"It's been so hot," Cora said. "They should be ready by now."

"You forgot, Granddaughter, it's the moon that ripens these. The moon is watery, and it makes water in the plums."

What is this place? I thought, walking back into the river and diving down into it. What is this place where everything is all of a piece, where tobacco seeds and stars are linked, and the moon ripens plums? What is this place and who are these people, I wondered, touching the silt at the river's bottom—until a child, a mischievous muskrat, swam close to tickle my ribs and sent bubbles out of her laughing mouth.

We drank cold wild mint tea from jelly jars and ate the sandwiches we had packed. Then we lay, spent from swimming, with our backs on the earth. Cora, aloof again, put her glasses back on and plopped her head in Granma's lap. Granma talked about the importance of avoiding otters while swimming in the river. "We Crows have always known never to let an otter brush alongside you. It would be very bad if that happened," she explained in her soft voice. Cora closed her eyes. "Very bad for your future." Jim nodded in assent.

I imagined the sudden slinky feeling of being brushed by an otter, and I believed that such an encounter would be ominous. In this place, where all aspects of creation seemed tied together, every living thing had its own significance within the system of symbols and stories through which people had once understood their lives. And some people, like Granma, still understood. The Crow world was a complex one. It wasn't that otters were inherently bad—no animals were—but that brushing alongside one in a river could be.

We heard a drumming on the leaves of the trees, one that started slow and gentle and then grew stronger, and soon drops reached our heads and shoulders. "Rain!" Cora cried.

"Ah, thank you, *Iichihkbaalia*,* we need this." Granma tilted her head back and let her face get wet.

"Let's pack up," Jim said. "It's really going to come down." We gathered all that we had brought, and we were happy rushing around the bank, laughing like children being chased. By the

---

* God

time we reached the truck, with towels and jelly jars and cattail shoots in our arms, we were soaked. We were a sticky, shivering foursome on the drive back. Big, bluish veins of lightning ripped through the sky, and we kept the radio off to hear the thunder. This is what I know, I thought. I know this place and these people. What had that other life been?

It was very confusing, the way my thoughts tipped so steeply in one direction and then another. I remembered the old-fashioned scale I'd noticed during my last visit to Dad. He had pulled it from the attic and placed it on top of the television set. He'd dropped the keys to the Skylark in one of the brass pans, and I'd absently transferred them to the other and watched the scale tip. My thoughts and feelings were similarly vacillating. One minute I envisioned my departure from the reservation; the next, Crow Country's charms captured me in a velvety embrace (the velvet of river water and cattail) from which I didn't want to escape. But I was fatigued, I supposed, from all the heat and the swimming.

THAT NIGHT, JIM AND I COOKED AGAIN. I had chosen a recipe for Pot Pie with Peas from *Three Hundred Thrifty Thirty-Minute Meals!*, and we'd decided to make two, filling one with some of the buffalo meat that was stored in the freezer and another with only vegetables. With Granma's guidance, we would make the crusts using wild turnip flour.

After the thunderstorm, the prairie was fragrant, and the innumerable droplets that lingered on everything (the yellow truck, the Pronghorn and her parts, Belly's fur, each blade of grass) refracted the rays of the reemerging sun. I stood, dried and dressed, in front of the open kitchen window, waiting for Jim and watching the curtain blow in and out like something breathing.

"Did I get all the right ingredients?" he asked. He looked scrubbed and shiny and wore a fresh white T-shirt.

"Yes, it's all here," I answered.

For a full minute, we stood and stared at the food, which I had spread upon the countertop. A spider, tiny and brown, crawled out of the droopy green carrot tops, paused, and made his way down the cabinet to the floor. We watched him go. The bright label on a can of mushrooms cried "Low Sodium!" at me six or seven times. Jim peered at the recipe and cleared his throat. "Well," he said. Again, I heard the faint shake in his voice, the same one that was there the night he'd brought the cookbook home and handed it to me. When he picked up a potato for washing, it disappeared for a moment in his hand, just as my own hand had the one and only time he had touched it in greeting. We got started.

We had prepared six meals together and in recent weeks had agreed upon a kind of unspoken choreography. I had learned to anticipate when he would move right or left, or forward or back, and he, it seemed, had learned to anticipate the same in me. So we no longer collided while we cooked.

"Did you used to do much cooking?" Jim asked. "Before you came here and we put you to work in the kitchen?" He smiled.

"Oh, sometimes." In Simon's spotless kitchen, the curtains had not breathed. To mention it—the meals, little Annette, the mourning doves—was pointless. "I was pretty busy. With the Operation."

"Yeah, I can imagine. What was it called again? The group you were leading?"

"Operation H.E.A.R.T." For the first time, I felt self-conscious saying it. "It stands for Humans Enforcing Animal Rights Today."

"That makes sense." Jim nodded. "You know, I think I understand. About the animals and all. My dad—"

"Ray?"

"Yeah! I guess Mom's told you about him. He was the greatest. He used to tell me that animals are our relatives, that they have things to give us and teach us, that we should pay attention to them and respect them. We're not supposed to hold ourselves above. And I think he was right. Of course, he did hunt sometimes. And so do I."

"Oh?" I cut through a carrot. My scale tipped again. Tomorrow, maybe. Maybe tomorrow would be the day to go. Of course, there was the problem of a car.

"We try, Mom and I, to be respectful. Most of the meat we eat comes from animals we've hunted ourselves. Once a year, I take a buffalo. Josie hunts deer. We share what we get with family and friends, and we use it all. The buffalo meat we're using tonight, it's from the one I got last summer. I hope it doesn't bother you too much—"

"N-no—I mean—I grew up eating meat with my Dad, and it was all straight from the supermarket. You know, the flesh of some poor animal who had led a horrific existence on a factory farm. At least you are sometimes willing to . . ."

"Kill it myself?"

"Well, yeah . . ." In truth, I hated it, to think of his hands hurting anything.

"Do you want to come to the buffalo hunt in a couple of weeks? Granma, Cora, and Josie are all going to be there."

"Oh, I don't think I could."

Jim and I were quiet for a long time. Then he said, "We've been doing it for centuries. It's part of who we are—"

"I understand."

The air between us was pulled into a taut ribbon. The curtain in the window hung straight and flat. The spider, who had been taking his time traversing the linoleum, froze. What was it? He didn't like me after all. I didn't like him. He appeared to radiate care and gentleness, but he killed animals. No, I would not stay much longer. I would leave before that hunt.

We worked for a long time in silence. I ignored the cubes of blood-red meat thawing in a bowl. Then Jim spoke again, cautiously.

"So, what did you *do*, anyway, if you don't mind my asking? Before you came here, what did you do to upset the feds?" He was wondering just how much trouble I was in, I thought, and how much longer it would take me to conjure the courage to leave. My face grew hot and my eyes welled, just as they had on that root-digging day when I'd told Granma I knew Jim didn't want me around. He chopped an entire stem of celery before I answered.

"I got caught," I said shakily, "talking to a crowd of people at a café called Gelato Amore about how to make an incendiary device—a firebomb. An undercover FBI agent in a newsboy cap"—Jim raised his eyebrows—"was there, and he recorded me on his cell phone."

Jim shook his head. "Oh, that's so ridiculous," he said. I couldn't tell if he was referring to my public talk about how to start a fire or to Agent Fox with his cell phone. I looked at him with big wet eyes. "Oh, no, I mean, that they recorded you. It's just so tricky. Is this upsetting you? You don't have to talk—"

"They—the feds—called it 'teaching the making or use of an explosive.' But there's other stuff, too, that they could charge me with down the road. Before that, I set fire to a restaurant that specialized in wild game. They served peacocks and—"

"*What?*" Jim stopped chopping. "Did you do much damage?"

"It burned to the ground."

"Wow, Margie. That's serious. I can see why they're eager to cart you off to jail. But I'm glad you've managed to stay out, so far. Jail's not a good place to be. And I can't picture you there at all." Could he picture me anywhere, I wondered, if he had never so much as looked directly at me? "My ex is there," he added.

"Your ex-wife?"

"We weren't married. Well, maybe we were, in the Indian way. For a while. But she had moved on long before she went to prison. Cora's mom, Isabelle."

"Oh. Cora has mentioned her. Once." I thought of the peach pit stashed in Cora's jewelry box, watched over by the ballerina. Its surface had grown quite smooth, its inner seed had been removed, and it was starting to resemble a ring. "She came from Georgia?"

"Yeah. Cherokee. You know, they're supposed to be the most civilized of all us Indians?" Jim let out a mocking laugh, but the line between his eyes deepened. For the first time all day, I noticed a stubborn speck of red ink tucked in the crease, impervious to our afternoon swim. It gave him an injured look, and my left ovary ached. And where, where was the spot where that vertical line and his horizontal grin met? Cora would likely pinpoint the place exactly, without even offering her textbook. "It is utterly simple," she would say, peering over her starry spectacles. "Just imagine them as two perpendicular lines and visualize the point where they intersect." But I couldn't allow myself to know for sure. "Well," he went on, "Isabelle was not civilized. Isabelle was wild."

"How wild?"

"Wild enough to keep making and using and selling methamphetamines after she had already been arrested and jailed because of it twice. Wild enough to walk away from Cora without a second thought."

I remembered the resignation in Cora's voice on the day she'd acknowledged that no letter had been waiting for her at the post office. "Why was she so wild?"

"I don't know. I didn't know her that well, to be honest. When we met, we were just seventeen. We were both drunk, and we stayed that way for the duration of our relationship. But I never got into drugs like she did. I'm grateful for that."

"How did you meet her?"

"She came out here one summer for Crow Fair. She was with a bunch of friends, on a road trip. Then she just stayed. We had Cora within a year. Isabelle was my first real sweetheart."

"And after her?" I wanted to know how many sweethearts his hands had known, his hands that might have cared but also hurt.

"After she went to jail the last time, Cora and I moved out here from Crow Agency to be with my mom. We've visited her some, though not recently."

Either Jim misunderstood or pretended to misunderstand my question about sweethearts. Was it that he'd had so many he was too abashed to discuss them? "What about you?" he asked. "You have any exes in jail?" He grinned. "Wouldn't surprise me."

"No. I'm the only jail-bound person I know," I said, thinking of brilliant and brokenhearted Anna, who had wanted to see Simon punished, and who had not even known there would be a me, a lonely bicycle pusher with the flu in a sundress covered in stalks of wheat.

"She went from She-Bird to jailbird," Jim intoned in a dramatic TV voice, and we laughed. "Aw, I think you'll be fine," he said. "I'm glad you have a safe place here with us. And I hope you don't feel like you have to be in any kind of hurry to leave," he added.

My hand grew damp as I twisted a stiff can opener. Jim hummed and turned a turnip root to fine granules against a grater.

"I know my mom is very, very glad to have you around," he said. "And Cora, too."

"Cora? I'm not so sure . . ."

"She is. Don't be fooled. It's just her way to act a little prickly sometimes. She's really tender. She'd probably be sweeter if she thought you were staying forever." I nearly lost the can opener. "Wait till you see her do the Fancy Shawl Dance at Crow Fair. It will break your heart, it's so beautiful."

"How come you aren't going to dance during Crow Fair?" I asked. "Or are you?"

"No, I'm not. I don't dance anymore."

"Why not?"

"I gave it up after my dad died twelve years ago. I gave it up as a way to honor him, because it was something I really loved. But that's also when I started drinking. I traded a good habit for a bad one."

"Was it bad? The drinking?"

Jim nodded. "Oh yeah. I drank to drown my grief."

"I know somebody like that," I said. I missed him. I missed him so much, and I had left him alone in a house turned upside down with nothing but photo albums for company—one containing some baby teeth and a miniature gold ring. "How did you stop?"

"With my mom's help. She never talks about it, but she knows a lot about healing. And after a certain point it really had become a physical illness more than anything else. I wanted to stop because of Cora." Had Dad ever wanted to stop because of me, I wondered? Was that why he had cried during our dance?

"What kind of dancing did you do?"

"Oh, Grass Dance. I was just about to start Fancy Dancing when he passed. Ah!" Jim stopped grating. He balled up one hand and covered it with the other. "Mom and I made all my regalia," he added.

"Are you okay?"

"Yeah, it's nothing. Little scrape."

I could almost picture him dancing, dancing in the same way he swam, big and splashy, but precise, too. If he danced now, I would be able to anticipate his movements, the way I had learned to predict them beside the stove, before the sink. "Did you love it?" I asked, but Jim misheard me.

"Yeah, I really loved him." He moved his hands apart, and I saw the smear of blood.

"Oh! What happened?"

"I shredded my knuckle on that grater. It's all right."

"Here." I reached my hand out, touched his. "Sorry," I said.

"For what?"

I held his hand under the faucet. The blood ran off of him and spiraled down the drain. Several short strips of skin hung off the knuckle. Underneath them, I could see, he was pink, glossy, like the interior of an oyster shell.

"What is that song you're always humming?" I asked. "I feel like I recognize it."

"I'm always humming?"

"When you work on the Pronghorn. And other times . . . just a few minutes ago . . ."

"Oh, I guess it must be that old song by Karen Dalton, a Cherokee singer from the sixties."

"Yes! I used to know someone who liked her."

"That song—'*in the evening, in the evening, darling, it's so hard to tell who's going to love you the best*'—it's always in my head." Jim's voice, usually so deep and strong, was quavering and uncertain when he sang.

"It's a nice song." I wondered if Jack Dolce really had been the hinge between one life and another. There was so much he had predicted, without knowing it.

I laid Jim's loosened skin back over the exposed places. "Ouch," I said. "You need a bandage."

"I don't think we have any." He looked intently down the drain, as if searching for a wayward spoon, a stray bean.

"You don't?"

"Uh-uh."

"Well." I pulled three paper towels off the roll on the counter. I twisted them and wrapped them around his hand, tying the two ends together in a knot. A few rosy blots bloomed through, then stopped. They stopped the way Rasha's poppies never had.

"Thanks," he said.

"It was nothing."

We stood for a few minutes looking out the window. The sun began to sink, and the curtain fluttered up again, and the air moved.

GRANMA WANTED TO GO OUT and gather chokecherries. "It's been hot, and the *baáchuutaale* are ripening. I saw some the other day, like pretty round rubies." She took up her flour sack. "This will be much easier than getting turnip roots," she said. "We just pick." We left Cora and Josie at the table, surrounded by beads and deerskin, hard at work on the leggings and red-cheeked in the heat.

"Get extra," Josie said. "My birthday's coming, and I want chokecherry cake!" And I understood the reason for her leonine carriage and proud, pretty ways, for she had, like Rasha, been born in the Leo time of late July.

We weren't far past the chickens when Granma began pointing out all kinds of plants we could eat, growing right under our feet. "There's burdock," she said. "And over here is some Indian lettuce—those thunderstorms and all this heat have made everything so lush for us—here, try a dandelion." Granma broke the spiky yellow flower from its stem and handed it to me. "Go ahead. It's good, I promise." It tasted like its color—bright and sweetly tart.

"Mmm, not bad."

"We eat the leaves, too. They're so nutritious. We'll get some of these greens on our way home and make a salad with them tonight."

"It's really wonderful," I said, "that all this is here."

"I know," Granma replied. "Can't you feel her throbbing in every living thing?"

The fuzz on my arms rose, but I didn't know just why. "Who do you mean?"

"Your mother," she said, looking straight ahead. "And mine."

I was quiet. I knew Granma didn't mean her own birth mother, who had been lost to her, or my Rasha of the red poppies, of whom I'd never spoken.

"This is what I've been knowing you would understand, honey," Granma continued. "It's why I wanted you to come stay with us, and to come with me on these walks. When I heard about you and what you were doing with the animals, I wanted to share it with you. Share *her* with you."

I remembered the tendrils of the gourd vines that had grown in the Community Garden where I'd sat during many mournful Middletown nights, how they had reached out so intelligently toward what was nearest to them and coiled themselves around it in the most accurate of embraces. I considered my lifelong Mary musings—the tendrils might have been strands of Mary's hair. And now Granma was talking about a "her"—a mother who throbbed in every living thing.

I told her about what the CCD sisters had said. The mother of God, they had called her. "But I have always thought of her as the mother of all creation."

"Yes, Margie, I feel the same, that there is one mother for all living things. We call her *Káalixaalia,** and she never stops giving birth." I looked around us and of course it was true. The prairie,

---

* Old Woman

which to my unaccustomed eyes had initially seemed so stingy
with its beauties, was almost unfathomable in its abundance of
animal, vegetable, and mineral offerings—the soil, the stones,
the grasses and the occasional trees, the plants and their roots,
the prairie dogs, birds, snakes, antelope, and deer, the insects, the
river and the cattails. "All of it just keeps unfurling out of her,
always," Granma said, "so long," she added, "as we care for
her and what she births."

She looked hot and out of breath—partly, I thought, because
our subject so excited her. A few strands of her spun silver hair
had escaped her bun and hung around her face in a girlish way,
an Evelyn way.

"That's why, honey, when I take roots, or berries, or any plants
at all, I'm careful not to take too much. And I always thank her.
Jim and Josie are the same when they hunt. We can't just do
whatever we want to her. This is what I want Cora to understand,
and remember, and to share when she goes into that other world
off the reservation."

Granma drew her wrist across her damp forehead. "Think of
this: if people had never started viewing animals as strangers
instead of relatives, as below themselves on some"—she paused—
"some imaginary ladder, then there would be no reason today for
you and your friends to try to save them or fight for their rights.
But people forgot that they and the animals—along with everything else—are so interconnected."

"You mean," I said, "like all of a piece? Like stars and tobacco,
or the moon and plums?"

"Yes! All these lives—from the littlest plants to the biggest
people—are knitted together. It's just the same as what I do with
my yarn, you see? I make a sweater for a baby. It has a body, it
has arms, it has a hood, it has a collar, all these different parts,
and I make it all with one long, long strand. Yes, I knit it up.

"And this world, Margie, is just like that. *She's* the yarn. She knits us up, connects us, holds us together. That's why we're never alone, never separate from each other, or from anything that lives."

We walked in silence for a few minutes. "What sorts of things were you doing in your group, honey?" Granma asked.

"Well, some of it was kind of silly, to be honest . . ." I hesitated, thinking of how we'd released the birds from Azar's, liberated lobsters from restaurant tanks, and dumped purple paint on fur coats. I knew how inconsequential those campaigns would seem to most people, yet my heart had been in all of them. I told Granma about some of our exploits.

"It really meant something to you, didn't it?"

"Yeah," I said. "It really did."

"And I think you were right—are right—to feel the way you do about animals. You know," Granma's voice took on a tone of fascination, as if she were recounting a particularly provocative episode of her favorite soap, "a magpie once told my aunt her children were in danger. The kids had made their own raft, not a very good one, and were using it in the river, and the magpie called to my auntie and told her about it. Sure enough, when she went to them, the raft had tipped over, and the littlest ones were underneath. She arrived just in time because they couldn't swim. And, do you know," she continued in a low, confiding way, "the prairie dogs helped my grandmother after my mother got so sick with drinking and was lost to us all? Grandmother was sad, so sad. The prairie dogs came to her in a vision, and they gave her a message that healed her heartbreak and helped her to move forward. She never told me what they said, but the prairie dogs became her helpers after that."

"I believe it," I said. "I think animals have so much to share with us, but most of the time we're too proud or preoccupied to listen."

We reached a thicket of tangly trees adorned with hundreds

of scarlet jewels. "Here, oh my," Granma murmured, "these look good, don't they?

"But that old understanding," she went on, "has really almost disappeared, replaced by a very different way of thinking. I first encountered it in the boarding school, this other way of looking at the world. You can't imagine how foreign it was to me." She shook her head. "When I was out in the city, working, it was just how everyone thought—that animals and the earth are ours to do with as we wish. I never could get used to it. And nowadays, honey," she said, popping a chokecherry into her mouth, "even among most Indians, I'm kind of a freak." She laughed. "There's not enough connection with the animals or the plants around the rez today. My son and I, we're not perfect, but we still try to keep some of the old traditions."

Granma hooked her arm over a branch. "When we see animals as brothers and sisters, we can never abuse them. I'll bet it was hard for you to see any kind of sadness or abuse. I can tell how much your sensitivity has been a burden to you. You just ache under the weight of it. But it doesn't have to be that way forever, Margie. Sensitivity can be a gift, too. You just need to find the right way to live, the right way for yourself."

"I have no idea what that is," I said. "Or where." I reached for a few cherries. They were firm and cool in my hand. "I want a feeling of home, but I don't know how to get it."

"Part of that is not having your mom. I don't know where she is, and you don't have to tell me, but I know she's not around," Granma said. "That's from one motherless girl to another," she added. "You might feel lost because you don't have her—but that's what I want you to know, honey. You have another mother always with you." She tapped the ground with her puffy sneaker. "This beautiful woman. Go to her, go to her creations, for anything you need, if you are sick, or sad, or when you are happy."

"But having a real human mother helps—" I felt the old

ladybug who, since her first appearance on a rose corsage, had been the frequent reminder of Rasha's absence. She began to stir behind my eyes, and I tossed a few cherries into my mouth to distract myself. They were so sour they made the tears come faster, and I wondered how Granma could gobble so many of them in their raw, unsweetened state.

"It does help, sometimes, but how many people do you know who don't have theirs, and they go on? I don't have mine, Cora doesn't have hers . . ."

I considered Annette Mellinkoff, whose mother had died of cancer, and Jack Dolce, whose mother had abandoned him to run away with the travel trailer salesman from Tucson, and Raven, whose mother had perished in the paragliding accident. There were millions of us.

"But Cora—at least she has that umbilical cord." The amulet inspired enormous yearning in me. Its very existence had sucked the mystique out of every one of my under-the-bathroom-sink Rasha relics.

"We all have another umbilical cord," Granma said, "one we can't see, that links us to the mother of all mothers. It can't be severed. And everything we do to her, we do to ourselves." I squeezed a chokecherry until it turned pulpy in my fingertips. I knew Granma was right, and I no longer felt so unorthodox for seeing Mary as a symbol of the earth and all its features, the way I had since I was a girl gazing at the ceiling in church, or for leaving the oyster shells as offerings at Mary's marble feet back in Little Italy while Jack Dolce stood and shook his head. And I realized what it was he had been missing. He already knew so much about living down close to the earth. But he didn't know who or what she was. He didn't know that she was beating in his own heart, that she animated him, that she was the roses in his cheeks, that she was the love—the feminine love—he longed for. I saw that once he understood, he could have her face filled in, and he, in all his bright-hearted brilliance, would be whole.

Granma glanced into her flour sack. We had filled it with a mass of red fruits. "*Look* at this!" she exclaimed. "Yum!"

Back at the house, I wrote him a letter with no return address. "You must fill in the face of your Mary," I wrote. And I saw why Jack Dolce had so captivated me. We were twins of a sort, alike in that the very thing we had been craving was right beneath our feet—there, all along.

THAT EVENING, CORA WENT OUTSIDE and practiced her shawl dancing in preparation for Crow Fair. There were lots of different kinds of dances, she had told me. "Fancy Shawl Dancers," she'd explained, pushing her glasses back professorially, "must keep their feet and their shawls constantly in motion." She had already shown me her shawl. It was bright pink, emblazoned with roses, and trimmed in long white fringe. "See, it billows out when I dance. I'm supposed to look like a butterfly! Escaping its cocoon!"

Josie had left behind a CD of the Hawk Heart Singers, a local drum group. Cora inserted the CD into her portable player, donned her headphones, and rehearsed on the grass.

She used the small knitted blanket from the back of Granma's recliner as her practice shawl. An assemblage of multi-colored squares, it looked like a whirling stained-glass window. While Granma, Jim, and I watched, Cora spun and fluttered and reminded us, yelling over the drumming in her ears, to imagine her in her regalia, in her "real" shawl, her flared skirt, her moccasins, and her leggins. "Remember!" she shouted. "I won't be dressed like this! I'll move differently in my moccasins!"

The sun began to sink and the Bighorns stood blue and benevolent against a pink sky. Grasshoppers had recently come to Crow Country, and dozens of them, delirious from heat and hunger, leapt up with each of her footfalls.

AFTER DINNER, CORA DISAPPEARED behind the closed door of
her bedroom to continue practicing. Granma wanted to take a
long shower. "My hands are so stiff from all that picking today."
She held them up for us, and her fingers resembled the knotty
branches of the chokecherry trees, the joints bulbous from years
of knitting, picking, digging, and, in her secretary days, typing.
"The hot water will help."

"Come back when you're done," Jim said. "I'll rub them for
you."

Jim and I were left alone in the kitchen, with only the grasshoppers outside to supplement our occasional words. We washed
the dinner dishes, put them away. He had come home with a real
adhesive bandage on his wound, which was almost healed, but
after we washed the dishes he peeled it off. "I figure the fresh air
will do it some good," he said, and I blinked at the rawness of his
revealed skin.

Then, sliding shut the silverware drawer, he said, "I brought
you something." He stepped into the living room and returned
with a paper sack. I leaned against the sink. It wetted the back of
my shirt, but I couldn't seem to move. "It's a thank-you," he said,
"for fixing my hand."

"Oh, no, I didn't do anything."

"Yes. You did. You were very kind."

The paper sack crackled with my anticipation. Jim unveiled a
small orange, the first one I'd seen since leaving home.

"Oh, an orange—"

"—It's just an orange." Nerves pushed our words on top of
each other. "Reminded me of you," he said. "I imagine, being
from Southern California, you must miss having lots of good
oranges around all the time." His usually sonorous voice was the
softest and quietest I had ever heard it. "Here. Sit down."

The grasshoppers whirred. Jim broke into the skin of the

fruit, and its sunlit scent filled the house. He scooted his chair close to mine and then, before I knew what was happening, he slipped a segment into the space between my lips. I closed my eyes in shyness and surprise. I let it rest for a moment on my tongue, and its sweetness suffused my mouth. When I chewed and swallowed, he fed me again.

The entire orange disappeared that way. Each time I felt a piece gently nudging my top lip, I opened for it. I kept my eyes closed and rested my face in my hand, no longer sure if I was at home, or on the prairie, or if Jim's present had made them one and the same.

"It's gone," he said, and the shower shut off in the bathroom with a shudder that shook the house. I opened my eyes. Jim was smiling, looking out the window, and there wasn't any line at all between his eyes.

11 🌿 BUFFALO *(Bison bison)*

ON THE MORNING OF THE BUFFALO HUNT, Josie came to the house with an elderly woman, one who really resembled Granma in spite of the fact that her hair was colored and tidily coiffed, she wore slacks and a polka-dotted blouse, and she had on bright lipstick, which contrasted with what appeared to be a slightly sickly cast to her otherwise comely skin. When she came through the screen door she paused and looked around as if appraising a favorite place she had not seen for a long time.

"Ruby!" Granma said. She embraced the woman tightly.

Ruby was Granma's older sister. As Granma had explained to me, after their mother had been lost to them the two sisters had led very different lives, but had reconnected as grown women and become close. I could see it in the trusting way they leaned their soft bodies into each other.

"Sweetheart!" Ruby said. "I'm so glad to see you. I'm ailing, Evelyn. I thought I should come down here and ask you for some medicine. I said to myself, 'My sister, the root digger, I know she'll be able to help me.'"

"Of course, *basakáataa*.* What is it?" Granma and Ruby

---

*   big sister

walked hand in hand toward the kitchen, murmuring in Crow. Then Ruby spotted me, the stranger carefully embellishing Cora's Crow Fair leggings (after much guidance from Granma) with a single rosebud in the place where Cora's right knee would be, and her sunken eyes sparkled.

"Hello there," she said with a vivacious smile, giving her cane a twirl.

"Ruby," Granma said, "this is our friend Margie. She's visiting from California."

Ruby exhaled a long whistle. "Wooooo, California, eh? Mighty far away from home now, aren't you?" Turning to Granma she commented, "Oh, she's so pretty! I wish I'd been born in California." Granma spoke a few sentences in Crow to tell Ruby something about me, and the words, though foreign, sounded soft to my ears: *kalée . . . bíakalishte . . . báthe . . . táachiiate . . . dakáake.** Ruby nodded her head as if she comprehended a secret. She shot me a wink.

Jim emerged from his bedroom with a book warming in the crook of his arm. Ruby exclaimed, "Here he is! Young James. My, my," she clucked. "I can never believe this tall drink of water was once a chubby little boy following his dad around, always covered in dirt, always asking all kinds of questions— could never keep quiet."

Jim darted a glance my way and a deep blush spread over his face. "How are you, Auntie?"

"I've been better, son. But your mother is going to fix me up."

Granma said she and Ruby would need just a minute, "and then we can all"—she placed a hand on my shoulder—"go to the buffalo pasture."

I felt nauseous about the hunt. I looked at Jim. He had sat in a sweat lodge with Josie's brothers in Wyola the previous night, and his skin had a translucent gleam. He looked even more

---

* runaway . . . young woman . . . fragile . . . bright . . . bird

lambent than usual, alive and anticipatory—like the young James to whom Ruby had nostalgically referred. But he avoided my eyes, and I felt as though my looking at him sapped some of his boyish excitement, so I turned my face away. Something in my chest clamped closed when I saw him carry a rifle out to his truck.

I looked into the kitchen, where Granma opened the cupboard of mysteries below the silverware drawer, the one that I never disturbed. She pulled out several coffee cans and a few old greenish glass jars with metal lids. As Ruby confessed her complaints in a pained and plaintive whisper, Granma, the prairie apothecary, pulled a few unfamiliar roots and stringy plants out of those most common of containers.

I thought about medicine, how it had so many forms. There was the medicine men made, and the medicine the earth gave birth to—Granma was adept at using that kind. There was the medicine Rasha had studied, which had also been tied to the fruits of the earth, and resulted in an invisible kind of beauty. And there was the kind of medicine that Granma's mother had used, which had made her lost. It was the same kind Jim had used, too, and the kind in which I had also overindulged during the months of my Middletown malaise. And, for as long as I could remember, it had been Dad's medicine of choice.

I wondered if Granma could use her kind of medicine to heal Dad. A few days earlier, I had told Granma about him, about his Maker's Mark with a splash of water.

"I'VE KNOWN LOTS OF PEOPLE WHO TRIED to dull their pain with drinking," Granma had said, "even Jim. The problem is they end up creating more pain for themselves eventually, and plenty for those around them, too."

"But," I was quick to say, "I know he loved—loves—me."

I couldn't bear even the slightest hint of criticism to be directed
Dad's way. He was too defenseless in his crumbling house, in
his robe, with his sweetly swooping eyelids. He came to my mind
so clearly in all his broken beauty, his black hair, his Ivory-soap-
and-cigarettes scent, his green eyes. "Maybe you could help him,
if he could somehow meet you," I said. "Do you think you could
fix him?"

"He has to want it," Granma answered. And then, more
seriously, she added, "Don't romanticize me, honey. I don't
work magic. Anyone can do what I do. I used to be lost, too,
and feel disconnected from everyone and everything. I made a
choice to live close to the earth. I feel like I have more strength
here, hidden away on this patch of land, than I ever did anyplace
else. I get it from her. And from my prayers. It's yours for the getting, too. And you might be able to help your dad someday, if he
is ready."

WHEN THEY EMERGED FROM THE KITCHEN the sisters were smiling. "Okay," Granma said, "are we all set?" Cora and Josie came
out of the bedroom.

". . . never seen a ring like that before," Josie was saying.

"I want to wear it for Crow Fair, but I don't know if it will be
ready in time," Cora said.

Josie and Ruby followed us out to the buffalo pasture in the
big brown truck. On the drive, I was overwhelmed with dread.
Even though Granma explained, "We've lived in close relationship with the *bi'shee* since the beginning. They sustained us for
a long, long time. That's why the tribe keeps its own buffalo
on the reservation now, because they're sacred to us, and they
are a traditional food for us," and even though Cora beside me
knocked her pointy knees together in buffalo-excitement, I was
pale with misgivings.

I didn't know what I would do once we got to the pasture. Possibly I would be like Marilyn in *The Misfits* when Clark Gable and his gang capture the wild horses, and run far, far away from the hunt, and hurl anguished screams at Jim across the prairie, and call him a murderer. Possibly I would close my eyes, or be sick.

But I was going along because Granma had beseeched me—had been compelling me to come, in fact, for weeks—and because there was some promise implicit in her asking, some treasure tucked into the mellow timbre of her voice, a treasure that—underneath all my dread—I dared to hope might become mine.

When we arrived at the pasture, Josie split from us and drove off with Ruby toward her brothers' truck in the distance.

There were dozens of buffalo ambling over the grass. They looked like boulders covered in dense, shaggy coats of reddish brown. For a long while, we just drove slowly around them. They were the first buffalo I had seen in the flesh, and I was as awed by their stature as I was by their stillness. They impressed me with their unexpected air of peace, and their confidence and composure, which made each of them seem ages old. If our presence was a disruption to their contentment, they did not show it. They perfectly echoed the placidity of the prairie and seemed an integral part of it. Never before had the marriage between a place and a creature been so plain to me. I thought again, as I had that day in the river, about everything being all of a piece, knitted together, as Granma had said, with a single long strand.

"How about him?" Granma pointed, and Jim stopped the truck.

"Beautiful!" Cora exclaimed.

The buffalo was enormous. He watched us sideways out of his melting chocolate eye and breathed heavily through his nostrils. I was shocked to see a stripe of pink on the underside of his long gray tongue, which he revealed to us when he licked his nose—

a line of pink like a wound. It was as pink as Jim's underskin had been when he'd scraped his knuckles with the grater. He was so rumpled, so large, plodding, and dark. But his tongue with its pink stripe seemed to me to be the symbol of his secret sensitivity. That stripe hinted at his essential nature, and when it appeared, curling carelessly out of his mouth, there was something almost unbearably naked about it. It was the symbol of what was inside of him and, I thought, inside of everybody, inside every alive thing—a crushing softness, a bare beauty, a pure vulnerability beneath fur, skin, and skeleton. It was the most immediate representation I had ever seen of the quality that always made me ache when I perceived it in a person or animal. And when he showed it, my left ovary contracted like a hand closing.

Far away from us, Josie's brother fired at a buffalo from inside his truck, but Jim wanted to get out.

"Are you sure, Dad?"

"Yes, it'll be okay. Just stay behind me." We all stood on the grass. The grasshoppers jumped over our shoes.

I watched Jim. He blinked at the sight of the buffalo's striped tongue as if suddenly struck by its beauty. I thought he might lower his rifle, but he kept it raised, and then Jim's belly burst outward with a big breath. I sucked in my own, and held it.

AMONG HIS REAL ESTATE LISTINGS, Dad had once counted an ostentatious Spanish-style house with a black-bottomed swimming pool in its backyard. In one of his rare but characteristically romantic flashes of inspiration, he suggested we go swim in it one Saturday (the owners had already moved away) when he was done mowing our front lawn. And so, in the manner of two trespassing teenagers, we climbed, snickering sneakily, over the side gate—a needless maneuver, since Dad had a key to the front door. He lounged poolside in a plush chaise and sipped his

usual beverage, iced, from a thermos while I showed him my
dives and, when I tired of that, practiced holding my breath.
"Time me, time me," I asked him again and again. I took in all
the oxygen I could and swam down to sit on the pool's bottom,
staring straight ahead with my cheeks puffed out. After my fifth
effort, I resurfaced to find Dad snoring lightly, his cheeks burning
in the sun. I got out of the pool and stood, dripping, in front of
him to shade his face while he slept, and still I practiced holding
my breath until the puddle of water that had gathered at my
feet completely evaporated and he awoke. That was what I
remembered when I breathlessly watched Jim and the buffalo. I
waited for the buffalo to become aware, to wake up, to somehow
save himself.

HE NOSED THE GRASS, LOOKING FOR appealing pieces. I wondered why he didn't move away to be separate from us, far from
our strange two-legged figures and our unusual smells, which
must have seemed dissonant against the odor he knew best, the
dusty green fragrance of the prairie. But he seemed undisturbed,
his inscrutable lashy eyes calmly blinking while he chewed.

Cora's hands hovered like hummingbirds at her sides.
Granma prayed in Crow.

Then the buffalo stopped blinking, stopped tearing at the
grass with his square yellow teeth, stopped licking. He turned
his head so that he faced Jim and his rifle. The buffalo stood still,
and he stared, as if waiting. Granma prayed, Jim fired, and Cora
started at the sound. The buffalo pitched forward. His front
legs, so slender compared to the rest of him, buckled and folded
beneath his body when he fell. He made a low sighing groan, like
a big man snuggling into a soft bed.

. . .

I LOOKED AT JIM'S FACE and saw tears leaving fat tracks down each of his cheeks. "Thank you, *baaláax*,"* he said.

"Come, Margie," Granma beckoned. We crouched around the buffalo. They all put their hands on him and at Granma's request, I did, too, tentatively. At first I put only one near his throat, but then, feeling the warmth of him, and the secret pink stripe of his nature, I put down the other, too. I wanted to feel as much of him as I could, to catch his life.

Josie, Ruby, and the brothers drove over to us. "He's a beauty," Ruby said. Granma cut his belly open and pulled out his kidney. She tasted it, and they all did, one after another. And then it was my turn. I couldn't refuse him. I had *seen* him fall down for us. I just grazed the kidney with my lips. It was still hot.

I touched him again and tears splashed my hands, but I scarcely took notice of them in all my wonder. Here he was, transferring himself to us. He had stood and waited and watched as if to give himself to us. Whether he had actually meant to give himself, I couldn't know. But Granma, Jim, Cora, and the others seemed to believe so. And he would dissolve into us, when we ate him. His strength and placidity, his sensitivity and sturdiness, his thoughts, his grass delights and prairie dreams—all would be a little bit ours now.

It was a kind of communion, like the ones in which Father Murphy had always led us back home at Holy Rosary. He would be resurrected in us. And that was my treasure.

ON THE DRIVE BACK TO THE HOUSE, Jim said, "I'm grateful for him, but that was hard. I felt different this time. I almost feel like a drink."

---

* brother

IT TOOK DAYS TO BUTCHER, prepare, and preserve all the parts
of the buffalo. Granma made a big stew with his meat, and she
made pemmican with some of the chokecherries we had picked,
and sausages, too, and I ate those creations and many
others that he had made possible. Later, Granma gave me his
furry hide to lay on my bed.

I felt more connected to him than to any other animal
I had ever, in my pre–Operation H.E.A.R.T. days, eaten.
And (excepting my Charlotte) I felt more connected to him
than to any of the creatures I had, as a member of the Operation,
saved.

Sometimes, lying supine on the floor of my Middletown
studio, when Charlotte had perched on my chest and licked my
face as she often did, I had felt that in even her simplest gestures
she was giving me a glimpse into a realm I would be better for
entering, if only I could. Rescuing lab mice and protesting pony
rides weren't drawing me any closer to it. We weren't in relationship with the animals when we did those things; we were still
imposing our will. It was still, always, us in our realm and them
in theirs.

Now, I felt that realm was not so closed off to me—not
because of anything I had done, not any campaign, but because
of a centuries-old understanding, one in which I'd been invited
to share. It was because I had come to this other place, an invisible kind of place, a seemingly bleak place in what felt like
the middle of nowhere, a place pulsing with the richness of
its own life. Maybe that was what I had unknowingly sensed
on the day I first arrived, when I'd fallen fast asleep on the
hood of Bumble's blue rental car. I had been cradled in its arms,
though I had not known. And what was coming from those
mountains they all cherished so much, the Bighorns? What
was in the roots, the wild fruits, the moon's white light, and the

sidelong glance of the buffalo's brown eyes? What was it there, so loving? So lovely? It was her, it was her, she was woven through it all.

"Are you glad you came to the hunt?" Granma asked, and I told her the truth—I was.

CORA STIRRED ME OUT OF SLEEP with her rustlings. It was barely past dark face time when I heard her scoop up her glasses, pour food into Daphne's dish, brush her hair, and put on her clothes. She accomplished the last task with unusual effort. She wasn't, by the sound of it, simply slipping into her summer uniform of shorts and a T-shirt. Her breaths bespoke a particular kind of concentration. She shimmied and strained, and shook the bunks when she plopped down to pause from her exertions.

I dropped my head over the edge of my bed, one woozy eye open, and saw her. She was partway into her dancing regalia. When she looked up to see me spying, she quickly crossed her arms over her bare top half, then covered herself more completely with the stuffed fawn. "How dare you!" she whispered. And then, "Get ready."

"Hmm?" I rubbed my other eye open.

"Get ready!" she exclaimed.

Crow Fair was beginning. There would be, as Cora had explained to me again the night before, a powwow every day for four days, a rodeo, and horse racing, too. ("But you're probly against that, right?" she'd added.) We would go today and we would go again tomorrow. And today had not come fast enough for Cora. "Come on! Get up!"

She'd hoped to take the Pronghorn, but Jim said she wasn't quite ready to be driven yet. So, a few hours after Cora woke, and subsequent to a big, long breakfast (during which she jumped out of her seat several times), we rode in the yellow truck to Crow Agency, the site of the fair.

On the way, I saw that some of the prairie's verdant juiciness had disappeared. Though it was still a month away, a hint of September hovered in the air, bronzing the grass here and there, and I wondered where I would be at summer's end, when I would turn twenty.

Crow Agency bustled with a rough kind of beauty. A pony carried a boy down the sidewalk past the Crow Mercantile, and her hooves sounded hard on the cement. The tangly cottonwoods were capricious in the breeze and gave away big and small bits of shade before snatching them back again. And many of the cars that crowded the streets were dented and rusty, but each in its own way, like inadvertent works of art. Jim, Granma, and Cora traded waves with countless people as we drove through town. I only waved to one person—a speck of a girl no older than two riding in the bed of her parents' truck with a pair of teeny friends. She, after staring at me with inexplicable and intense fascination, had waved first.

Suddenly, an unwelcome tide of dread flooded my chest. I was going to be around people, lots of them, and if the wrong person saw me, someone, perhaps, who recognized my face from the wanted poster I often imagined . . . I pulled down my sunglasses and chewed on a fingernail.

"Don't be nervous, Margie," Granma whispered. "This will be so much fun. I almost forgot, I have something for you." She reached into her tote bag and pulled out my long-lost navy blue baseball cap. "I know you'll feel more comfortable wearing this."

The fabric above the bill had been intricately beaded, and the beads formed a gorgeous buffalo. I gulped, remembering Rasha's buffalo belt buckle, and opened my mouth, but Granma said, "Shush, I know you like it."

"I love it!" I finally sputtered. "It's breathtaking. The most beautiful—when did you do this?"

She delighted in her own sneakiness. "In my bed at night," she said.

"But your hands—no wonder they've been so achy."

She clasped them in her lap and said with conviction, "Everybody needs something special for *Baasaxpilue*."

"What's that?"

"Crow Fair, honey. It means 'to make much noise.'"

Cora studied me thoughtfully when I donned the hat. Tipping her head she said, with the great simplicity of manner she sometimes adopted when deeply satisfied, "Incognito."

We drove into a camp crowded with teepees. They were grand and white and supported with tall tree trunks, some of which still had leaves shooting out of them. The camp was crawling with people on horses, kids, dogs, and dancers in clothes that were ribboned, fringed, feathered, and belled.

"How come you don't come down here and camp like these people?" I asked.

"Yeah." Cora turned to Granma. "How come we don't?"

"It's a lot of setting up," Granma said. "And I'm not much help to your dad with the teepee. Maybe next year. Our relatives will help us. We used to do it, when your grandpa was alive and your dad was small." This image—her dad, small— plunged Cora into a dreamy state, and as she stared at cowboy-booted Crow boys of just three and four who straddled ponies and squinted at our passing truck, she seemed to try to reconcile the sight of them with the reality of her father, ink-stained Jim, towering and powerful behind the steering wheel,

Jim the rumpler of her hair, the restorer of her future car. She
smiled.

He parked among a hundred other cars. Nearby, there was
a big grassy dance arbor and, surrounding it, rows of bleachers
filled with expectant faces. A ring of vendors encircled the
bleachers, enterprising folk who had come from all over to sell
food and souvenirs from lopsided tables, splintery wooden stands,
and tiny travel trailers. Hand-painted signs and banners rippled
in the wind and announced their offerings: fry bread, Indian
tacos, popcorn, snow cones, funnel cakes, beef and buffalo
burgers, pizza, Thai food. There were balloons, feathered head-
dresses, chintzy tomahawks, drums and dream catchers, stuffed
animals, plastic toy machine guns, and plush blankets featuring
the faces of the famous, including Marilyn, and also shirts screen-
printed with the outline of the Bighorns. It was such a motley mix
of stuff, and a scene of such ramshackle charm, that I—after my
months of quietude—was dazzled.

As we strolled, friends and relatives stopped to visit. Some
of the women, old schoolmates of Jim's, looked at him with the
same sort of fawning, forlorn gaze I had so often seen directed
at Dad. They reached out to him proprietarily with their long-
fingered hands and brushed his shoulder, his chest. They flipped
their sleek hair back over their brown shoulders, let loose throaty
laughs, called him Jimmy, and teased him about his adolescent
exploits and endearing quirks (the fastest runner, the best basketball player, the math whiz, the most talented writer of poems,
the quietest date) with glints of hope and desire in their carefully
made-up eyes. I stood back, tracing crescent shapes, which I knew
were really orange slices, in the dirt with the tip of one shoe. Cora
glowered at them from behind her glasses and possessed Jim's
hand all the while. She was resplendent in her flared pink skirt,
her leather leggings blooming with wild roses, her tall moccasins,
her silkily fringed shawl, and her tightly braided hair, and she

received many compliments. I got a few, too, on my buffalo hat, along with ten times as many curious glances.

"Those girls," Jim said, shaking his head. "I've known most of them since I was three years old."

Considering myself in contrast to the indigenous beauties, I felt ridiculous in my heart-printed sundress, my lucky red Chinese shoes. "They're all so pretty," I offered. An inexpressible jealousy made my face hot. Jim shrugged.

We spotted Josie at a distance, standing near the Indian taco stand. She shimmered in her silvery Jingle Dance dress, which dripped with the rolled-up lids of countless chewing tobacco tins. Pete Sings Plenty, he of the sparse and silky mustache, stood beside her, his jaw opened in adoration of the big-boned beauty. Cora giggled. Then she and Granma saw Miss Crow Nation and little Fern, who had been deemed Tiny Tot Crow Nation, holding court over by Feast from the East and moved to join the crowd of admirers surrounding them. Cora turned to Jim and me. "You guys want to come?"

"No thanks," Jim said. "I'm going to get a snow cone. Anybody?" I nodded, still secretly steamed about Jim's coterie of admirers. Cora didn't want to risk dripping any food on her regalia, and Granma said the coldness of the shaved ice hurt her teeth. "Okay, I'll catch up with you in a bit," Jim said.

"You and Granma go ahead," I told Cora. "I just want to stand here and watch everything." Before she departed, I pointed to the empty dance arbor. Its grass glowed so green in the sunlight, and it looked like the perfect place for Cora to mimic a butterfly. "Will you go out there soon?"

"Yes, but only for Grand Entry, when everyone who will dance walks around in a big circle. I'm not actually dancing today. I'll dance tomorrow." Cora stared up at my face for a few moments. Then she added, "I know my dad doesn't like any of those ladies."

I shrugged.

Smiling to myself, I meandered through the bleachers, teeming with visitors from the world I'd left behind at summer's start. But their figures were a blur to me because my thoughts were turned elsewhere, and I was dizzy with a new delight. I didn't care about their conversations, their clothes, their cameras. I wandered, wondering at perceptive Cora and what she had seen in my face, and why she had said what she had when she could have just as easily walked away without those parting words. There was a heady smell of funnel cake in the air, and someone began to beat steadily on a deer-hide drum.

I found Ruby leaning on her cane. She was no longer as frail as she had been when she visited, and her coloring was more gold than gray.

"You look better, Ruby," I said.

She clasped both of my hands in hers. "You look radiant yourself, my friend," she replied. "Your cheeks are rosy. And why are you smiling so big?"

On the other side of the dance arbor, I saw Cora talking to Fern, who was garbed in elaborate garments befitting her new title. Cora leaned down and said something that made the chubby child toss her head back and laugh convulsively. It was a brief moment, but in it I saw Cora pull back the curtain around her heart and give a little portion of it to someone smaller than herself. And I realized she had done just the same for me a few minutes earlier, for she'd seen that I'd been feeling small, too. She had been so defended against me—the invader, the kook, the stranger in a series of crazy sundresses—that when she let one portion of her most protected organ show, it was ten times as significant as it would have been had she simply worn it all the time on her sleeve. And as I watched her whisper funny secrets to a child, my own heart melted for her. All the difficult and darling facets of her nature, which I had studied all summer long, coalesced, like the rough ridges covering the surface of a peach pit. I considered:

the way she sometimes peeked at me so suspiciously through her slightly slanted eyes, which tilted so prettily upwards, echoing the shape of her glasses;

the way her arms appeared to be too long for her body and dangled with gangly helplessness at her sides until they lifted to facilitate the occasional avian flights of her hands;

the endearing mannerisms of her speech, including her frequent use of the word *utterly* and the way she said "leggins" instead of "leggings," or "Granma" (for she had been the one to give Evelyn that name), not "Grandma";

the elfin look of her pointy-tipped ears when they poked through her long cascade of hair, which she kept so scrupulously clean with apple-scented shampoo;

the smallness of her experience, for she had neither seen the sea nor smelled it, and had visited no city outside the reservation other than Billings—had never, in fact, stepped a single twinkling toe outside of Montana;

the largeness of her expectations for her own life, which included being "brilliant" at college, solving the world's "most perplexing" problems, and wearing the most "*utterly* exquisite" clothes;

the sharpness of her mathematical mind, which sometimes amazed me with its power to penetrate matters and see down to the heart of everything—yes, to see the pit when she looked at the blushing fuzz of a peach;

the shrillness of her voice when she was excited, and how quickly it retracted to taciturn seriousness when she was not;

her habit of staring, sans spectacles, into the mirror above her dresser to assess what she looked like without her cat-eyes, and her subsequent sighs and shoulder slumps because her nearsighted-ness rendered her unable to make out her own reflection;

and, most of all, her aura of something fledgling, for in spite of her stuffed fawn and ballerina jewelry box, she was hovering for the briefest of intervals on the threshold between girlhood and adolescence, and being so positioned, she was both fragile and fearsomely full of potential and power.

I had an urge to hold Cora in my hand and to close it tight around her, to allow nothing to hurt her. But of course, I was too late. The wounds of her life were evident in the hang of her arms, and especially in the way the insides of her elbows faced forward, exposed for all to see, rather than inward—as if she had already grown resigned to the inevitable injuriousness of the world.

Pondering all these things, and tucking them away into my heart, I walked on, away from Ruby. Stepping through the crowd, negotiating my way past chairs and feet and roaming toddlers, I bumped right into the front of him.

"Margie, are you all right?"

"Hi." We stood so close I had to tilt my head back to see his face. "I thought we'd figured out how to stop bumping into each other," I said.

"In the kitchen, we have. Out here . . . maybe not. You were looking kinda lost."

"I'm not," I said. "Just thinking. Cora's really something. I like her so much."

"I do, too." Jim wanted to take me for a walk. "Let's go see what else is going on," he said.

He took big greedy bites of his snow cone and tipped the cup against his lips to sip the juice. It stained his lips violet, which only heightened the strength of his features. It seemed, I thought once again, that Jim must always be embellished, marked, as if the universe conspired to draw attention to his bold beauty through the accidental application of colors.

We came to some horses near the camp. They were tethered and stood in the shade, snuffling and scraping the dirt with pleasure. Jim rubbed the white lightning bolt dividing the face of one. I saw a faint and flickering image of a divided face, one that filled me with a vague sadness, but in the heat of the afternoon and the noise of the fair, with pastel clouds of cotton candy all around and Jim beside me, the image faded as quickly as it had come. Jim stroked the length of the bolt, petting from the top of the horse's head down to the velvet of her nose. He took unself-conscious delight in it, the way he did in petting Cora's long locks.

"I'd like to have a few someday," he said.

"Hmm?"

"Horses."

"Oh, yes."

"Do you like them?"

"Yes, of course I do. I love them. I think Cora would love one."

"She'd disappear on it, though. I'd have to go out looking for her."

"It would be better than her driving a car."

"Ugh." He looked pained. "I know, but that's unavoidable. And here I am rebuilding that Cutlass for her—and I named it after one of the fastest animals in the world! But I hate to think of it. I dread it."

"You really love her so much," I said.

"I do."

"She's lucky."

"That's what it's like when you're a dad. You feel so much love it hurts. A man's lucky if he can find a woman he feels that much love for."

"Have you ever?"

In silence, we walked through the camp and came to a tall wall of stacked hay bales. On the other side of it, we discovered a boy of ten and a girl a bit younger, whispering and holding hands. When they saw us they shrieked with exaggerated alarm.

Laughing at us and then at each other, they ran away, the boy pulling the girl behind him.

Jim took my hand and guided me so that my back was pressed against that wall of hay. It smelled very golden in the heat, like it contained half earth and half sun in equal measures. I closed my eyes and inhaled.

"Open your eyes," Jim said. But I could not.

Then two explosive little laughs rang out. I opened my eyes and saw the boy and girl, the kid sweethearts of Crow Fair, peeping at us from around the corner of the haystack. "Time for Grand Entry!" they yelled, and Jim tugged me along toward the dance arbor.

We heard the amplified voice of the Master of Ceremonies (a tribal elder with a smooth, sultry cadence fit for a late-night radio show specializing in songs for the lovelorn) beckoning all the Crow Fair dancers into the arbor. He called them in groups, and they slowly covered the grass with color and movement. And there was music, too, because several groups (including the Hawk Heart Singers) sat around the arbor beating drums and singing in vibrating voices that sometimes exploded into shouts or stretched into falsettos, shaping a sound so rich it gave me goosebumps.

Cora, with a few fine hairs having escaped from her braids and a fan of eagle feathers in her hand, made her entry with a group of other shawl dancers. She gave us a sly sideways smile as she strolled slowly past. It took a long time for all the dancers to enter and parade around the arbor, and all the while I thought of the wall of hay, and wondered what had been about to happen against it.

MANY HOURS LATER, we made the drive back to the house under the night sky. Granma, thoroughly spent from so much sun and socializing, slept beside me with her head tilted back and her snoring mouth wide open. Cora, sleepy after several sugary soda pops and snow cones (her craving had eventually overwhelmed her desire to stay spotless), snoozed beside her. "Did you have fun today?" Jim asked me.

"Yes, did you?"

"Yes."

"You're probably really used to Crow Fair, since you've been going to it your whole life."

"I am," he said. "But it's always good to see old friends. And there's always a lot of them there—" He suddenly swerved the truck around a black cow who stood on the dark road. "But," Jim added, "I like new friends the best."

13 OTTER *(Lontra canadensis)*

THE NEXT MORNING, JIM ROSE EXTRA EARLY and worked on
the Pronghorn. At noon, he was still outside, half hidden under
her hood and humming, when Cora, fully garbed in her regalia,
stepped through the screen door and cleared her throat meaning-
fully. The ground was wild with wakeful grasshoppers.

Jim clanged and hummed, and did not look up.

Cora stepped closer to him and executed a few hopping shawl
dancer steps. Jim was otherwise absorbed.

"Dad!" Cora cried. "Let's go!"

But Jim, who bonked his head on the Pronghorn's hood upon
hearing Cora's shrill cry, still had to shower, and to dress, and to
join us for a healthy lunch (Cora unable to eat a bite), and to gulp
down a second cup of coffee before we could all leave. And then,
before Granma, Cora, and I could climb into the truck, he had to
clear it of all the scraps and symbols of the previous day's Crow
Fair fun: two snow cone cups, three soda cans, numerous napkins,
a stray ribbon from one of Cora's braids, a schedule of fair events,
and an informative pamphlet entitled *The History of the Apsáalooke
Nation*, which was intended for tourists but which Cora had read
with critical interest (checking it for accuracy) before falling asleep.

"Just let me get this stuff cleared away—hold on—just a second—sorry, ladies, I didn't sleep well last night, and I'm a little out of sorts—"

"Dad, we're going to be late!" Cora flickered in her fair finery. Belly, evidently in agreement, barked three times. "Grand Entry starts at one!"

"Don't fret, Cora," Jim said. "Crow Fair runs on Indian time. You know that."

"Indian time?" I said.

"Yep. That means everything happens when it happens, and nobody hurries. Okay," Jim said. The truck was clean, and he held unruly bouquets of debris in both hands. I waited for Granma to hop in and take the spot that would be nearest to him, but she just stood—waiting, it seemed, for me to do the same.

"After you, Granma," I said. I couldn't sit beside him. Too many haystack thoughts had woken me in the night, along with unsettling dreams about black cows and other prairie phantoms, and in the morning Jim had shown the indifference of old, eye-ing his invisible angel when he bade me a brief hello. The scale had tipped again, though who had tipped it I couldn't tell. The mystery exhausted me. The air between us was wound into a tightrope.

"No, honey, after you," Granma replied.

Cora expelled a big breath in exasperation, moved past Granma and me, and climbed into the truck. "Come *on*," she said. She was electric, nervous. It was her dancing day. As Jim drove us down the dirt road, and Belly yipped and sprinted after us, Cora lowered her head in prayerful concentration and whispered to herself. "I want to have wings," she said.

THE ACTION AROUND THE DANCE ARBOR was audible from a great distance. We heard the MC's deep voice through the

sound system. Grand Entry had begun, and he beckoned all
the remaining dancers into the arbor. "If you dancers aren't
out here yet, come join us, come join us, for Gra-a-a-nd
Entry-y-y-y . . ."

Parking spots were scarce. As soon as Jim shut off the engine,
Cora clutched his arm. "We've got to find Josie so she can braid
me. Granma's hands are too stiff today." She dragged him away.
Granma looked ruefully at her own bent fingers, and I touched
the buffalo on my baseball cap with guilty gratitude.

"We'll catch up with you later," Jim called to us over his
shoulder, and as they hurried toward the crowd they looked like
two figures dissolving into the melty fragments within a slowly
turning kaleidoscope.

"There's so many people here today," I said. "Way more than
yesterday." Granma slipped her arm through mine as we walked,
and I was glad to have her close. I felt uneasy, like the frayed end
of the ribbon from Cora's braid that Jim had scooped from the
truck's seat.

"Because it's a Saturday, honey," Granma said. "Yes, people
come to Crow Fair from all over. Especially to see the dancing."
The bleachers surrounding the dance arbor were overflowing.
"We'll be sitting down there today." Granma pointed to a collection of comfy canvas chairs on the grass below the bleachers.
"That's where the dancers and their families sit. Ruby is saving us
seats." We walked, stopping every few moments so Granma could
greet endless friends and relatives and cuddle a dozen different
babies. An hour passed. I wasn't sure if I'd quite understood what
Jim had meant by "Indian time," but I felt we must be in it, for
that hour had seemed like a mere minute. "Men's Grass Dance!"
the MC called. "It's time for the handsome Grass Dancers, ladies
and gentlemen . . ."

I squinted into the arbor and saw men fringed in hundreds
of ribbons that resembled windblown blades of prairie grass when

they danced. But I didn't watch for long. Unlike the day before, when I'd been too distracted by other novelties to pay it much attention, the crowd in the bleachers now fascinated me. There were more people than I'd seen in a single place for months. Their accents were varied. They shouted at each other to be heard over the drumming and singing, pointed and marveled at the dancers, fiddled with the video recorders, bit into hamburgers, and spilled relish on their T-shirts. As disquieting as they were, I couldn't stop looking at them.

"You coming, Margie?" Granma asked. Ruby waved to us from the distant grass. She wore a dress covered in hundreds of elk teeth. "Look at her," Granma clucked, "all fancy and proud. She's had that elk tooth dress since she was a newlywed!"

The MC announced the next group of dancers. "Jingle Dancers, come out here. Look at these beautiful ladies! They simply take your breath away . . . Ladies and gentlemen, the Jingle Dancers are filling the arbor . . ."

"Ooooh, Josie's going to dance," Granma said. "Come on—"

"I'll catch up." I wanted to look longer at the crowd, to absorb the sights and sounds. I knew it would be best for me to hide, to lower my cap until it bumped the top of my sunglasses, and to sit safely between two aged Crow sentinels, the sisters Evelyn and Ruby. But I had a feeling something was there for me, in the wheeling kaleidoscope, maybe one of the phantoms from my dreams of the night before, something that might relieve the expectant tension I felt. The little curls at the back of my neck tingled and rose.

"I'm going to go get a drink, I think," I said.

"Okay, honey." Granma squeezed my arm. Then she raised one twisted hand and touched my face. "Don't go too far," she said.

. . .

I WALKED PAST THE FOOD VENDORS. Outside Thai Treat, I saw a man wearing a windbreaker that boasted "I've Seen Fifty Nifty States From My RV." He held a camera aloft to capture the dancers walking by in their regalia. His wife noshed on a hot dog and grunted approvingly at the most colorful garments. When the MC intoned, "Fancy Dancers! All Fancy Dancers, you're up! Friends, you cannot miss these fellows, they are truly a sight to behold," she tossed the remains of her hot dog on the ground and pulled her husband toward the arbor. A boy banged a toy tomahawk against a stick. A pair of Native teenagers displayed an array of beaded earrings on a card table, all of them in the shape of birds.

"Hey." I felt a tap on my shoulder. "I'm going over to get some fry bread." There were dark splotches of sweat on Jim's shirt, and the line between his eyes was deep. "Bring you back some?"

"No thanks." He stood close, looking at the passing faces, saying nothing. "Did you find Josie?" I asked.

"Yes, Cora's with her. Sure you don't want anything?"

"Yes," I said, but I wasn't sure. Maybe I wanted endless orange slices slipped between my lips, and bits of hay in my hair.

Jim lingered. "Okay," he said finally. After he left, I realized he had wanted me to go along.

I WAS THIRSTY. MY SUNGLASSES KEPT SLIDING down my slick nose. The hair at the back of my neck now lay flat with damp. I had a brushed-by-an-otter sensation. And then, while I stood in line at the lemonade stand, the atmosphere around me changed. The vibrancy of the colors and the vitality of the beating drums became diluted, as if a drop or two of water, or tears, had trickled into the kaleidoscope and clouded my view.

I smelled him before I saw him, a teary hyacinth note that sneaked through the cracks in the thick wall of fair food scents, stole into my nostrils, and spoke of sadness and silver hair, of silver charms and the metal of train tracks so cool against the neck.

And I heard him after I smelled him, speaking a name I knew, and speaking it with great familiarity and intimacy because it was the name of the little lass he stirred from bed each morning and folded back in each night, whose hand he now held. "What size do you want, Nettie?" he said. They stood in line, a few spots in front of me, he in his black-and-white-checkered trousers, she with her yellow hair crowned in a feathered souvenir headdress. I watched them get their drinks. Simon pushed his wallet into his pocket. Just before they turned, I left the line and walked away.

I forced my legs to carry me once more past all the vendors' stands. Could it be, could it be, could it be that he had come for me? I stopped at the fry bread trailer, but Jim was not there. I looked toward the grass on the outskirts of the arbor, where Granma and Ruby sat in matching chairs. Beside them, Josie, flushed from dancing, stood and wove Cora's locks into twin braids. Cora craned her neck first one way and then another, looking, squinting through her spectacles, her mouth an opened oval of worry, and Josie clasped her head firmly in her hands and centered it again. "Ladies and Gentlemen," called the MC, "it's time for the Hoop Dancers. All you lovely Hoop Dancers, this is your time to shine."

"Margie!" A small, hot hand clasped mine. "Hello!"

"Hello, hello!" I bent down to embrace her. Her feathers stuck to my damp face. "What are you doing here, Annette?" I looked up at him. "What are you doing here?" I asked again.

He hugged me hard, sighed into my neck, said my name over and over. I hadn't been held so close for so long, I almost swooned from the sweetness of it, and from a simultaneous sick feeling in my stomach. The ladybug left her station at the back of my neck and resettled in her usual spot behind my eyes, and she was still, and so was I.

"Let me see you," he said, lifting up my sunglasses and staring into my face.

He, I noticed right away, was not wearing any sunglasses. I looked into his eyes and discovered that the once-impenetrable gems had developed little inclusions, little openings, and I could see sentiments shining through them, like sunlight through the slits in shut blinds. I wanted to hug Simon again.

"You look different," I said.

"Let's go," he replied.

In a way, it was a relief. This was the end to the queasy anticipation. This was the "old friend" I would find at Crow Fair. Of course everything would come full circle, I thought, glancing at the Hoop Dancers twirling their closed rings. Of course everything would come back to Simon, who had, I supposed, started it all. Still . . .

"I want . . ." I said. "I wasn't . . . expecting . . ."

"I drove a thousand miles to get to you, and it's a thousand miles home."

"Is this the place where you brought my Strawberry Shortcake suitcase?" Annette asked.

"How did you know I was here?"

"The long letter you wrote me. I got it after I gave Bumble the one I wrote to you. You told me you were on the Crow Reservation. We've been driving all over this godforsaken place for three days." Annette nodded. She looked pale, and there were bits of blue cotton candy glued to her chin. "When I heard this big fair was happening, I thought maybe I'd run into you here. And here you are." He pulled me close. "My Margie, come. You're so tan and lovely, how long your hair is, come, I want to eat you up."

Annette looked away, entranced by a Fancy Dancer's fluorescent clothes. "Dad, what are all these costumes?" she asked.

"But, I'm not . . . I don't know if I'm ready, today . . ."

Simon didn't hear. "We're going to get you out of this mess. I'm going to try to get into Nettie's trust fund. We'll pay for a good lawyer. We'll get you back in school." He paused. He poured his eyes straight into my mine. And, just as it had been in those crushy classroom days when he had called me "beautiful, more beautiful, most beautiful," it was heaven to be seen. "You must have felt like you were dying here," he said. "It's so empty. Count on Bumble to arrange for you to come to a place like this." He shook his head. "Surely there were better options. Who have you been staying with? Have they treated you well? Are they here?"

"Simon, I—"

"You have a lot to tell me. I can see it in your face. You've been lonely. I've been lonely, too."

"I can leave tomorrow," I said.

"No, today. What reason could you possibly have to stay? Come, Margie. We've spent three nights at a strange hotel in Billings called the War Bonnet Inn, and tonight will be our last. That will have been more than enough—"

"There are so many bunnies at that hotel, Dad!" Annette noted.

"This is true."

"Can we get one when we get home?"

"Maybe, sweetheart. If Margie wants." He squeezed my hand with his cushiony palm. His own hand shook. I was moved, captured, entranced. I remembered our jasmine nights. "Come now," he said. "Our car's not far."

SIMON'S TOMATO RED 2002 was haphazardly parked, blocking the entrance to one of the teepees in the camp. He opened the passenger door for me, and I slipped in and rolled down the window.

I was hot, so hot, so thirsty, and it was hard to see anything clearly through my foggy sunglasses, and my heart pounded in my ears, but still I could hear the MC calling, calling over the sound system, for the "young ladies, lovely young ladies from near and far who will do the Fancy Shawl Dance for us at this fabulous Crow Fair, ladies, you butterfly girls, young Fancy Shawl Dancers, come into the arbor and out of your cocoons . . ."

I turned my face away from Simon beside me. I pressed it into the nook between the passenger seat and the door. I pressed my wet face into the sliver of space there, bending the bill of my buffalo hat.

"Okay, Margie." Simon stroked me. "Okay, don't cry. It's all over. You're coming home."

"Go," I said. "Let's go. Let's just go."

FIVE MILES OUT OF CROW AGENCY, I pulled my face out from the space between the seat and the door. I took off my cap and placed it on my lap, upside down so I couldn't see the buffalo. I grabbed Simon's hand. Annette reached forward and petted my hair. "I'll brush your hair and you can brush mine," she said.

ANNETTE HAD BEEN RIGHT about the War Bonnet Inn. It was inexplicably populated by an abundance of bunnies. There were hundreds of them hopping all over the hotel grounds, their calico colors vivid in the late-afternoon light. They hopped in the parking lot, on the sidewalk outside the lobby, and in the outdoor corridors between rooms. "I'm tempted to devise some plan to save them," Simon said, "but they actually seem to be doing quite well. Maybe they don't need saving at all. And anyway," he gave me a weary glance, "those days are over."

I told Annette about Charlotte. "Perhaps she can be our pet when we get back home," she said.

"I hope," I said. "If Ptarmigan is willing to give her back."

"A rabbit—in the house?" Simon asked. "You lived with a rabbit in your house?"

"My studio apartment," I said. "After I left your place." He bowed his head, and I felt sorry for mentioning it. "There are house rabbits," I added. "Many people have them."

"Is that sanitary?" he asked.

I recalled the scoured, snowy surfaces of Simon's shadowy abode, the way the big heavy outer doors led to a second set of inner doors, which opened to a spotless, solar-powered realm of closed windows and white walls, everything clean, everything "green." It would be nice, at least, to sleep in a big bed again, I thought.

Simon had left the DO NOT DISTURB sign hanging on the doorknob of their hotel room. Inside, his suitcase was opened, and his and Annette's clothes spilled out onto the floor. The beds were unmade, and in the bathroom all the complimentary soaps and pocket-sized shampoo bottles were scattered about in disarray, while a soaking wet towel languished on the linoleum.

"Sorry it's not very tidy," he said. "I guess I've been pretty preoccupied with tracking you down."

"I don't have any of my things," I said, picturing the Strawberry Shortcake suitcase and all of its contents tucked into its usual corner in Cora's bedroom. I could never ask Jim and Granma to ship it to me. I could never speak to them again after the way I had left. I felt gray inside, not rosy or healthy, but gray with shame.

"It's okay," Simon said. "You can wear something of mine. And *you*"—he coaxed the TV remote gently out of Annette's hand—"need a bath."

I stood in the bathroom and watched the dirt of the day, along with a few fine cotton candy filaments, slide from her slim sylph's body into the water. She told me about the seahorses in the nature documentary she'd watched on TV the night before.

"Did you know seahorses are raised by their fathers?" I asked.

"I wish I had that kind of tail," she said, "to curl around whatever I wanted. I would curl it around you right now."

Simon called me back out to him. The air conditioner droned, and the whole room smelled of Annette's teensy bar of strongly perfumed hotel soap. He sat me down on the bed, pushed my hair behind my ears. "Did you get my letter?" His voice was low and intimate. I nodded. "Did you understand everything?"

"Yes."

"Margie, I made a mistake, pushing something special out of my life because I was afraid of losing it. I mean you. I'd rather have you, and face my fear of losing you, than be without you. I want to do the brave thing. I've worked through my troubles. I've missed you, my *rara avis*.* I want you."

I stared into Simon's face. The new lights in his eyes sent sharp sparks into my left ovary, as did the familiar shakiness of his smile. "Thank you," he said, "for coming with me, and for giving me a chance. I think we can be a family."

I pressed my face into his neck.

"Who was it you were with?" he asked.

"A family," I said. Impossible—it was impossible, I thought, to speak of them, to speak of her soap opera, to speak of his ink stains, to speak of her spectacles.

I ran my fingers over his strong Russian cheekbones, pinched his earlobes. We lay down beside each other and embraced. A long time passed. Just by lying there beside me, fully clothed, he coaxed all the loneliness out of my limbs and brought blood back into my touch-starved body, but there was nothing, nothing to be done about the stifled sob that had formed an enormous lump in my throat.

"Simon."

Annette splashed and sang to herself in the tub. "She's okay," he said. "She won't hear." But I pushed him away. When he got up to answer her calls ("Dad! How do I do this drain?"), I rose

---

*   rare bird

and looked out the window. The room was on the second floor.
It was already almost dusk, and in the pearl light I could see, not
too distant, the new strip mall where we had gone to get the supplies for Cora's leggings. I had to turn away. The dusk was the
same no matter where it happened, I thought. It held the secrets
of all hearts and made them visible for a few minutes, held them
suspended in the air like thousands of tiny beads.

ANNETTE SNORED IN THE BED BESIDE OURS. Simon pulled me to
him and we pressed close together as we had in days of old, noses
touching. I felt his pulse quicken, and he stirred in secret and
familiar ways beneath the sheets.

"No, Simon," I murmured. "I can't—"

"Oh, dear," he said in his bone-dry way. "It's like we're already
married."

"I'm sorry," I said, "I just can't. I'm too tired. My heart—I
mean, my head aches."

"I know, I know. It's all right." He pressed his mouth into
my cheek and whispered, "Go to sleep, go to sleep," and I
breathed in his hyacinths. He stroked my forehead and my
hair. "My girl," he said, "my dear girl." And as I drifted off
(it was easy to sleep in his remembered arms), pondering those
words, I recalled what Granma, what Evelyn, what the root
digger had told me about being a girl. "You're a girl," she had
said, "as long as you allow life to happen to you." And when
I woke up hours later at dark face time, for no reason other than
it had become my habit, and I heard not Granma's soft sneakered
footsteps but only the whirr of the air conditioner against a sterile
silence, I remembered the rest of what she had said. "You become
a woman," she had told me, "when you start living according
to your own instincts, your own intelligence, and your own
desires. You're a woman when you take hold of yourself." And

though it terrified me, I knew, staring into the dark, which one I wanted to be.

I HAD GONE TO SIMON, both the first time and the second, because he had demanded it of me in his warm way. What if I went to Jim, even though he had not demanded, not even asked, because it was what I wanted, because I desired it? Ever since the sweetness of the orange, and even long before then, I had been waiting, passive, nervous—waiting for something the way a girl waits.

All summer, I had loved to step into the bathroom when he was done and steep in the steam of the shower he had taken. Doing so reminded me of the feeling of the hill houses—a humid intimacy, so safe. All summer, I had listened for the sounds of him. I had catalogued each one in my mind—the friendly rumble of his truck approaching the house, the slow squeak and click of the screen door when he came through it, the jangly racket of his lunch pail and thermos when he laid them down for the night, his footfalls, which, in spite of his size, were only slightly heavier than his mother's, his voice, his contented humming, and especially the rich mellow tone of his "hello," because the last "o" sound was as round, full, perfect, and pregnant as the letter itself, and always lifted up in a lilt, as if the end of the word liked to take a few steps up a prairie hillock to stand a bit closer to the sun.

What was it, to pay such attention to the most everyday tokens of another person's existence? Why could a clanging lunch pail carry such charms?

WE PULLED OUT OF THE HOTEL PARKING LOT amidst a confusion of rabbits, who zipped around with the elated energy of prey awakening to find they had survived to see another day.

"Goodbye, War Bonnet bunnies!" Annette called out in her scratchy morning voice.

"Is there anything you want to stop and see on our drive?" Simon asked. I knew he meant landmarks or national parks.

"I want . . ." I said. I could not look at him, at his new eyes, at his hopeful face. "I want . . ." I could not say I wanted to see prairie dogs, grasshoppers, and Bighorns, that I wanted to see a lone old woman standing on a little hill in darkness to pray, to see lightning tearing through the sky, to see a full moon rising with a child jumping up to reach it, or that I wanted to see a man who was splattered with colors, a happy man suffused with the sap of life, and shy—I knew it, just like me—shy. "I want . . ." I began again. Simon and Annette waited. Simon even laughed. I took his hand. "I want to go back," I said.

His face was like a still lake with a single stone thrown in.

"I know," he said. "We're on our way back—"

"No. *Back*."

After a long pause he spoke. "Margie, I don't understand. What could there possibly be for you in that place?"

"Please," I said. "If you love me—and you've never said it, not once, and you didn't write it in your letter to me, either." Simon's face crumpled, and I was instantly sorry I'd said those words. "But if you really love me, or even if you don't," I was crying then, "you'll take me back."

"Dad?" Annette said. She looked at me and back at him.

"I'm so sorry," I cried. "I didn't know for sure until I left. I never expected it. I think my heart really is there."

They looked at me with confounded eyes.

"I'm knitted in," I said.

HALFWAY DOWN THE DIRT ROAD leading to the house, I asked Simon to pull over. I wanted to walk the rest of the way. I took off my charm bracelet and put it on Annette's wrist. "This is for you," I said.

She examined the silver bird and the half of a heart. Then she looked up at me, petted my hair in the soothing way she sometimes had, preternaturally parental, and said, "All right, don't be sad." I kissed her.

I kissed Simon. I kissed his mouth, his cheekbones. I kissed the plump lobes of his ears, one after the other. I kissed both of his shut eyes. His salt and mine mingled. "I don't have any regrets," I said.

"Margie." He choked on my name and sucked in his breath.

"It's only because of you"—I couldn't speak very well at all—"that I found it."

WALKING TOWARD THE HOUSE, I noticed something unfamiliar, something that hadn't been there the morning before. Vivid patches of dark and light pink had emerged all over the land and lined both sides of the road, and a new, fragile fragrance was in the air. Looking closer, I saw countless five-petaled flowers of fuchsia and antique rose rising out of leafy shrubs, some exuberantly opened to face the sun, some still shyly hidden in tight buds; I realized they were wild roses, and that they had just begun to bloom.

ALL WAS CALM AT THE HOUSE. I stepped past Jim's truck, past the Pronghorn. Belly lay on the porch with the mangled remains of one of my lucky red Chinese shoes in her mouth. I patted her head, but she was in such a red-shoe reverie she didn't look up. I took a few deep breaths, for I was afraid, and went inside.

The house was quiet. There were two coffee cups on the table

and some dry plates standing in the dish rack. Granma's room
was empty. I looked into Jim's, and it was empty, too. In Cora's,
Daphne was the sole sign of life, snoozing under a blanket of
cedar chips.

I walked outside. "Belly, where is everyone?" Maybe,
I thought, I had been deluded in thinking I should come back,
and we really were all of us Always Alone. Simon and Annette
were each alone in their small red capsule, traveling overland at
seventy miles per hour. It was a heart-piercing picture, and for a
second I shut my eyes hard against it. I lay down on the hot hood
of the Pronghorn, which was finally closed.

"Margie?"

"Jim—"

"Is everything okay? Where were you?"

"—where were you?"

"I was out back," he said. He held a chicken in his arms,
and he promptly put it down. Belly, feigning aggression she did
not truly feel, so satisfied was she after my shoe, chased the bird
around to the coop. "But what about you?"

"I was . . . confused," I said.

"My mom and I were very worried. You can imagine what we
thought."

"I know. I'm sorry. Where are they?" I asked.

"With Josie. They went to watch the horse races at Crow
Fair. I wanted to stay home." He looked at my clothes—a pair of
Simon's trousers, which hung so long my flip-flops barely peeked
out from under the hems, and Simon's button-down shirt—but
said nothing.

"I'm sorry," I said. He nodded with acceptance, but he had a
discouraged look.

"Jim," I said.

"What?"

"Jim." I pulled off my buffalo baseball cap.

"What is it?"

"I love it here. I love Granma. I love Cora . . ." Tears came with her name, tears and more of the awful gray shame.

"Margie, Margie." He steered me into the house and down the hall into the one room I'd never actually entered—his. "Lie down," he said. I sat on the edge of the bed, sniffling. I stared at him. "It's okay to lie down. I'm not going to hurt you. I'll be right back." I fell back onto the brown woolen blanket. His buffalo skull regarded me from one corner of the room. His basketball rested on the dresser.

Jim returned with a handkerchief tucked in his hand.

"I missed Cora," I wailed. "Dancing."

"Here," he said. "Blow your nose." I turned sideways and blew, embarrassed by the honking sounds I made, and by what must have been—after a morning filled to the brim with tears—my disheveled appearance. And when my nasal passages were cleared, I smelled it again—the smell of both love and home, the smell of neroli, the same bright essence of orange blossoms that had announced itself so boldly when Jim walked through the front door on the night I first met him.

It confused me. I sat up, frowned, looked around. Was it coming from him? "Margie," he said again. He pressed the handkerchief lightly, so lightly, to each of my eyes. They were badly swollen, and so was my mouth, and my face was hot, and having Jim's big hands so close to it gave me an incongruous impulse: I wanted to kiss them.

"What happened yesterday?" he asked.

"Someone came for me."

"Who?"

"An old friend. It was just like you said—there are old friends at Crow Fair. I thought I would go with him, but I couldn't. I want this."

I saw a brief blaze in Jim's off-to-the-side eyes, but he quickly extinguished it. "You need some water," he said. "Your cheeks are so red. I'll be right back." I heard him in the kitchen, choosing a glass, running the tap. I turned to examine his uncluttered nightstand. There was an alarm clock, a lamp, and a simple wooden box with a hinged lid. I lifted the lid up to peruse the box's contents. I had already embarrassed myself completely, I thought, so it would hardly matter if I got caught snooping.

There was a snapshot, curling at the edges, of Cora and Granma taken years earlier. Cora was hummingbird-small, only three or four, and wearing pink-framed eyeglasses with lenses no bigger than quarters. Granma had not changed at all. There was a handful of loose tobacco, redolent of leather and earth. And there was a twisted bandage made out of paper towels, the very one I had fashioned for Jim when he'd grated his hand in the kitchen. It was blotched with brown blood. When he rounded the corner into his room, I blurted, "Jim, you still have the bandage."

He eyed the open box and froze for a moment. The buffalo watched from his corner. The basketball rolled forward a fraction of a millimeter. "Yes," he said. "I saved it."

I tasted the essence of orange on the back of my tongue. "But Jim," I said, "you don't even look at me."

He sat on the bed. He put one hand on each of my cheeks. He dipped his head, low enough to hold my eyes with his. And he held them, and held them. "This way?" he asked. And then I saw it. I saw the spot where Jim's pair of perpendicular lines met, where the vertical line between his eyes and the horizontal line of his smile intersected. It happened at the very center of his bottom lip. And what was buried there, under that place? Tobacco seeds shining like stars? I held it for a moment between my top and bottom teeth, then between my lips. There was warmth there, and health, and kindness—all the same qualities that inhabited his hands. Jim made a sound. Then the words came out.

"I have been looking at you, Margie, from the first night I came home and found you here. I may not seem like I'm looking, but I promise you, I am. I saw the kiss you drew on the ground between us that morning, not long after you arrived—"

"The kiss?"

"Yes, you made an X in the dirt with your toe while you stood next to my mom, talking about root digging—"

"Oh!" I cried. "But I didn't know that I . . . I didn't mean . . . or maybe I did?"

"I'm just nervous," Jim went on. "You know, I don't really have all that much experience with women. And being so close to the one I want—it's overwhelming sometimes." Watching him closely while he said these things, listening to his words, I lost my breath.

"But I've been looking at you," he said, "looking with all of my senses. When I taste the food you make with me, you're in it—you, you just melt into everything you do, you're so tender. When you're close enough for me to smell, what comes through your skin is pure, prairie pure, but unfamiliar to me, too, like California flowers, and it's the most delicious"—he paused—"distraction. When I hear your voice, it's like your soul's right there vibrating under every word, and I could lie down and dream, listening to it—I'd dream of all your life, your experiences, the things I don't even know about you, the sadness and the sweetness. And when I turn my eyes on you, when you're looking away and I can study you that way, well, I see just what all my friends at Crow Fair told me they saw, what I've seen from the very start: a beautiful woman."

"What about when you touch me?"

"When I touch you . . . when I touch you . . ."

We folded into each other. Minutes, skin, eyelashes merged. The grasshoppers outside grew louder.

. . .

AT DUSK, THE SECRETS OF ALL HEARTS were once again suspended in the air. And what was suspended in the air between us? The tightrope that had so often hung there slackened, and that slackened rope turned to the softest of all yarns. And then I was found, and so was he, and for a while, Jim and I—just Jim and I and nothing else—were all of a piece. We were knitted together by that yarn.

"WHAT DID YOU THINK WHEN I CAME HERE? And you didn't even know me?"

"I thought that my mom wanted someone to keep her company, and that she also wanted someone for Cora. A young woman. Someone who could be a friend to her—"

"I doubt Cora will ever want me for a friend—"

"—and then, not long after you got here, I wanted you for myself. I'm glad you came back today," he said. "So glad."

LATER, JIM DID WHAT NO ONE outside of dreams ever had. He held the back of me against the front of him in a spooning embrace. He was the dark-haired stranger of so many of my dreams, but I was not asleep.

THAT NIGHT THE TWO OF US SAT AT THE TABLE listening to the grasshoppers. The star-shaped ceiling lamp shone down on us, and the flecks of glitter in the Formica shone up.

"I missed it, too," Jim said.

"What?"

"Cora's Shawl Dance."

"What? Why?"

"Because I was so worried about what might have happened that I went looking for you."

"That's terrible," I said.

"I know." Jim's vertical furrow was deep. "She didn't even ask why—that's the worst part. She wouldn't speak to me at all last night or this morning."

I laid my head down on the table, wondering what I would say to her.

Soon, Josie's truck rolled up to the house, radio blaring, and deposited two figures outside—one aged and slow, one young and quick.

"So, she's back," Cora said before the screen door slammed shut behind her. Her hair had been freed from its braids and fell in wild waves all around her face.

"Cor—" Jim started.

"Did she just come back to get her things?" she asked him.

"No," I began, "I—"

"Or is she going to sleep in my room a bit longer?"

"Cora, we're so sorry we missed your dancing," Jim said.

"It's all my fault," I added. "I left, and your dad felt like he had to look for me."

"I *knew* you were the reason." Glaring in her regalia, with her hair so full of static and smelling so smokily of the fires from the teepee camp, her skin shimmering with prairie dust and slightly ghostly from the powdered sugar that covers fry bread, she frightened me. But then she tucked her lips into a small tight line and her eyes went stormy behind the spectacles.

"Grandchild—" Granma said, but the sobbing sprite stole swiftly into her bedroom. Granma sat down. She reached for me, and I noticed how much like Jim's her hands felt. The same blood warmed them. "Where did you go yesterday, honey?"

"I'm sorry and ashamed. I was so confused, Granma. I felt so uneasy and sick." I told her all that had happened.

Granma nodded. "I know that sickness you had. It's called *daásduupe*—two hearts. It makes a person feel uncertain, insecure, faltering. Do you still feel it?" She stared into my face, studying it for signs.

"No. I got better. In the night, while I slept, and at dark face time. I knew what I wanted, and where I wanted to be. I want to be here with you," I said. "But I won't if it's not okay with Cora. That means everything."

"I'm glad you feel that way, like you belong here," Granma said. She smiled at Jim, and then winked.

"Mom," he said, shaking his head.

"What?" she asked. "I'm happy she wants to be with us. I love her."

The grasshoppers called. We looked at each other across the table. "*I* love her," Jim said.

THE ROOM WAS DARK. She was visible only as a slight shape
in her twisted sheets. She had carelessly strewn her fine clothes
all over the floor, and I stumbled over a moccasin before I made
it to the bunk ladder. I ascended and lay flat on my back. The air
felt compressed, as if Cora and I were inside of a watch that had
been wound too tight. And sensitive Daphne was unwilling to
release some of the tension with even a few squeaky turns of her
wheel.

"Cora." In the silence after I spoke her name, I thought about
it, for the first time, in a Latin way, the way Simon had taught
me. *Cor,* I realized, meant *heart*—"Cora, I'm so sorry I caused us
to miss your dancing. I'm so sorry"—and mine hurt for her. She
was quiet.

"I want to be here," I said, "to watch you dance next year. I'm
kind of like you. My mom hasn't been a part of my life." I felt her
turn over in the bed below me. I couldn't tell if she was listening,
or if she meant to give the bunks a see-if-I-care shake. "And I've
been looking for my place for a long time. I think it's with you,
and your dad, and Granma, but only if you think so, too."

Cora offered not one peep. "And if you don't think so," I said,
"I'll go. But I want you to know that I have loved the time I've
had with you. And I love you. I know you don't like me at all
right now. But I think you're amazing. You're brilliant, strong,
gorgeous, funny, completely unique. I'm in awe of you. I know
you're going to end up doing incredible and unexpected things
with your life. You're going to make a difference, I just know it."
A breeze blew through the window, and I turned my face toward
it, thinking of what Jack Dolce had called my "desperate" drive
to make a difference. I realized that it had mellowed, mercifully,
that make-a-difference mania, and it wasn't any longer so misguided. "That was something I tried to do myself," I said to Cora.
"Make some sort of difference. And I hope to be around to see
you do it better."

Daphne took a few tentative steps on her wheel. Then complete silence cloaked the room, and we all—me, Cora, the hamster, and the ballerina upside down in her jewelry box—slept.

AT SEVEN, I WOKE TO THE SOUNDS of Cora's precise morning routine. She rose, scraped her spectacles off her dresser, brushed her hair, poured pellets into Daphne's bowl. I heard her pick the various pieces of her regalia up off the floor, shake them out, and arrange them on her bed. Then all was still. Granma had breakfast sizzling in the kitchen—I smelled it. But Cora didn't open the door and bound out for a bite. Minutes passed, during which all I could hear was the regular rise and fall of her girlish breaths.

I opened my eyes and saw her standing in the center of the floor, staring at me. "Hi," I croaked. But she just looked a little longer and left the room.

IT WASN'T LONG BEFORE THEY CAME. Still bedbound, I lay and listened to the muffled sounds of Granma and Cora in conversation.

"... so many more of them today."

"... know where they all come from?"

"... only the males who make that sound."

A car pulled up to the house. I pushed back the daisy-printed pillowcase curtain, peeked out the window, and saw a sedan, black and shiny as a wet stone despite the dusty terrain it had traversed. For a short, sleepy moment, I was intrigued. But when I saw the brown and green splots all over its windshield and hood—dozens upon dozens of dead grasshoppers—I knew.

"Who's this?" I heard Cora ask. "And where did Dad go?"

Granma said, "Let me go to the door, Cora."

I sat up and stared at my hands. Panic seeped from my palms. Simon's letter was right. They had started watching him before they'd begun watching me. Maybe they had lost track of me for a while, but they had always kept their eyes fixed on him, and when he'd come all the way to Crow Country to retrieve me, they had followed.

I watched them get out of the car: two men in suits. How strange it must be, I thought, for Granma to see once more what she had first seen some sixty years before, two men in suits stepping over the prairie grass, coming to knock on her front door. Now I was the one hiding beneath a buffalo blanket.

I heard a man's voice, the same one that had sounded outside my Middletown studio so many months earlier and called me out of bed by my first and last names.

"Ma'am. I'm Agent Fox with the Federal Bureau of Investigation, and this is Agent Jones . . ." The introductions, the reason for their visit, rolled into my ears and out of my pores, slicking me with sweat. "We have reason to believe that this woman is living with you." I knew the photograph (they were showing it now, pressing it up against the screen), the one they had snapped at the San Diego County jail when they booked me, the one that was published in the *Sun*—me after a long night of wine, with worried eyes, uncombed curls, and a mournful mouth. "Her name is Margie Fitzgerald, but she may use an alias. Do you know her?"

Granma let spill a long string of sentences—all of them in Crow.

"Do you speak English?" asked Agent Jones.

"*Baaleetáa!*"*

I discerned a little bell through the bulk of the buffalo hide. It was Cora's ringing voice. "Can I help?"

I buried myself deeper still. I imagined her studying the photo with her mathematician's intensity, squinting through her cateyes. There was a long, long pause during which I knew she was

_____
* No!

constructing the succinct and sword-sharp statement that would seal my doom: *You are utterly correct, gentlemen. That woman is living here. In fact, she is sleeping on my bunk bed right now.*

"This is what she looks like?" Cora asked.

"Yes, miss."

An eternity passed. A thousand times, the sun set and the moon came up and ripened the wild plums, and all the Crow children jumped and grew up strong.

"I'm sorry," Cora said, "but we've never seen anybody like this. Right, Granma?"

"*Éeh.*"*

"Are you sure?" Agent Fox's high whine was dubious and exasperated.

"Utterly," Cora said.

I WAS ALREADY TRIPPING DOWN the bunk ladder, saying "thank you". over and over, when they burst into the bedroom. Granma hugged me. Cora stood apart with one hand slipped into the other. Still, a smile repeatedly threatened to break open on her staid face.

"They're going to come back," I said.

"That's right." Granma nodded. "They always do."

"They'll have a search warrant," I said. Cora wouldn't let me catch her eye. Her decision to preserve me had made her shy.

Then a pervasive purr rippled through the air and hummed through the house, as if the lions sleeping beneath the prairie had finally awakened. It was the Pronghorn coming down the dirt road, and Jim was behind the wheel. "She drives!" Cora exclaimed. We awaited him on the porch.

"Who were those guys I passed in the black car?" he asked.

"Where were you?" I said.

---

* Yes!

"Test drive. Want to go for a ride?"

"I'm afraid I might need to," I said. "A long one."

OVER A BREAKFAST THAT NONE OF US ATE, we made the plan. I would go to San Diego and show up in court. Rather than being taken, I would take myself. I would take hold of myself.

"Let's resolve it," Jim said. "Go through with the trial."

"How can you live any kind of good life," Granma asked, "always hiding?"

"I know," I said. "But how will things be any different now than they were when I left?"

"Now you'll have us," Jim said.

Cora echoed, "You'll have us."

And it was hard to be terrified then.

"They'll be back, Margie," Granma said. "You'd better hurry. Don't let them take you."

I carried the Strawberry Shortcake suitcase into the living room and clicked it open. I pulled out the rose-scented rosary—"Ah," Granma said, "you have a *baaluukáate*. I love those!"—and the porcelain palm. "I'd like to leave these here," I said, and Cora stilled her fluttering hands and held them safe. I found my remaining lucky red Chinese shoe, opened the screen door, and tossed it out onto the grass, where it flowered for a brief moment before Belly, barking and bouncing, took it up. I lifted out the long-unfinished letter to Dad, the one begun so long before in Middletown. I considered, as I had been doing for months, the P.S., and realized that, like all my postscripts, it would be long. But I couldn't write it yet, because I was still living it. "Save this for me, too," I asked Cora. "I'll be ready to finish it later." And then, from the very bottom of the suitcase, where it had slumbered all summer, I pulled Rasha's recipe.

"Now, that looks interesting," Granma said, her intrigued eyes falling on the fine paper. "What is it?" she asked.

"Remember," I said, "how you told me about animal helpers, about your aunt and the magpie? And your grandmother and the prairie dogs?"

"Of course, honey."

"Well, a long time ago, for nine perfect months, I was loved and cared for by a gazelle, and this is what she left me."

THE SUN WAS HIGH when Jim bade Cora and Granma goodbye and started up the Pronghorn. "I know this is the best way," I told Granma.

"We'll be here," she said. "When you need us to come, we'll come." I kissed her.

Cora stood at Granma's side, arms dangling. "Thank you, again," I said.

"It was nothing."

"Everything I said was true."

She nodded.

"I'll see you soon, I hope," I said.

"Okay." I waited for a moment, my own arms tingling for her, but she stepped closer to her grandmother and clutched her hand. I slid into the car.

Just as Jim shifted out of park and into drive, Cora cried, "Wait!" She dashed into the house. When she reappeared, she opened the passenger door and stood close to where I sat, so close that one edge of her starry spectacles brushed my cheek. She sucked in a big gulp of air, glanced down, and took up my hand. "Now," she said, finding my finger and adorning it with a ring sculpted from the pit of a peach, "you're mine."

Epilogue

Fortuna feminae est magna.*

---

* The fortune of the woman is great.

P.S.

I NEVER IMAGINED I WOULD GROW so fond of snow, Dad, but the prairie has such an iridescent beauty in the winter, especially at night under a swollen moon when the white icy granules shimmer. And the house feels so cozy in the winter, too, so warm and snug, and even with Mary Bear and Mark Ptarmigan it's not too small for us. Evelyn Bee is still little enough to sleep in our bed, but soon she'll be ready for Cora's bottom bunk.

I was so surprised when Cora handed me the first part of this old letter. She found it yesterday while cleaning her room and packing up her things. This morning she left us—back to college for her second semester. Jim drove her, and I'm expecting him back any minute. She didn't want to take the Pronghorn. She prefers to get around on her bicycle, which must be a stunning sight for all those college boys—Cora brown and willowy, with her long hair flying behind.

I already miss her, even if she is only a few hours away in Bozeman—and not just because she is such a big help with the children and the garden, the chickens, horses, rabbits, goats, dogs, cats, cows, llamas, and pig. She's still so much the girl she was when I met her, scarily sharp, with a sly sense of humor, and she

still teases me about my criminal past, though I suspect it was
the trial that first inspired her to dream of being a lawyer. She
was fascinated by the entire process—by the brass-embellished
courtroom, by the bemused judge, by the wide-eyed but generous
jury, by the showy but smart way Ronald Clack defended me, and
by the testimonies of my friends in the crew, and of Simon, who
insisted I had been unduly influenced by him and tried to take the
blame for everything.

Of course, you remember—you were there for most of it.
Jack Dolce was characteristically sweet, helping us pay for
Ronald Clack's services with money nobody ever suspected he
had. ("When my mom took off with the travel trailer salesman
she wanted to make sure I was taken care of. You know
I don't have any use for it! Why don't you take some?") Those
six months of community service in San Diego weren't bad.
Rooming with Raven was fun, and so was spending time with
the rest of the crew and visiting you. But my memories of
Montana made me hurt in the most exquisite possible way,
the way memories of certain sights, sounds, smells, and smiles
do. You know. They make an invisible kind of beauty inside
of you.

I guess I've kept my promise to the judge to find a more
constructive way to help animals—here we are, surrounded by
adopted strays and the ones nobody else wants. We're developing
a reputation as a sort of refuge, but I don't mind.

In spite of the fact that I've kept my promise and lead a
very quiet life, I did make it into the newspaper again last summer (PRAIRIE ORANGE THRIVES, CONFOUNDS AND DELIGHTS). A
reporter from the *Billings Star* came out to interview me about my
orange tree because orange trees don't, as a rule, survive out of
doors in Montana. Mine is bright with blossoms, heavy with fruit,
and no one can figure out why. For the photograph accompanying the article, I wore a striped sundress and stood next to the

tree with the four kids, several dogs, and our pig. The reporter wanted to know my secret. I admitted to blanketing the tree on cold winter nights but didn't mention that I had planted it right beside Granma's grave, and that I suspected its success had something to do with her—and, of course, with *her,* the most beautiful woman of all, the one Granma taught me about.

I'm glad you had the chance to meet Granma before she died. I can hardly believe it's been two years since we found her in her favorite thicket of chokecherry trees, lips stained red from the juices.

Evelyn is tugging again at the peach pit ring. I wear it on a chain around my neck now because it's too tiny for my finger. After three babies and enough love I am not the Audrey type I once was, but not quite a Marilyn type, either. I make my sundresses a bit bigger these days (though lately I'm knitting sweaters) and gave all the old ones to Cora. Jim says my cheeks are even pinker than they were when he first saw me, and that I smile a lot more, too. He's right. I know I'll hear his truck coming up the road any minute. I'm listening for it, and listening to the sounds of the twins' breathing as they sleep here in their side-by-side beds, and listening to the cat cry hello as she nudges my calf.

Josie and Pete Sings Plenty are going to look after the animals for us while Cora has her spring break and we all make the trip down to Orange County. I'm warning you now: we're going to try to convince you, again, to move to Montana. We can even work together to build you a little house close to ours. I think you should go for it, Dad. Last time we were there, I could see you considering. Yes, I could see it in those green, swooping eyes, and in the way you tried to hide your smile by taking a big swallow of your soda. I think it's time. I want to drive back up here with the lone lovebird I had to leave behind so long ago.

We're going to ride down to you in the Pronghorn because the truck isn't big enough for all of us. And I can hear the truck now, coming up the road. He's almost home.

And I can hear the familiar sound of him opening the door, and the soft stomp of his boots as he shakes the snow off before he steps into the house. (I hope he'll have a few bits of snow in his hair. I love to find them melting there.) I can smell his orange blossom odor, which is the smell of the fulfillment of all my life's longing. I can hear him say my name the way he always does when he comes inside, because he calls me, he calls me. And I can hear him ask, the way he always asks, every time, "Margie, are you home?" And I, growing rosy, rosier, the rosiest I've ever been, answer the way I always do. "I am."

Acknowledgments

I'm grateful to my daring and dedicated agent, Terra Chalberg; my enthusiastic and insightful editor, Jenny Jackson; everyone at Doubleday whose work and expertise have helped me turn a dream into a reality; the kind communities I found in Bozeman, Livingston, and Iowa City; the Crow Tribe of Montana; Tim McCleary of Little Big Horn College; the dear friends and teachers—Ben Leubner, Angela Kinley, Lisa Aldred, Jessica Bunn, Marie Thomas, Mark Murphy, Greg Keeler, and Andy Fahlgren—whose good cheer, encouraging words, companionship, and affection meant so much during the years I spent working on this book; Michael Konsmo, whose belief was a gift for which I will always be thankful; Carl, Anne, and the rest of my family, who have showered me with reading materials, writing tools, and love from the very beginning; and, finally, the bright green snake, who emerged through a crack in the sidewalk at just the right moment.

Natalie Brown grew up in Orange County, California. She earned a BA in Literature from the University of California at San Diego and master's degrees in English and Native American Studies from Montana State University. She lives in Iowa. *The Lovebird* is her first novel.

A NOTE ON THE TYPE

This book was set in Granjon, a type named in compli-
ment to Robert Granjon, a type cutter and printer active
in Antwerp, Lyons, Rome, and Paris from 1523 to 1590.
Granjon, the boldest and most original designer of his
time, was one of the first to practice the trade of type-
founder apart from that of printer.

Linotype Granjon was designed by George W. Jones,
who based his drawings on a face used by Claude Garamond (ca. 1480–1561) in his beautiful French books. Granjon more closely resembles Garamond's own type than do
any of the various modern faces that bear his name.